PLUM CREEK

PLUM CREEK

A NOVEL

W. W. McNEAL

FORT WORTH, TEXAS

Library of Congress Cataloging-in-Publication Data

Names: McNeal, W. W., author.
Title: Plum Creek / by W.W. McNeal.
Description: Fort Worth, Texas : TCU Press, [2016]
Identifiers: LCCN 2016016743| ISBN 9780875656410 (alk. paper) | ISBN
    9780875656474 (e-book)
Subjects: LCSH: Country life—Texas—History—19th century—Fiction.
Classification: LCC PS3613.C585943 P58 2016 | DDC 813/.6—dc23
LC record available at https://lccn.loc.gov/2016016743

TCU Press
TCU Box 298300
Fort Worth, Texas 76129
817.257.7822
www.prs.tcu.edu
To order books: 1.800.826.8911

Cover and Text Design by Preston Thomas
Cover image ©iStock

FOR TOM

CONTENTS

ACKNOWLEDGMENTS

I have made use of several works of history for the historical background of this book. They include the following published works:

Lone Star: A History of Texas and the Texans, by T. R. Fehrenbach
Comanches: The Destruction of a People, by T. R. Fehrenbach
The Great Comanche Raid, by Donaly E. Brice
Goodbye to a River, by John Graves
Texas Ranger: Jack Hays in the Frontier Southwest, by James Kimmins Greer

ONE

T HE RIVER WAS A ROILING CHOCOLATE AND HAD BEEN FOR days. That was why his father's body had lain in the front parlor for over forty-eight hours before it was finally declared safe to ford to the Highsmith Church and cemetery. His uncle Wonsley had swum his horse across to take word, so his relatives on the Guadalupe County side were waiting, too.

On the way home from Dilley's Saloon two nights before, his father had accidentally hung himself in a forked branch of a tree. So since the body was pickled anyway, his uncle John said, "Let it keep on. We damn sure need the rain."

Billy's sixteenth birthday was still a week away, on the fifteenth of November, 1869, and he had been wondering if his daddy would be buried on his birthday, spoiling it. But the reports from up river were that it was no longer raining in the Hill Country and the Blanco was receding, so the dry goods wagon that doubled for a hearse, its tarp flapping in the light wind and rain, led the procession—the men mounted, the women in buggies and wagons, and the Negroes on mules—across the waist-deep brown water of Sam's Ford and up the deep-rutted mud road to the little church at the top of the hill on the other side. There the Baker side of the family was waiting, huddled at the far end of the church by the wood stove near the pulpit—the men smoking and chewing, the women seated in a semicircle between the stove and the pulpit, knitting and talking about children, his grandmother Baker smoking her corncob pipe.

Elder Baker, his grandfather, had his black preacher clothes on, his vest and string tie a sharp contrast against the bleached white of his starched shirt and the silver of his hair and beard. He greeted them at the door, his tousled string tie lying uneven against the clean, worn linen of his shirt. Elder Baker shook the hands of the McCulloch men as they entered and grasped the hands of the women in both of his gnarled, calloused farmer's hands, finally taking the black-gloved hands of his daughter in his, his knuckles red against them.

"He's finally at rest, Laura," he whispered. She pulled her hand away, looking at him with a strange expression that Billy had seen only once before, then she lowered her head. She looked at Eli Baker's hands, suspended where she had withdrawn from them, then back to his face.

"I hope so," she said.

The night his father died he heard the sounds of the men bringing his body into the house and ran down the stairs expecting a tragedy. The house was never awakened in the night but for tragedy. His mother had that look about her as she passed him on the stairway, the men holding the dark, wet body on the porch until she reached the door. His father's sisters were at the door, frozen in shock at the scene on the porch. Laura ushered the men into the front parlor as if she had been expecting them, as if she had dreamed the entire scene beforehand, the subtle lines around her eyes shadowy in the lamplight.

And the following night, when Lily Poe and her daughter came in widow's weeds to view the body, her daughter, four years younger than Billy was, clutching the black folds of her mother's dress and crying, his aunts held the pair at the doorway in the blowing rain, calling Lily a hussy. From the room where the body lay came his mother's voice, soft and firm: "Let her in." Her voice at such times was like her eyes, knowing and quietly determined.

He was sitting on the staircase while the aunts still hesitated and Lily Poe said, "I just want to see him. Then I'll go." A small woman, she looked up at his tall aunts as she spoke. He was disappointed in her. She looked nothing like the notorious Lily Poe, whom the older boys talked of in whispers, and the girl looked like a frightened animal clinging to her mother's side, her eyes wide and scared.

Laura's voice from the front room once again told them to let her enter, this time more insistently, and they stepped aside and let Lily and the girl pass. His mother stood at the door of the room and motioned them in, her solemn look following them into the room; then she followed behind them and closed the door, the widow admitting the mistress and her daughter to the room she had been sharing only with the body of her dead husband. Now sharing him willingly, resignedly, with the woman she had not acknowledged for so many years, whose existence had been almost a fiction to her. Silently acknowledging, by admitting her into the room, what she had never acknowledged while he was alive.

The silence in the room went on for the better part of an hour as the boy waited alone in the dark hallway. When the door opened and they emerged, Lily was leading Barbara Ann, who had fallen asleep, by the hand. His mother held the door open for them, the small woman leading the sleepy girl.

As he watched his mother slip his grandfather's grasp inside the doorway of the church, in his mind's eye he saw her again in the hallway with Lily Poe and her daughter, who were now back in the town on the other side of the river and the creek. Lily's husband had been buried in the cemetery that lay between them—a point of land high above the confluence of the two now-rushing streams, headstones silhouetted in the cold rain and wind.

Eli Baker led the widow to the front pew on the right and saw to her seating, then the Baker clan and the rest of the group from across the river found their seats. Scripture was read and a hymn was sung, unaccompanied by any musical instrument, which was the way of the Primitive Baptists. Elder Baker read a brief biography of the dead man, about his birth in North Carolina, his marriage in Tennessee, his arrival in Texas, his children, grandchildren, and other survivors. There was a prayer and another hymn. The congregation always sang a bit off-key, and Billy was always a bit embarrassed for them. He never understood the ban of musical instruments in the church. His grandmother Leonie had a piano in her parlor. If the Lord only wanted to hear voices in church, why would he want to hear the piano in the parlor? But this time the hymn was about finding a resting place beyond the river, and the voices all seemed to blend together.

The black casket was dripping water onto the hardwood floor, and the wind was whipping the last dying rain around the corners of the small church building as the sound of the voices died away. Suddenly the door at the rear slammed open. A wiry, bearded man wearing a black oilskin slicker entered the room, slowly took his black hat off and poured water from it out the open door before he closed it. He pulled off his slicker deliberately. It did not seem to bother him that the entire congregation was turned and looking at him. He was roughly dressed in a brush jacket and dark brown pants under the slicker, his pants stuffed into his high boot tops. His long black hair was matted wetly against his forehead in front and against the sides of his head below where the hat had creased it, and his beard showed a touch of gray at the chin. His hazel eyes surveyed the room as he hung his slicker and hat on a peg by the door.

He took a seat in the back row. Most of the mourners turned back and faced the front where Eli Baker stood motionless, staring at the man who had just entered. Only Billy and one or two more still looked at him.

"It's Hays," his uncle John whispered from the opposite side of his mother, and she grasped her brother's arm.

Billy found the man's eyes staring at him from the last row, past the heads of the people who sat between them, as if the man had known beforehand he was going to turn and look at him. The eyes were calm and somewhat cold, so out of place in the room that Billy sat and stared at them until his mother's gentle tug on his sleeve finally turned his attention. Some of the men wore slight smiles of recognition.

After the final prayer, when the coffin was being carried out, Billy tried to pick out the man in the crowd, but he could not find him. The congregation followed the pallbearers out of the church to the adjacent graveyard, and the break in the service caused by the man's appearance seemed like a dream to him. He began to wonder if he had imagined it. His mother held his hand firmly in the short procession to the gravesite, so he gave up turning to look for him, but standing at the grave, she finally let go of his hand to take a handkerchief from her purse, and Billy slowly backed away from her until he found a break in the crowd. He looked but could not find him in the faces he could see.

Then, as the coffin was being lowered into the grave, Billy saw him on the hillside where the railroad track would later be laid. Standing next to a buckskin horse, he was looking down on the graveyard, bareheaded in the light, blowing rain, his hat held at his side, as if he had been sent to witness the fact of Wesley McCulloch's death—and was there to carry away a visual record of the burial. There was something about the man's movements in the church, the way he stared back at him, the way he stood motionless by his horse in the rain, and the tone of his uncle's whisper, "It's Hays," that was frightening and upsetting and yet comforting, as if this man was not governed by the laws of physics and probability like most of us, as if he was one who could turn the tide of events by his will alone. Before the last shovelful of dirt had been thrown on the grave, his uncle John Baker, who had been standing by his side as he watched, said quietly, "You see him, don't you? Seen him in the church, didn't you, boy?" Uncle John was looking at the man with admiration, his face solemn.

"You take a good look, Billy. So you can tell your grandchildren. That's Jack Hays." His uncle's voice rose slightly when he said the name, which caused several men standing nearby to look in the man's direction. Hays saw them. He replaced his hat, mounted his horse, and soon disappeared over the rise.

After the funeral, the families gathered at Elder Baker's house, across the road from the church. The women busied themselves in the stone-floor kitchen. The men sat around the cast-iron stove in the parlor.

The Baker house was one of the best in the area, with large rooms and French doors in the parlor, facing southeast. It was filled with warming light in the fall and winter, although there was little light the day of Wesley McCulloch's funeral. Billy longed for those summer days when the wind came across the parlor from the southeast and across the cool stone of the kitchen floor.

The McCullochs and Bakers were linked by two marriages, one between Billy's mother and father, Laura Baker and Wesley McCulloch, and one between two of their first cousins, a Baker son and a McCulloch daughter. Of the families that had been in the area since before the days of the Republic, the Bakers and McCullochs had intermarried late. Billy was the oldest child of the Baker-McCulloch unions.

The Bakers had more kin among the Copelands and Morrisons and the McCullochs more among the Wades and Bowens, but Wesley McCulloch and Eli Baker had been partners in a cotton gin. Although the Bakers lived on the west side of the river, the Guadalupe County side, and the McCullochs lived on the east side on land that was first in Gonzales County and later in Caldwell County, the two men had met soon after their arrival in Texas in the twenties, before Green DeWitt was granted the title of empresario and founded the town of Gonzales.

They had been close ever since, although Wes McCulloch retained the wildness of the early days, and Eli Baker got religion and founded a church. Both had prospered, but the estate of John Wesley McCulloch was hampered by debt from the aftermath of the war. Once a respectable holding, by the time his handwritten will was read, her "widow's allowance" had to be used to save Laura the two hundred acres of homestead and the tools of the farming trade. These the state exempted from the writs of creditors.

The portion of his will that left his interest in the cotton gin to Lily Poe, however, would establish the seed of a great Texas fortune. The residue of his estate, of such great value on the night he drunkenly scrawled his will on the top of a whiskey keg, would be largely depleted to pay the debts and taxes he had assigned to it, leaving his widow and children with the bitter dregs of his bold appetite for risk, and his mistress and her daughter with a status and influence he did not foresee and would not have intended. He left the widow Poe his half interest in the gin, at the time saddled with debt of its own and facing an uncertain future, because of a sardonic pleasure he had in anything he could do to throw Eli Baker off his steady, confident course. On the day of Wes McCulloch's funeral, Eli Baker had a new partner.

Laura showed Eli Baker the will while still at the graveyard, after the others went back to the shelter of the church. She was respectful of his feelings, saying only, "He left this," sheltering the paper from the rain and holding it before him to see and take hold of if he wished. Eli looked at it for a long time, then gingerly took it from her fingers, as if the paper itself was fragile. Holding his hat over it, he read it in silence, his lips pursed, and his clear blue eyes unblinking. She looked at his face as if it held the answer to something she little understood and was unable to articulate. The genius of her husband. His patent denial of his mortality. His vitality.

After reading the will, Eli looked up at her. He had to look away quickly, over her shoulder, at the church and the wagons and buggies leaving the curving drive, at the men on horseback, hunched over in the whirling mist. He handed it back to her.

"I guess you'll be seeing Ashley," he said in his preacher's voice, and she knew that he was not going to tell her anything.

"I guess," she replied.

"Let me know if you need anything." His body had already turned toward the church, to step around her. Then, as if it was an afterthought, halfheartedly, he touched her shoulder. She turned away from him.

"I'll be all right," she said quietly.

He squeezed her shoulder lightly and went back to his wife Leonie and his sons and other daughters. Later, with the men in the parlor by the stove and the women in the kitchen serving the meal which had already been prepared, Laura and Leonie sat at the large, hand-hewn table and talked about old times. Billy sat in the doorway between the kitchen and the parlor, listening.

His grandmother and mother were dressed alike and were about the same size, but Leonie's jet-black hair, dark features and prominent cheekbones made her seem larger next to her daughter's delicate lightness. Laura had light brown hair that looked blonde in summer, light green eyes, and a thin nose. Both women were small, but Laura's small hands were dwarfed by Leonie's long, slender fingers, which were constantly in motion as she spoke. She was reminiscing about Wesley McCulloch.

"I don't know if you know about Wesley before you was born, when he was a boy with the Rangers."

"I've heard, Mama," Laura said, folding napkins. "About how wild he was. Is that what you mean?" Her eyes smiled as she tended to the napkins.

"I first met him when I was a girl," Leonie said. "He helped save me."

Although she said it softly, the voices from the kitchen quieted down. The two women became the center of attention, sitting at the table between the young women laying out the plates and dinnerware in the kitchen and the men around the stove in the parlor. Billy's perch was between the women and the men, closer to his mother and grandmother than any of the others. The two women, talking quietly, were being given the respect of silence. A couple of men looked through the doorway when Leonie mentioned Wes McCulloch's name.

"I was sixteen then," she said. "I had forgotten English."

Eli Baker stood up from his rocker and slowly walked to the doorway where Billy was sitting and leaned against the doorframe, tilting into the kitchen. Leonie looked at his sullen face and smiled.

"It'll be on the table in a minute, Mr. Baker," she said to her husband. "Just hold your horses."

"No hurry," he said, with a softness in his voice Billy was not used to hearing.

"You remember when Wesley and the others brought me back, don't you, Mr. Baker? It was in the spring and the hill was covered with bluebonnets."

"I remember," he said.

"I bet you didn't think I remembered that day, but I do," she said.

At once Eli Baker was back in the field behind the plow. She was tied to the paint pony she called Feather and Wes McCulloch was leading her up over the crest of the hill from the west. He remembered how she sat the horse, the look on her face, and how she had grown since he had last seen her, before she escaped and went back to "her people," as she herself put it.

Before she, a ten-year-old, slipped out of the blue dress and under-garments her Anglo mother had made for her and crawled naked in the cold December night to the river and then swam down it to where they were waiting for her with a blanket made of buffalo skin. They covered her and warmed her and eventually her shivering stopped. She had seen them that day across the river, after they had sent out a call that only she would recognize, and she had known they would be waiting for her there that evening. Her father's people. The people the Spaniards had named Comanche.

Her hair, braided and greased with animal fat, black as her Indian for-bears, glistened in the late morning sun on the day Eli saw Wes McCulloch leading her over the hill and down to the ford to rejoin her Anglo family. Her dark eyes stared at him from the saddle, hostile and unafraid.

She looked at him now in the same way, but her tears were there too, holding back, but there—and her smile was there for reassurance and comfort. It was a small part of the dance they had danced together for so many years. It was a day that called forth things that were not talked about. In spite of her concern for his feelings, she was determined.

"We never talk about that," she said to Laura. "But you ought to know how good Wesley always was to me. And a gentleman, too. I never thought about him not being around. Today when I saw the coffin, my heart stopped."

Laura was staring at her, her eyes soft, as she sat with her right hand resting softly on the pile of folded napkins, her back straight in the wood chair, the black lace over the top of her hand, curled in a way Billy would always remember. The clatter of dishes and utensils from the kitchen stopped, and the house was quiet enough to hear the wind outside. His aunt Jane and his aunt Elizabeth, whom everyone called Sis, were standing near the table where Laura and Leonie sat. Leonie looked at them.

"Is it ready?" she asked.

"Yes, Mama," Jane replied.

"Then we'll talk some more after the meal," she said to Laura. "It's time to break bread." She stood and extended her hand to her husband, who leaned out of the doorway and gently took it.

The children and young women ate at the kitchen table. They could not see the older ones through the door between the kitchen and the dining room, but they could hear the sound of the voices from the main table answering an inquiry or agreeing with a statement. The voices were quieter, subdued, not as lively as they usually were when the family gathered for Sunday dinners after church, and Billy had to remind himself that this was Thursday, and the occasion was his father's funeral. He could hear the clock in the hallway as it punctuated the quiet conversation from the dining room.

Sally, his red-haired cousin, made faces at him from across the table. She was almost fourteen, two years younger, and making faces at him at Sunday dinner was a tradition with her, although she was too old for it and knew it. She would soon discover that there were other and better ways to get his attention, but on the day of his father's funeral she was still acting like a child.

"Shut up," he said crossly, which produced her usual laugh. It was a game with them, and although he thought it was silly, he still played it. Sally would make a face and he would tell her to shut up, just as he had that first time years ago, and she would laugh just as she had then. Sally was his third cousin on the Baker side, "too close to be a kissin' cousin," his uncle Wonsley warned him the summer past, when Sally began to fill out. She was the granddaughter of Cass Baker, Eli's brother, and got her red hair from her mother's side of the family, according to Laura.

Little Tad McCulloch was his first cousin. He was six years old and was named for Tad Lincoln, which did not make him a favorite in the family. The McCulloch men, in particular, found naming a son after Lincoln's child galling, but Tad's mother was from Indiana, Lincoln's birthplace, and had stood her ground. Tad's father, Isaac McCulloch, was killed by the Yankees at Shiloh in the year of Tad's birth, and was not around to contest the naming of his only son after the devil Lincoln's spawn.

Tad was as devilish as his detractors had long predicted. He was a spoiled child who constantly tested the limits of his mother's forbearance, always finding that there seemed to be none. His mother Elizabeth was a beautiful, vain woman, whose northern accent did not help her with the other women, and whose flirtatiousness with married as well as single men made the women of the area wonder why she did not return to the state of her birth and take her problem child with her. But she stayed on, as if to spite them, running Isaac's little general store with a hard Scottish hand and granting her son his every wish.

Joe Baker was two years older than Billy McCulloch. His dark brown hair was long and unkempt and always fell over his eyes. He was a dirty boy who never seemed to wear clean clothes. Even now his Sunday clothes were wrinkled and soiled, his white shirt yellow with stains down the front. He knew a lot about how to hunt and fish and could tell good Indian stories.

The other children at the table were younger and, unlike Tad, reasonably well-behaved. Billy paid little attention to them.

Midway through Billy's last helping, the outside door opened and Gruder stuck his head in. The old black man had been a slave of his father and was faithful to the family even after Juneteenth, the day when Texas blacks learned about the Emancipation Proclamation that had been signed years earlier. Since his birth, he had been known as "McCulloch's Gruder" whenever his name was written down, in the traditional manner of identifying slaves in court documents and newspaper articles describing runaways. When Thomas Coddington, the carpetbagger from Ohio, registered him to vote, Gruder claimed not to know he had any name other than Gruder, and Coddington did not know how to properly ask for it, being unaware of the local custom and practice. After receiving a cursing from Coddington, who was drunk at the time, Gruder spoke up and said Mr. McCulloch was his boss, and he might know his name. A Texan assisting Coddington in registering black voters knew enough to write his name down as "Gruder McCulloch" for the first time and told him, "Your name is McCulloch."

"Do say," Gruder answered, with feigned wonder. "Do say." He was proud to bear the name, but the Texan noticed the sarcasm in his tone that was lost on Coddington. If he had been aware of Gruder's usual correct manner of speech, he would have also noticed the contempt behind the sarcasm.

Gruder had *raised* Billy. From the time Billy could walk, Gruder had been in charge of his care whenever his parents or grandparents could not be in attendance. Once Billy was old enough to go into the woods, Gruder became his mentor. The old black man was in charge of many things for Wes McCulloch and had plenty of petty cash to spend as he saw fit, for "necessaries." Gruder thought the world of Billy, so Wes McCulloch made him Billy's surrogate father, telling him to take care of him, which greatly pleased Gruder.

Gruder did not know his age, only that he came to Texas when he was in his twenties with Billy's father and had been born on a farm in West Tennessee. He was slim and muscled and quite agile in spite of his gray hair and stooped walk. Unlike most former slaves, he could read and write and keep books of account. He had held a very high position before the war, always dressing well, much like the young white men of property. He had more money before the war than afterwards, when there was no money to be had.

Gruder leaned into the back doorway around the edge of the kitchen fireplace and gestured at Billy with his hand and a nod of his head. Billy leaned back in his chair to see if any of the adults were moving that way from the dining room, then slid to the side and around the table to the door. Gruder took him by the shoulder and pulled him through the doorway and out onto the back porch. There was a break in the rain, but the north wind was cold and biting. Gruder leaned down and looked in his face, grinning.

"You want to see somethin'?" He was grinning the way he did when they were hunting and he had seen or heard something that Billy was not aware of. The boy was used to hearing, "You want to see somethin'?" from him, as if Gruder could imagine that one of these days Billy would say no.

"What?" Billy asked, as he always did.

Gruder turned and gestured with his arm and hand as he usually did in the woods, indicating that Billy should follow. They walked from the porch to the edge of the muddy road between the house and the church and graveyard. Gruder stopped and turned sideways and pointed across the graveyard fence toward the first row of headstones where the man who had barged into the church stood beside Wes McCulloch's grave, his black hat in his hand, his head down, looking at the wooden marker. The buckskin was tethered to the iron gate near the circular driveway.

"It's Hays," Billy said, with the same inflection and tone of voice his uncle had used in the church.

"Sure is," murmured Gruder. "The baddest white man that ever lived."

"He ain't bad. He was a friend of Pa's."

"I don't mean that kind of bad. I mean deadly." He looked at Billy, his expression serious. "That little man has killed more Injins and Meskins than all the rest of Texas put together. That's the Captain."

"Come on," Billy said, and stepped lightly across the road, avoiding the puddles.

"I'm not sure you should disturb him now, Billy."

But Billy was already across the road, heading for the cemetery gate. The horse snuffled at him as he approached, but the man stood as still as stone. When Billy entered the gate, Hays's back was to him. He tried not to walk too quietly for fear that Hays might think he was trying to sneak up on him, but the brown brush jacket did not turn, and as Billy drew closer, he could see the pattern on the red bandana around his neck, blowing in the wind. The rest of him was still. Billy leaned against a tree ten feet or so back.

It seemed like the man remained motionless for an eternity, and Billy began to doubt the wisdom of coming up on him from behind. He might turn suddenly and shoot him without seeing that he was only a boy, dressed in his Sunday suit. And if he was the killer Gruder said he was, he would not miss. As Billy began to think seriously about backing out of the situation and took a step away, Hays spoke without looking up.

"You'd be Billy," he said, in a voice that was not so deep as it was steady. Hays did not turn around or give any other indication that he had even seen him. "I heard he died on horseback at night. That so?"

"Yes sir."

"Was he drunk?"

Billy hesitated and the man half turned to look at him. His hazel eyes had the same calm, cold look as in the church. There was no emotion in his face, only thought.

"Well?" he asked, waiting with his hat in his left hand.

"That's what they say."

"That's what they say, huh?" A slight smile crossed his thin mouth. "Well, he probably was." He turned again and looked at the grave for the last time. It was a look of finality and completeness, his form moving ever so slightly. The grave was covered with fall wildflowers in bunches—yellows and purples—carefully placed from the service. After a pause, he turned and replaced his hat and began walking toward the gate. Billy fell in beside and slightly behind him.

"How's your ma taking it?"

"Oh, all right, I guess."

"How about your grandma Leonie?"

"She's doin' okay."

When he reached the horse, he untied it and Billy stopped, staring at him.

"You know who I am?" he asked.

"Yes sir. I think I do."

"You tell your grandpa Baker I'll be back tomorrow."

He pulled himself up into the saddle and nudged the buckskin to the north. It seemed like only a few seconds before he disappeared over the rise. Billy turned and ran to tell his grandfather.

Gruder walked back to the house mumbling to himself, "I don't like this. I don't like this at all."

His grandfather Baker took the news quietly, but the women made a fuss. His aunt Sis kept saying, "Wonder what he wants?" to no one in particular. Laura and Leonie sat in the parlor with the men, and they spoke in hushed tones. After a while, the McCulloch clan loaded up and crossed the river.

Gruder was on horseback ahead of the buggy Billy drove for his mother. After they forded and were headed up the road, the sun low behind them, he dropped back even with the buggy.

"Miss Laura?" he said, his voice lifting up on her name.

"Yes, Gruder."

"I hear Cap'n Jack came back to Texas to take revenge. I hear he had kinfolk killed, and he came back from California to find the ones that did it. Course that's just what I hear."

"Who says that, Gruder?" she asked, with a harshness in her voice.

"Oh, just folks. Folks."

"Who was killed? Do they say who?"

"No. Just kin. That's all they say. But they say it was that half-breed that did it. And his bunch."

She looked at him for a long moment, then looked away. She said nothing the rest of the ride home.

When Billy was helping Gruder unhitch the horse from the buggy and put it away, he asked him about the half-breed. Gruder spoke quickly as he worked.

"You ever heard of the Yellow Rose of Texas, Billy?"

"Naw."

"Well, the story is she was one beautiful woman. A high yaller. She was the highest-priced woman of pleasure in the old days, during the Republic. They say Santa Anna bedded down with her at San Jacinto and that General Houston put her up to it, to keep him occupied." He stopped with a harness and reins in hand. "They say she had a hundred children from most of the fathers of Texas, all outside the law, of course. They say she's the mother of Leo Morgan, the half-breed, and that Spoon Dog, the Comanche chief, was his daddy. Her name was Emily Morgan. They say she hired a man to kill him once. Her own son." Billy had heard of Leo Morgan. All of the children had heard of him. In games, Tad McCulloch was made to play the part of Leo Morgan by the other children his age, as a condition of letting him play. He came to like the part. Morgan was a renegade and a murderer, known for torturing his victims. Tad McCulloch liked the respect the role brought him.

"Anyway, they say that Leo killed a young family and captured a girl that is kin to Cap'n Jack and that's why he's come back to Texas. To get revenge and find the girl. He's probably gonna call in some chips from your grandpa Baker."

"Grandpa Baker's too old to go hunting Indians."

"Oh, he won't ask him, exactly. You be at your grandpa's tomorrow and you'll see. Cap'n Jack doesn't ask favors. He'll just tell what he's up to in a quiet way, and your grandpa Baker'll do the rest."

"But he's too old."

"I know, Billy. But that's what families are for. He's got two sons that are able."

That night, he dreamed he was riding with a group of men up a shallow stream, and there were bird sounds all around them.

TWO

THE DAWN CAME PAINFULLY FOR ASHLEY MAITLAND. HE WAS PAST
the age when he could sleep much beyond it, no matter how hard
he tried. It was mainly thirst that always woke him, but when that was
quenched, his mind was awake and busy. No matter how hungover he
was, he could never quite find sleep again, so he had taken to reading
classics in the dim light from his east window, sitting on the deep sill
until the sun's rays crossed the page. At first he tried to be conscientious
about it, but lately he had taken to turning to some passage that he knew
almost by heart and reading it aloud in his sing-song actor's voice.

The morning after Wes McCulloch's funeral, he stood looking at the
crude homemade shelves that lined the wall between his two east windows. The passage he had in mind, he knew by heart anyway. He'd always
had the ability to remember verse, even the ability to write it, but he
lacked discipline. He remembered the night before and the gathering at
Friedman's after the funeral. The whiskey. The singing. The recitations.
The oral tradition.

The cracked leather bindings of the old books seemed to stare at him
from across the room. There were no new ones. He had no casebooks and
had to go to Gonzales or Lockhart to really research a case, but Thomas
Harwood in Gonzales was effusive in his offers to share his library, and
he had a good one, in a quiet room on the second floor of a limestone
building overlooking Saint Joseph Street. Harwood would often drop in
between clients and talk law with Ash, saying it was Ash's payment for
the use of the place.

"Besides," he said, "these books could stand some reading."

He looked through the window to the right of the shelves of books. A cow grazed beyond the oak tree, among golden-leafed elms. The sunlight streaming through the trees silhouetted the cow amid the translucent, bright, swirling leaves and branches. The rain of several days duration was over, and the early November morning was starting out clear and fresh and clean, like an overture.

On another morning he might have felt a softness, a kind of contentment because of the color and the contrast and the movement, but his gut would not accept it this morning. He remembered Wes's face when he first saw the body. There was no discernible contentment in it. It looked cold and impersonal, not like a human face at all—more like a death mask that someone had made up to look like a human face, to fool you.

He felt a cold, fearful thing that threatened to take him over, and he had a feeling like you first feel when falling from a tree limb or a bluff. Even if you know it is going to be safe, you still get that feeling. Your heart in your throat.

He did not want to think about his wasted life again. He had been through that before. Moaning and groaning to himself about the waste, the missed opportunities, the stupid decisions. But this was not that. It was not self-pity. It was deeper. He did not feel bad, he thought. Only disjointed. Thrown off. And in a way, it felt good. Almost good enough to offset the pain in his head. All he recalled eating were oysters and crackers.

He thought he must still be drunk from the cannabis and whiskey and then realized that his cheeks were moist, and his eyes were filled with warm tears.

He had come to Texas because of Wes McCulloch, because Polk had investments, or at least interests, and he had always been fond of Polk. Or because, like so many, he had failed in Tennessee, as his father had failed in North Carolina before him. Twenty years later, Wes was gone, and he was no richer and no more famous than he had ever been. Maybe wiser, but probably only more cynical, less trusting, warier. And still given to sentimentality, the curse of his line. And whiskey.

He found his pipe and saw that there was some left in the bowl, found a match and lit it. The first full pull on it filled his lungs with the harsh cannabis and choked him slightly, making him cough and wheeze, but after a few puffs his throat settled down, and he felt better.

Menudo and coffee would help. Garcia's would be open and ready to serve. He pulled on a pair of wool pants and his boots, tugged a sweater over his head, and walked into the street bareheaded. The morning air was brisk but quite bearable, and the north wind felt good against his head. He walked in the middle of the street where there were fewer pools and puddles.

He had been here since the town began to take shape, crude buildings cropping up on either side of the road because Ike Webb had liked the spot and put his horse pen here, east of the creek on high ground. Then came a lean-to occupied by Ike's man George, when he was tending horses. Then Ike and the woman he found and brought there added onto it as the children came. When Ashley showed up the next year, in 1850, there were already five structures built by those who had purchased farmland along the creek from Ike. He said they were welcome to build along the road if they wished, although no lots had been surveyed or deeds or leases drawn until Ashley came.

The blacksmith shop that started as the lean-to had turned into a full livery stable by 1869. It was one of three commercial establishments among the dozen or so buildings. There was also Webb's store and Garcia's place, unless you considered Maitland's law office a commercial establishment, which he did not. The closest doctor was in Prairie Lea, ten miles upriver.

Mrs. Webb had opened the store and could be seen through the small front window with broom in hand. Ike was probably sleeping off the gathering. Ash could hear George banging on a piece of iron long before he reached the shop. The sound made his ears ring, and he was suddenly dry mouthed from the cannabis. George did not look up from the forge as he passed, although he knew George was aware of his passage. George did not look up until spoken to and sometimes not even then. Ike referred to him as a "smart nigger." George never visibly reacted to that statement, although Ash always thought there was trouble brewing in his silent defiance. He never heard George say "Yassuh" or "No'm" like the other blacks. Ike said George came from Georgia with him in the days of the Republic because he had heard that slavery was illegal in Mexico and, Texas being part of Mexico, there were not any slaves. He acknowledged, though, that George had never told him this and was his legal servant when he came with him from Georgia and could not have refused anyway.

"He could have run off, though," Ike said many times. "That nigger ain't going nowhere he don't want to. You can bet on that."

Ike named the village Atlanta.

Garcia's was off the street, on the only trail that could be considered a side street. The place began only as Garcia's house and was not intended as a restaurant. It was hardly that now. When Garcia's wife had begun to make and sell tortillas and tamales from her kitchen, she talked Garcia into adding a small room with a dirt floor onto the side of their two-room shack. There were two crude homemade tables, a couple of benches made out of split oak logs, and a few apple boxes for additional stools. You just came in and sat down, and in no time Mrs. Garcia would bring you strong coffee and a bowl of menudo with hot tortillas, if she knew that was what you wanted, or a plate of Mexican eggs with bacon. There were seldom any strangers there because there were no signs to indicate it was a place to eat, and nobody who lived in the area ever had any company that dined out.

Ash had credit from representing Garcia, and he was careful not to irritate Mrs. Garcia about it. It was because of hog thievery that she had to cook for Ashley Maitland, and she did not feel that it was always her duty to be in the mood to do it, particularly if the conversation was not to her liking. She never spoke English and professed ignorance of the language, but if Ash should make the mistake of joking about hog thieves or even horse thieves, she would likely clear his dishes away before he had finished, without saying a word.

Garcia could not even mention pork. He spent thirty days in jail at Lockhart because of the case. The hogs he contended he had raised from his original stock were proven to the satisfaction of the jury to have all sprung from a sow belonging to the widow Nichols and were ordered turned over to the county, over Ash's strong protest. After entering the judgment, Judge Daughtry gleefully chastised Ash over whiskey at Friedman's, saying that he should have known better than to rely on payment with stock that was the progeny of stolen property. "I hereby grant judgment for the plaintiff and hereby impose a constructive trust," the judge had intoned in the courtroom. "The sheriff is directed to seize all the hogs. The defendant will not be allowed to keep his ill-gotten gains. Your exception is noted, sir." The Judge thus decided the civil case brought by the widow at the same time as the case of the *State v. Garcia*, even though there had been no trial setting of the civil matter. He knew Ashley wouldn't appeal.

From across the table at Friedman's, Ash told the judge he at least wanted to be invited to the pig roast, and that he was certain even a widow should have to pay court costs. The table quieted while the judge paused for effect, but he laughed, finally, and told Ash he was going to order him to buy a jug for the party to pay his part of the court costs.

At least he got some free meals out of the deal, and it led to Maria, Garcia's daughter, cutting his hair and trimming his beard when he needed it, and, if he could continue to bear her silent hostility, Garcia's wife's cooking was something he'd just as soon not give up.

This morning two of Webb's cowhands were in the place, as well as a Mexican *vaquero* who had been staying with the Garcias. None of them were talkative. Ash was relieved. He was able to sip the coffee and menudo in silence. Mrs. Garcia even brought him a glass of buttermilk, which was very unusual. It was cold and went down easy. By the time he finished, he was no longer convinced that the top of his head was going to blow off.

When he got back to his office, Laura McCulloch was sitting on the bench on his front porch with the leather case that held Wes's will in her lap. Gruder leaned against the McCulloch buggy across the street. Ashley let her in and built a fire in the stove without saying more than the usual pleasantries, then sat with his back to his rolltop desk and waited for her to begin. She handed him the leather case. It had Wes's initials on the flap, and Ash knew it well. He opened it and drew out the handwritten document that he had not seen since the night he and Ish Friedman witnessed it. He had advised Wes that it was good enough in his own handwriting, without witnesses, but Wes insisted that his two friends put their names on the document.

"With a lawyer and a Jewish merchant on there, nobody will question it," he had said, winking. Ash, knowing how drunk Wes appeared to be and knowing Wes McCulloch wanted it to be that way—to have the will written in drunkenness and witnessed on a stump table in a saloon by his two closest friends, the hard-drinking lawyer and the quiet Jewish store-keeper—as if it was destined to be that way because whatever he decided was foreseen anyway, and he was only playing out the story. And he said as much, in his deep twang.

As he unwound the string and opened the flap on the case, he had the sense of being at a certain point in time that he would remember, like the night of the will's execution five years before and the more recent night that saw Wes McCulloch leave the warm bed of Lily Poe for a game at Dilley's that he never came back from. So as he pulled the browned paper out, he sensed not only the moment but also the swift passage of time rushing by him as he unfolded the will and held it out to the light from the window.

Wes McCulloch's broad hand was steady and sure, as sure as any could have been. Those familiar with it could have detected the trailing off at the end of some words, where the hand moved too gracefully for the pen and paper because of the whiskey. They had just returned from a hunt, with deer meat and turkey outside on the horses in the cold night, the men's feet by the stove in the middle of Friedman's, passing the earthen jug between them—Wes, Friedman, and himself, loosened by the whiskey and buoyed by the thrill and satisfaction of the hunt. Wes had asked Friedman for the pen, inkwell, and paper and wrote it out on the stump without saying what it was. He handed it to Ash when he was finished.

Ash had not remembered anything but the part leaving Lily Poe the interest in the gin, and his and Friedman's signatures did not look right, but it was Wes's will, and when he looked up at Laura, her look said, *See? I didn't destroy it,* and they both knew she could have but would not have, no matter what the cost to her. She asked, "How much can you save?"

He hated to answer. "Most of the stock and two hundred acres around the house and barns," he said. "And your furniture and personal clothing and belongings."

"There's not much more," she said.

"The debts on the gin go with it," he said. "They're Lily's concern."

"'I wondered about that."

"There is a widow's allowance."

She looked insulted. "I'd appreciate your getting it over with as soon as you can get to it."

And that was it. She shook his hand firmly before she left. As he watched this small, hard woman stride off his porch and onto the damp earth of the crude lane that passed for a street, he again thought of the waste of his and other lives, of the impractical dream that was called Texas and the blood that had been spilled, the lies told, the hardship endured for the promise of a piece of something that could be salvage for faded careers and starting points for new ones. He thought of Houston, sick and despondent in Tennessee and longing for the last great adventure. Of Polk, convinced that they all held the key to destiny in their hands. Of the men he had never met who had so influenced all their lives. Austin, frail and childless, with so little to gain. De Zavala, with so much to lose. Fannin, realistic to the point of indecision, which became so deadly. And Travis, intentionally blind to the obvious consequences of his so-called bravery.

He thought that if he were to write about it all, he would have portrayed it as the adventure of fools and scoundrels, dreamers and failures—one of the most impractical and improbable undertakings in the history of the world. But fortune had smiled on Texas for some reason. Mere circumstances delivered their enemy, Santa Anna, to Houston's firm hands and, bankrupt as they had been and were again, they were still here. Men like Ben McCulloch, Wes's cousin, had been impractical enough to fight for a stake they believed destiny had handed them. Men like Jack Hays came along and significantly altered the balance of power between the Anglo settlers and Mexicans and Comanches through legendary courage and the innovative use of the Colt pistol. Ash had looked into the eyes of the adventurers and followed them. It was like looking into the windows of Hell.

Wes McCulloch had been one of them, so it was fitting that all of his labor and investment had dwindled to a trunk full of Confederate scrip, his homestead, some cattle, horses, and implements, and half a working interest in a debt-ridden cotton gin. Most of his former field hands and servants, his former property, still lived in the same shacks they had lived in for so many years, as did the Mexican braceros and vaqueros, though there was no money for them, only their lodging and what sustenance could be scraped from the land, and this produced only because of the sweat and strain and endurance that remained their only commercial assets. They had nowhere else to go. So the blacks took the McCulloch name and stayed apart from the Mexicans as they always had, and they all continued to stay on the land and somehow survive.

Thirteen hundred acres would be reduced to two hundred. There would be an involuntary splitting off to other owners and de facto masters. Eventually the bankruptcy, for Southerners the most significant feature of their defeat by the Union, would stimulate the beginning of the long climb toward a more diverse and fairer society. Hardship and hatred would eventually give way to a degree of tolerance, perhaps through identification with all who suffered. At that time and place, on the edge of the prairie, where the farming economy of the South and the ranchos of the West met, overlooking Plum Creek in the autumn of the fourth year after Appomattox, the seeds of a reawakening had been sown. But the stagnancy of the old had not yet expired.

He watched Laura, in her black dress and bonnet, as she crossed the street to the wagon where Gruder waited to help her up, her head bowing only slightly as she stepped around the low spots, her dress held up with one small gloved hand to avoid the mud. She was the best part of what had been, of what was still holding on. From making do on rough corn bread cooked in a skillet and cleaning up after her childbirth, to holding together the inheritance of her only child amid the scattered detritus of her man's ill-managed life, she would continue to endure.

THREE

HAYS SAT IN THE STRAIGHT CHAIR BY THE FIRE. LEONIE SAW THAT his collar was frayed and the front of his vest was spattered with dried mud. He had obviously been traveling.

"Not very good weather to travel the last few days," she observed.

"Not too bad," he said.

Eli Baker cleared his throat. "What brings you to Texas, Jack?" He glanced at Leonie as he spoke.

"It's a family matter, Eli," Hays said.

"You need some help?" Eli asked quickly.

Hays looked down at his boots for a long moment. "I'd count it as a favor if a couple of your boys could go along with me. I have an errand that might involve a fight, and I need a good tracker. I was thinking of John and Wonsley."

"You know they'll help any way they can," Eli said. "When do you need them?"

"You better know what it is, Eli," Hays said, looking up again.

"I know you, Colonel. You wouldn't ask if it wasn't important."

"It's Leo Morgan," Hays said, with the old coldness in his voice.

Eli shot a glance at Leonie. She was staring at Hays as if he was telling her about the death of her sons. She had a stiff look, like the one she had when they brought her back from the Comanches.

"He's got a niece of mine," Hays said, returning Leonie's look. "He was in Seguin a couple of months ago. He killed her parents and the servants and took her with him. She's fourteen."

Leonie stood up suddenly, started to speak, then turned just as suddenly and walked through the doorway to the kitchen with short, breathless steps. Eli looked after her, and Hays again looked down at his boots.

"Then you'll be wanting to leave right away," Eli said.

"Yes," Hays said, without looking up.

"I'll ride over to John's with you. Wonsley should be there helping him with fencing."

"Eli," Hays started.

"Don't say any more, Hays," Eli interrupted. "You and I go too far back to start questioning each other now on the main things. And we're not old enough to start adding up accounts yet. If we did, you'd still be ahead."

"I appreciate it, Eli," Hays said quietly.

Susan Baker was slopping the hogs when she saw the two men coming over the hill between the barn and the river. They came slowly, their horses' hooves barely splattering the ruts in the road, as if the mood of the two men had been transferred to the horses, and they were resigned to the task ahead of them. She stopped with bucket in hand and watched their approach, her face registering her growing concern. When they were within hearing, she did not wait for a greeting, but yelled out, "He's at the hay patch." Hays tipped his hat to her. Eli Baker dismounted and slowly approached the hog pen.

"You want him for fighting, don't you," she said. It was not a question.

"Yes, Susie," Eli said. "Colonel Hays needs some help."

"Then go on and get him," she said, her voice rising with emotion. "I knew that's what it was when I saw you."

"It's a family matter," he said.

"Oh it's always something like that, isn't it?" Her voice was sharp and quick.

Eli stood still, holding his hat in his hand. "I want you to know that he could not be with a better man than the Colonel," he said. "He'll look after him."

"Where are they going?"

"Up on the Medina," he said. "At least to start with. A renegade has run off with a girl. He's a bad man. They're going to find her."

She stared at Hays, who stared back. His hazel eyes were steady.

"I'll pack some things," she finally said. When she looked back at Eli, there were tears welling in her eyes, but she did not say anything. After hesitating a moment, Eli looked back at Hays, who was still staring at her, almost coldly, sitting back in his saddle as if he was reliving a familiar scene.

"I'll bring him back to you, Miz Baker," he finally said, without altering his stare.

"Where were you during the War?" she asked suddenly, then stiffened at the harshness of her question, as if someone else had asked it. She grasped the bucket handle tightly with both of her reddened hands, tears now running down her cheeks.

He spoke slowly, forcing out the words.

"I was in California."

Her jaw dropped into an expression of extreme disgust, and her lower lip quivered.

"He came back in one piece then," she said. "He'd better come back the same way again." Then she turned sharply toward the shack that they had made their home.

Hays and Eli Baker watched her walk across the hog pen, lifting her skirts out of the wallow, her auburn hair blazing in the morning sun as she went through the gateway and shut it behind her. She did not look back.

John and Wonsley Baker were repairing a wood fence at the edge of John's lower hay field. Billy McCulloch was helping. His uncle John paid Billy fifty cents a day wages, which was as much as any hired hand was likely to make and more than most. His mother wanted him in school, but Billy had recruited John Baker to convince her that he needed Billy's help for at least another week. John identified with the boy's aversion to school. Besides, Billy was in his last year anyway and could read faster and write better than anyone in the family.

Hays and Eli were talking to John when Billy and Wonsley returned from the creek bottom with a load of fence rails. Billy knew what they were there for. As they approached with the mule and wagon, John was looking at his pocket watch, and Eli and Hays were riding away. John turned to them with a grave look.

"What'd they want?" Wonsley asked.

"Hays needs some help," John said, without changing expression.

"Shit. It must mean some killin'," Wonsley said. "From what I heard, he ain't no missionary."

John was stone faced. "Leo Morgan ran off with his niece. She's fourteen."

Wonsley was in his early twenties, nearer Billy's age than his brother's. He was shorter than the other Bakers, and fairer. His blond hair was long and fell across his forehead. His light blue eyes sparkled out at John. He was the best shot in the entire area and had taught Billy to shoot. He was adept at tracking and often went off hunting by himself for days, taking only gunpowder and a bag of salt. Billy followed him around and often went hunting and fishing with him. Although Wonsley had refused schooling and could barely read, he was wise in the ways of the land and was invaluable as a guide.

"Where's he holed up?" he asked excitedly.

"Up on the Medina."

Wonsley looked at the sky. "It's gonna be cold. We better get going."

They unloaded and stacked the post oak, loaded their tools, and started back to the house before Billy uttered a sound. He wanted to talk to Wonsley, and after they had walked a good distance and Wonsley was out in front of John, Billy caught up with him and spoke in a low voice, looking down at the trail.

"I wanna go," he said.

"Shit," Wonsley said, without looking at him. "Your mama ain't about to let you go."

"I can take care of the horses, you know that. And I can shoot better than anybody but you."

Wonsley grinned. "Your mama would bust a gut."

"Maybe not if you said you needed me."

"What about school?"

"Aw, that's a waste of time. I'm not in school now anyway."

They walked in silence for a while. Billy kept looking up to see if his uncle's look had changed, but he was still grinning, looking straight ahead. Sometimes it seemed as if Wonsley was thinking of something funny when everybody else was cold serious. When they approached the barn and pens, he looked at Billy with a familiar sparkle in his eyes.

"If your mama says it's okay, it's okay with me, but what about Hays and your uncle John? They ain't gonna like no kid goin' along. I can hear 'em now."

"Hear who?" John asked in his usual serious tone. He had let go of the mule that was heading for the water trough on his own, and had gained on them until he was close behind.

Wonsley did not look back. "Billy here thinks he's ready to be a man killer," he said lightly.

"Not likely," John snapped.

"If Mama says it's okay," Billy said.

"That'll be the day." His voice was sharp and final.

Billy glanced at Wonsley, who was still grinning.

FOUR

L ILY POE AND HER DAUGHTER PULLED UP TO THE ENTRANCE TO the gin road in her buggy. She held the horse back and looked at the overgrown road that wound down to the river bottom from the edge of the main road. A handmade sign that read SAN MARCOS GIN COMPANY—J.W. McCULLOCH, PROP. hung crookedly on one of the gateposts. The wooden gate was off its bottom hinge and leaned across the entrance. Without being told, Barbara Ann jumped off the buggy seat, ran to the end of the gate that lay nested in the weeds, and tried to lift it. Her mother said, "Hold on," dismounted, and came to help her. Between the two of them they managed to drag the gate open. Barbara Ann stayed on the ground as her mother drove through, then hopped on the back of the buggy, hanging on to the seatback as they drove under the hanging branches of pecan trees down to the loading area.

The gin had not been in use for years, and its condition showed it. Lily pulled up in the tall dead bloodweeds next to the loading shed. A dilapidated wagon sat under the shed directly beneath a chute where the raw cotton would be sucked up into the gin. The corrugated tin of the building itself appeared to be in a decent condition, but the overall appearance of the place was disheartening.

Wes McCulloch had not been around when the gin closed. He was in Virginia. The bottom dropped out of the cotton market in Texas at the end of the war and was only now beginning to recover. There had been thousands of acres of fields in Mississippi and Alabama with no one to plant them, much less pick them, and there was no money for seed.

Gradually demand improved with the restoration of shipping and river traffic, but the railroads were just now being rebuilt in parts of the South, and the market was still sluggish. Lily's brother in Macon kept her abreast of the situation in the East, and she had saved some money in gold, but the appearance of the property was worse than she had expected. She sat in the buggy as Barbara Ann jumped off the back end and ran through the bloodweeds to the loading dock.

Lily had visited the gin once when it was still in operation. She had been there on business. Wes McCulloch owed her a gambling debt that she was determined to collect. Gruder saw her coming from his foreman's place on the loading dock and went out to meet her before she reached the gin, hoping to head her off before trouble resulted. The gin was a beehive of activity that morning. She saw it in juxtaposition now: on the loading dock negroes rolling the large bales down the ramps into the wagons; others, field hands, the property of farmers, waiting in the farm wagons full of raw cotton picked and loaded the day before. Others had their wagons at the seed shed, receiving cottonseed from the trapdoors open above them.

She dropped from the buggy as she had that morning and made her way through the bloodweeds toward the small office by the scales, feeling the past as if Gruder again walked beside her, trying to slow her down with polite questions and remonstrances. The near window to the office was boarded up, and the glass in the half-open door was broken. She had to straddle a broken step as she pushed the door aside and looked in. The desk he sat at that morning was still there, covered with the excrement of birds and rats. And his chair was still there, overturned in the corner, its undercarriage an obscene *X*. How he had turned to look at her and the expression on his face came back to her vividly, for the first time. The longing in his eyes. The pain in the set of his mouth. She felt suddenly dizzy and leaned against the doorway. That morning came back to her with all the smells and sounds of the gin and the field hands, the water rushing over the dam, and the bird sounds in the pecan trees, as if every sense had been transported back in time. It was a reminder of the connection between past and present in her life.

She continued to look in his eyes and felt the same swelling in her breast and weakness in her knees. She'd had a sudden realization of the blind injustice of fate on that fall morning long ago, and it engulfed her again now: the recognition that she had finally met the man she had always known in her heart she would someday meet, at a time when they were both inextricably tied to other lives.

She stood there until the smell of the decay around her returned and brought her back to the present. She looked around, half expecting to see Gruder, hat in hand, standing behind her as he had been that morning, and she knew that he was a key to her future, as if some force had brought the vision to her, as if fate had a hand on her elbow now and was propelling her forward. She stepped back down off the small porch and explored the rest of the property, her mind suddenly alive with ideas. The millrace was still in good condition. There was one break in the dam, on the far side, which could be repaired with some effort. A belt needed mending. The rest was cleanup and hard work, and she was used to that. Gruder could recruit and straw boss for her, and she possessed the one rarity that would fuel her endeavor, that would enable her to lease land with sharecroppers, buy wagons and supplies. It was in a safe place, hoarded through her stormy marriage, the death of her gambler husband, and the ravages of war and Reconstruction. The gold she had been collecting from soldiers and planters and cowhands would finally be put to use. She would begin to turn a profit in a remarkably short time, and the business Wes McCulloch had built from nothing would be resurrected by it.

As she looked at the river flowing over the dam, she was aware that her life had reached a turning point. She was in control of her fate for the first time, and her daughter would be the inheritor of the good fortune that had been hiding in her life, below the surface, for so long.

FIVE

E LI BAKER HELPED HAYS LOAD GRUB BAGS ON THE GRAY MULE.
His sons, John and Wonsley, tended to their saddlebags and bedrolls. Wonsley wore a look of excitement. John Baker was his usual solemn self as he tied his saddlebags on. There was a gray light in the east
and they could now see without the lanterns. Wonsley walked to where
they hung and, one by one, blew them out. Billy stood by his father's bay
mare, Julie, his pack ready. His grandfather glanced at him while lashing
one of the bags to the packsaddle frame, thinking he would probably
grow another couple of inches if he returned from their ride, and he was
already about six feet.

Eli was still surprised that Billy's mother had allowed him to go along.
He could tell the boy was anxious to get going before she changed her
mind. Billy shifted restlessly in his tracks, which caused the mare to move
away from him, so that he kept pulling her back by the reins. When
Laura had consulted Eli, he had only said, "There comes a time, Laura."
She looked at him for a long minute, but he would not say any more, at
least not without her asking him more. And that would do no good. Billy
was fifteen, almost sixteen. It was time for him to go.

"He'll hold the horses?" she asked.

"He'll stay with the horses and tend to the mules," he said, but there
was a vacancy in the way he said it.

Before they reached Staples Store on their way up the river road,
Gruder caught up with them. He was wearing the old brown hat Wes
McCulloch had given him that Billy had only seen him wear on Sundays

and at horse races. He had a full bedroll and saddlebags on his rig and was riding Laura McCulloch's four-year-old gelding, Jimmy. He was coming at a trot up the road, kicking up dust. He rode past Billy waving his hat and caught up with Hays and John, who were riding ahead, following Wonsley, who was in the lead farther on.

John looked at him inquisitively. Hays nodded in his direction.

"Okay if I go along?" he asked, without any "boss-man" in his voice.

"Glad to have you," Hays said quickly.

Gruder's smile broadened, and he rode along with them for a while. He remembered hauling Hays and Wes McCulloch back from a Comanche fight once, with Wes drunk from the "medicine" he took for the poison he kept saying the Comanches cooked up for their arrowheads while Hays endured the wagon ride without the benefit of bourbon.

"Where's he holed up, Cap'n?" Gruder's high hoarse voice sounded almost matter-of-fact. He persisted in calling Hays by his earlier rank.

"A storekeeper from Bandera saw a young girl with some renegades while out hunting deer. I thought I'd look up at Snakebite."

"Just what I figured. You gonna want somebody to come in from over the top, aren't you?"

"I was figuring you'd show up for that job, Gruder." Hays was looking down the road, smiling. "In fact, once the boy came along, I knew you'd be here."

"How did Laura take it?" John Baker asked.

"You know, at first she didn't see no sense in the boy goin', but Mr. Baker had a talk with her, and she changed her way of lookin' at it."

"Uh-huh." John glanced at Hays. "I'll bet she did."

They came around a bend in the road and up a rise and they were at the edge of the village called Staples Store and the old army camp, Camp Clark, where two companies of troops, one infantry and one cavalry, had been stationed during the war. The Bakers had kin in each unit, Company D of the Fourth Texas Infantry, Hood's Brigade, and a unit of the Fourth Texas Cavalry under Will Hardeman.

They rode at a walk under the edge of the oaks by the parade grounds in the dappled morning light. In 1862, privates made eleven dollars a month, officers fifty. The enlisted men lived in pup tents, the officers in rooms provided by local farmers. The men were kept there for an inordinately long time before being sent to join other units in the killing going on back East, because the Texas military men believed there was a danger of uprising in Texas among unionists in Austin, San Antonio, and Fredericksburg, mostly German people who had never owned slaves and believed too strongly in the idea of the States—the Union, as it was called by Northerners during the war—to support a rebellion against it. They had fled a Europe that was oppressive and intolerant for a land that promised freedom, particularly economic freedom, and they were minding their own business and had no stake at all in a fight that was said to be over states' rights and independence. So the Texas leaders, Ben Mc-Culloch and Albert Sidney Johnston among them, kept troops stationed nearby, and the town grew up around the camp.

The rail fence that once bordered the parade ground had fallen and was partially scattered, but it still outlined the old ground where the men marched and rode in review on Sundays. The oak grove where the locals came and picnicked was still there on the far side. Billy remembered the Sundays, after church and chores. The polished brass and leather, the groomed horses, the rowdy young men, whooping and hooting, vying for the lead in any game, garrulous, grinning at the girls, their chests out with pride and youthful enthusiasm.

The stone foundation of the commandant's quarters was the only evidence of structures remaining, other than the fence rails, scattered though they were, and the oak trees, where the troops were entertained after parade. There was not a lot to share at times, but the folks who lived within twenty miles or so would come regularly, bringing what they had, laid out on portable tables, set up by the blacks that remained. And the boys, like Billy, did the busywork, as his cousin Ada would say. He was eight, and Ada was fifteen.

One Sunday, there was a secret horse race, secret not just because horse racing was illegal on Sunday; secret because the participants were using army horses and tack and in some cases parts of other army gear, mostly gray campaign caps, which were prized by many of the younger ones, some of whom had worn caps and hats all their lives and were not in the habit of going bareheaded. Few of them had ever worn a new cap or hat, and they were hard to part from them. The third race that day produced a fight between a young private, who had come in second, and a sergeant, who had come in first. The young man claimed he had been fouled.

He was thin and fair, and the sergeant was burly and mean. By the time Billy and several of his friends came upon the circle of men, the boy was on the ground with a bloody nose. The sergeant stood over him, his large fists clenched.

"You better stay put if you know what's good for you," he said, but the boy did not hesitate. He jumped to his feet and took another blow on the chin that put him down again. When he tried to regain his footing, a kick from the sergeant's boot caught him on the side of his head and sent him sprawling again.

"I'm tellin' you. You better stay down," said the sergeant, his voice now raised.

The young soldier, dazed by the blow to the head, wavered as he sat up, but leaning on one hand he pushed himself to his feet again and lunged at the sergeant's middle. His movement was quicker than expected and caught the larger man by surprise. The boy's head hit the sergeant's groin low and knocked him back with enough force to take him down, but several bystanders caught him and broke his fall. The older man gave out a low moan and doubled over in pain. The boy began to swing wildly at the sergeant's head, landing every third blow, until several bystanders pulled him off.

They held his arms and he fought them fiercely, trying to break loose and bring more to the fight, but it was over. The sergeant remained bent over in pain and was led away by several of his friends to a stump, where they helped him sit down to wait for it to subside. The boy stopped struggling and watched the older man, who was groaning involuntarily. The boy's friends gathered around him and began to compliment him on his bravery, but the boy pushed away from them and went back to his horse, picking up his campaign cap on the way. The older man, seated on the stump, was surrounded by his friends, who commented on the foul the boy had committed by butting him in the groin. After a while, the pain subsided enough for him to stand and haltingly walk away.

The young private rode by Billy on his way back to the camp. His face and shirt were bloody, and dirt clung to the blood. He wore a proud look. His friends rode beside him, commenting from time to time on the fight and the race.

"He fouled you. I saw it."

"You got him good, Ev. You see his face?"

The private did not respond, his light blue eyes staring ahead as he rode. As he passed, he wiped his face with his dirty sleeve and looked at the blood on it, as if he did not know he had been bleeding. He was the center of attention in his group of cavalrymen, all below the age of twenty, all eagerness and clumsiness, most of them beardless because they could not yet grow facial hair. He acted as if he was used to being there with his friends looking to him for example.

Billy saw him again the following Sunday, riding in the rear of the company. He had a deep bruise on the side of his face from the sergeant's boot and rode his mount as if he was born in the saddle. Billy was standing with Ada and some other cousins at the edge of the parade ground where they usually watched, beside their parents' wagons. He had told the others about the race and the fight, and Ada seemed greatly interested in the exploits of the young private.

"That's him, isn't it?" she whispered.

"That's him," Billy responded proudly. Ada beamed as the line of horsemen rode by, the young private second from the near end.

"Oh, he's quite handsome," she whispered. "You didn't tell me that, Billy, how handsome he is."

Billy shushed her. He did not want his parents finding out he had been to the races and had been reluctant to let Ada know about it, but she had overheard him in the schoolyard relating the story to a group of boys and forced him to tell her by threatening to tell his mama about what she had heard him say. If she made a scene, it might be discovered that he had been going to the races after the picnic on Sundays instead of hunting like he had claimed.

"I think you ought to introduce me," she said in a loud voice.

"Shh. Shut up."

"I'll tell," she said, even louder. His mother was just behind them, sitting on the wagon seat with his aunt Sadie. He quickly walked away from Ada, down the line of bystanders in the same direction as the parade. She came running after him.

"What's his name?" she asked as she caught up.

"I don't know."

"You do too. You said they called him Ev."

He stopped at a gap in the crowd lining the parade ground and turned to her. "If you tell about me, I'll tell about you," he said.

"There's nothing to tell. You'd be lying."

"You know I'll tell."

She blushed. He had her.

"I found out his name. But you got to promise me."

"What?"

"You won't tell about the horse races."

"I promise."

"Okay." He began to walk along again behind the backs of the spectators. She followed closely behind and to his side. "He's Everett Hardeman."

"He's a Hardeman?"

"That's what I said."

"So is he Will Hardeman's son?"

"No. His daddy's dead."

"So who was he?"

He stopped again and turned to her.

"Why do you want to know?" he asked. "What difference does it make who his daddy was? Why do you want to know that?"

She looked down the parade ground, toward the line Ev Hardeman was riding in, which had passed them. Her face was bright and her eyes were as wide as the sky.

"It doesn't matter," she said. "It doesn't matter at all."

Later, after the parade, when the women were setting the tables, she approached her mother, who had the gout and was seated on a milking stool, giving directions to her help.

"Mama, can I invite a soldier to our table?" she asked, trying unsuccessfully to hide the excitement in her voice. Her mother was visibly surprised.

"What soldier?"

"Oh, just a boy that Billy knows." She blurted it out without thinking and was suddenly shocked by her mention of Billy, her involvement of him. She had not intended to mention Billy, because she feared that Billy would tell what he knew about her, and she could not allow that to happen.

"What's his name?" she asked.

"Everett Hardeman," she stated proudly.

Her mother looked up from a picnic box she was unloading. "Walker Hardeman's boy," she said with a softness in her voice.

Ada was surprised by her mother's reaction. She did not normally allow anyone to notice that she cared about anything, particularly since Ada's father, Tom Moore, had gone off to join the army.

"Why do you want him to come and eat with us, Ada? How do you know him?"

"I don't really know him, Mama," she said. "But I'd sure like to."

Her mother looked at her carefully. "You would, huh?"

"Yes ma'am. I would. So could you invite him?"

"Ada, if you'd been paying attention, you'd know the troops march in here and take their places at random. There are no invitations. And we've had the same bunch eating with us the last four Sundays."

She could see the disappointment in her daughter's face.

"Maybe you should sit here and help me with this table for a change and you might catch his eye as he comes by."

"Does he come by here?" Ada asked.

"Well, he might. You never can tell." She turned on her stool and looked around. "Here they come now," she said.

The cavalrymen had begun to stroll into the picnic ground from the opposite side of the grove. Their horses were left hitched to the rail fence on the edge of the road. As they passed into the shade of the oaks, the dappled sunlight touched their grey uniforms here and there, causing them to appear to shimmer. Ada came around the end of the table where her mother was sitting until she stood at the edge of the open area between the uneven rows of tables. She was a beautiful girl, with long black hair and blue Irish eyes, and most of the boys teased her in every way they could think of, trying to outdo each other in their small juvenile cruelties.

He saw her as soon as he stepped into the shade of the oaks. She was standing near the opposite side of the grove, wearing a light blue dress. He had eaten with a family he knew on past Sundays, but he walked past their table toward the young girl, who he could see was bravely standing in the open area and looking straight at him. At first, he thought that she must have mistaken him for someone else, but as he came nearer and she did not look away, he began to feel a strange excitement. She was very bold in looking straight at him, without so much as a glance to the side. She was not smiling. Her expression was very serious, and she looked as if she had been waiting for him for an eternity.

The Sunday before, he would have hesitated, unsure of himself, but since the incident with the sergeant, he had become a hero to the other young enlisted men, and he was still full of pride and instilled with a sense of chivalry. The girl, standing still in the wavy light beneath the oaks, was destined to be there. It was *his* destiny not to waver.

She could feel herself shaking as he approached, and she suddenly realized how frightened she was, but she gripped her hands together tightly in front of her waist, determined to act bravely. He stopped a few feet from her. Neither could find words. He broke the spell by looking at the table, where her mother sat staring at him.

"G-good afternoon, ma'am," he stuttered.

Mrs. Moore hesitated, unwilling to make it too easy for him. He looked back at Ada.

"Won't you join us, Private?" she said suddenly, glancing at her mother, who finally relented.

"Yes, please, Mr. Hardeman. Won't you have a seat?"

He took his campaign cap off quickly and looked at the table. Ada saw other soldiers approaching from behind Private Hardeman, including one freckled-faced boy who had been trying to attract her attention for weeks.

"Yes, please have a seat," Ada said lightly, trying to sound nonchalant. She stepped behind her mother and took a seat on the bench next to her stool, making the space across the table from her the obvious choice for the private. He turned and saw that the others were approaching and quickly sat down.

Billy sat on the top rail of the fence at the near edge of the grove, watching. The other soldiers came and exchanged greetings with Mrs. Moore and Ada, and grudgingly with the new man at table. They took their seats just as the servants were finishing the last table preparations. Billy could see that Ev Hardeman could hardly keep his eyes off Ada, and that she was sitting upright, acting in a manner that told him she was determined and single-minded, just as she could sometimes be when involved in a game she wanted very much to win.

As he rode by the grove behind the three men, his uncle John Baker, Gruder, and Jack Hays, he stared at the spot where he sat that day and the place where the table had been, now overgrown with weeds and briars, and he thought about the boys who had gone to fight and did not come back, and about those who came back changed. About the men who came back with their spirits altered, as if their boyish enthusiasm had been sucked out of them by some ominous, unseen force. When he was eight, he believed that his *country* was being threatened. Not the South, which was a concept that was unfamiliar to him, but Texas—home—and that foreigners were trying to take away the freedom that Texans had fought and died for. Now, seven years later, the foreigners had come, but few of them. For the most part, those who held the reins of power were Texans who had not gone off to fight, who had been there all along, invisible to him for so many years, along with a few who had come home after fighting for the North.

The men who fought for the South had no money and little property, could not vote or run for public office, and had only leftovers, things that had endured because they were of little value and could not be sold for enough to buy food or seed. There was no money of value, except that which the carpetbaggers brought with them and the Union soldiers' pay and the return on Northern investments that a few had secretly made in the early days of the war. Nothing that could be called government in any normal sense existed. Texas was occupied territory—a territory rather than a state or nation.

He did not learn of the battle of the Nueces until years later, when he was a young man. The killing of Union loyalists, most of them of German descent, came to be called a massacre during Reconstruction. It was said that Confederate troops intercepted lightly armed men attempting to flee to Mexico to avoid the draft and killed them without mercy or quarter. Later in life, he was told the fuller version of the story in an angry confrontation with a drunken, aged German scholar. Sometime later he heard the tale of a survivor of the massacre, who told him of the young Germans' stubborn refusal to surrender in the face of overwhelming odds, until only a few remained alive. Nor did he know until later in life of the folly of his father's cousin, Ben McCulloch, at the Battle of Pea Ridge, where his indecision led to his own death and that of many of his men; nor of the removal of Sam Houston by the secession convention because, as governor, he refused to take the oath of allegiance to the Confederacy. Or of Kaiser, who set fire to hundreds of acres in the Big Thicket in the last days of the war in an attempt to destroy suspected draft evaders. He learned instead of the heroism of Albert Sidney Johnston, killed at Shiloh, of the steadfastness of the men under John Bell Hood at Antietam and Gettysburg; and of the pyrrhic victory of the men under Rip Ford at Palmito Ranch in the Rio Grande valley after Lee's surrender at Appomattox.

He also learned, much later, that beliefs were the real stuff of wars and that the strength of a belief can overcome reality until complete disaster renders the remaining believers an ineffective and meager force, left to spread their creed in secret among the remaining believers; there were also others, those who once followed in step with the firebrands because it appeared that their homes and their society were indeed threatened by outsiders bent on destroying their way of life and not because of an un-swerving, blind adherence to undying principle. Those were the ones who ultimately survived and adapted and achieved a perspective that could admit, at least tacitly, that the whole sacrifice had been for nothing— nothing more than an unrealistic ideal.

But he was not to come to this understanding until much later in life, when he was past the age of adventure. At fifteen, riding behind the three men who would most influence him, he believed in the justness of his kin and therefore the justice of their cause. The black man who rode ahead of him, a willing participant in the search they were undertaking, was a product of the society that Ev Hardeman and others had so willingly fought to save and was therefore living proof of its validity and worth— and of the injustice of its demise—as much as the white men who rode beside him, or so he believed.

It would be years before he learned about the early Texas law that forbade the immigration of "free negroes" and provided for their sale at public auction and criminal penalties for any who harbored them, on the theory, expressed in the statute, that the presence of free blacks in Texas could not be tolerated because the slaves would be encouraged to seek their freedom, thus destroying the institution so *necessary* for commercial survival. Just as it would be many years before he came to know the truth about secret organizations and broken promises. Gruder could read, which relatively few whites his age could do, and he knew more about more things than anyone Billy knew. Things like how armadillos crossed rivers and how a cotton gin worked. And he used good English, generally.

The morning was sunny and cool and they made good time as the road climbed through rolling pastureland until it forked at the base of the escarpment that forms the southern edge of the Edwards Plateau, the Texas Hill Country. They headed west along the edge of the escarpment.

Gruder had fallen behind the two leaders and was riding even with Billy, who had the three pack mules in tow.

"So how many's he killed?"

"His share." Gruder acted unconcerned, but Billy knew how much he loved to tell tales, particularly about old times. And he clearly loved and revered Hays.

"How many's that?"

"Enough," he said with a slight smile.

"Were they all Mexicans and Indians?"

"Mostly."

"Why'd he go to California?"

"Guess he was seekin' his fortune."

"Did he find it?"

"Don't know. Don't look like he's dressin' real fancy though, does it?"

Hays and his uncle John rode ahead of them, no longer talking, which was not surprising. They matched each other in their quiet ways. Earlier, Hays had informed John Baker that he thought they should be able to reach Leon Springs by nightfall, and he expected them to camp there and be on the Medina by the next day. He was keeping a pace that would just about do it, pushing his horse along in a trot.

John Baker knew that the information about Morgan which Hays possessed was weeks old and that they might be in for days of riding before they caught up with him, if they did at all, but the way Hays talked about reaching the Medina had a certainty, a deadliness about it, as if he knew where and when he would run onto Morgan.

"I figure he's holed up on Wallace Creek," he had said. "I plan on camping on the Medina tomorrow night." His voice had the old tone of command in it.

His history with the Comanche was not only as a Ranger, but also as a scout and surveyor. He had studied Comanche camps, burial grounds, and watering holes unknown to the white man. There is a place where Wallace Creek turns upon itself a few miles above its confluence with the Medina. There are two ways in and out of the broad canyon it flows through. The approach from the south, alongside the creek where it cuts through steep hills, is easy to sentry. The way out to the north is steep and hazardous. The Comanches had used horse trails up the sides of the sloping, rocky hills for decades and could even escape up the northern draw at night, when it was impossible to follow them. During the day they would have a two-hour head start, and the white man and his horses would not find easy going even in daylight, giving the Comanches every advantage. Unless you could kill their sentry before he could raise an alarm.

The Comanches had holed up for generations in this little valley, where there was normally an abundance of winter grass for horses, plentiful game, and the clear, cold water of Wallace Creek—particularly when they knew they were being followed by an inferior force of whites. Then, after running before their pursuers as if afraid for their lives, they would lay in ambush along the path from the south and kill every man in the party pursuing them. If pursued by an equal or larger number, they would rest as long as they felt safe, then escape to the north, on a trail which took the better part of a day to reach by going around the hills surrounding the valley. If Morgan was where Hays believed him to be, he would know of their approach long before they were near and would be waiting for them.

Morgan's Comanche name translated to Swift Rider. He was known as an excellent horseman among an entire band of excellent horsemen, the Antelope band, or what was left of it. The Antelope had not signed the treaty to enter the reservation two years earlier, as other bands had. Leo Morgan, as the son of a chief, was a natural leader whose following included the wildest and deadliest of the young warriors, but he was considered a renegade who had adopted many of the ways of the whites. He liked white women, the younger the better, and neglected his Comanche wife and children for them. He had taken many white women in raids and turned most of them over to others when he tired of them. He had only killed a few. While he was enjoying them, he kept them from the other women and would not allow them to be worked, but this was usually for only a short period, at most a few weeks. The other half-breed Antelope, Quanah Parker, steered clear of Morgan.

Most of the half-breed Comanches, including Quanah, were from a union of a captured white woman and a Comanche warrior and were born and raised Comanche. Leo Morgan was born in a whorehouse in El Paso and did not see a Comanche until he was five years old, when a "friend" of his mother, a fortune hunter called Bad Jack, took him to a Comanche camp outside Fort McKavett, where Jack was doing some trading. The boy had felt an instant sense of belonging and sneaked back to the camp after dark, leaving Bad Jack asleep in his roll nearby.

There was no council fire that night. It was a summer moonlit night, and the old people were sitting around without a fire, talking about the day and telling tales. He had never heard Comanche spoken before that day, but he was fluent in Spanish and English and the band that camped that night was a group of Yap-eaters who had broken off from the larger band to attempt peaceful trade with the whites. They told the trading post man at McKavett that they were Kiowa Apaches and he was too ignorant of Indian ways to know the difference. A sergeant stationed at the post recognized the Comanche signs in their clothing and gear, but he said nothing, judging them to be a harmless collection of old people and women and children—as they were—posing no threat to the fort. Some of the women spoke Spanish to each other when the men were not speaking. The boy crawled to within hearing distance and lay there listening to the voices in the moonlight until he was discovered by an old woman returning from the spring.

She dragged him into the circle of women by the scruff of his neck and threw him down before them. Although dressed in white man's clothes, his black hair was long and straight, his skin was dark, and he looked like a Comanche boy in the moonlight.

"*Amigo*," he said. "*Yo soy un amigo. No intento molestar.*" He stood up immediately and began to talk to them as if he was a grown man. He was used to living among groups of women; even at age five he had a certain arrogance about him when speaking. He told them he was an orphan whose father was a Comanche chief named Spoon Dog and whose mother had been a great white lady, that he was seeking his father and wanted to learn the ways of the *People* so that he would know how to look for his father among them. He knew little more about his connection to the Comanche than his father's name, which he had learned from his mother one night when she was drunk in her confinement with her monthly curse. She had come and taken him from the pallet in the storeroom down the hall and put him in bed with her and told him the story of his father, a great warrior, who had paid well for her at Cross Timbers and wanted to take her with him that very night and would have, but for the drunkenness that finally overcame him and put him to sleep.

The Comanche women did not believe him, but they could see that he was a breed. They told him he could come along with them if in the morning the leader, Hook Nose, approved, but he would have to do the dirtiest work in camp and take orders from everyone. The next morning

Hook Nose, in a bad mood, disputed that he could be the son of Spoon Dog. This boy had a short nose and green eyes. He was not Comanche.

But the women had already made up their minds, so Hook Nose ignored him for a few days, acting as if he did not see him following along with the women, until the boy gradually began to understand enough of the language to take orders from some of the old men who would not speak Spanish as a matter of pride. By the time the first norther came he was, although not accepted as a member of the little group, accepted as a fellow traveler who would be allowed to look for his father's band as he traveled along with them. He would not see his mother again until he was fifteen.

SIX

LILY POE POURED COFFEE FOR ASHLEY MAITLAND WHILE BARBARA Ann stacked the dishes and cleared the table. Ash watched Lily hold the coffee pot with two potholders as she poured. He knew that the invitation to dinner was more than social. Lily Poe had always impressed him with her attention to business.

"So how are you and Eli getting along?" he asked, as she drew back the pot.

She hesitated and her eyes narrowed. "How was supper?" she asked, smiling.

He had already complimented her profusely. "You bought him out," he said suddenly, reading her. She stopped smiling.

"It was a good deal for both of us," she said, looking Ashley straight in the eye.

"You want me to take notes?" he asked.

She laughed.

"Ash, I do love you. Do you think I've imposed on you too much over the years?"

He stood. "You're a fine one." He smiled and took his cup to the window. "What's the deal?"

"Ten thousand over fifteen years. Ten percent of the profit, as interest."

"And you keep the books."

She turned abruptly when he said that and walked through the kitchen doorway.

He immediately wished he had not said it. He had never known her to cheat a friend. He walked in behind her and touched her arm. "I'm sure he'll get every penny."

When she turned he could see from her moist eyes that he had unfairly dredged up something that should have remained buried.

"I'm going to make a go of it, Ash. And it's going to belong to me and my daughter. Nobody's going to take it away from us. I've paid for this opportunity, many times over. And I know you're a friend and I'm grateful for it. It's sad that Wes had to die for it to happen."

He was silent. Her chestnut hair was pulled back in a bun, revealing the curve of her neck as she turned back to the washbasin.

"Any way I can help you I will," he said. "You know that."

"I didn't know about the will. You know that, don't you?"

"I didn't think you did."

She began to take dishes from Barbara Ann, who was washing. As she dried, she talked about her plans. She had decided to use very little of her cash, keeping a reserve for contingencies. She had calculated her labor costs and made an estimate of materials she fully intended to buy on credit against future mill rates from merchants who also farmed cotton. Some of them owed her gambling debts, which she agreed to credit against half of her purchases. She had lined up enough sharecropping deals to pay back her initial outlay in capital within a year and clear a small profit, with any kind of market and any kind of luck. She had also figured out how to make interest on debts and favors due her. It would take a minor disaster for her to fail to make a profit in the first year.

"I'll have to wait a few days for Gruder," she said.

"Why's that?"

"Laura sent him with Billy. To watch out for him."

"And Billy went with Hays?"

"Indeed he did. To take his daddy's place." She looked at him with the same glistening eyes.

Ash finished off the coffee. "Wes would have approved."

"He would have certainly gone if he had been here."

He was afraid she was going to break down.

"Gone where, Mama?" Barbara Ann asked, looking up from the basin with concern.

"Billy's gone with some men to find a lost girl," she answered. "They'll be gone a few days."

SEVEN

THEY CROSSED THE GUADALUPE AT INDIAN CROSSING, WHERE the cypress trees stood high above the banks. They skirted the town of New Braunfels, a quiet, orderly German community, because Hays did not want to discuss their mission with the inhabitants. Although the German farmers were honest and minded their own business, some of the townspeople still traded for buffalo skins with the Indians and Hays preferred to avoid them. These men were friendly with renegades, who helped them locate wandering bands. If they were seen, and Hays was recognized, Morgan and whoever was with him might be warned, so they stayed on the old San Antonio Road south of the town until they came to the trail that branched off toward Leon Springs.

It was twilight when they reached the springs, an ancient campsite surrounded by post oak and mesquite, a regular camp for Hays and his Rangers in the old days. Hays noticed a paint pony grazing on the far side of the clearing. The pony wore a rope halter and looked up at them as they approached. Hays and John Baker dismounted. Gruder veered to the right around the edge of the clearing and showed his open hand to Billy—a signal for him to wait. Billy sat saddle at the near edge of the clearing while Hays walked steadily toward the other side, leading his horse, with John Baker following. The light was dim, and the camp within the post oaks, around the springs and the curving creek bank, was not clearly visible to them.

The paint did not look up again from its grazing as Hays passed it halfway across the clearing, his eyes scanning the tree line ahead. He dropped the reins short of the wood line and his horse stopped. Hays stopped at the edge of the clearing, peering into the darkness, waiting, until John Baker reached his side. He stood perfectly still for several minutes, then slowly walked into the campsite, his right hand held near his belt. He disappeared from Billy's view for a moment, then Billy heard a whoop from within the grove. It was not a war whoop. John Baker entered the trees, then came back out smiling and waving to Billy and Gruder. When Billy entered the camp, Hays was standing near a small fire talking to an old Indian man who squatted before the fire. Wonsley sat on a stump stool nearby. Hays turned to Billy, who was the last to enter the woods. The old man stared into Billy's eyes, unwavering.

"This is Wes McCulloch's son," Hays said, in Spanish.

The old man said, "I thought so."

"And these are his uncles," gesturing toward John and Wonsley.

Gruder walked up slowly and stopped still.

"Who's this old Indian?" he asked in Spanish, looking at Hays with arched brows.

He then looked back at the squatting old man, who said in a strangely accented English, "Who's the old man?"

Gruder glared at him, but his features quickly softened.

"I can't believe you're still alive, Luis," he said, and began to smile.

"You either, Gruder."

After they had made camp and were sitting around the fire, Hays told Billy about Luis. He was an Apache who had been jailed by the Mexicans at the time of the Santa Fe Expedition almost thirty years ago. He had scouted for Hays along the Nueces and Rio Grande after he was brought back to Texas by the survivors of the expedition, who had freed him when they escaped prison. He fought alongside Hays and the Rangers to pay the Texans back for his freedom, then returned to his people. That was in 1842, the last that Hays or Gruder had seen of him until this evening.

Luis then told of his life after he left Texas and went back to New Mexico, in soft Spanish. The Mexicans arrested him again, although he was vague about the reason, in 1845, and he spent the next two years in prison. By the time he was released, New Mexico had become a territory of the United States, but he had a score to settle against the Mexican who had arrested him, an irregular by the name of Garza, who was reported to have gone to San Antonio. Luis spent the next ten years looking for

Garza over most of South Texas and Northern Mexico, but never found him. When he returned to the mountains, the home of his people, he found that his wife and son were dead, killed by a half-breed named Juaro. He had been looking for Juaro ever since.

Luis said he had dreamed that he would meet up with Hays, whom he referred to as Capitan Jack, and that Hays would lead him to one of the men he sought, though he could not tell which one. He also said that in his dream the Capitan needed him because he too was looking for a man, and Luis could help him find his man.

He had been looking into the fire while speaking. "Whom do you seek, Capitan?" he asked softly, still speaking Spanish.

"A bad man, *un hombre malo*," Hays replied. "I think he is in the Hill Country to the northwest."

"I have seen," Luis said, still looking into the fire.

"What have you seen, Luis?"

"I have seen a river or creek, surrounded by hills, and a man with a scar on his left cheek. He is angry. I also see a girl with red hair. She is crying."

Hays looked across the fire at Gruder, who looked back with a sign of recognition.

"The creek turns upon itself and looks like two creeks, like Sister Creeks, but it is not Sister Creeks."

"Have you ever seen Wallace Creek, Luis?" Gruder asked.

The old man hesitated, still staring into the fire. "That is where Bigfoot once was," he said. "He is not there right now."

"That's right," Gruder replied. "You ever been there?"

The old man turned to look at Gruder. He said something Billy did not understand. It was not Spanish.

Gruder turned to Billy, for the first time acknowledging his presence in the circle. "He said only in the dream world."

Luis looked at Billy for a long moment, then spoke to him slowly.

"There is another world that most men are too busy to visit," he said, again speaking Spanish. Then, in English, "I have had a lot of time."

He then spoke of how he had seen his wife and son many times and how much he wanted to join them, but he could not, until he had found and killed the man who had killed them. It had been his thirst for revenge that had killed his family. He spat out the word, *venganza*. It was his burden in life that he was to carry until he could find the killer and kill him. That was not revenge, he explained, no *venganza*, but his penance.

He had seen a man with a scar on his cheek in his mind's eye, but did not know if he was the killer of his family. He sensed that he was too young, but he did not know if he saw him in his dream as he was now or had been then. He felt that he might be Juaro, the man who had made his life a living hell, and he expected that if he came along with Capitan Jack he would find the man and kill him. He pronounced Hays's early nickname like the Comanches did, a border lingo, *Capitan Yack*.

Hays had also been looking into the fire. He seemed to be in a trance. Billy later learned many things from Gruder about the exploits of the famous Capitan Yack. He could sense how Hays had evoked wonder among the early Texas settlers by his quiet forcefulness, but this trance had nothing of that coldness in it. It was a totally relaxed state, in which Hays appeared to be somewhere else. A long silence passed.

Gruder finally stood and tended to the fire. Later, he told Billy about how fearless Hays had been in battle. Of about ninety initial Rangers, whom Hays joined shortly after San Jacinto in '36, only a handful, including Hays, were still alive at the beginning of the Mexican War in '46. Six out of ninety. Yet Hays had been at the vanguard of almost every battle. The Comanches had come to believe he was an evil spirit incarnate and called him *Diablo Yack*. Evil because he was sent to exterminate the People. But for such an evil influence, the *Nermenuh*, as they called themselves, could have survived all those battles.

They thought they had him at Enchanted Rock in '41. He had climbed the rock alone. None of the others in his surveying and scouting party, including Henry McCulloch, wanted to make the climb. Enchanted Rock is an extrusion of granite which heats up during summer days and, when cooling at night, makes sounds that the Indians said were the voices of spirits. Hays was on top when he was surrounded by a party of Comanches, who recognized him. He crouched in a small rock crater at the top, while the Comanches shouted, "*Diablo Yack*" and "*Diablo Blanco Silencioso,*" another Comanche name for him, trying to taunt him out of his lair.

He had lost his powder horn, emptied his two five-shooters and his rifle, and had pulled his Bowie knife for hand-to-hand combat when his men—hearing his shots—finally arrived and drove off the remaining

Comanches. Although he had only eleven shots, fourteen Comanches lay dead around him, one killed by his men as they approached. He had killed two with the butt of his rifle.

Almost immediately, the story of Enchanted Rock became embellished, and it added to the growing mystique of Hays. The earliest version had him fighting off an entire band of one hundred Comanches without rescue by his men. His legend among the whites was therefore as deep as that told by the Indians, with one important difference. The Comanches believed that a warrior was invincible only through magic. The whites believed in a different kind of heroism.

Luis followed them at dawn as they left the camp. No one said a word about it, as if it was understood that he would be coming along. They followed the old trail that led past the camp on Ranger Creek, near Boerne, which Hays had used as a regular ranger camp because it was convenient to many of the old Comanche trails. His job in the early forties had been to discourage the Comanches from raiding the whites, although the only way to discourage them was to eventually kill off so many of their warriors that they could no longer field an effective fighting force. After Plum Creek, the Comanches seldom raided east of San Antonio, but they still held to the belief that *Comancheria* was their territory, and any white or black man who ventured into the Hill Country was an invader, subject to torture and eventual death. It was not an idle, vainly sadistic thing to torture one's enemies. It was part of the strategy of war. The fiercest were the most feared.

The Comanche attacked in large bands many times after 1840, but the Rangers had the five-shooter by then, and the Comanches soon learned that stealth was the only weapon effective against men like Diablo Yack and their weapons that could spit bullets as if from the fingers of each hand. The Comanche raids became lightning quick, by moonlight, against small ranchers and settlers. There were few buffalo left for them, and they had no other means of survival but the horses and other livestock they could steal. Stealing from an enemy was honorable, particularly if it could be done in a brazen manner. Leaving mutilated bodies was also good medicine, as was carrying off women, particularly young girls, as slaves. The warriors were fascinated by red hair, and a red-haired woman was likely to survive, although the degree of mutilation and torture she endured was often a matter of chance.

They took the trail from Ranger Creek toward the Medina and Bandera by way of Pipe Creek. The Medina was broader and deeper beside
the town of Bandera, which they avoided. They crossed well above the
town and proceeded up the opposite bank on the old trail that was no
longer in use until they passed most of the outlying farmhouses. The
stream, clear and cold, narrowed above the town. They stayed on the
overgrown trail to avoid being seen. If Morgan was on the Wallace, he
might have confederates in Bandera. It was late afternoon when Hays
led them up a ravine to the top of a hill overlooking the Medina Valley,
where they were to camp for the night. There were no signs of anyone
having been there recently, which is what Hays had counted on. He rode
the perimeter of the hilltop looking for signs on the ground. It was evident that he was familiar with the place. Gruder later said that it had
been at least twenty-five years since the Colonel had been to this site.
Gruder had been with him, but would not have known he was within
five miles of the place from the lay of the land. Hays's surveyor's eyes,
however, remembered every rock and hill.

They camped without a fire in the cold wind that swept across the
hilltop, lying in a depression below some rocks that gave partial shelter. The three-quarter moon rose early and illuminated the camp. Billy
dreamed of his cousin Ada, swimming nude in Plum Creek. She was
fourteen again and he was seven, but this time she swam away from him
toward some older boys on the opposite bank, and he could not swim
fast enough to catch up. Then he looked down and realized that no matter how hard he paddled, he could not move in the water. The current,
instead of coming from upstream, came across the creek from the other
bank, where the boys, also naked, were cheering Ada as she swam effort-
lessly toward them.

Then he realized that someone was holding him back by pulling on
his shoulder and he felt that he should open his eyes. When he did,
Gruder was pulling him by the shoulder onto his back. The moon had
set, and the stars were starkly outlined above him.

"We're movin'," Gruder said softly.

"What time is it?" Billy groaned.

"Early," Gruder said. "Come on." And he turned to roll up his bedroll.

Hays planned to ride up Wallace Creek into the hidden valley before
dawn, although he had not bothered to mention this the night before.

They saddled up quietly, each of them sobered by the early wakeup and the danger that awaited them. Billy checked the saddlebag for his father's Colt that he had brought with him. He pulled it out holstered, checked the load in its cylinders, and strapped the holster belt on. They could see by starlight the rough outline of the horses and the trees on the edge of the hilltop, but Billy wondered how they could possibly pick their way through wooded country in the dark. Even Wonsley would have difficulty in strange country in this darkness. But they all followed Hays as he led his horse down another overgrown trail that seemed to follow a ridge, never dipping as low as the river valley below but keeping in a relatively open space where the ground could be faintly discerned ahead of them. They walked for a good hour along this high trail, then stopped. Gruder, who was ahead of Billy and the pack mules but behind the others, led his horse to the front to confer with Hays. They had reached the point where Gruder was to separate from them and from what he had said earlier, Billy knew that they were about to go down into the valley, where danger waited. He could hear Jimmy snuffle as Gruder led him on up the high trail, and the rest of them began to descend.

Billy followed behind the others, leading the pack mules as well as his own mount. Luis brought up the rear. Billy had the two mules tied in sequence with ropes of varying length, so that they could follow his horse in single file, with one rope strung through the rigging of the lead mule to keep them in line. They treaded quietly, as if the animals sensed the danger of being heard. The trail soon began to dip, and they moved up and down small hillocks among junipers, gradually descending into the valley of the Medina. Billy could not visualize how the Wallace came into the Medina and wondered whether they would have to cross the Medina to get to it.

Luis followed quietly, leading his paint. Billy could occasionally see his outline against the sky when he looked back. The old man seemed to have trouble standing, and it was hard to understand how he was able to walk down this semblance of a trail in the dark, but he was never far behind.

Billy was at the rump of Wonsley's horse before he knew it. The others had stopped ahead of him. After a long pause, they started moving again. After twenty yards or so down the trail, the path opened up onto a worn trail, devoid of underbrush. They bore to the left. He heard rushing water to the right as they moved among cypress trees, and at times could see the river between broad spaces among the cypress branches. After a while they stopped again, and word was whispered down the line to mount. They entered the river edge slowly, coaxing their mounts into the water by leg action and soft sounds. The crossing was shallow, and the water did not reach their boots. Once in midstream, Billy could see the outline of the ridge behind him against the stars, a dark, ominous, sleeping-animal shape that the Indians might well have named for a recumbent buffalo cow or blanketed woman.

The starlight over the river was unimpeded by trees, and he could see up and downstream as far as the nearest bends in the river. The river was wide at this point, and the cypress trees stood starkly as dark outlines against the banks on each side.

The horses and men ahead of him were also visible. He wondered if Hays knew whether they were being observed from the hills across the river. They were heading for a low place, with the dark outline of hills on either side, and dark borders of cypress trees below the hills. When they reached the far side of the river, they veered left, upstream, and toward the middle of the low place where Wallace Creek emptied into the Medina.

Here, the cypress branches extended over the banks of the creek until they almost touched, forming a canopy that shielded the creek from the hilltops on either side. After a few hundred yards, Hays led them into the shallow water of the creek, and they moved upstream at a slow walk as the first light began to appear in the sky ahead of them. They moved in slow motion, a soft breeze moving the cypress branches above them in a low rustle, the rushing of the stream a gurgle that played against the sound of the wind in the branches. The plodding of the horses and mules in the stream blended in, making their progress silent and timeless, their movements ethereal, as if they were disconnected from the world of the hills and the trees and animal life around them. As the light grew, birds began to awaken and sing in the branches of the trees all around them.

Billy felt a cold chill. He was staring ahead at the hats of the men and the heads of the horses moving slowly from side to side as the horses felt their way up the stream, framed by the density of the trees on either side, with bird sounds all around them. He had an uneasy feeling in his belly. He held the reins slack, giving Julie her head so that she could keep her balance in the current. As the light in the sky increased, he could see through the tree lines the hills that bordered the creek. They became gradually steeper, approaching the banks precipitously until there was no place for a trail on either side, and the horses were moving up a steep canyon between high cliffs. He thought of Gruder for the first time since he had split off and wondered where he was. Was he above— on the top of one of the bluffs— or ahead of them, or at the place where they were heading?

They rode in a slow calm way, and Billy gradually began to nod. He had been wide awake the whole time, fear and uncertainty stimulating him, but now he was very drowsy and had to fight to keep his eyes open. He tried to concentrate on Hays, three horses ahead. The black hat bobbed and swayed in the soft morning light. But this seemed to be counterproductive, causing him to fix hypnotically on the movement of the hat and drift off. He shook himself awake after an uncertain period of unconsciousness, took his hat off, leaned down to dip it in the cold water of the stream and bathed his head in a splash of cold which washed over his shoulders and onto Julie's neck and forequarters, causing her to start. There must have been a noise, for Wonsley turned in his saddle and looked back at him with a puzzled expression, but the cold water had done its work well. He was awake again.

They continued upstream for about an hour, until the cliffs on either side gradually widened and gave way to gentler slopes. Here they left the stream. Hays signaled to them to dismount in a grove of cottonwoods, close by the left bank of the stream and sheltered from view from above by a large boulder which formed a part of the hill on that side of the creek. They gathered around Hays as he squatted and drew markings in the sandy soil.

"Here's where we are," he said, pointing to a place where two lines in the dirt came close together around a third. "We are at the bottom of a valley that runs a mile or so upstream before it narrows up again, here," indicating with a stick. "There are falls the horses can't get up. The camp is here." He put the point of the stick on a small circle he had made on the far side of the line that represented the creek, just below the upstream canyon.

"The only way into it is across this field, which this time of year will have low grass. We will be in the open for a space. There's no other way in. If Gruder's done his job, and our man's in the camp, we'll have to ride hard and fast across the field and the creek to get to him. If he had warning of us coming, he won't be there."

He looked at Billy sternly. "You stay here with the mules. If we flush him and don't get him soon enough, he may come back down this way. You can't count on what he's going to do. So it's important for you to stay here and be alert."

Billy suddenly felt that Hays knew he had fallen asleep downstream.

Hays turned to the Bakers. "We'll ride in at full gallop. The creek's shallow, but there're big rocks in it over there, so you'll have to rein in when you cross. If he's inclined to fight, he'll try to knock us off as we cross. And we don't know who's with him."

Luis was sitting on a rock behind Billy. "The man with the scar is here," he said softly. "I think he is the one I seek."

"You stay here too, Luis," Hays said. "I need you here."

Luis said something that Billy did not understand, and Hays replied tersely in the same language, the words punctuated with gestures. Luis said nothing, but stared at Hays without expression. Hays stared back for a moment, then stood.

"We will know soon who is here," Hays said in Spanish. "Let's go."

Billy watched the men mount and move slowly to the edge of the grove at the low end of the clearing. They sat and checked their weapons, first the rifles, then the pistols. Then they nodded to each other and spurred their horses into a gallop across the clearing toward the line of trees in the distance where the creek meandered to the northwest. Billy watched, holding Julie's reins and the lead ropes to the mules. Luis left his paint with the reins dropped and walked to the edge of the clearing where he, too, stood watching the horsemen gallop away.

"He will not come here and Capitan Jack knows it," he said. "He is trying to save you from harm." He turned and looked at Billy. "You will stay here."

He made a sound with his lips, and the paint followed him into the clearing.

Billy started to remind him that Hays had told him to wait, but stopped himself. It would have done no good, and it was not his place. The old man walked erect, and the paint followed behind him, the hats of the riders ahead barely visible in the distance. After they had disappeared from sight, the old man whistled to his horse and mounted, then proceeded at a trot after them.

Up ahead, the tree line grew larger as Hays and the Bakers galloped until they could make out in the pale light the darker recesses where the creek lay among the cypresses. They could detect no movement, and Hays, his eyes steady as he rode, concentrated on one particular area, below a place on the hillside where embedded rocks could be seen between the tree branches in a narrow field of light.

They crashed through the underbrush and line of trees on the near side and into the water with a sound that for the first time seemed to exist outside of the rumbling and pounding of the horses and their hearts. They danced across the narrow span of shallow water, the horses lunging competitively now and covering the width of the stream in a couple of bounds. In seconds they were on the other side, pistols drawn, crouched in their saddles to hang over the necks of their mounts, intensely aware of the movement of every leaf around them. There were some post-oak logs leaning against the side of the hill ahead of them, overgrown around the bottom, which at first appeared to be a narrow stack left after cutting, but soon they could see the matted reeds woven into the upper portion of the stack, reeds darkened by smoke and dried by the sun. They reined in, slowing their mounts before they ran headlong into the bouldered hillside. The lean-to was under a rock overhang. Its outer edge was almost overhead when they pulled their horses to a stop.

Hays swung down as his mount slowed and in the same motion lifted his rifle from its scabbard. He moved quickly to the opening on the left side of the structure, thrusting his rifle inside ahead of him. Wonsley was on the ground before Hays reached the opening. John Baker was slower, dismounting and moving in a crouched run to the opposite end of the lean-to, his pistol drawn. Wonsley, in the middle, scanned the rocky hillside above them from right to left, his rifle in hand.

"Cap'n," he said in a low voice.

Hays backed out of the opening and looked his way.

"They went up there," he said, gesturing to the hillside where a barely visible trail snaked among the boulders.

Hays backed out from the overhang to look where Wonsley pointed with his rifle.

"I'd say they left this mornin'," Wonsley said. "Those tracks are fresh."

He was fifty feet away from the portion of the trail where the nearest bare ground was visible, staring up at it with wide blue eyes. The trail, almost vertical in places, seemed impossible for a horse to climb. John Baker returned to his horse and grabbed the reins.

"Then we better get on up there," he said.

Hays went first, patiently leading his buckskin up the trail, so narrow and steep at some points that the stallion slipped back and was in danger of falling off the edge of the hillside, but slowly he followed Hays's patient coaxing. Wonsley and John Baker followed, leading their mounts. Wonsley had climbed many a trail, but this one was particularly difficult. The horses were reluctant, and the men could only move a few steps at a time before pausing to coax their horses another few steps. Finally Hays had reached the uppermost part of the trail where it was not as steep and there was more space between the worn path and the down break in the hillside. He paused and looked up and down the ridge that now lay slightly above him, where the trail branched off into north and south. He crouched his way up the final few yards to the top, where he waited for the others. Before Wonsley reached the top Gruder came into view, leading his horse up the ridge trail from downstream. His hat was tied to his saddle. He came along the trail with his head down, reading tracks, although he had seen Hays before Hays had seen or heard him. He was solemn and obviously disappointed.

By the time Gruder reached the spot where Hays stood, Wonsley and John had made their way to the top and were waiting beside him.

"I don't know how he knew we were coming," Gruder said. "Whoever he was, he could see in the dark."

"How long you figure?" Hays asked.

"No more than an hour, Cap'n. I was almost on top, and I heard him move. He hardly made a sound, but I heard him. But I was too far down the trail. I couldn't get to him. He had to see in the dark. I didn't make any noise."

"Then they got an hour on us. Wonsley?"

Wonsley walked the upstream fork of the ridge trail a few steps, looking down at bent blades of grass and thin accumulations of soil that were barely discernible. At one point he kneeled, looking at a bare place between flat rocks where there was no grass.

"Four horses," he said, looking at the ground. "Three came up from below to about here. The other one came up this high trail ahead of Gruder."

"Then let's get going," Hays said.

"What about the boy?" John asked.

"You go get him and Luis, Gruder. We'll meet up at Brown's."

Gruder looked down at his boots. He knew that it would be the next day before he and the other two could get to Donald Brown's cabin on the Guadalupe if they had to double back down the creek to the Medina and make their way cross country to get there.

"Whatever you say, Cap'n," he said slowly.

Hays studied him.

"You think you can get those mules up this hill?" he asked, skepticism in his tone.

Gruder walked over to the point where the trail reached the ridge top and looked down at the steep incline and the barely worn path that angled down the side of the hillside. He turned and looked at the three men.

"You got those horses up here, didn't you?"

Hays shot a glance at John Baker, then looked back at Gruder.

"We'll go ahead, and you come on with the other two and the mules. We'll see you when we see you."

Hays nodded at Wonsley, who swung into his saddle and headed up the ridge trail. Hays and John Baker followed and soon disappeared over a slight rise. Gruder tied his horse to a juniper limb and began to descend the trail toward the creek. When he was a third of the way down, he saw a flash of sunlight from the far side of the creek that did not look right, and he squatted beside a small boulder, watching and waiting. In a few seconds he saw a spot of blue among the cypress branches over the creek. Then he saw Luis's bandana-wrapped head as he rode across the stream. When Gruder reached the bottom of the hillside, Luis was waiting for him in the small clearing in front of the lean-to.

The old Apache was looking at the ground around him and at the logs tied together under the rock overhang. He stood still and did not look up at Gruder as he approached.

"They gone up the ridge," Gruder said. "They must have heard us coming."

Luis looked up at him. "How was that?" he said, in English.

"Don't know. But they pulled out before dawn."

The old Apache squatted, picked up a handful of grass and threw it into the wind. "They smelled us," he said in Spanish. "The wind changed this morning."

Gruder made a sound that was almost a chuckle. "They didn't smell us," he said.

"How do you know?" Luis asked.

"What are you doing here, anyway? The Cap'n told you to stay put."

Luis, ignoring him, stood and walked slowly to the opening at the side of the lean-to where he poked his head in and took a deep breath. Then he stood erect and faced the creek, his eyes closed. Gruder watched his impassive features for several minutes, then turned and waded the creek to go after Billy and the mules, leaving the old man standing there with his eyes still closed.

When they returned with the animals and packs, the old man was seated on a cypress root at the edge of the water, staring into the moving stream. He looked up at them as they crossed, then stood and came to them.

"They are doubling back," he said. "We should wait here."

Gruder, who had been leading the mules ahead of Billy, stopped and looked at him.

"What do you mean?" he asked. "How do you know that?"

"I can smell them," Luis said. "They are coming back. I cannot tell when, but they are coming back."

Billy approached the lean-to slowly, carefully looking at the post-oak poles, which were tied together to form a wall under the edge of the rock outcrop. The reeds used as ties came from just downstream, the clay chocked between the poles from the creek bank. Everything used in its construction came from materials immediately at hand. He crouched into the opening on the left and pulled aside the deer hide that covered the entryway. The smell of fire ash and something musty and mysterious filled his nose. The darkness was at first complete. It took a full minute before his eyes adapted to the low light in the lean-to and he could see spots of sunlight on the dirt floor. Gradually, he could make out a fire ring containing a small amount of ashes and hollowed-out places where buffalo robes had lain. The rear of the lean-to was a low-ceilinged cave, darker than the area by the doorway. There was something light against the darkness of the cave floor. He crept over to it. He hesitated to reach down in the darkness. A fear of bats and creatures of the night overcame him for a moment, transporting him back to early childhood. Then his curiosity took over. The object was small. He slowly reached his finger down and touched it. It was soft. A piece of cloth. He picked it up between his thumb and forefinger and carried it out into the light.

The white cotton was stained with blood. He held it up as Luis silently approached him, a frown on his face. He grabbed the cloth away from Billy and brought it to his nose. His scowl deepened. He squinted at the red stain, then looked at Billy, his eyebrows arched.

"*La muchacha es una mujer,*" he said, nodding slightly.

Gruder snatched the scrap of cloth away from him and stared at it, holding it away from his body in the sunlight, his face a grimace of disgust.

"Bullshit," he growled, and threw the cloth into the creek. "Let's get going."

He and Billy took the mules up the hill first. They were easier than the horses, once they decided that they wanted to go up the hill. When they came back for Julie and Luis's paint, they found Luis sitting on a flat rock beside the stream. He insisted on staying there, and could not be reasoned with. After he had managed to get Julie up the hillside, Billy went back down to try again to convince him to go with them, but Luis was adamant.

"The one I seek is with them, but he will not stay with them," he said. "I will wait here for him."

They left him there. The last Billy saw of him he was still seated on the rock on the bank of the creek, staring down into the water.

Gruder led them up the ridge trail, keeping his eye on the ground and yet measuring his gait and looking up from time to time. At first Billy thought the pace was too slow. They were a good hour behind Hays and his uncles, who were probably losing ground on Morgan and his companions because they had to go at a trailing pace, and he did not want to fall farther behind. The sight of the bloody underwear gave Billy an ache, a feeling in his guts that he had not felt before. He wondered if this was the feeling that made men kill. Although he had no conscious thought of killing the men they pursued, he was now urging Julie ahead until she had to shy away from the mule in front of her. Gruder looked back over his shoulder and gave Billy a disapproving look.

The trail followed the ridge for several miles. The sun became hot when they dipped below the ridgeline on the leeward side for the last mile or so. At the northwest end of the ridge, the trail curved around the high point. The valley that lay before them was spotted with small cedars. They could have seen anyone on horseback for at least three miles ahead, but they saw nothing. Gruder dismounted and stood scanning the horizon. The bottoms of the ravines running up the hillsides were hidden from them, so Gruder waited for a few minutes and looked for any movement. He did not move on until it was clear nobody was there.

The valley floor below them was already in shade. They had about an hour and a half of daylight left. Gruder remounted and led the mules down the trail into the valley, where they would be visible to anyone on the ridges on either side. The trail followed the valley floor for about two miles, then forked. The left fork led up a side valley that was not discernible from the ridge they had been on. After getting down and squatting for a closer look, Gruder remounted and led them down the left fork, where darkness soon overcame them. Although they could have followed the trail farther, they would not have been able to see the tracks in the dark. They made camp under a mesquite tree. The narrow valley shut off the wind, and Billy was soon asleep in a warm bedroll. Gruder stood the first watch. The moon was up when he shook Billy awake by a hand on his shoulder, raising his finger to his lips as Billy sat up. He gestured toward the horses and mules, which were tied in a row to a growth of huisache. They were restless, moving back and forth, their ears back and their nostrils flared.

"It's probably a cat," Gruder whispered in his ear. "But I'm not sure. Those people might have doubled back. Follow me."

He crawled toward the horses and mules and Billy followed, after strapping on his pistol. He made sure the rawhide thong was looped over the hammer, keeping it from being pried up by brush and accidentally setting off a discharge. Gruder kept in the shadows of cedar trees until he reached a point a few feet from where the first mule was tied. He silently crossed the moonlit area between the last cedar and the patch of huisache in a crouch to where Jimmy was tied. Billy scooted across to a spot by a nearby bush, then moved in a crouch under the edges of the huisache until he came to where Julie was pawing the ground. She was more excited than Jimmy or the mules, moving her head up and down and pulling away from the bush where her end of the line was tied.

Billy was sure it was a cat, a cougar, from Julie's actions. She had caught a whiff of the cat and instinct was telling her to run. He had to try to keep hidden in a dark place, but also needed to be where he could have a clear view. If it was a cat, the best thing to do would be to make a racket or even light a fire, but if it was not a cat, that would expose them all to detection. He looked around. A big rock was barely visible in the shade of a cedar a few yards away from Julie. It looked like it would be a good place to sit and watch. He raised up on his haunches to dash across the moonlight when he saw something on the leading edge of the rock that did not look right. He could make out a perfectly still shape that protruded above the rock edge and did not look like rock. Its lines were somehow wrong.

He thought of reaching for his pistol, but his hand was frozen. He tried to swallow, but the sudden dryness in his throat that seemed to demand it, prevented it. He felt a cold sweat break out on his forehead. The thing he was looking at did not move, but he was convinced it was alive. It lay in darkness above them. He was frozen in a half crouch, a few steps from Julie's head.

Suddenly the cat sprang from the rock, a blur in the moonlight. Julie tried to pull away and succeeded in tearing the rope end away from the huisache, but the cat landed on her just as she pulled away from the bush. Billy could see the cat clearly now in the moonlight, but it was a blur as it tore at the horse above him. Julie's cry went through him. He tried to pull the pistol, but the safety thong held it in the holster, and he pulled on holster and all. He rolled on the ground away from the horse and the cat tearing at her. Julie reared up in the moonlight, the cougar clinging to her. He found the thong with his thumb and unholstered his pistol as he came to a crouch and fired instinctively at the shadowy figure on the horse's neck. The cat made a screeching sound and came off her neck as Julie bolted toward Billy and leapt over him in the moonlight, dragging the rope behind her.

She pulled the mules along with her until she had passed where Gruder now stood with the other end of the rope in his hand. He pulled some slack around his butt and leaned away from the direction of Julie and the mules as the rope came around, then held on as it tightened. Julie was jerked around momentarily at the far end of the rope, but Gruder gave with it to soften the pull, and she came around without losing her balance.

The cat had disappeared into the huisache. Billy moved quickly to

Gruder and then along the rope, making low comforting sounds with his voice until he reached Julie's head. She was still frantically pulling on the rope, and it took a while for her to settle down enough for him to touch her. Her forequarters were wet with her blood. Billy took off his cotton jacket and daubed it against her neck and shoulders. In the moonlight the blood appeared to be everywhere. She moved away as he daubed at it. Gruder slowly came up from her other side and took her head, talking softly to her the whole time, in the same way he often did. She finally quieted to the point that she was standing still. She let Billy hold his jacket against her neck and shoulders, but it was already soaked. His hands and shirt were wet with it.

"Let's see if we can get her around a little so I can hold her better, then you go get my little blanket," Gruder said quietly and calmly. Billy did not want to stop daubing with his jacket. Gruder said, "Billy. You need that blanket." He said the words with a familiar inflection, but one he seldom used with Billy. It waked him from his obsession with the jacket and he stopped daubing and looked at Gruder over the mare's neck.

"I'll hold her. Don't worry," he said, looking at Billy steadily.

Billy ran back to the camp area, grabbed Gruder's blanket from the ground next to his saddle and ran back to where the black man stood holding the mare's head, his hand extended toward Billy. When he hesitated Gruder thrust his open hand toward him until he handed him the blanket. Gruder had cut a length of rope. He wrapped the blanket around Julie's neck and shoulders, then wrapped the rope around it several times, drawing it into a series of loops that were increasingly larger as they reached her shoulders. It slowed the flow of blood.

When he had finished, Gruder looked to the east, where there was a slight glow. "It'll be another hour before we can see enough to do any good," he said, with kindness in his voice. "I got some salve we can put on, if we can stop the bleeding."

"I'll stay with her," Billy said. He was petting her nose.

"I'll make some coffee," Gruder said.

When it was light enough, they unwrapped the blanket. They could see the work the lion had done. There were long gashes on each side, more on the left, from the shoulder area halfway up her neck. They were deep enough to require stitches. Gruder went back to his saddlebags, and Billy held Julie's head while Gruder stitched the worst wounds closed with a needle and thick cotton thread that he always carried with him. He smeared salve over the wounds and packed clay from the dry bed of the ravine on top of the salve. The clay was dry and powdery until it came in contact with the bloody salve. It softened then, and he slowly worked it over the top of the wounds until it lay in red steaks across the mare's neck and shoulders. He rolled a smoke and looked at his handiwork.

"It'll dry, but it'll take a while. You hold her still and keep her from breaking it loose."

The sun was now high enough to show they had lost a good two hours tending to the mare. Billy first thought he would tell Gruder to go on without him, and he would stay with Julie, but then thought that it would be a childish thing to do. The mare might die. Their job was to catch up and help his uncles and Hays. When Gruder returned he had a cup of coffee that he held out to Billy, who took it, and Gruder turned to look at the clay, which had already begun to lighten as it dried.

"It won't do to take her with us," he said. "She'd open up and bleed." He turned to face Billy. "I noticed a place where there may be a hidden spring a mile or so back. We could leave her there, tied. There's probably enough water and grass to give her a chance until we get back."

"Better to leave her loose," Billy said, his head against the side of hers. "She'll follow us."

"That's better than staking her out for another cat. Or wolves."

"I can tie her so she can work free after a while. Hell, she gets out of pens by herself all the time. But by the time she unties herself, we'll be on down the trail. She'll likely stay with the grass and water."

Billy could feel as well as hear her uneven breathing. He knew that Gruder's lies were intended as a kindness.

"It'd be better to shoot her," Billy said. He felt the warmth of tears running down his cheeks and moved his head to the left side of the mare's neck to hide them.

"We're a good half day's ride from Brown's," Gruder said. "Longer if we have to walk and lead her. But if you want to do that, we could cut up the Guadalupe and camp there tonight when we reach it instead of following Cap'n Jack's trail. They'll come back to Brown's eventually, and we're not likely to catch up with 'em now anyways."

Billy did not move his head away from Julie's. He tried to keep his voice clear.

"We can't just quit because of a horse," he said, trying to sound adult.

Gruder shrugged and said, "You want to do it or you want me to?"

"No," Billy said involuntarily, before he had even realized what Gruder had said. It was not conversation, but a reaction, and it came with the unmistakable sound of grief and sorrow, the very sound he had been trying so hard to hide, to hold back. The sound of his immaturity. To his mind, his cowardice.

Gruder felt bad about getting the reaction even though he had anticipated it. He knew better than to say anything else or to move, so he stood and sipped his coffee from the tin cup and looked at the surrounding hills. He saw Billy's hand shaking on the side of the mare's neck. After a while, he drained the coffee and threw the grounds away with a flourish.

"There's a wet-weather creek up ahead a few miles, and the valley's wide there. If we leave her there with a slip knot tyin' her, she'll head toward the Guadalupe when she gets loose and she'll have a chance. A good chance, really. She's a pretty smart mare. Odds are she'll stay on this side of the river and graze upstream, which'll bring her up to Brown's sooner or later."

Billy did not really believe him, but it sounded reasonable. If she reached the Guadalupe, she might be able to survive. If she didn't break open her wounds, and if she was lucky.

"How far is Brown's from there?" he asked.

"From the creek up ahead?"

"Yeah."

"'Bout a half day's ride."

They left her tied to a willow by the creek, which had a good flow that would last for the rest of the day and leave pools in the deep spots for a week. She was far away from the hills and would be able to see and smell a predator before it could get close. Gruder tied a knot to her halter that would work loose after a while, if she did not pull it tight from shying away from it too soon. She should have the rest of the day before she was in any danger from predators, except for Comanches, who would not hesitate to butcher her for the meat if they ran across her. It was the best shot she had. Billy did not look back at her as they rode off. He sat astride the gray mule in spite of Gruder's insistence that he take Jimmy and let

Gruder ride the gray. Billy was adamant. He would not let Gruder give up the mount his mother had entrusted to him. He did not feel worthy of riding the best mount. What had happened to Julie should not have happened. He had frozen, had forgotten to release his pistol, had acted in a panic, like a boy, and he was determined that he would not be catered to.

Wonsley was on his haunches looking closely at the ground, holding the reins to his horse in one hand. Hays and John Baker sat their horses and waited for him to speak. He stood, dropped the reins, and walked back toward them, his head down, tracing a trail that was invisible from where they sat. He searched the ground until he came even with John's horse, then turned and walked west toward the ridge, his eyes on the ground. When he finally looked up, his eyes followed the top of the ridge to the west. He squinted in the late afternoon light.

"They split up here," he said, his eyes scanning the horizon. "I figure two of them went to the west over that ridge. Or along it. It looks like two horses went straight down the canyon from here."

"That makes sense. Morgan wouldn't be going east at this point if the girl is still alive. He won't go where there are whites, if he can avoid it," John said, his voice low and soft.

He was looking up trail to a point where the canyon veered to the right. There was a glimpse of cottonwood branches, yellow in the slanting afternoon light. "There's probably a trail along that ridge," he said, gesturing to the hilltops on their left. "If they're following that, they'll be in a good position for an ambush up ahead."

Wonsley was still studying the ridge. "We can go that way, too."

Hays looked at him, but his eyes seemed to be seeing some other image. If they followed the ridge trail instead of continuing down the canyon, they would lose time, and Morgan might be far enough ahead that he could lose them. Once he hit the trail north of Mountain Home he would be almost impossible to track. Hays was not familiar with the ridge trail, but he did not think that Morgan and his band had split up permanently. If they had, their trail would likely have forked at the Guadalupe, and they would have taken the trouble to ride down river for a few miles to cover their exit points. This would have caused the pursuers to take much more time and would have made it far more difficult to track them. It was obvious to Hays that Morgan was not concerned about being followed, which could only mean that he knew of a good ambush spot or a shortcut to the Llano, where his tracks would be lost in the main trail. If they had split up to form an ambush, however, it was hard to imagine why they waited until this spot to do it.

Although the Lipan Flacco had taken him up and down the hills and canyons of the upper Medina—the Lipan's one-time home—Hays was in an area he had never visited, though he had ridden across the Llano to the northwest, where the North and South Llano join. The trails in this area were ancient and largely unknown to the white man. The encroachment of the whites drove the Lipans this way, and those that were left lived in the valleys of the Llano and the San Saba. The Comanches liked to winter their horses in the valley of the San Saba, and Morgan probably knew all of the snake holes and rocks to hide under between Kerrville and Fort McKavett. He was likely to be heading for the San Saba Valley, where a group of Antelope would probably be staying for the winter. If that was his destination, he would not want to be followed that far, but would prefer to stop his pursuers before he reached the valley.

Hays said to Wonsley, "Looks like four horses. What do you think?"

"That's what I been thinkin', Cap'n. It looks like the ones that went west got two horses. Then there's the two that went straight down the canyon."

"Don't look to me like any are overloaded. But I could be wrong," Wonsley grinned.

John Baker got down off his mount and squatted in the dirt. "You figure one of these might be a mule?"

"Either a mule or a Spanish pony," Wonsley replied.

Hays dismounted and came over to take a look. He stood beside John, squinting at the marks in the dirt and the flattened grass, then looked up at Wonsley. "And the smaller animal went over the ridge?"

"That's what it looks like to me, Colonel. Maybe carryin' a little more of a load."

Hays looked at the ridge. The sun was at the crest, and the ground five feet from him was in shadow. "We've only got a couple more hours of light," he said, looking at Wonsley. "I need you to get up on that ridge and find the trail. Then come back and let us know if it looks like it doubles back. Unless you run into them."

"Yes sir." Wonsley straightened up fully, almost as if he were standing at attention. He had an exaggerated, solemn look.

"Then you got to watch for them real carefully. I figure there's a spot up ahead with a good ambush point. I'd look for a narrow spot with some high rock. They'll want to catch us where we're hemmed in and have no place to hide."

"That's what I figure," Wonsley said.

"We'll wait here," he said, looking at John. "If we go on up the trail, the moon won't be up 'til late, and we'll be in the dark before we know it. Then Wonsley wouldn't be able to find us. Wonsley, if you see the trail leave the ridge for sure, or if we're wrong and it heads up the east side, come on back here right away."

"You figure Morgan and the girl are still on this trail?" John asked, still looking at the marks on the ground with a puzzled expression.

"I don't know, but that doesn't make a lot of sense," Hays replied.

"That's true," John said.

"Why's that?" Wonsley asked, hesitantly.

"Because he wouldn't split up his band and stay on the same trail," John replied.

Hays did not say anything. He was looking down the canyon trail to the point where it curved to the east, which was now in the shade of the hills to the west. The cottonwoods meant a wet-weather creek with enough alluvial soil to hold water during the dry season, which meant there was at least another canyon branching into this one, if his feeling about the lay of the land was right. He had always skirted this area in the past. He knew there were no rivers between this place and the Llano, but he was not sure about how many trails there might be up ravines, or whether the country would allow Morgan to strike out across the hills northwest in the direction of the Llano without following a trail. And he would be smart enough to switch mounts, if what Hays had heard about him was half true. He could be a long way from them by now just by using his knowledge of the land. If they stayed on the trail, they would never pick up his tracks, and he could go where he pleased. It also made sense that he would not want to be moving on a well-traveled trail where there was little cover, like the one between Mountain Home and Junction City, especially with a fourteen-year-old white girl, and especially if he had to keep her tied.

"What if he gave the girl to one of the others?" John asked. "What if he gave her away and took off with one of his compadres up that high trail? Leavin' the girl might be smart at this point."

"That's possible, John, but I don't think so." Hays had been looking at the ground but then looked John in the eye. "If he got tired of her, we would have found her body by now. It would have been hard to miss."

Hays turned to Wonsley. "Go find that trail, son, and we'll wait here until we see you on the ridge."

"Yes, sir," Wonsley said. He mounted his horse and headed toward the ridge to the west, leaning out of his saddle, his eyes on the ground.

Hays and John Baker dropped their reins and sat down on rocks facing the sun. John was uncomfortable about the situation. He was not fond of unknown factors.

"You figure they split up to slow us down?" he asked, looking up at the hill ahead of him.

Hays was looking down. He remained silent for a moment, then looked up at John. "Doesn't matter much what I figure," he said coldly. "He's slowed us up, sure enough."

They sat for more than an hour, until there was no more sunlight on the east wall of the canyon. Hays stood up and started picking up dried ocotillo stalks. "We might as well build a fire."

John Baker almost questioned him about that, but held back out of respect. He could not understand how Hays could be so careless as to build a fire after they had been so careful all along to avoid detection. Hays walked in front of him and laid some stalks down. He saw John's puzzled look.

"They'll know where we are," he said, "if they're waiting for us. When we don't show up-trail. They might be coming back. You got a pretty heavy bedroll, don't you?"

A look of recognition crossed John's face. He stood and began to help gather wood. After they had accumulated a large pile, mostly juniper and mesquite, they laid their bedrolls out carefully, placing their saddles down where they would normally rest their heads. They rolled up their blankets with the ocotillo inside and carefully adjusted them until they would look like bodies in the dark. When they were finished, with rocks at the feet of their rolls to serve as fake boots and their hats over their saddle horns, it was almost dark. John was lighting the fire when they heard Wonsley's whistle from the top of the ridge to the west. When he saw that they were looking his way, he took his hat off and held it low against the side of his saddle, moving it back and forth. Hays signaled for him to come down. Wonsley dismounted and led his horse down the hillside and across the narrow valley.

"That trail heads off northwest like you thought," he said to Hays. "I followed it until I was sure they didn't double back."

"Was it two horses?" Hays asked.

"Looks like it, Cap'n. Only one of 'em's loaded down a lot more than the other one."

"So they got the girl and provisions on that one," said John.

"That's what I figure," Wonsley said. "And there's two of them on this trail."

"You might as well tie her up and have something to eat," Hays said.

They dined on hardtack, dried bacon, and coffee, then propped themselves under mesquites, out of the firelight. Wonsley had added his bedroll to the other two. They kept their horses tied next to them. Wonsley could not stop thinking about the signs he saw on the ground and their possible meanings. The girl could be with one rider on either trail or she could be riding double, which would mean there were four of them, two having gone down each trail. Or they could have slit her throat and tied rocks to her and sunk her in a deep pool of the Medina before they ever got up there. How were they to know that the girl was even there?

When John Baker shook himself from sleep, not realizing he had been sleeping, there was a gray light in the sky. Hays was rebuilding the fire. Wonsley was thirty yards away propped up against a stunted old mesquite, his head down, dozing. John realized that he had not seen Hays sleep since they left home. He had heard tales of Hays going days without sleep, but had dismissed them as exaggerations. Now he was not so sure.

They had coffee, then saddled up and moved the horses up the west hillside where Wonsley had descended the previous evening. They left a trail sign for Gruder and Billy, indicating they were going up the ridge to the west.

The ground still had enough moisture from the recent rains for there to be a discernible trail, and they were able to follow it at a fair pace. They rode over a high, uneven plateau, then down into a broad valley filled with post oaks. It was one of those fall days when, after a rainy period, the air feels light and the woods are quiet. They rode in silence for hours, until they came to a place where the trail they were following met the main trail to Junction City, a place they would have reached hours earlier if they had stayed on the canyon trail. Morgan, by splitting up, had cost them valuable time because they could not take the chance of trailing at night. He was now far enough ahead of them that they would not catch up until he chose to stop.

They reached the crossing at the South Llano in mid-afternoon, waded their horses across with the sun sparkling on the water upstream, and rode down a dirt road into the little village of Junction City. Now that Morgan knew they were following him, there was no longer a need to avoid the settlements. They looked for the general store to seek out a man Hays had met before, a man named Marshall, who was supposed to know everything that went on in town. The store was a single-room hut, dingy and dusty. It was one of the few commercial establishments on the dirt lane that served as the main street. Marshall was sitting on a keg near the door with an earthen jug nearby from which he had obviously been drinking. His dirty brown hair hung long over his eyes. When Hays walked in, Marshall squinted up at him.

"I knew you'd come by here again sometime," he croaked. "What took you so long?"

Hays stared down at him.

"It's been a while, Cap'n." He looked past Hays to John and Wonsley. "You got a pretty good lookin' posse there."

"We're looking for a renegade that took a girl. You seen anything of him?" Hays asked calmly.

Marshall reached down for the jug, pulled the cob out of it and lifted it over his arm with one motion, then took a long pull, wiped his mouth on his sleeve, recorked it, and sat it back on the dirt floor. He spoke while still wheezing from the whiskey.

"Came through last night. One of my boys saw him. The girl was with him. Ridin' double."

"Anybody else?" John Baker asked from the door.

"One other one. Dark man, the boy said."

"They headin' for the San Saba?" Hays asked.

The man looked down at the dirt floor, as if thinking about saying something he thought would get him in trouble.

"Cap'n, you probably know where he's headed as well as I do."

Hays turned immediately and stepped through the doorway so quickly he bumped Wonsley as he passed him. John and Wonsley followed him to the horses and down the lane to the trail that led across the North

Llano. They crossed rapidly and rode for an hour at a fast pace. Hays said nothing, but kept looking at the hills ahead. His eyes were steady as always, and his companions did not speak to him. There was an unspoken tension that had not been there before. Wonsley wanted badly to ask him what he had learned from the man in the store. He could not fathom what information could have passed in the brief conversation without his being aware of it. He decided to bring up another subject.

"Cap'n. How far back you reckon Billy and Gruder and that Apache are?"

Hays seemed to be oblivious. He was still looking ahead.

"Cap'n?" Wonsley said this a little softer, his resolve wavering. John was riding on the other side of Hays. When Wonsley looked over at him, John frowned and shook his head.

Hays had no need of Wonsley's tracking now. Although the main trail from Junction City to the San Saba was not as well trod as the one from Kerrville to Junction City, several wagons and numerous horses had passed this way since it had rained, and it was impossible to make out any recognizable tracks in the middle of the trail, which was over fairly open ground. It was also wide and provided easy going. It was now apparent that Morgan had been headed for the San Saba all along. He had gained considerable time by splitting up his party. When he and the other man reached the San Saba, they would be in Comanche country, with more allies—if Morgan had any allies. It should have been obvious that he was headed that way all along, but Hays had hesitated when confronted with the split trail. He was determined to make up for it by not resting until they reached the valley of the San Saba, but they would need fresh mounts if they kept pushing on the way they were.

The trail passed over low hills, traversing country that was open and bare of trees. At the crest of each hill, they could see for miles. They met no one on the trail. It was apparent that there were few settlements—little need for a renegade to avoid the main trail. Morgan must have felt more comfortable in this country, less afraid of running into someone who would question the girl's presence. Or the girl was no longer with him.

They passed Teacup Mountain and Red Creek at a steady lope. Gradually, Hays stopped pushing his mount so hard, and the horses slowed down to a walk. The trail narrowed between two ridges and wound down to a narrow valley where a dry creek bed lay in a stand of willows. Before they reached the point where the trail crossed the creek bed, Hays turned off to the left and around a hillside. About a hundred yards away, they spotted a small corral and shed and farther on, an adobe shack. Hays rode up to the edge of the corral and dismounted. It was empty and over-grown. The poles that were used as a gate lay on the ground, abandoned.

Hays looked at the shack for a long while motionless, standing and holding the reins to his horse. Weeds grew high around the adobe walls. The rough wooden door was half open. A stone well stood on the side by the creek, a broken leather bucket dangling from the well rope against the side. Hays walked up to the door. John followed. The weeds they walked through were thick around their legs. Hays pushed the door. It dragged against the ground as it opened wider, and they looked inside. A rough wooden table stood in the middle of the dirt floor, a single wooden chair turned over on its side beside it. Uneven, dilapidated, empty shelves lined the wall on one side of the small, crudely built stone fireplace opposite the doorway. A ray of late afternoon light from a half-shuttered window played across the table and fallen chair, illuminating the thick layer of dust that lay upon them.

Hays stood at the doorway and looked over the room. John Baker peered from behind him into the dimness within. After a long while, Hays turned to look at him.

"You know this place?" John asked.

Hays turned and looked around at the willows and the creek and the corral. "I used to," he said.

John stood aside as Hays walked around the side of the house by the well and the creek to the back, up a small rise. There, on a piece of level ground, a headstone reclined against the side of an anthill. They walked up to it, and Hays leaned down and squinted, trying to make out the faint scratches on the surface of the weathered stone. He took a bandana from his pocket and wiped off a layer of dirt. John Baker leaned over beside him.

John made out several letters, but not the entire name. The stone was crudely carved and had weathered to the point that it was impossible to read all the letters. Hays straightened up and turned to go, but John, looking at the stone, read aloud, "Died 1856."

Hays looked back at him.

"Looks like it says, 'A faithful wife.' It's pretty hard to read."

Hays turned and looked down at the stone again. "Maggie," he said solemnly. Then, looking John in the eye, "That would have made her about thirty-seven."

"Who was she, Jack?"

Hays looked back at the stone. "A friend. An old friend."

He turned back to the corral, and John followed. They reached the horses where Wonsley was waiting. Hays walked up to him.

"The folks that lived here were friends of mine. I got word about the wife getting killed by Comanches years ago. I thought the man might still be here. But he's gone, too."

Wonsley stepped back a step. "Cap'n, I . . ."

"Just thought you might want to know. And I think there are four of them if they rejoined, and they'll have the girl with the Comanches by about now. Morgan might have been easier on her than they will, if he gives her to them. On the other hand, he probably wouldn't have taken her all this way to give her up, unless he has to, to get in with them."

"Cap'n, I was just wonderin'."

"It's all right, son. You got a right to know what I'm thinking."

He turned to John Baker.

"I know our mounts are tired, but if we ride all night we might catch up to them. I was hoping to get some fresh horses here. I hear there's a man named Lewis up ahead a ways, though, that may let us have some fresh mounts."

"Then let's do it," John said.

They mounted and rode back to the trail, across the creek and up the rise on the other side as the sun on their left threw a rose-colored blanket across the sky.

Billy and Gruder rode into Junction City about dark. They turned upstream after they crossed the South Llano and headed for the shack and corral of a Mexican Gruder knew named Cayetano. Gruder called him Ki. His place was on the left bank of the stream a mile from the edge of the village. They found him sitting by the fire in a stove he had made by propping truncated sheets of roofing tin against each other on the dirt floor of his one-room shack. The roof of the shack had a slit at the peak for the smoke to escape. The man squatted before the stove like an Indian in his lodge, smoking a cob pipe. He stood and came to the rough opening that served as his doorway as they rode up.

"Who's that?" he asked in a high voice.

"It's Gruder," Gruder responded.

"Gruder?" The little man stepped out of the doorway. He appeared to be looking in their direction, but over their heads. First Gruder, then Billy dismounted. Although it was dark, they could clearly see him standing under the sagging roof of his porch, but it was apparent as they approached that he could not see them.

"Ki," Gruder said. "You're still in the same spot."

"Yes, Gruder. Who is that with you?"

"It's Billy McCulloch. Wes's boy."

"Come on in by the fire," the little man said. "It's chilly out here."

They entered the small room. Cayetano squatted before the tin stove. Billy and Gruder stood near it. The room was warm.

"So how is Mr. McCulloch?"

"He's dead," Gruder said, glancing at Billy.

"Oh, I'm sorry to hear that. A good man."

"We're helping out Colonel Jack Hays," Gruder said. "He's trailing a renegade. The colonel should have come through here yesterday or today."

"I heard about it," Cayetano said, his eyes staring ahead. "He was here today with two other men."

"My uncles," Billy said.

"Ah. They went up the trail to the San Saba, by way of London ranch."

"Okay if we bed down here tonight?" Gruder asked.

"But can't we catch up with them tonight?" Billy asked.

"We've come a long way today, Billy. The animals need food and rest. So do we." He was already through the doorway heading for the mule and horse and their bedrolls.

EIGHT

A SHLEY MAITLAND RODE HIS HORSE OFF THE NEW PONTOON bridge at the foot of Congress Avenue among milling horses, carriages, wagons, and shouting hostlers. The avenue was full of deep ruts after the rains. He remembered days of rain in Austin, when the avenue ran like a stream, and he and his fellow congressmen spent days at poker at Remington's hotel bar while waiting for the Colorado to go down and the ferry to start running again. That was at the end of the session in '43, when the only serious topics of the year were proposals to generate enough income to pay the past-due debts of the Republic and somehow finance the military resources necessary for survival. It was a similar situation now, with a near-bankrupt state treasury and a pervasive sense of gloom, but now the mood was darker. Few of the men who had been in the Congress of the Republic were entitled to vote in 1869, and they were ineligible for public office. Even the hope of regaining political control of the state, which seemed so plausible in '66, was gone. There was a bitterness and hostility that did not exist in the latter days of the Republic.

Of the men who had sat in the Constitutional Convention of 1866, only six attended the convention in Austin in June of 1868, which passed the Reconstruction Constitution. It was later approved by a slim margin of the voters, even with their numbers diluted by disenfranchisement and a Democratic campaign to boycott the election.

Under the new Constitution, most power was to be placed in the hands of the new governor, yet to be elected, and taken away from the representatives elected by the minority who were allowed to vote. The race for governor was a contest between E. J. Davis of the Radical Republican faction and Jack Hamilton, a Conservative Republican, who had the respect of a great many former soldiers and officeholders.

The Radicals were intent on making over Texas to fit their idea of a fairer society, which was based on a slanted view of what a Northern state, with only good Unionists and freedmen allowed to vote, was supposed to be like. The carpetbaggers, those who came from the North, and the scalawags, those resident Texans who had supported the Union, were allied under the Radical wing. Davis made pacts with the most extreme of their leaders, including G. T. Ruby, state president of the Union League, a secret society whose members had come south to educate the Negroes to vote Radical Republican. Pease, the puppet provisional governor, resigned in disgust, saying in a letter to President Grant that eight-tenths of all educated (meaning white) Republicans were for Hamilton, and that Davis represented a "carpetbagger and Negro supremacy party."

With Davis men acting as voting registrars, it did not look good for Hamilton. Ashley had known Hamilton for a long time and respected him. He had come to Austin in response to a letter from Hamilton asking for his help. The letter did not say what kind of help was needed, and Ashley needed no explanation. The Democrats who could get past the registrars to vote needed to do it and not boycott the election, as they had done in the election to ratify the Constitution. Ash had been to five secret meetings since October. The secrecy was necessary. Any public meeting of known Democrats was likely to be broken up by the army, with the consequent arrest of the leaders of the meeting on charges ranging from theft to treason, although most of the specific charges, wrung out of the army only after days of effort by lawyers, would be dropped. Ashley had been reluctant to meet in secret, a practice which placed the men at the meetings in the same bad light as the Klan and tarnished their reputations to some degree, but he finally came around to the view of the others. The rules of near-martial law in a land occupied by a bitter former enemy required it. They could see Texas slipping away from them, the last vestiges of their society being destroyed.

Hamilton Stuart, editor of the *Galveston Civilian*, was the Democratic nominee. It was widely known that he did not have a chance. A vote for Stuart would be wasted. A vote for Jack Hamilton was a far better alternative than the abandonment of the political arena to the Davis faction. The election was coming up on November 30. There was little time.

The old hotel had a musty smell. The lobby was dark and cold. The desk clerk was lethargic. Ash had to clear his throat loudly, three times, before he was heard.

Then the bald man behind the counter acknowledged his presence with a scowl and turned the stand on which the desk book lay to face him.

"I am supposed to meet Mr. Paschal," he said.

"Room 215," the clerk said.

He walked down the familiar hallway to the winding staircase and followed the old blue and purple woven carpet up to the second floor, over to the suite where he remembered seeing Sam Houston, and opened the door without knocking. The windows opposite the door were open, as was the transom above the door, but a haze of smoke filled the room. A tray with glasses, a pitcher of lemonade, and a bottle of bourbon lay on a small table between the windows. The men in the room were all standing. Most of them were fairly well groomed and wore dark suits and ties. A few wore brush jackets and cotton pants. Most had long beards that had not felt scissors in years. A slight man with a bald pate and closely cropped gray sideburns turned to the door as Ash walked in. He showed a pleased look of recognition and came up to greet him, his hand extended.

"So glad you could make it, brother Maitland," he said.

George Paschal was a respected man of letters and the law and the chronicler of the legislature. He had a good sense of humor and was often the host of gatherings of a political nature.

"You know most of the men, here, Ashley. Help yourself to some refreshment and make yourself at home."

Paschal turned away as they crossed the room. Ash walked to the table and poured himself a glass of lemonade. Nine in the morning was a little early for whiskey, and the ride from Atlanta had taken two and a half hours. He was thirsty, but not for whiskey. He turned and surveyed the room.

Colossal Jack Hamilton and Rip Ford, who were near the fireplace, stood a head above the others. Engaged in an animated conversation with Hamilton was Thomas Coddington, a man Ash was surprised to see there. He did not feel Coddington could be trusted and could not understand how he had been invited to attend. The rest of the room was filled with Democrats and Conservative Republicans, the latter being part of Hamilton's wing of their party, men who had been Unionist during the war, but who had kept the respect of the secessionists by making their stand on the issues one of principle. Most had obeyed the law, including the conscription laws, but had not been hesitant to express their view that secession was a mistake.

Hamilton Stuart was on the other side of the room visiting with a couple of former legislators from North Texas. Two of the three leading candidates for governor were in this room. Ashley walked over to say hello to Stuart. He had admired his editorials, some of which had drawn threats of arrest from the military authorities. An old friend of Ashley's, Richard Coke, had defended Stuart brilliantly against these threats. Coke's letters to General Griffin were published in more than a few Democratic newspapers around the state. His argument about the First Amendment right of free speech was laced with subtle sarcasm that placed it in context with the self-righteous hypocrisy the army continued to display. Coke made the point that Stuart was advocating change by political means, not by rebellion, and that the support of the ideals of the people was not treason, by definition. It was a point that in normal times would have been taken for granted, but in 1869, everything was upside-down. Texas was having its democratic government usurped by people who were traitors to the ideals they expressed. Habeas corpus was ineffective in the courts, where the judges, recently appointed and inexperienced, were afraid to enforce it. Unscrupulous officials could effectuate arrests that would wipe large swaths across the Texas population. Once jailed, a man might stay for weeks before being freed on a writ. Texans considered Texas a nation, not just a state, and the nation had been made captive. It did not sit well with those who called themselves conservatives.

As Ash approached the group, Stuart saw him and brightened. "Hey, Ash," he said. "What brings you to this den of wolves?"

Ashley shook his hand. "Came to register my illegal vote for you, brother."

Stuart put his arm around Ash's shoulders and hugged him.

"Good to see you, Ash," he said, grinning. "So you came to register your vote, huh?"

"I suppose so. It's the only one I have."

"How you figure to cast it?"

"For you I guess, but I may want to hear some logic about it first. What's the word around here?" Hamilton Stuart was a journalist, not a politician. Ash knew him to have few pretenses.

"That's a good question," Ham replied. The other two men laughed nervously.

"It's a question we may not have an answer for this year," Ash said. "Hard to know who to listen to."

"Good ol' Ash," Stuart said softly, after a long silence.

"Gentlemen," Ashley said, bowing slightly, "I must find Mr. H. I have something to tell him."

"Good to see you, Ash," Stuart said again.

Ash moved over to the group standing around Jack Hamilton and Rip Ford. Ford, tall, thin, and gray-bearded, stood there listening quietly to the conversation. He saw Ashley walk up to the edge of the group and immediately smiled at him. Ford was a good soldier and a man of letters. His name was John Salmon Ford, but during the Mexican War he had been given the job as a Ranger to keep records of those who had fallen in battle. Beside every name and date he put the letters *R.I.P.*

Hamilton, a graying, big man with a prominent nose, looked down at his boot tops. He was rocking back on his heels impatiently. He looked up as Ashley approached. Hamilton's big blue Scots-Irish eyes beamed at Ash.

"It's a lovely morning, Ashley, and a pleasure to see you," he said. Hamilton was strangely hesitant for a political candidate. And for a big man, with his ruddy complexion, unexpectedly reserved. He was not one to extol his own virtues.

"Ash, I'd like to visit with you privately," Hamilton said. "Gentlemen, I hope you'll excuse us for a little bit." He did not succeed in his obvious attempt to conceal his feeling of relief. The other men standing around him politely excused themselves, with further expressions of support. Coddington turned abruptly and walked away.

Ashley followed Hamilton to the refreshment table by the window. The screens had been taken off in late October, and Hamilton leaned out to look down the avenue, which was full of ruts and water-filled holes. It was a crisp, sunny day, but you could still see where water had receded from higher levels. There was a considerable amount of traffic: a couple of carriages; four wagons, one with oxen; and an assortment of men on horseback and people on foot. All having someplace to go. He could see the wagons pulling off the end of the bridge five blocks to the south, their drivers coaxing the horses along. He turned to Ash.

"There's a lot of commerce going on out there," Hamilton mused. He poured himself a lemonade from the cut-glass pitcher. "As you can see, my speech today will be well-observed by all. I am going to speak about unity, of course, and say the Republican Party can be a Texas party, which is true. You can predict every word."

"It does sound a little familiar."

"What I want to tell you, Ash, is that all I want to do is to help save Texas. I don't care what it takes to do it or who does it."

"I already know that, Jack."

"If the Democrats will get out and vote, I'll drop out and leave it to Stuart. That's what I mean." He looked over the lip of the lemonade glass while drinking, his red nose disappearing behind the rim.

"But how can you make a man vote? Hell, I don't know how to get them out," Ashley said.

"I know," Hamilton said, the glass lowered to chest level. "But when the time comes, some may try."

"Yeah, well, I guess some might, but would their votes be counted?"

Hamilton turned and looked out the window again. "You and I both know what most of those Radical bastards are after. Other than the few who are true zealots. It's right out there, being hauled up and down Congress Avenue."

There were wagons loading and unloading goods all along the broad avenue and more pulling into and out of side streets, carrying goods.

Hamilton turned back to Ash. "We want the same thing," he said. "But we believe in working for it. Not stealing it. They'll take everything they can get and take it back north. They're not for Texas."

Ash did not know what to say. Hamilton's expression revealed his reading of Ash's face.

"Don't worry, old friend," Hamilton said. "I just have to try. Don't let it worry you. There's not much we can do about it right now, but I've got to try."

He put his glass down and took Ash's hand again, shook it firmly and looked up at Rip Ford, who had walked up to the table grinning.

"Ash, I heard a mutual friend has been in your neighborhood lately," Ford said. "That true?"

"Indeed it is," Ash replied. "Only he's probably on the Medina by now."

"I heard," Ford said, his grin disappearing. "Sorry I missed Wes's funeral. I was in East Texas."

"I heard, Rip."

"How's the Colonel look?"

"He hasn't changed much at all. A little heavier, but still pretty wiry."

"I heard he was after someone."

"That's true."

Ford's eyes froze. "Then pity the poor devil," he said.

There was a long silence. Finally Hamilton cleared his throat

Ford patted Ash on the shoulder. "It's good to see you, Ash. Real good."

Ford had commanded the last Confederate unit in the last battle of the war, at Palmito Ranch, near Brownsville. There were noticeable periods of quiet that now sometimes engulfed him. He looked down at his boots, still muddy around the edges. Hamilton broke the silence.

"Well, it looks like Mr. Stuart is finally going to speak."

A group of men crowded around the fireplace where Stuart now stood. Ash could just see the top of his head. Stuart began to speak in his usual quiet manner. Though it was difficult to hear him, Ash heard enough to know that it was the speech that he and everyone else expected, a speech about Texas and its institutions, the suffering of its people, the need for unity.

Hamilton was straining, trying to hear. He finally excused himself and left Ford and Ash at the lemonade table alone. They stood side by side and listened. Stuart's voice rose as if he had gotten his second wind.

"I know that some of you feel that the Republican Party is the way to go, and all of us should respect that."

They could hear only parts of what followed, over the sound of shifting feet and throats clearing. Ford and Ash exchanged a long look.

"You know, Ash. We're going to look back on this someday as a bad dream. The whole damn thing." Ford again looked across the room at Stuart.

Ash turned and retrieved his lemonade glass from the table, took the bourbon bottle and poured a liberal amount over the rest of the lemonade, swirled it around a bit, then took a long swallow. The bourbon hit him immediately.

They were all gathered in that room out of mutual respect. All except Coddington and a few who were there because it seemed that it would help their personal prospects. All of them had fought together against common enemies. All had suffered personal and financial tragedies. They were scattered remnants that could not come together. It was as if the war had permanently sundered them. Society had broken down, and there were enormous forces set against its reconstitution. And these men made no difference whatsoever. It did not matter what they did, except perhaps to posterity. And it was hard to think of responsibility toward posterity when it appeared that everything was collapsing around them.

Ash set his glass down, patted John Salmon Ford's shoulder and shook his hand, then quietly moved across the room and out the door. When he reached the street in front of the hotel, he could feel the whiskey in his legs. He had the urge to piss and started to go back through the lobby to the privies in back, but decided he would cross the street to the Pinto Bar, where you could drain your bladder in a trough that ran in the back corner. And a beer might taste good.

NINE

WONSLEY CREPT ALONG ON HIS ELBOWS AND KNEES THROUGH a stand of dry grass. He could hear the sounds of chopping ahead, the dull thuds punctuating the bird sounds of the early morning. The previous day and night had been warmer than the last few days, and the morning was starting with a vigorous breeze from the south, which rustled the leaves in the live oak above him and gave a full backdrop to the chopping.

He came to a large root of the tree and, sensing that he was on the edge of the slope of the river valley, pulled his leather cap off with his left hand and instinctively ducked behind the root. He had crawled fifty feet or so after first hearing the sounds. They had startled him at first, until he took the time to think and be still and listen. There were only the chopping sounds, and they were hollow and relatively light. Dry wood chopped with a small axe.

He peered over the root. Between the thinning blades of grass he could see the narrow river valley, but could detect no movement. He raised his head higher to see downslope and saw the black head of a Comanche woman, then her hide-covered shoulders and the small axe she held in one hand. She bent and laid the axe down out of his field of view, then reached behind her for something. He anticipated her drawing a knife, but he raised his head a little higher and saw her pull a long hide thong from behind her. Then she stooped out of sight. He pulled himself up a bit onto the root so that he could see better. She was bent over a stack of sycamore limbs, tying it with the thong. When she had secured the thong around the limbs, she moved sideways, reached and pulled another piece of hide from behind her, then stooped to tie another pile.

The woman was not young. She was short and rather wide. He had seen Comanches before at a camp near Dripping Springs when he was ten. His father had taken him along to look for stolen horses. An old Comanche chief had been lying under a tree, manacled. There were several Rangers standing guard over the chief. Two Comanche women were locked in a corn crib. He could not help staring at the old man, whose left ankle was rubbed raw by the iron manacle. The old chief looked at the ground in front of him and only looked up once, directly at Wonsley. His dark eyes were full of anger and something else that Wonsley could not quite make out. Their own horses were not there, and his father refused the offer of one of the Rangers to take some anyway.

"They's a lot more of these horses than there are owners, now," the Ranger said. "You might as well take a couple." The man's beard showed dark tobacco stains around his mouth.

How the old chief looked at him was still in his mind. He had always wondered what the chief saw in his face. And he could not forget the look in the old man's eyes. Wonsley would come to consider that it was hatred he saw there.

The woman's face was similar to the old chief's. The broad forehead and high cheekbones. The full chin. Her lips were pursed, as if she was deep in thought.

She tied the thong around the second pile and moved to still another. Her movements were deliberate, unhurried, and smooth. She tied five stacks together in all and piled them onto a couple of longer limbs that were tied together, ladder-like, making a travois. It seemed she had worked a small amount of magic in making up her load. It had been done so quickly. She moved to the far end of the travois, lifted the pole ends up, and dragged the wood down the slope toward the river. He could see her axe hanging from the back of her belt until she entered the taller grass along the near bank. He watched her until she was out of sight.

Wonsley had feared there might be children with the woman until he saw her face and realized she was probably past childbearing age. Children could be a problem when you were trying to sneak up on somebody. They had a way of wandering about and stumbling onto you when you least expected it. But the woman was obviously alone.

She headed downstream in a northeast direction, crosswind. It was not safe to follow her, but it told him where her camp was. She would not go far for firewood. It was plentiful in the lower river bottom. The stream was brown and running swiftly, high up on its banks. The fall rains had been good up here, too. Tiny white flowers topping long stems covered the slope below him. Cattails lined the opposite bank, their tops waving in the stiff wind. Crossing the river would be the best way to approach their village, at least until the wind changed. The sky to the north seemed to be a darker shade of gray, and the wind from the southeast was steady, not gusty. There was likely a blue norther on the way.

They had come up from London ranch, where London Lewis had given them some corn for the horses and loaned them three extra mounts so they could take the weight off for a few miles. They traveled at a slower pace until dark, when they made camp a few miles upstream from where Wonsley now was, where a man named Adam Bradford and his family lived and made do in the cattle business. After talking to Bradford, they accepted his invitation to spend the night before resuming their pursuit. The Comanches had wintered in the San Saba valley for many years before any Europeans had set foot in the area. The first, the Spaniards, built a stone fort near the river across from a broad pasture where Bradford cattle with an *A* brand now grazed. Bradford had set up a store in a lean-to on the south side of the river. He had been in the area since 1863.

Fort McKavett to the west was some protection from the Comanche, but they still came to the valley in the late fall, in decreasing numbers. Bradford led Hays to believe that there were no Indians for miles until you got to Pegleg Crossing, about twelve miles downstream, but Wonsley discovered the squaw only about five miles downstream, near where the Spanish Mission had once stood. There the valley began to broaden out into a large pasture that ran down both sides of the river, near where the Ditch reentered the river. The Ditch, dug by the Spanish to supply water to the mission, was a shallow, narrow canal that had been opened up by Bradford and the others to water their fields. White men had planted and harvested crops in the area for several years without any interference from the Comanches, except for a few raids now and then. The settlers left the Comanches at Pegleg alone, and the Comanches had thus far allowed the white people to survive in their small numbers, although they would ambush any white man who strayed too far from his fields.

It was therefore a surprise to see the woman so far upstream and so near the Bradford ranch and store. The Comanches were almost never seen, partly because the white men did not look for them and were willing to share the water and grass in the valley, although they were always on the lookout for danger and kept their cattle in areas where the Indians were not expected to roam. It was most dangerous to go coon hunting alone at night. The Comanche would wait until they heard the dogs bark "treed." They killed a number of white men in this way, coming on them while they were absorbed in approaching a treed raccoon. They were interested in horses and rifles and would occasionally attack a cabin, but most of the time the few white men in the area and the small Comanche bands that passed through in the late fall and early winter avoided each other.

Wonsley was careful returning to the Bradford store where Hays and John waited for him. He had left his mount at the edge of the Bradford pasture and went on foot along the riverbank. In a way, he was relieved that he found the woman so near. They had not seen any Indians for days, and he was tired of pursuing an unseen prey. He rode across Bradford's field at a lope, anxious to share his information.

Hays and John Baker were seated under one of the oak trees by the lean-to, where they had camped for the night. Bradford and three other men were there, standing around. Wonsley described where he had seen the woman and her hair and dress. A thin, swarthy man dressed in dirty buckskin listened intently, then asked him several questions about her appearance, particularly about feathers on her axe. Wonsley replied that there were two turkey feathers, tied with dark leather.

"Sounds like a Honey Eater," the man said after pausing and rubbing his bearded chin. "*Penatekah* is the Comanche word. They haven't been around here for a while."

Bradford kicked at a rock. He was burly, with long red hair and beard and bandy legs.

"If they're that close, there'll be a lot of them," he growled. He had once scared off a war party by acting crazy—singing, dancing, and laughing loudly when the Indians came upon him alone on his way back from Austin, where he had driven hogs for sale. He looked at Hays. "There might be hundreds of 'em, if they're that many left."

Hays looked up at him from his coffee cup. "There used to be plenty of them."

"They've been thinned out some in the last few years, Colonel." Bradford used Hays's last rank in addressing him, as did most who did not know him in the old days. The thin, swarthy man cleared his throat before speaking again. His voice was raspy and high-pitched. "That half-breed is supposed to be part Antelope. *Kwaheerkeina*. They ain't been seen around here ever, as far as I know." The man spoke as if he was proud of his knowledge of the Comanches. "But if he's part Comanche, they'll take him in. What's the one with him?"

John spoke up. "We don't know. There may be more than one."

"There's usually a few down at Pegleg this time of the year, but I don't know which band," Bradford said, giving the swarthy man a quick glance. "They're Comanches, though. Sooner kill you than not."

There was a moment of silence. Then Wonsley spoke. "Looks like there's a norther on the way. Maybe by tonight."

Hays tossed the dregs of his coffee in the fire. "How far is it around to Pegleg?" he asked, looking at Adam Bradford.

"You mean going on the south?" Bradford asked.

Hays nodded.

"It'll take two, maybe three hours if you avoid the river valley completely."

Hays looked at the gray sky. "Then we ought to have plenty of time," he said, and stood up.

Hays and John went to the pack mules and finished packing their gear while Wonsley saddled Hays's horse, as he had been doing on the few mornings they had actually awakened from a real sleep. The local men stood around, commenting on the probable location of the Indians and disputing the timing of the norther. When the horses and mules were ready and the men mounted, Adam Bradford walked up beside Hays's horse.

"We've managed to get along pretty good out here without bothering 'em," he said in a low voice, although all the men could hear him. "And we got women and children here. But I feel like we ought to help you," he said.

Hays looked at him for a long time before speaking. When he did it was in his characteristically matter-of-fact voice. "You have family to attend to here," he said. "You don't want the Comanche seeking you out. It wouldn't be the smart thing to do. But you can help us by telling the rest of our party where we're heading. A boy and a Negro man. They should be here later today or tomorrow. If they're coming."

"I'll see they get the word, Colonel," he said, his bright blue eyes looking straight into Hays's. He watched them ride off to the south, through the pass they had come in by, the one the Spaniards called *Puerto de Baluartes*, Haven of the Strong. Wonsley took the lead, with Hays and John Baker following.

"You figure Morgan don't know the Honey Eaters are here," John said.

"That's right," Hays said.

"So he must be headin' for Pegleg." John said it with finality. Hays did not comment.

Although they had heard about Pegleg before, Adam Bradford and the man in buckskin had filled in more details. It was a place where the Comanches had formed a corral for horses by using a high riverbank on the north across the river, a steep rocky bluff that curved around on the east at the water's edge, and their lodges and a rock wall on the west that extended to the south river bank. There was little grass for the horses, but the river was shallow within the enclosure and it was therefore easy for the horses to drink. It was also easy to defend because it could only be effectively approached from the west, where there was no cover for several hundred yards, only the tall grass that bordered the river. This provided cover, of course, only if someone approached in the river itself. Bradford told them the way to Pegleg from the south and suggested they approach the river valley from that direction, through a pass used for many years by Indians and Spaniards, but if the Comanche had sentries, it would not be easy to avoid detection.

Billy slumped in his saddle. It seemed that they had been riding for days since they left Junction City, and they had not tarried long at Adam Bradford's. Once Gruder had heard how close they were, he was for moving on immediately, only giving the horses half the time they wanted to drink. The moon had not yet risen, and the trail in front of Billy was dark and forbidding. He looked up at the dark sky and could detect no starlight. He could only sense dark movement above him. He could tell that Gruder was only a few paces ahead of him by the occasional sound of Jimmy's hooves, but he could not see him. The mule was a rough ride, though steady and seldom needing coaxing, and the jarring helped keep him awake. He was not so much sleepy as he was exhausted. He found it difficult to concentrate on the sound of Gruder's horse ahead. His mind wandered, and he found himself thinking of things over and over again—insignificant things, like the feel of his pocketknife in his pocket and the creak of the saddle.

The wind from behind their backs had been gradually picking up for hours. Now there was a rumble that went with it that turned into a growl and then into discernible thunder. Once the lightning began, its flashes momentarily lit an outline of the figure ahead of him, so he could see Gruder gesture for him to pull off the trail and under the edge of a fallen-away hillside. It provided a slight overhang for them to stand under and hold their mounts.

The wind swirled around the top of the bluff with such force that it blew tree limbs and dirt down and into their faces. The lightning flashed with such regularity that the trees nearby seemed constantly illuminated, and the thunder turned from a low rumble to harsh, loud cracks. Jimmy and the mule were spooked and tried to get their heads. It was all they could do to hold them. Billy held the mule around the neck and placed his bandana over his eyes, which calmed the animal after a while. Jimmy, however, was moving back against them in a threatening way. The mule sensed his closeness even with the bandana. He tried to move back against the earthen wall of the bluff. Billy tried to calm him, but with the loud thunderclaps, it didn't seem the mule could hear him, even when Billy spoke into his ear.

The rain came in large drops. The wind blew it under the overhang and it splattered against them, stinging the side of Billy's face. The rain somehow calmed the animals, as if they now understood that they were in a natural environment, rather than the unknown and frightening place where the lightning came and went. The mule still shivered under Billy's hand, but the bandana masked the lightning flashes and he no longer tried to pull away. After a while, the scattered large drops turned to a driving rain. It blew against them with such force they had to lean into it to remain standing. The lightning was no longer as fierce, and the thunder was again a low rumble rather than the deafening claps that came before.

He heard Gruder shouting something but could not make it out, Then Billy saw him, in a lightning flash, gesturing for him to follow him out into the driving rain. Billy thought he had taken leave of his senses. It was hard enough to stand under the overhang of the bluff, but then he noticed rivulets of water running off the edge of the earthen overhang and realized why they had to move. He made a hand movement signaling Gruder to go on, and Gruder led Jimmy slowly out from under the overhang. Billy tried to get the mule to follow, but he would not move. He dug in his front hooves. Billy remembered the bandana and removed it. At the first flash of lightning, the mule shied into the earthen bank and lurched forward into the space just vacated by Jimmy. The sudden movement caught Billy by surprise. He failed to set his boot heels, and the mule dragged him forward. He stumbled in the strong wind, lost his balance completely and fell, but he did not let go of the reins. He held on as the mule careened against the bank, which was now wet with rain. The mule lost his footing momentarily, kicking out in an attempt to regain his balance. Billy felt a searing pain in his shoulder, but he held onto the reins. After slipping a few times, Billy managed to clamber to his feet. He was now on the wet grass beyond the edge of the concave underbelly of the hillside. He grabbed the bridle near the bit and brought the mule's head down, slowing the animal enough to fully regain his balance. He steadied the mule's head long enough for the mule to give in.

Clenching the reins together in his left hand and the bridle in his right, Billy led the mule steadily away from the bank. The mule did not follow easily, but no longer dug in his front hooves and seemed resigned to Billy having the upper hand. Billy peered ahead into the darkness. The rain swirled about him now, pelting first his face and then his back, then came in strong from the side. The lightning did not come as often. In the occasional flashes, he could sometimes make out Gruder and Jimmy ahead, although he could see only a few feet in front of him because of the rain. After a while, he could no longer see Gruder ahead of him, but moved slowly forward in the darkness, hoping he was going in the right direction.

The ground felt uneven, and he began to worry about falling off a cliff or into a hole. The slightest incline was exaggerated by his blindness. He slowed his pace and felt carefully ahead with each step, paying more attention to the ground beneath him than what lay ahead. Then he realized that his right hand, which still gripped the bridle tightly, had lost all feeling. It was as if it was no longer there, although he could feel the pull against his body as he moved slowly forward with the mule. He had lost his hat, and the rain ran down his face, matting his long hair against his eyes and further impairing his vision, but he held fast to the reins with his left hand and the bridle with his right. He squinted at his hand on the bridle and in a flash of lightning saw that his jacket sleeve had been torn away at the shoulder and hung loosely from his elbow. The mule lurched then, and he felt a sharp pain in his shoulder that made him gasp.

The pain almost blacked him out. He stopped and tried to remove his hand from the leather of the bridle, but he could not. He felt very dizzy and weak and was afraid he was going to pass out. The mule had stilled, and Billy leaned against the side of his neck, touching the mule's wet coarse mane with his matted forehead. He tried to think of what he should do and began to doubt what direction he should go. The rain was not swirling now, but fell straight down. He thought about Ada in the creek for a moment, then was mad at himself for letting his mind wander at such a time. Realizing that the mule was calmed, he reached his left hand, still holding the reins, to his right and felt his fingers around the leather of the bridle. Although he had thought that he was gripping the bridle, his fingers seemed to be loosely curved around the side strap. He decided that he should move his hand away, but the first movement caused excruciating pain in his shoulder, and he was engulfed in blackness.

Ada swam away from him in the brown water. It was early spring, and the creek was up. Little bits of sticks and leaves swirled around her black hair as she swam. His eyes were just above the level of the water and he was holding his breath. He thought it was strange that he could hold his breath for so long. She swam for a long time, but she did not swim away from him. It was as if she was treading water, but she looked like she was swimming. Then, she turned and stood up until the water was at her waist and he could see her small breasts, the nipples hard and crinkled. He thought they were smaller than he remembered and then he realized that she was younger than he was, rather than older. She looked at him solemnly and reached out her hand. He looked up to her and he tried to stand up, but could not feel the bottom. He could not even feel his legs. Yet he did not sink, but stayed at the same level, his eyes just above the brown water. Her brow furrowed, and she said something, but he could not understand what she was saying. She gestured impatiently to him with her outstretched hand, but he could not move. It was as if he was there only to observe and could do nothing that would move him in her direction. Then he heard a low sound. It must have been her voice, but it was too low, as if she was an old man speaking. He still could not make out what she said, and he realized the sound did not fit the movement of her lips. The sound of the rain came back, and he heard the voice more clearly. It was Gruder, saying his name.

He opened his eyes and saw only darkness, but he could feel Gruder near him. Gruder was telling him to wake up.

"There," Gruder said. "Now you're awake."

He was lying under something that kept the rain off. He heard the rain falling against it and he began to make out Gruder leaning over him.

"You passed out, Billy."

"It's my shoulder," he said. His own voice sounded strangely hollow to him.

Gruder leaned forward and felt the shoulder. The sudden pain made Billy catch his breath.

"It's dislocated," Gruder said, feeling around his shoulder with both hands. "I'm gonna have to raise you up, Billy. And I'm going to have to hurt you, but it's got to be done."

Billy felt Gruder's large hands, one behind his head and the other around him in the small of his back, lifting him gently and slowly. When Gruder had Billy upright, his head was against the canvas shelter Gruder had thrown over the limbs of a tree to shield him. Gruder moved his hands and arms until he held Billy fully in his left arm with his left hand under Billy's right armpit. Gruder's other hand felt slowly and gently around the top of Billy's right shoulder until he found the spot he was looking for. Gruder took a deep breath and for a long moment he was motionless. Then he moved suddenly and powerfully, and the pain caused Billy to black out again.

When Billy opened his eyes once more, the rain had stopped and there was a faint light in the sky. He was lying in his bedroll under the canvas shelter. Gruder was sitting on a rock with his back to him. He did not recall any dreams this time, only blackness. He opened his eyes and saw the large shoulders and back he had known for so long. His wet clothes were hanging on a limb beside him. His mouth was dry. Then he remembered his shoulder and recalled the pain, but it was no longer there. His shoulder was wrapped in cotton cloth that came over his forearm in a sling, his forearm resting across his bare chest. He raised his head slightly to look at it, and Gruder stirred and turned around to look at him.

"Well, now," Gruder said. "How you feeling?"

"It don't hurt anymore," Billy said weakly.

"That's good. Glad to hear it."

"But I could use some water."

Gruder reached for a canteen that lay nearby, pulled the cork out of the neck, and put it to Billy's lips. Billy tried to rise up to meet it.

"Watch out now. Don't put pressure on that shoulder just yet. Just lay back and open up."

The water was cold. Gruder dribbled it into his open mouth at just the right rate of flow, and he drank eagerly. When he stopped swallowing, Gruder stopped the flow. After a pause, Billy again looked at Gruder's handiwork. The cloth was from Gruder's spare shirt, and it was still clean. It had been torn into wide strips and expertly tied around the shoulder and arm in such a way that it not only made a sling, it supported the side of the shoulder from the weight of his wrist, or would when he stood up. The knots around the wrist were unlike any Billy had seen before.

"How'd you know how to do all this?" he asked, looking up at Gruder.

Gruder smiled gently.

"If you get to be old, you get to learn things," he said. "Or at least that's the hope we have."

After a long while, Billy convinced Gruder that he could sit up. Gruder lifted his upper body in his arms until Billy could lean back against his saddle, which was propped on a log nestled against the tree trunk. It was full light, and the norther had hit full blast. The wind from the north was cold and strong, and Billy wrapped the bedroll around him. Gruder got wool sweaters for them both and Billy's spare shirt from the bedroll, which had remained dry, wrapped in another piece of canvas. Gruder said they could not light a fire because they were close to the San Saba and it was too dangerous. They ate some jerky and cold biscuits for breakfast.

Wonsley figured they were a few miles southwest of Pegleg. He was leaning from the saddle, looking at the ground, when he noticed part of a hoof mark in the edge of an ant bed and dismounted to take a closer look. The red dirt was depressed in an uneven fashion where the left edge of the hoof had made its mark, indicating a large fissure in the edge, a pattern he had seen before. Crouching, he looked over a broader area and found more marks which indicated to him that the horses they were pursuing had passed over this ground. Hays and John were intentionally spaced out a few horse lengths behind him. By the time both of them came up he could tell that the tracks led into the valley ahead. John dismounted and stood looking at the tracks as Wonsley pointed them out. Hays looked at the ground from his saddle.

"They're not very old," Wonsley said. "And they're headin' where we thought."

They heard the faint rumble of thunder from the southeast.

"We got plenty of time 'til dark," John said, looking up at Hays.

They had been traversing low red hills that were sparsely covered with sage and huisache. They could make out what appeared to be a gradual slope about a mile ahead.

"We'll keep on," Hays said. "We need to get to the river ahead of the storm."

"You think they got a sentry posted?" Wonsley asked.

"Don't know," Hays said.

John and Wonsley mounted up. They rode single file to the place where the trail, such as it was, descended into a shallow pass between two small hills that were part of the ridge above the river valley. Unlike the hills for miles behind them, there were dwarf cedars here and live oaks growing on the crest of the ridge, providing cover for anyone who wanted to watch the trail.

Hays, in the lead, stopped for a moment and looked at the hill to their right. It was rocky, but rounded on top and relatively low, with gullies caused by runoff etching its face. It was thick with cedar and huisache but there were relatively few mesquites. There were no horse trails visible. The low brush made it undesirable for horses. Hays dismounted and started leading his buckskin up one of the low places. They had changed horses, and the buckskin had come along riderless after watering and resting long enough for the sweat to dry on him. The horse had brought Hays from California, and although Hays never said anything to anyone about him and spoke to him only in low, unintelligible murmurs, he would not leave him. The buckskin continued to display his stamina and loyalty as he followed Hays up the shallow ravine toward the top of the hill, brushing between cedar and huisache limbs in belly-high grass.

John and Wonsley followed, dismounting and leading the bay mare and the paint along in single file. The mare shied at the first cedar tree, her eyes showing high white, but John held her around the neck behind the ears, and she gradually began to move under his gentle guidance. The paint was used to following Wonsley through thick brush. He dipped his head under the first cedar limbs and with characteristically adept footing, matched Wonsley's pace up the rocky slope of the gully.

When they reached the top they found that the cedars were spaced farther apart under the shade of the live oaks, and there was enough room to move between them easily. There were very few huisache. They remained dismounted and moved northeast along the edge of the river valley and over many small hills, each with its crest relatively clear of underbrush. By necessity, they followed a curving path up and down the hillsides, following low places between the cedars and searching for gradual approaches. There were signs of coyote, raccoon, rabbit, and possum, as well as deer and antelope, but there were no signs of horses.

After going a few miles along the edge of the river valley, they reached a crest that appeared to be longer than the rest. It extended into a ridge. The ground remained fairly level along the top of the ridge for several hundred yards, and they could see a curve in the hillside through the limbs of the oaks ahead. A long bluff curving to the north looked like the one Adam Bradford and the others had described. Hays looked around, then tied the buckskin to an oak limb. The others tied up and followed him toward the edge of the hilltop where the ground began to drop off gradually before it reached the edge of the bluff. The river had worn against this hillside in flood stage for centuries, leaving the rocky bluff that ran from west to east, then curved to the north. The top of the bluff was a third or more down the hillside from the crest and was covered with cedar and huisache like the other hills, giving good cover to anyone who wanted to see into the valley without being seen. Below the bluff was a pasture between the bluff and the river where the Comanches pastured their horses.

Wonsley did not understand the lack of evidence that the Comanche had ever been there. It seemed like the logical place to put sentries. Unlike Hays and his brother, most of what he knew of the Comanche was based on what others had told him. But he was unfamiliar with the tales some Rangers told of coming up on Comanche camps and completely surprising a whole band. For centuries the Comanches had been lulled into a sense of security in their encampments by their superiority over their enemies. Any tribe they had not completely vanquished kept a wide distance between themselves and the possible range of the Nermernuh, which was what the Comanches called themselves. It was also contrary to Indian tactics to pursue an enemy from the battleground. It was customary for each side to carry their wounded and dead away from the site of the battle. They had no strategy that included the concept of gaining territory through force of arms.

They could see grassland on the other side of the river from the top of the hill, but not the river itself or the land on the near side, where the Pegleg camp was reported to be. The cedars blocked their view. Hays gestured to Wonsley, and Wonsley nodded in recognition. He began carefully creeping down the side of the hill, crouching below the branches of the cedars and closely watching his footing. It was a rocky, well-eroded hillside. A slip could send a cascade of rocks over the edge of the bluff and alarm the people below. John Baker and Hays came behind, careful to follow Wonsley's path.

About fifty yards down the hillside, he saw the edge of the bluff where the cedars stopped and a place near the edge and a bit to his right where a large boulder appeared to form some cover. He crawled from cedar to cedar, staying close to the ground and under branches until he reached the flat place behind the boulder. The boulder jutted out from the edge and tapered down to only about three feet above the ground where he now lay. He crawled over to the downstream side of the boulder and, taking his cap off, peered over the edge.

The river curved below the bluff downstream. On the near side of the river horses were grazing in a flat pasture bordered by cottonwoods. There must have been two hundred head in his view, and he could only see a part of the valley. Many were paints, which the Comanches strongly favored, but there were a number of bays, sorrels, and blacks among them. Some of them were larger than Indian horses, but most were the small, hardy ones the Comanches had bred for years. Wonsley crawled a little closer to the edge and surveyed the river. A few horses were wading and drinking. On the opposite side, the river had cut a steep bluff out of the pasture about twelve to fifteen feet high, just as the swarthy man had described. The near side appeared to be gravel bar. The water was shallow where the horses stood.

He could not see anything closer to the bluff on his side because of the weeds growing out of the side of the bluff, so he crawled back over the level space behind the boulder to the upstream side, where the edge of the boulder stopped at a bare place. Here, there were smaller rocks and no tall weeds below him, so he was able to pull himself right up to the edge and look over into the valley below.

Upstream about a quarter of a mile stood twenty lodges, the streamers at the top of the lodge poles flapping in the strong wind from the southeast. He could make out some of the rock wall, visible between the structures. There were men, women, and children all about, some carrying water from the river in hide bags, some tending to their lodges. They all seemed to be moving with some haste. The thunder in the southeast came louder and more frequently, but the people in the valley below did not give any sign of alarm. They went about their tasks as if they knew their allotted time.

He was a couple of hundred feet above them and well downstream. Below him there were more horses but no visible Comanches. Judging from how the people in the camp looked, he decided he was practically invisible to them, and it would be possible to carefully search the bluff for a passageway down. He crawled back to the downstream side and into the weeds at the edge. He felt his way along until he came to an indentation in the top of the bluff that indicated some erosion. Parting the weeds, he saw a place where the bluff had eroded over a period of years, causing a natural trail that curled beneath him in an upstream direction to the left, under the overhang of the boulder. He crawled to the other side of the indentation to get a better view. The rainwater had followed a gradual path diagonally down the face of the bluff, leaving a space just wide enough for a foothold. It would enable a man to make his way down the side until he was near the bottom, or at least it seemed so. He could not see all the way down; the natural path turned out of sight over halfway down, which could mean a drop-off of almost a hundred feet or only a change in the direction of the natural path. There was no way to be sure without crawling down there, and there was no cover. The bluff was spotted with clumps of buffalo grass and small cottonwoods that were only a few feet high. They grew in the areas where runoff had deposited soil from above, so that it looked as if they bordered the paths made by the water, but they were mere shoots, most no more than a foot high, probably with little root structure and not likely to give good handholds.

He crawled back behind the boulder where John waited. Hays was on the upstream side, leaning out in the rock-strewn grass, looking in the direction of the Comanche lodges. He had pulled his hat off. Wonsley noticed for the first time that he had a bald spot. John was looking at the hillside above them and the way it curved downstream until it reached the place where the river entered a small gorge. The cedars lay low and thick against it, without a break.

"There's a natural trail down, over there," Wonsley said, pointing, "but it's hard to tell if it goes all the way down." He spoke in a low voice, although the wind and the distant thunder made it difficult to hear a voice at any level below a shout.

"I guess that's why they feel safe down there," John said, in a normal tone.

Hays pulled a spyglass out and looked carefully at the area where the people were, upstream. He was motionless, cradling the end of the telescope in his left hand, which he steadied in a clump of grass, and holding the eyepiece with his right, against his right eye. Only the grass and the edges of his hair that had not been matted by his hatband moved in the stiff breeze. Normally, there would have been Indian children playing among the horses below, away from the tipis, but even the children were carrying firewood and putting up things in preparation for the coming storm. The horses below moved about restlessly, seldom stopping to graze or drink. It would not be long before they stopped grazing and drinking altogether.

Wonsley stared at Hays until he became restless and sat back from his squatting position. John had seated himself on a patch of grass. He had been with Hays before and knew better than to hurry him. He knew he was studying every part of the Comanche camp and would remember every detail.

Hays finally lowered the telescope, but remained looking over the top of it at the line of tipis. After a long while, he collapsed the telescope, slipped it into its leather case, and slowly pulled himself over the edge of the bluff until he was leaning out over the edge in the short grass, his head dipping below his shoulders, studying the valley below. He looked at every detail, from the lay of the far bank of the river to the narrow spot on the northeast side as the river curved, to the land on the other side of the Comanche encampment, a slash of low, level ground where crops had once been planted before the Comanche discouraged further intrusion into their private area. When he had seen what he wanted to see, he pushed back and rolled in one motion, came to a crouching position, and made his way back to where John and Wonsley sat behind the boulder. Holding his black hat in one hand, he crawfished over the small rocks with the aid of the other. His movements were quick and precise. When he reached them, he squatted and placed his black hat on his head, looking down as he spoke to them in a calm, sure voice.

"They're down there," he said. "We'll wait until dark. Better get our mounts settled and ready for the storm." He said it with a coolness that John had heard before, but not for a long time. It was the voice of a man who had made up his mind what he was going to do. It was clear from his tone that he expected the same determination from those who were with him, who would follow him, and it never failed to have a calming effect.

"There's a trail that goes down the other side of the rock," Wonsley said. "We can get most of the way down, I think."

"Can we get back up?" Hays asked.

"I think it goes all the way down, but it's hard to tell from up here. We may have to use ropes to get all the way down and then use them to get back up."

Hays's gaze was piercing.

"You may have to come up this hill carrying a girl," he said. "They got their horses tied near the second tipi from the river. One of the men there is scanning this ridge."

Wonsley did not respond. It was a while before he realized he had been thinking about crawling up the side of that bluff at night with the rain pummeling them and the girl crying. A silence passed, then Hays began to crawl back up the hill between the cedars. The brothers followed. They made it back on all fours, and when they reached the top of the ridge they tied their horses securely at a distance apart so that they could do no harm to each other during the storm. They unwrapped their slickers and checked their pistols and cartridge belts, then waited, apart from the horses, as night began to fall and the lightning storm began.

At dusk, the sky in the west had a golden tint. The cloud cover was thinned out on the edge to the north and west and the roiling grey clouds above turned purple. The men made their way back down the hillside to the top of the bluff as the lightning began to crackle in the darkening sky, and the first big drops of rain pelted them. Wonsley led them to the edge where the natural path began, pointing out the way in the lightning flashes, but Hays took the lead down the side of the bluff, grasping his way in a crouch before them. They wore their slickers and did not carry their rifles. Wonsley followed behind Hays and had trouble keeping up. He occasionally looked away from the steep incline and the handholds he grasped for to see the valley below them illuminated in the stark silver flashes of lightning. John followed behind, unhurriedly grabbing cottonwood shoots and finding footholds in grass clumps. Wonsley slipped once and slid a few feet down the slope before he grabbed a shoot that stopped him. He found a foothold to push his way diagonally downward until he reached the path again. When he thought he had reached the place where the path disappeared during his first reconnoiter, he saw that a small boulder created a drop of five feet or so to a fairly wide spot below. Hays had already traversed it. Wonsley slid off the rock and down, a little more quickly than he would have if he had been alone. He didn't want to fall too far behind the older man. The descent was exhilarating.

It was full dark now. The rain was holding off as if to allow them time to get to the valley below, while the wind and lightning hurried them along. A bolt of lightning struck a tree on the ridge above with a crack like a rifle shot. There was no time to think about what they were doing. Wonsley moved much faster down the hillside than he thought possible, alternating his attention between the hand- and footholds he half saw and half felt and the scene below him, the dark figure of Hays moving eerily ahead and below on the thin path, the river reflecting the flashes of lightning, the green pasture dotted with horses moving about in the storm.

It was as if he was suspended in the air just below the source of the lightning, above the earth, half sliding down the dark side of a giant being that seemed to move in the night. Then the rain came and blew against him, pelting his leather cap with a sound that contrasted strangely with the sound of the thunderclaps all around him: a staccato punctuation between the flashes that pushed him faster down the hillside.

Then he could see the trunks and branches of large cottonwoods and knew they must be nearing the bottom. The branches were swirling in the wind and rain, throwing leaves. The slope leveled out gradually, and he could see Hays ahead of him at the edge of the cottonwoods, moving swiftly from one to the other. By the time he was at the line of trees, Hays was well within them. Hays turned, waiting for him. John was not far behind, and when they were all at one spot at the edge of the thin grove, partially sheltered, Hays gestured toward the end of the line of tipis near the riverbank. He moved out immediately across the level pasture. Wonsley and John followed close behind. Horses were running across the field as they crossed, circling them in the lightning storm. The rain came harder, cutting down their visibility. Wonsley felt a horse rush past him between the flashes, a large dark force that almost touched his side as it went by in a slippery lope.

He thought he was still between Hays and his brother John, but he could no longer see clearly enough ahead to know which direction he was going. Although he ran at what he thought was Hays's pace, he could not be sure. The wet, grassy pasture was level and smooth, and his boot heels dug in the turf, allowing what he estimated was good speed.

He was not winded and felt he could run at that pace all night, but he slowed gradually. He had the feeling he had run the distance he had seen from the cottonwoods to the tipis, or close to it. Then he felt a slope and slowed to a walk. Now he could see the river's edge and soon came upon Hays, who was standing on the gravel bank waiting. They stood and waited, looking around for John. He realized for the first time that he was breathing hard from the descent from the bluff and the run across the field. John came up along the water's edge, and they followed Hays upstream, crouching as they moved, until the ground sloped upward slightly, and they were off the gravel bar. Hays squatted, and when they came up to him, he pointed ahead and a bit to the right. At first Wonsley could not see anything; then he made out the outline of the tipis, some twenty yards away. Hays gestured toward the second tipi from the river and gave a sign for them to follow him and surround it. Wonsley would go left and John right.

They came up to the tipi from the rear, opposite the flap that served as an opening. The rock wall was constructed so that the tipis could be placed in the openings in the wall, and other openings could be closed with lodge poles, making the walls and tipis together an effective fence. The wall was about five feet high and made of large limestone rocks that had been hauled there from up and down the San Saba valley. The stones fit together tightly and well without mortar, but it was not worth the risk of dislodging a rock by attempting to crawl over it. In the intermittent light, Hays found an opening down the fence line, and he motioned for John and Wonsley to crouch behind the wall while he moved around to the opening and lifted the lodge pole that barred it. Wonsley crouched beside the lodge and put his hand against the buffalo hide. It was warm to the touch, and he could make out smoke coming out of the top opening, which was half-flapped for the storm. He unsheathed his Bowie knife. The skin of the tipi was fairly fresh and translucent before the firelight inside, and he could make out silhouettes. The second closest tipi to the water would belong to a chief or medicine man. There were four figures seated around the fire. There were probably more, lying down where he could not see.

He turned to look for Hays on the other side of the fence and saw his black hat moving toward the tipi. Then, one of the flap poles moved. Hays was shutting the flap over the chimney hole. The pole moved slowly and steadily until the flap closed. Wonsley crouched around the rear edge of the tipi, looking at the lower silhouettes. It was only a minute or so before he heard the first coughs.

He stood ready with his knife for the first sound of gunfire from Hays. There was more coughing and one of the figures inside stood up. Another moved toward the entrance and crouched there. It would not have been unusual for the strong wind to have moved the chimney flap. It was likely that at least one of the men would come out to fix it, and the others would come out for air. The coughing had become widespread inside the tipi. One man said something to another. Then, the door flap hit the outside skin of the tipi, and they moved toward the opening, except for one that remained crouched by the fire. He saw some movement down low near the rear of the tipi, a head moving and coughing in a higher pitch. Hays's pistol rang out as the figures came out of the front opening. The figure that had remained huddled by the fire moved swiftly away from the entrance. Wonsley raised his knife to slash into the buffalo skin of the tipi, but before he could bring his hand down, a blade from the inside cut through a few feet to his left, and a man plunged out.

Wonsley jumped back, and the dark figure blew past him. He went to the opening the man had cut. Inside, amid the smoke, he saw the small coughing figure.

He stepped inside and grabbed her with both arms, then dragged her out of the opening. She began to scream. Someone came toward them from the inside as he dragged her out. Outside, he dropped the small person he assumed was the girl and tried to reach inside his slicker for his pistol, but missed it. He still had his Bowie knife in one hand, and he raised it as the dark form lunged toward him. A pistol shot rang out from a few feet away and the figure turned back toward the sound, then sank before him, falling at his feet.

There were three more pistol shots from the front of the tipi. He could barely see the ground below him in the glow from the tipi's fire, but he could hear the girl coughing, and felt for her. He had dragged her out in the buffalo robe on which she had been lying, and he found the wet fur. He wrestled with her, turning her over, and she pushed against him hard.

"Stop," he yelled. "We've come to save you."

In a flash of light he saw her face: wild blue eyes staring at him. She had a red streak across her forehead, a slash mark. He grabbed her wrists. She tried to pull away. He pulled her to her feet and out of the buffalo robe. She was in the dirty gingham dress she had been taken in, half of the left shoulder ripped away.

"I'm takin' you back," he yelled into her face. He shook her.

Suddenly, John was beside him. The girl saw him in a lightning flash, which spooked her again. She broke away from Wonsley's grasp and tried to run, but slipped. Wonsley was on her heels and fell over her, pinning her. Then Hays was there. He grabbed the buffalo robe as Wonsley picked her up bodily, and they wrapped the robe around her. She momentarily stopped struggling. Hays gestured, and they moved out in the direction of the cottonwood grove and the bluff.

The lightning was letting up and the rain intensifying. The direction Hays took had to be pure guesswork. They had not caught sight of the cottonwood grove in the storm. It was more difficult than ever to follow him. In the complete darkness and the rain, there were no landmarks, nothing to see or feel or hear to indicate the right direction. The girl was over his right shoulder. She had kicked him in the groin once, causing a shooting pain that staggered him, but she finally stopped struggling. He had the impression that the buffalo robe was as heavy as the girl, and it got heavier as the rain soaked it. He thought of it as carrying a sack of feed. A hundred-pound load was not so bad, but he had never carried one through a rainstorm at night. His forward foot had a tendency to slide as he put it down, and he came close to falling over backwards with the weight of his load until he dropped into a crouch. This allowed him to lean into his step and anticipate the slide.

After what seemed like an hour, he realized he had no idea where he was headed. His concentration on maintaining his balance could well have thrown him off his path. The rain was coming down harder than ever, and the girl in the robe grew heavier with each step. He was panting and his right arm was aching when he brushed up against something on his left side. It seemed to be solid, but when he stopped and tried to reach back with his elbow to touch it, nothing was there. It could have been a tree or a horse. He took a step back and tried to once more to touch it, but nothing was there. If it had been a horse, it had moved, but he had not heard anything above the sound of the rain hitting his slicker. He stood still and listened. The girl was dead weight. She had not moved for some time. If she had fainted, he did not want to put her down and risk waking her up, although stopping had brought his attention to an aching pain in his right shoulder and a numbness in his right hand.

He stepped forward tentatively, wondering if he had come near the river instead of the cottonwood grove. The ground still seemed level, but it was hard to tell in the dark and the rain. He picked up his pace again and noticed that he was not sliding as much with his steps. Either he had adapted to it or the ground was firmer. He tried to feel more of the surface with his foot, and after a few steps sliding his foot forward, felt something against the toe of his boot. He raised his foot slightly to better feel it. It was a small tree branch, lying flush to the ground. He must be in the grove. He stepped over it and felt with each step until he felt another one, this one slightly above ground, a curve in the limb raising part of it where it lay.

Then he heard something other than the rain, a low whispering sound, barely audible amidst the patter against the ground. He turned his head slightly, freeing his right ear from the wet surface of the buffalo robe. The sound was above him. The wind and rain hitting the cottonwood trees sounded like the whispers of old women.

In his mind he pictured the depth of the grove from where they had crossed it. He tried to estimate how long it would take him to get through it, but the grove covered the entire south side of the pasture, and he was not sure whether its depth was uniform. As he moved forward, he occasionally felt more fallen limbs. He stumbled against a rather large one that hit him mid-shin as he stepped. He thought of the bluff ahead and wondered how he could find the slight path and whether it would still be there in the rain or if it had washed out to a steep fall that he would be unable to ascend.

He had not thought of John or Hays for a long time, but now he wondered about them. John had started out behind him, but there was no way he could have followed his path, and Hays, who had been ahead, was completely lost to him now. The best thing to do, once he got to the bluff, was to try to find the path on his own, but he was not sure which way to turn. He would think about that when the time came. For now, he had to get across this grove and get to a place where he could set the girl down. He did not think he could go much farther without resting his shoulder.

After a while, it seemed like he should have come to the base of the bluff. But carrying the weight of the girl and the robe in the rain might have slowed him down more than imagined. He would stop thinking about that. He would keep going forward, and he would come to the foot of the bluff and put the girl down. There was a sharp, high sound. At first he thought he had imagined it, it was so faint. Then, after a few moments of just the sound of the wind and rain, he heard it again. It was coming from ahead and slightly to his left. He turned in that direction. After another twenty paces it became clearer. It was a whistle that sounded like the call of a bird. He was moving toward it. For a moment he thought it might have been a Comanche, perhaps the man who had dashed out of the tipi past him in the dark, but that made no sense. He would have had no one to signal to, as far as Wonsley knew. Then, he heard it again and whistled back. He had learned to whistle and make bird calls when he was very young and had practiced whistling without using his fingers. He whistled against his lips, holding his lips tight against the front of his teeth and blowing hard with his tongue set against the roof of his mouth behind his front teeth.

The shrillness of his whistle caused the girl to stir. She began to kick her legs and beat her fists against his back. She wriggled with renewed energy and his weakened arm was losing its hold on her. She slipped off his shoulder, and when he tried to grab her with his left arm, he lost his balance, and they both fell. She was up in an instant, before he could get a good hold on her. She slipped out of his grasp, leaving him clutching the buffalo robe. Before he realized what had happened, she was gone, her steps plodding wetly against the soaked, leafy ground. He stumbled to his feet and went after the sound, staggering against the change in balance the lifting of her weight from his shoulder had caused.

He had run only a few feet when he heard a thud and the sound of the breath being knocked out of her, then the sound of scrambling in the wet leaves as she tried to get back up. He was almost to her as her steps began to splat against the ground again. But there was another sound, as if she had run into something solid. It had a sharp sound, not like the sound of her hitting a tree trunk. He heard a low voice saying, "Hold on," and Wonsley was close, almost within reach.

He stopped and waited. He heard the girl's feet stabbing the wet ground, but she was not moving. Then, he heard the low, male voice again, saying, "Hold it, girl," and he recognized it as Hays's voice.

"Cap'n?" he yelled. The girl screamed.

Hays held the girl as she sobbed. There was no finding the buffalo robe in the dark, and she was soaked and shivering.

"Hold on to her," Hays yelled, and thrust her toward Wonsley. He reached out in the dark for her, felt the side of her head and grabbed her by the neck. She turned and bit his hand. He managed to get his arms around her and held on. She struggled, pushing against his chest with her elbows.

"Dammit," he yelled into her ear. "Don't you know we're tryin' to save you? That's your uncle there."

She stopped pushing against him, but kept her elbows up. He sensed Hays nearby, although he could not see anything in the dark. He felt the girl shivering against him. Then Hays let out another loud whistle, which caused her to jump. There was no response at first, but after a minute Hays whistled again and this time, there was a faint whistle from the direction of the pasture. After a few minutes John's voice could be heard calling out their names, and in a few more, he was with them.

They followed Hays by the sound of his footsteps, Wonsley half dragging the barefoot girl along and John Baker following behind him. They came to the slope that led to the foot of the bluff and then, magically, to the foot of the trail. Wonsley never understood how Hays could have found it in the dark. Suddenly Hays was standing close in his path.

"This is the bottom of the trail," he said. "Can you get that girl up?"

"I can if she'll ride my back," he responded. "But I don't know how I can hold onto her and climb up."

He could feel Hays's breath on the side of his neck as he spoke into the girl's ear.

"Martha. I'm Jack Hays, your uncle."

He felt the girl turn in his arms.

"You've got to hang onto this man's back because we got to go up a hill." His voice had that coldness that Wonsley had noticed before, but it was calm and steady. The girl sniffled and shivered, but she did not move away. "Do you understand?"

"Yes." It was faint and barely audible although their heads were close.

Hays put his arms around her, and Wonsley loosened his hold on her, then turned around and the girl put her arms around his neck from behind and held on. At first, she was choking him, but he lowered his chin and got his neck down in the buttoned collar of his slicker until he was able to stand the pressure. She drew her knees up and hung on, and they started up the steep trail.

He had to stop four times before they reached the top and fell three times. Each time he thought he was going to slip and fall down the face of the bluff with the girl on his back, but he was able to grab a rock or a cottonwood shoot and steady himself. The trail carried a narrow stream of water, but the footing was surprisingly good. The rock and clay of the bluff had already eroded down to hard places, and he was able to find footing, although he moved at an agonizingly slow pace. Each time that he stopped and put the girl down to rest he was on the verge of falling, and each time he fell, he realized that he should have rested. John was close behind and a couple of times, he could feel the girl lighten as John supported her from the rear.

Once he slipped on a flat rock, and the girl slipped off his outside shoulder. He thought he had lost her, but John apparently grabbed one of her legs. She hung in the air until he regained his balance and could shift her weight back to the right where he could lean against the hillside.

When he came to the last few feet before the ledge next to the flat boulder, he had trouble finding a foothold. The ground was steeper here, and they had slid down when they descended. He could feel Hays's hands grabbing the girl's upper arms from around his neck, pulling her up the last few feet to the ledge. He barely made it up, and Hays had to give him a hand. He fell, exhausted, when he had finally reached the level spot.

John pulled himself up to the ledge and sat beside Wonsley. Hays had opened his slicker and placed it around the girl. He leaned with her against the side of the boulder, which gave some protection from the blowing rain. They sat for a long while in silence, listening to their heavy breathing; then Hays said they had better get up the hill. Wonsley expected to be given the girl to carry, but heard Hays's steps ahead of him, so he crawled up behind him through the cedars. Hays had placed a canvas shelter over some low limbs of a live oak tree. When they reached the top, he took the girl there and laid her down under it. There was no room for a fire, and they had no dry wood, but John had brought a small kerosene miner's lantern which they had left under the tarp. He retrieved his metal matchbox and after a few failed tries, lit it. There was a blanket. Hays took the wet dress off the girl and rolled her in it. She was shivering hard in the lantern light, but pushed herself up into a sitting fetal position.

The three men positioned themselves around her like a windbreak. Their heavy breathing gradually slowed. The wind and rain slacked off a bit, as if giving up on them. None of them exchanged a look. Each one fixed his eyes on the small figure huddled before them, her wet red hair showing over the edge of the brown blanket, which shook steadily. Wonsley was not sure if he could get up again. He was leaning against the live oak trunk. John was seated just outside the edge of the tarp, the rain running off the front of his hat brim down the front of his slicker and onto the ground between his long, outstretched legs. Hays was under the tarp on the other side of the girl, staring intently in the lamp light.

They sat until the rain stopped, and the wind picked up again, blowing a cold warning from the north. Wonsley was not aware that he had closed his eyes, and when he opened them, there was some light in the sky in the east. Hays had gone to check on the horses. The girl had stopped shivering and seemed to be asleep, lying on her side. John went to his pack and brought back some pants and a shirt. He had thought to bring them along, which amazed Wonsley. They were boy's clothes, hand-me-downs that had been in the family since long before Wonsley had been able to wear them. He gave Wonsley a look, then touched the girl's head. She jerked upright, clutching the blanket around her. He extended the clothes to her.

"You better put these on. Wonsley and I will leave and give you some privacy."

He laid the clothes on the damp ground beside her and gestured to Wonsley to move. Wonsley had difficulty getting up, but he got to one knee, then lifted himself by a knob of the live oak and stepped out from under the shelter half. Hays was at the horses with his slicker off and his wool coat on. The horses were still in place, and they had cached their goods well enough that they were dry.

"We better move on out," he said.

They repacked their loads and when they were saddled and ready to move, the girl came up to Wonsley, still barefoot but with the blanket wrapped around her. She stood waiting to get on his horse with him. She looked up expectantly, but her face was blank, as if she were in a dream.

"You better put on some socks," he said. "I got some in my pack."

The girl did not respond. When he reached in his saddlebag and pulled out a pair of clean wool socks and handed them to her, she took them in her hand and looked at them as if she was not sure what to do with them.

"Here," he said, and grabbed her around the waist and lifted her onto the saddle. He put a sock on her near foot and stepped around to the other side and put the other one on. He took the reins at the head of the horse and looked up at her.

"You're gonna have to lie down when we go through the cedars," he said. She nodded weakly.

Hays led them off on the trail through the cedars, the men leading their horses with the brown-blanketed girl ducking under the branches as they went. The north wind blew cold from their rear in the gray light.

TEN

AFTER BILLY HAD MANAGED TO STAND UP AND HAD SLIPPED INTO his cold, damp pants, Gruder came back from his horse with a package of oilcloth bound with string.

"Your daddy got you something for your birthday," he said, giving Billy the steady look that he usually gave him when he wanted his attention. He handed him the package. When Billy took it, its weight surprised him, and he instinctively reached and tried to grab it with his right hand, pulling against the cloth sling.

He had forgotten about his birthday and had lost track of time. He looked at the oilcloth wrapping and the string and thought of his father tying it with his own hands. He had often looked at those hands, large and callused, tying harness or rope. The thick string was tied in a tight bowknot.

"You had this in your saddlebag?"

Gruder smiled.

"Is it really my birthday?"

"It's the fifteenth. Ain't that your birthday?"

Billy pulled the string loose and unfolded the wrapping, revealing first the shiny barrel and then the frame and handle of a new pistol, its shape unlike anything he had ever seen. He took it by the grip and held it up to admire it. It had an eight-inch octagonal barrel and a sleek trigger guard that curved gracefully into the walnut-clad handle.

"It's a new one," Gruder said. "He got it in San Antone last month. It's not a Colt. It's a Remington New Model. A single action forty-four."

It was beautiful. The new blued steel shone in the morning light. Gruder showed him how to move the latch to allow the loading lever to drop down and how to remove the cylinder pin to free the cylinder so it could be taken out for loading. After Billy carefully examined the cylinder, Gruder pointed out the nipples for percussion caps and the recesses where the hammer would strike metallic cartridges or could lie in safety when the cylinders were loaded with percussion charges and balls. He then showed him how to load it from a new box of shells he produced from his back pocket, also a part of the gift. While Billy hefted the pistol in his left hand, swinging the tip of the barrel around to get the feel of it, Gruder took the old Walker Colt out of Billy's holster, wrapped it in the oilcloth and tied it with the string. It was larger than the Remington, but the oilcloth covered it.

"It's a good thing you can shoot with your left hand," Gruder said. "You gonna have to pull it backwards though. This holster's made for the right."

He gestured for Billy to turn around, and he tied the belt on him backwards, placing the holster on his left side.

"Now, try putting it in there and taking it out."

He had actually practiced wearing his holster this way. He rotated the gun inward in a circular motion and shoved it into the holster. He was surprised by the easy feel of it when he turned it around in midair. It dropped farther down into the holster than the Colt, causing him to jerk his hand toward it a bit as it dropped. Otherwise, it was a smooth movement. Then he dropped his hand to his side for a second and moved it in a smooth upward motion, caught the pistol handle on the way up and pulled it out to a pointing position. It felt balanced and smooth. It felt just right. He turned it in his hand and examined it carefully. The handle was smaller than the Colt, but fit just fine. There was more to the pistol in front of the hammer than the Colt because of the design of the mainframe, which gave it a clumsy look, but it did not feel at all clumsy.

"How's that shoulder feel?" Gruder asked.

Billy had forgotten about the shoulder. He moved his arm in the sling to test it.

"It's okay," he said.

"Then we better be on our way," Gruder said. He turned to take the canvas shelter down and folded it, then grabbed Billy's saddle and started for the horse and mule. Billy reholstered the pistol and tended to his bedroll, taking out his wool coat and putting it on. He felt a twinge in his shoulder every time he used his right hand, but he was not about to let Gruder know about it. By the time he made it to the gray mule, Gruder had his saddle cinched down and grabbed the bedroll from him and tied it on back of the cantle, over the saddlebags.

"Can you get up by yourself?" he asked.

"I expect so," Billy said and swung up smoothly with his left hand on the pommel. Gruder mounted Jimmy and turned him around.

"We best follow along the river bottom," Gruder said. "There won't be any trail after that rainstorm."

"Then how will we know where they went?" Billy asked.

"I figure they're downstream," he replied. "This is the way the Cap'n would have come, and we haven't run into them yet."

They wound down an overgrown trail into the valley of the San Saba. Here it was quite narrow on both sides of the river, with barely enough room for the trail. The river was yellowish brown and at the top of its banks. The ground was littered with leaves and broken limbs, and the cottonwoods and elms were half bare. Several trees had been struck by lightning, and a few cottonwoods had their tops blown off.

The gray dawn had turned into a bright morning, and the wind from the north blew in their faces with a steadily increasing force, numbing them. Billy had lost his hat in the night and had not thought to bring a cap. His long brown hair blew back from his reddening face in the wind. Gruder had jammed his old brown hat down on his head and tightened the leather thong that served as a strap under his chin.

Billy held the reins in his left hand, but if he had to draw his pistol he would have to drop the reins, and he was not sure how the gray mule would react. He had been ridden mostly by hired hands, and Billy did not consider him well trained. He had tied the reins, although he had always hated to ride with his reins tied. His father had made him ride that way for almost a year when he was first starting to ride because he had dropped them once. He considered it a childish thing to do, something for children and women, but he had tied them in case he had to drop them to pull his gun, and he might as well find out how the mule would react. He dropped them against the saddle horn, and the mule stopped in his tracks, as if he had been trained to do so. Billy unholstered his new pistol and waved it over the mule's head. It was out of the mule's line of sight, and he stood still. He reholstered the gun and lifted the reins. The mule stood his ground. Even a couple of kicks in the withers did not move him.

"Come on, Gray," he said in a soft voice, but the mule did not move. He popped the mule's left shoulder with the end of the reins, and he started to walk again, but it seemed an arbitrary, unpredictable movement instead of a trained response. After a few steps, he stopped. The mule had given him little difficulty since he had left Julie behind, except for getting spooked in the thunderstorm. It irritated him that simply dropping the reins would cause him to become mule stubborn. In less than a minute, Gruder and Jimmy were winding out of sight in the trees and brush ahead. He decided to try dropping the reins again. When he did so, the mule started up, moving at the same pace as before.

They wound through piles of driftwood. Because they were traveling upwind, they could hear anything loud ahead of them, but it was hard to judge the extent of their hearing range. There were no bird sounds in the wind, but they could hear the San Saba rushing against its banks. Billy thought he could hear Jimmy's hooves striking the wet ground ahead of them better than he could on a still day. The sound was faint. Then he heard a sharp crack to the right of and behind Gruder. It came from the wooded hillside, the sound of a stick trod on by a man or beast. It did not sound like the sound a wild animal would make. It was too incomplete, the sound of the break too tentative.

He dared not drop the reins. He slid his left hand down to his side, over his thigh and tensed his legs in the stirrups. Through the trunks of the elms and cottonwoods, he could see only the fluttering of leaves in the wind. Nothing else was moving. Whoever was there could pick Gruder off if he had a rifle or maybe even a pistol. He dug his heels in the mule's sides and urged him with a forward lean and the mule increased his pace. A couple of more touches and the mule responded again. Gruder was only intermittently in sight ahead of him, weaving along the trail.

He whistled, loud and clear. Gruder stopped and turned to look back at him. In the same moment, a rifle shot cracked out, and Gruder's body twisted awkwardly back the way it had turned. Gruder leaned forward in the saddle and kicked Jimmy strongly in the withers. Jimmy bolted forward as if shying from the shot more than anything, and Gruder was quickly out of sight behind a large stand of brush and trees.

The smoke from the shot was flowing in the wind from the point where it had been made. Billy gave the mule the maximum physical encouragement, and he began a jarring lope. In a few seconds, he covered the twenty yards or so up the trail to a point close to where the shot had been fired, then Billy pulled up on him hard and dropped the reins. The mule came to a straight-legged stop and almost threw him. When he straightened up, the Remington was in his hand. He smoothly threw it forward, cocking the hammer in the same motion, and fired at a place of unusual-looking movement in the maze of leaves and tree trunks. He then reholstered the pistol, dismounted and hit the ground in a crouch, his pistol swiftly into his hand again.

Billy could hear someone running through the brush in the direction of the hillside, probably thirty or forty yards away. Then he heard the sound of a man's heavy breathing, and he lunged into the brush after him. His bare head was slapped and scratched by limbs and brush, but he did not feel it. He ran swiftly, although the sling on his arm caused him to dip his right shoulder to maintain his balance, and this slowed him up. He could not hear while running and stopped to listen again. At first there was nothing, then two successive sounds of small limbs cracking, coming from the hillside. He was twenty yards away from the incline and could see the low green brush rising ahead and a glimpse of something else that did not fit in. He fired at it, leading just enough upslope to compensate for the movement of his prey. He heard a grunt and was sure he had hit him.

He ran in that direction until he reached the bottom of the hillside, then crouched in the edge of the larger bushes, which hid him from the hillside above. He looked carefully around the edge of the brush until he could see the top of the hillside. The brush there was lower and sparser, and he could see the entire area. Nobody was there. He moved out from under the bush, and a shot was fired. The bullet whizzed past his left ear. He dropped and crawled with his one good arm and hand, holding the pistol against the ground for leverage. He held the slinged arm close to his chest beneath him and was soon back behind the bush, but another shot went through the bush and just high, cutting through its fine limbs a foot over his head. He scrambled up and ran back in a crouch toward the trail and away from the hillside. Another shot pierced the brush three feet to his right.

The man was a good shot with a rifle, and he had been smart enough to lure him into a position where he had the high ground. When Billy reached the trail, the mule was still standing where he had left him. He crouched behind an elm tree and listened. He could hear nothing above the rush of leaves in the wind and the river. After a few minutes he was certain that the man was not pursuing him, but had been content to run him off with his rifle fire. He had no doubt retreated over the hillside and beyond the edge of the valley.

He wondered about Gruder. It looked like he had been hit by the first shot from the rifle. Billy stood up slowly and surveyed the area he had just traversed. He could detect no unusual movement and could hear nothing out of the ordinary. He reached for the reins and led the mule up the trail in the direction Gruder had gone. After a hundred yards or so, he saw Jimmy's head above the brush. He approached cautiously, and when he was near, he whistled the birdcall Gruder had taught him to use as a signal. After a moment, he heard Gruder's voice saying "Here," weakly. Billy hurried up the trail.

Gruder was on his back, propped up against a cottonwood trunk, his Navy Colt in his hand. The left side of his flannel jacket was a dark red. Billy ran to him and squatted before him.

"Where'd he get you?"

"Left side," Gruder grunted. "I think it broke a rib. But it ain't bleedin' too bad."

Billy pulled open his jacket and saw that Gruder had placed his bandana over his cotton shirt and had been holding it against the wound with his left elbow. When the jacket opened, the bandana fell aside, revealing his bloody shirt. It was soaked through.

"What should I do?" Billy asked.

"There's a little corn whiskey in my left saddlebag in a pewter flask," Gruder said, his voice still weak. "And I put the scraps from that shirt I used on you in there too. You might get them."

He went to the saddlebag and found the remnant of the shirt as well as the flask. He had never known Gruder to drink whiskey. He brought them back to where Gruder lay and helped him open his shirt. His flannel underwear was also soaked with blood, even more than the shirt, and the blood had wicked around in front to cover his abdomen.

"I think it went on through," Gruder said. "See if you can cut open that underwear and wash that wound off."

Billy pulled his Bowie knife and gingerly reached in with it, sliced a gash in the flannel and ripped it open wider. He tore off a large strip from the bandage shirt, opened the flask and soaked it with whiskey, then gently rubbed against Gruder's black skin, over his left ribcage and side, until he could make out the entry wound, a blue spot against the black skin. It had entered low in the area of the lowest rib and on the outside edge where there was no other bone to slow it up or stop it. The exit wound was larger and still seeping blood. After wiping it off with the whiskey-soaked rag, Billy tore off another strip from the shirt and made a pad by folding it several times, placed it against the wound area and asked Gruder to hold it. He twisted the remaining strip for strength, got Gruder to sit up and reached around his back with it, grabbing it with his right hand and pulling it forward over the exit wound and the pad, then brought the ends together in front and tied them across Gruder's belly.

"Looks like you know a few things yourself, Billy," Gruder said, smiling, his voice still with the slightly high edge to it that revealed his weakness.

"I seen you do it a few times," he replied. But it was never over a gunshot wound and never around the body of grown man. It had only been around cuts and nicks on arms and legs and then more for show than necessity, in Billy's mind. Gruder was always doing things that later in life Billy came to believe were not necessary, but were to show him how to do them. He checked the tightness of the binding against the pad and it seemed secure.

He picked up the flask again and handed it to Gruder. Gruder looked concerned. His brow furrowed as it did when he was hesitating to tell Billy some bad news, but after a pause, he took the flask, opened it and took a long swig, wiping his mouth with his sleeve when he was through, then handed the flask back to Billy.

"Now maybe some water," he said.

Billy took the canteen from where it hung over the saddle horn and brought it to him. He drank eagerly. When he was finished, he was a bit out of breath and sat looking down and breathing deep for a full minute. When he looked up again, it was straight into Billy's eyes.

"We gotta keep on going," he said. "Help me up."

He leaned forward and pushed against the ground with his right hand.

"Wait a minute," Billy said, reaching for him, but Gruder was on one knee before he could restrain him.

"Give me your arm," he said.

Billy helped him to his feet. Gruder moved unsteadily, but they made it to Jimmy, and although he had trouble lifting his leg into the stirrup, with Billy's help he managed to get up. He swayed forward in the saddle, gripping the horn with his right hand, his left arm hanging limp at his side.

"You gonna be all right?"

He did not answer at first, thinking. "I can make it."

"I think I winged him," Billy said. "I heard him when I shot."

"We're still a ways from where I figure we need to go," Gruder said. "Let's get moving."

They wound down the sparse trail for another two miles, Gruder leaning forward in the saddle ahead of him and favoring his left side. Billy had reloaded the Remington. He rode with his left hand near it. When they reached a slight bend in the river, at a place where the narrow bottom opened wider into a field, Gruder stopped. Billy pulled up beside him. Fresh blood was visible on Gruder's pants below his jacket.

"You're still bleeding."

Gruder looked down at his pants leg, then ahead into the stiff wind. His jaw was rigid.

"We need help," Billy said.

Gruder turned and looked at him. His face showed pain. "We need to get out of this valley and into some shelter from the wind," he said. He looked to their right at the edge of the valley where the hillside was steep and thick with brush, then downstream to a gravel bar that appeared to be shallow enough to cross in spite of the high water in the river. "There used to be a cabin a couple of miles north," he said.

"Can you make it?"

"Better get down and try to stop this bleeding," Gruder said. He dropped his reins over the saddle horn and weakly raised his right leg to dismount. As he swung down, his left foot slipped from the stirrup and he fell, landing on his back with a deep grunt. Billy quickly dismounted and went to him. Jimmy had shied away a few feet from the fall, but stood his ground.

"You all right?" Billy asked, leaning down to him. Gruder stayed on his back, his eyes wide, breathless, clearly unable to speak. Billy tried to unbutton his coat, but fumbled with the wooden buttons. He finally managed to get the coat open and pulled it away from the left side. His shirt was soaked dark red. "Can you get up?" Billy asked. Gruder struggled to get his breath.

"Think so," he said, and rolled to his right and lifted onto his right elbow. Billy got his arm around his shoulders and tried to help. After a struggle, Gruder got to his knees. He reached his right hand out to stop Billy from urging him up further. He stayed on his knees and reached around to his side, pressing his hand into the blood on his shirt.

"I got another shirt in my roll," Billy said. "I'll get it."

He went to the mule, who shied from his approach. He managed to grab the reins and hold him still, then moved around him to gain access to his roll. He returned to Gruder with an old cotton shirt he was outgrowing.

"You won't have to tear that," Gruder said. "Just wind it around."

Billy rolled the shirt and wrapped it around Gruder, positioning the rolled shirt body in the area of the wounds, and tied it tight by the sleeves in front. He stayed on his knees beside him. Gruder weaved a bit, then he looked toward the river.

"I could use a little more water," he said, then after a pause, "and a little more of that whiskey."

Billy retrieved the whiskey and the canteen. After Gruder had taken a large draft of the water, tipping the canteen up sharply, he uncorked the flask and deliberately took a healthy swig, grimacing as he brought it down from his lips. He was still facing northeast and looking across the river. His eyes narrowed.

"Somebody's comin'," he breathed, then struggled to gain his feet. Billy moved around to his right side and gave him support. When he stood, he weaved before fully gaining balance, then stood looking toward the northeast. The midmorning sun was behind them, and they could both see a horse and rider on the far side of the grassy meadow that opened out in that part of the valley. The rider came steadily on. He was not in a hurry. He was on a bay and showed a light brown above the dark horse in the bright sunlight, just a speck that gradually became larger. Gruder walked unsteadily around to the right side of Jimmy and pulled his Winchester out of its scabbard, dropped it to his side in his right hand and moved a few steps away from the horse. Billy was staring at the approaching rider and did not move right away; then, seeing Gruder with the rifle, he lifted the Remington out of his holster and held it hanging by his side.

As the rider drew nearer, they could make out a floppy leather hat and buckskins, but there was something about his appearance that did not look like an Indian. When he was closer, Billy could see that he was bearded, and the buckskin he wore was not fringed or painted with designs. The horse looked like an Indian horse, blazed on the nose with stocking feet. The man was tall and thin and dark. His long hair blew forward around his face in the wind. When he reached the edge of the river he lifted both hands up to show they were empty and urged the bay into the water, which got up to belly deep in midstream. The man lifted his buckskin boots backward out of the water, holding the stirrups up also. When he had crossed to the other side, he dismounted and led his horse the rest of the way. His look was solemn as he walked up to them.

"Name's Key," he said in a high, raspy voice. "Hobart Key. You have a little trouble?" He was looking at the blood on Gruder's leg and Billy's sling.

"We had a bit, Mr. Key," Gruder said. "This here's Billy McCulloch and I'm called Gruder."

"I figured you might need some help," Key said. "That breed do that?" He gestured toward Billy's sling.

"No. A thunderstorm did that," Gruder said. "But somebody with a rifle did this." He nodded slightly downward toward the bloody pants leg.

"I heard the shots," the man said. "You got some bleedin' goin on there, ain't you? We better get on over to my place. My woman will fix you up. I'm just on the other side of the meadow back there."

"We'd be obliged," Gruder said.

Billy helped him mount up again and the three of them crossed the river and rode side by side across the meadow.

"I was at Bradford's when the Colonel and the other two came through," Key said. "I figured it was either them or you when I heard the shots. You're lucky you're between the two bands. You didn't miss the Honey Eaters by much, though. Which way'd you come down from Bradford's?"

"Down to the Calf Creek crossing," Gruder said. "That's where we hit the thunderstorm."

"It was a dandy, wasn't it?" Key said. "Blew off part of my roof. I was just finishin' fixin' it when I heard that rifle shot. You fire the pistol back at him?"

"That was Billy."

"I hit him," Billy said.

"The hell you did," said Key.

Billy, not used to having his word disputed, just looked at him. At the edge of the meadow they entered a wood of elm and sycamore on a gradual rise that took them from the valley floor to the ridge above. After they reached its crest the ground gradually dropped into a creek bottom. They followed a well-worn winding trail down to a log cabin separated by a dog run which stood next to a shallow creek lined with cypress trees. The bottom was protected from the north wind and the smoke from the cabin chimney rose a good twenty feet before the wind picked it up and diffused it southward. Two cords of wood were piled up alongside the cabin and several hides were stretched out in the sunlight by the south wall of the east part.

Dismounting beside the dog-run middle, Key gestured toward the side with the chimney.

"Me and the missus stay in the side with the fire, but you're welcome to the other. There's a few hides and supplies stored in there, but it's fairly snug. But come on in now and get warmed up and fed. Minnie ought to have a pot of stew on by now."

They dismounted, followed his lead in hitching the horses to an oak log with several limbs sticking up and then followed him onto the porch and halfway down the dog run to the heavy plank door to the right. The door and part of the inner wall were fairly new, its wood contrasting with the dark aged wood of the rest of the structure. Key stepped in and they followed him. The room was dark and smoky. A candle on a small hand-hewn table added to the light given off by the fire, but it took an adjustment to get used to the dim light. When he could make out more, Billy could see shafts of light coming through shutters on the small windows on the outer walls, one to each side. They were shaped more like gun openings than windows, each one about six inches wide by a foot or so tall. Then next to the fire he saw the woman. She was Indian, wearing a blanket around her shoulders, seated hunched over on a low stool by the fire. She had a wooden stick in her hand which could have been called a spoon, but that would have been stretching it. An iron pot hung on a suspended steel rod, its ends wedged into crevices in the stone fireplace. Key said something to her in a language that Billy did not understand.

"She Comanche?" Gruder asked.

The woman looked at him quickly; then her eyes darted away and back to the fire.

"Yes she is," Key said proudly. "She's a Yap-eater. Came across her out near Cross Timbers. She's a big help to a man. Good worker. I've helped her cook some, though. I like a little more spice in my meat."

The woman gave no sign of understanding what was being said. She sat by the fire watching her stewpot. Key said something else to her, and she stood. She was barely five feet tall and round, with sloping shoulders under her blanket.

"Sit down here and let her take a look at you," Key said to Gruder, gesturing at another cross-cut stool that stood by the table. Gruder sat, and the woman came forward and stood close.

"*Abra su camisa*," she said in a quiet voice. Gruder started to unbutton his shirt, but fumbled. The woman gently removed his hands and deftly unbuttoned the shirt. She hesitated, looking, then untied the cotton bandage Billy had tied around him. She removed it slowly, reaching out with her arms to keep it from sliding down his back. The slashed, dirty underwear, the top half of his longhandles, was a faded rose against the dark wine of his blood. She pulled the remnants aside and tore them off, leaving the crude bandages, drooping now with the weight of his blood.

"*Vino*," she said to Key, without looking up.

"She says to get him some wine," Key said, watching from behind Gruder, not looking at Billy, but addressing him by his tone of voice. "I got some good mustang red here. I'll get him a glass."

Gruder's head was tilting forward. The woman went for a gourd bowl, filled it with water from a barrel in the corner and returned with rags. She bathed Gruder's midsection with care, then went into the dimness again and returned with a handful of large, rough leaves that she put into the water and, after soaking them for a minute, raised them out one by one and put them over the wounds—only two, one over each. She stood and gestured toward the side of the room where a cot stood. Gruder rose up heavily from the chair, the bone flagon of red wine now in his hand, and went to the cot. The leaves clung to him. Bracing his hand on the edge, he sank slowly into the hide. He drank the wine in one long draw and leaned back, turning, until his head settled on a rolled blue blanket, his feet hanging a good foot over the edge of the cot. He let out a sigh.

She put one hand around to the rear wound and her other on the entry wound and pressed against the leaves, which thickened with his blood. After a while, she removed her hands and grasped him by his left arm and pulled, gesturing with her other hand for him to turn on his side. After he had moved and turned, she pressed gently against the leaves again; then covered him with a blanket.

Gruder's head lay on a shuck-filled pillow, its ticking brown with stains. He was overdue lying down, and his eyes were quick to close. Billy sat slumped over on a stool by the table, looking at him. Key's woman touched the sling where Gruder had knotted it in front and asked him something in Comanche.

"She asks why you got that thing on," Key said from beside the fireplace.

"I threw my shoulder out," Billy replied, looking down at the soiled sling.

Key said something to the woman. She put her hand on Billy's injured shoulder and said to him, in Spanish, "I will look at it if you will let me."

He nodded, and she untied the sling and gently lifted it away. She unbuttoned his shirt and undershirt and pulled them over and away from the shoulder, then leaned over in the dim light to look, feeling it gently with both hands. She said something he did not understand, then went to the corner where the water barrel stood and, squatting, fumbled among some things in the dark of the corner and returned carrying something in one hand. She reached with the hand to his shoulder and rubbed in a circular movement. He immediately felt heat on his skin and moved away instinctively.

"It is good," she said in Spanish. "It will take out the pain."

She continued to rub in the ointment, her hands small and strong over his shoulder and upper arm. When the skin seemed to dry out from the heat, she stopped rubbing and took his wrist in her small right hand. She moved it in an arc, first away from his chest and then back. He winced at first, and she looked into his eyes knowingly, then kept up the motion until the hitch in his shoulder smoothed out. She replaced his undershirt and shirt and tied the sling back in place.

"Did the Negro tie this on?" she asked. Her Spanish had an accent Billy had heard before.

He nodded. She turned and looked at Gruder, who slept quietly on his side on the rawhide cot, then stood and went to the pot hanging over the edge of the fire. She filled a wooden bowl with stew and set it on the table and handed Billy a wooden spoon. She then returned to her place by the fire and sat in the same attitude she was in when they first entered. Billy wasted no time in spooning up a portion of the stew, which he had to cool before putting it into his mouth. It was probably venison with some kind of chiles and one or more unidentifiable vegetables. It was rich and filling. He finished the bowl and could have eaten more, but did not ask.

Key had lit his pipe and was standing by the fire.

"You run across that half-breed," he said. It was almost a question.

"Don't know. It was somebody who could handle a rifle."

"Bushwhacked your man there, huh?" His mouth around the pipe stem was stern.

"Shot him off his horse. I think I hit him, though."

"With what?" He took the pipe out.

Billy nodded down at the Remington.

"What you got there?" Key walked over to the table, peering down at the walnut handle of the pistol. "I'll be damned. You shot that with your left hand?"

"Yes, sir."

"I'll be damned."

They followed the same trail back to Bradford's and were descending through the Puerto de Baluartes by mid-morning. Hays was in the lead with Wonsley and the girl following, doubled up, and John Baker in the rear. Wonsley felt warm under the slicker and his jacket in spite of the stiff north wind. The girl's hold on him was strong, almost desperate. Unable to shift positions in the saddle, Wonsley's back hurt. After strenuous work, a long time in the saddle often lets the body calm down enough to feel again, and he was painfully aware of the rigors he had put it through the night before. The girl rested her head on the back of his right shoulder. She had not moved for so long he assumed she was asleep. He did not want to wake her up and risk her going wild on him again, so he endured the pain and stiffness that the rigid position accentuated and concentrated on the trail ahead. It seemed much longer than when they had come this way before, and that seemed like a week ago, not just a day.

Bradford and a couple of other men were standing in the dirt trail by his lean-to waiting for them when they made the last turn around a copse of elms, even though they had seen no one observe their approach. Bradford went immediately to Wonsley's mount and reached up for the girl, who raised her head as if signaled, even though he had said nothing.

"My wife'll be glad to take you in, girl," he said in his gruff voice. "Let me help you down."

Hays, turning in his saddle, gave the girl a look and she let go of Wonsley and reached for Adam Bradford's outstretched arms and let him take her down off the horse, his strong hands under her armpits. She weaved a bit when she hit her feet, but Bradford steadied her. She wrapped the Indian blanket around her in front and looked down at the ground in front of the men, who stared at her without any pretense of restraint. Bradford glanced at the two men, then up at Hays.

"If you'll allow it, I'll take her to my place and let Mrs. Bradford care for her. Y'all can come along if you want."

These men were not among the ones who had been there the day before, but they acted as if they knew of Hays's mission and about the girl. One of them, a long-haired, bearded man with a rough red nose and a potbelly pushing between his suspenders, was looking at her with evident disgust. Hays did not appear to hear Bradford, but was concentrating on the potbelly's expression.

"What are you looking at?" he said in a voice Wonsley had not heard before. He said it quick, with an emphasis that left no doubt about his feelings, not in the quiet way Wonsley had come to know. The man looked up at Hays with wide eyes and began to back away. Hays nudged his horse toward him and the man quickened his retreat. "Get out of here right now," Hays commanded him sharply.

The other man, a pale, mild-looking man of medium size, was frozen in place, looking from Hays to the bearded man. John and Wonsley sat their mounts and watched as Hays herded him backwards toward the nearest oak tree, which stopped his retreat.

"I didn't say nothin'," the man said. "Not a goddamn thing."

Hays looked at him for a minute, then his expression softened and he turned the buckskin away from him and turned back to Bradford.

"She'll be needing some care," he said. "I appreciate it."

After they unsaddled and watered the horses in the river, John and Wonsley walked the mile to the Bradford house to check on the girl. Hays said that he had something to do and stayed behind at Bradford's store. Bradford's house was of split logs with a dog run and a separate kitchen. A blonde girl of about twelve came out to meet them as they approached. She was barefoot and wore a homemade sack dress. She told them her mother had asked her to wait for them, and the girl was asleep, but they could look at her if they wanted to.

"She's in the big bed," she said, pointing to the right side of the house. They followed her onto the porch and into a low doorway. The room had a couple of windows with glass panes, a rarity in the area. The girl was asleep on a bed made of rough pine. The pine posts had been finished with oil and although obviously homemade, the person who made it had taken the time to try to make it look shiny. The girl was covered with a brown and red Indian blanket. Her red hair was damp and spread out on the white pillowcase. A small, dark-haired woman stood at a table in front of the fireplace.

The two men stood quietly looking at the sleeping girl until the woman said, "You are with Cap'n Hays and are responsible for rescuing this young woman, I guess."

Both men looked her way, but took their time in speaking. Finally, John Baker said, "Yes ma'am. I guess that's right."

"And where is the Captain?"

"He's back at the store," John replied. "Is she all right?"

The woman looked at the sleeping girl.

"She's alive," she said, and looked back at them. "Thanks to you."

"We'd better be getting back, then."

"Don't you want some breakfast?" she asked. "I got some deer sausage and eggs, and it won't take long to make some corn bread."

They had forgotten about food for a long time and after polite protestations followed Mrs. Bradford out on the porch to the rear of the house, where they were shown to the well and a washstand beside it where they could clean up. She busied herself in the kitchen. Before the eggs were ready, the thin, dark man they had seen at Bradford's the day before came up from the south on horseback. He saw John and Wonsley before he entered the clearing—before they saw or heard him. He came to where they were sitting on a log bench near the well, dismounted and took off his floppy hat.

"Met you boys yesterday. Name's Key," he said. "Got your nigger and boy down at my place. They're a little worn, but should be okay. The nigger was shot, though, but just looks like a flesh wound. My woman's takin' care of 'em."

John stood up. There was something about this man he did not like. Perhaps it was his knowing attitude. As if he had superior knowledge, better than anyone else's.

"Much obliged, Mr. Key. We appreciate it. They're family."

"I just come to tell you. I'm going on up to Bradford's store. Is the Colonel up there?"

"He was a little while ago," Wonsley said, curtly. He didn't like the man either.

"I'll tell him. Look's like y'all are waitin' for some breakfast there," he said, looking toward the kitchen. "I'll tell the Colonel. Got to get some supplies anyhow. I'll come back by in an hour or so if y'all want directions to my place."

They thanked him and watched him ride away.

ELEVEN

T HE STONE BUILDING IN LOCKHART THAT SERVED AS THE courthouse was two stories with a winding wooden staircase in the middle of the first floor hallway. The staircase led to the courtroom and the judge's and clerks' offices on the second floor. Ashley Maitland had difficulty keeping up with Laura McCulloch's quick pace up the stairway. When he reached the top, he was slightly winded. Laura, still wearing black, paused at the top step for him to catch up. Her lips were pursed and her face pale. She looked down at his feet as he gained the top step.

The courtroom was to the left, and he gestured with his outstretched hand for her to precede him. She nodded without looking up and walked to the courtroom door at a slower pace. Inside, a few people sat scattered among the mahogany pews. A small group of lawyers stood around a large potbellied stove to the left of the bench. Ashley showed Laura to a seat in the front row, pushed aside the swinging gate, and went inside the railing. He placed his leather folding case on one of the two counsel tables. As he proceeded to the stove corner, several of the lawyers turned toward him.

After handshakes and greetings, he turned to face the back of the courtroom and saw Lily Poe sitting in the last row by the far window. She was no longer wearing black, and her hair hung loosely around her shoulders. He did not think Laura had seen her. Laura sat impassively staring forward from her seat in the front row, lost in thought. Lily was looking his way when he turned around, with a trace of a smile upon her lips. He felt the urge to go and talk to her, but he held off. When he turned back around, one of the lawyers, Hadley Wilson, was facing him, smiling.

"I haven't had the chance to tell you that I represent Mrs. Poe, Ashley," he said, leaning back slightly with four fingers of each of his hands pushed into his vest pockets framing his large belly. "I am sure there is nothing today that we will question, but Mrs. Poe felt she should have representation. I'll be happy to work with you on this estate."

Ashley's immediate thought was of Wes McCulloch's extreme dislike of Wilson. He had confided many times that he did not trust him and considered him unreliable. Ashley was surprised to learn he represented Lily, but his face was a blank.

"Very well, Hadley. There shouldn't be much difficulty, except for creditors. Mrs. McCulloch will offer the will for probate today."

"I was gratified to read your application," Wilson said, in his attempt at a courtroom voice, his high pitch lacking the punch intended. "Are both witnesses here?"

Ashley looked around at the benches outside the rail.

"Friedman is supposed to be here," he said. "He said he might be a bit late. Doing inventory today."

"That's no problem, Ashley. No problem at all. I'll waive any conflict, and you can testify. You are the other attesting witness."

"Hopefully that won't be necessary," Ashley said.

He walked to the clerk's table and picked the brown cardboard file out of a stack, untied the twine that bound it, and pulled the folded papers from within. He checked the citation, which indicated that the clerk had signed the return stating it had been posted at the courthouse door for the requisite period of time. He replaced it along with the will and the handwritten application.

He could feel Lily's eyes on the back of his neck and was determined not to look at her. The previous evening, over dinner at her house, she had given him no clue that she would be in court that morning. The courtroom was still a bit chilly, and he returned to the warmth around the stove.

The clock on the back wall indicated that it was a few minutes past nine when Judge Daughtry entered from the door which led to the jury room and eventually to his office. He wore the same blue serge suit he always wore in cold weather, with brown areas on the elbows of his coat and the seat of his pants. His stubby legs quickly carried him through the side gate of the railing and up to the bench, where he sat down with a dull thud. He looked blearily over the pews outside the railing and then slowly turned his head toward the lawyers standing by the stove. They now faced the bench, some with their hands in their pockets, some with bemused looks.

"Well, it looks like we have a gentleman traveler here today," he said, his voice squeaking out from his tobacco-stained gray beard. "What brings you to town, Lawyer Maitland, another hog case?"

It was the cue they had been waiting for. Several burst out with laughter that seemed forced, including Wilson. Ashley stood quietly, his hands hooked under his coat lapels into the armholes of his vest. He waited until the laughter died down, then spoke in his deep voice. Although it could be heard from the back of the room, he appeared to put no more effort into speaking than he would a whisper.

"A little matter of probate brings me here today, Your Honor. It is indeed a pleasure to be among these esteemed gentlemen of the bar once again." Then a pause. "And to appear in this honorable court."

The judge fumbled in his coat pocket for his bifocals, placed them on the tip of his nose and peered down at the thick, leather-bound docket book before him. When he looked up, his bushy eyebrows were raised.

"I see. It is an honor to have you again, counselor. You should make an effort to grace us with your learned presence more often. And you, Mr. Wilson? I don't see a case on the docket with your name on it."

Wilson strode to the front of the bench.

"I appear here on behalf of Mrs. Poe, Judge, an interested party in the estate Mr. Maitland refers to."

The judge's eyebrows went up again.

"Mrs. Poe?" he asked, his voice going up half an octave. He searched the sparse crowd outside the rail over the rims of his glasses and squinted at the woman seated in the back row. When his eyes focused, a warm smile replaced his grimace. "Mrs. Poe," he said fondly, then, after a pause, turned to see the remaining lawyers by the stove staring at him. He quickly straightened up in his high-backed chair, his little eyes darting around the pews until they came to rest on Laura, who was turning to look at Lily Poe. All other eyes also turned to Laura, who quickly turned her head back to the front, then looked down at her clasped hands in her lap.

The silence was palpable. Then the rear door was slammed against the wall on its hinges. The sound caused several of the lawyers to jump.

Through it, stumbling slightly as he entered, came Ish Friedman, the rumpled collar of his coat upturned and one white cuff sticking out farther than the other, as if he had just pulled the coat on as he ran up the stairs. His shock of graying dark hair had scattered dandruff over the narrow shoulders of the coat and it sparkled like snow against the dull black of the heavy cloth. Making his way up the center aisle with his characteristic uneven, hurried shuffle, he stopped short of the gate in the railing and looked at the judge through his thick glasses.

After a brief moment, in which Friedman stared at the judge and then the lawyers, he turned quickly and sat in the front pew on the opposite side of the aisle from Laura. Ash turned back to the judge, who cleared his throat.

"I will call the docket," the judge said.

The remaining lawyers by the stove moved to the chairs inside the rail. Some used the spittoons by the counsel tables as they passed. Ash took a seat at the counsel table to the right. Wilson raised his bulk into the jury box to the left and took a seat in the first row. The judge asked for announcements, and lawyers stood and announced their appearances in the cases called. Several of them were not on the docket but were in court in the hope that they would be appointed to criminal cases that were called.

One, a tall, graying man wearing a brown suit, was in court at every session looking for appointments. He made his living, such as it was, off appointed cases. He had no real office, but shadowed the clerk's office down the hall and the benches under the pecan trees on the courthouse lawn, looking for something to fall his way. Matt Barton was his name. He could be counted on to plead his assigned charges guilty after only brief consultation. Another, Dean Turner, was a title lawyer, the best in the county. He had the reputation of being able to clear the worst title problem, if the money was right. He only appeared in court for probate matters and as second chair in the rare land title suit that was tried.

There were ten other cases on the docket, including a couple in which lawyer Barton was appointed to represent the absent defendants. They would be brought to court from the jail later in the morning, and Barton would confer with Billy Bandy, the prosecutor, and briefly with his clients before entering a plea of guilty for them. On the rare occasion that an indigent defendant did not agree to enter a plea, a jury would be summoned at the next session, usually a month later, and the defendant would be tried promptly and efficiently, with the jury assessing punishment instead of the judge. The sentence was almost always harsher than the judge would have meted out.

There were two other probate cases, both belonging to Dean Turner, and after calling the docket, the judge heard those first, followed by the rest of the cases: two criminal pleas in which the defendants had employed counsel and two suits for debt in which the defendants did not appear and default judgments were entered. He then called the McCulloch estate.

Ashley stood and gestured for Laura to come forward. Before Hadley Wilson could get out of his seat, Lily Poe had already reached the rail and slid beside Laura as she entered through the gate. The judge's face was impassive when they approached the bench together with their lawyers. The women stood side by side in the middle of the two men, both looking forward, not acknowledging each other's presence. Ashley, standing to the right, next to his client, thought that Wes McCulloch would have loved this scene—the two women in his life standing silently next to each other in the courtroom, one still in widow's weeds and the other in a royal blue dress, newer and more expensive than any other in the county.

Before Ash could speak, the judge said, "I was very sorry to hear about Wes, Mrs. McCulloch. He was a good man." He then looked around the almost empty courtroom. Only the bailiff, the clerk, and Matt Barton, who was waiting for his new clients to be brought up from the jail, remained, other than Ish Friedman and the parties and lawyers before the bench. He then glanced at Lily before saying, "You may proceed, Mr. Maitland."

Ashley called Ish as a witness. He came inside the railing with a jerky step, then hesitated, not knowing where to go. Ashley motioned for him to stand between himself and Laura, and Ish moved to a point a few steps back from Laura's flank, hesitating to come any closer.

"Raise your hand to be sworn," the judge said. He raised his right hand. "Do you solemnly swear to tell the truth, the whole truth, and nothing but the truth, so help you God almighty?"

"Surely," he replied.

"You may proceed, counselor."

"Did you know Wesley McCulloch?" Ashley asked sharply.

"I did indeed. Knew him for thirty years."

The judge picked up the will from the bench and handed it to Ash.

Ash displayed it to Friedman. "Do you recognize this document?"

Ish reached for it, grasped it at the bottom of the first page and peered through his thick spectacles at the sprawling cursive writing. A smile came over his face. Ashley had not shown him the will before that morning, and he had not seen it since the cold night that Wes McCulloch had written it and asked him and Ash to sign it.

"I surely do," he said. "That's Wesley McCulloch's will."

Ashley turned to the third and last page.

"Do you recognize his signature thereon?"

"Yes, that's his hand. He wrote the whole thing out in my saloon."

The judge's eyes twinkled.

"And did you and I witness it?"

"We did."

"Was he of sound mind when he signed it?"

Ish looked impishly at the judge. "He was a little drunk, Your Honor, but you know Wes. He never lost his senses from whiskey."

Laura turned and gave him a cold look.

"Beg your pardon, Laura, but it's true. He could hold his whiskey like nobody I ever saw. He was a brilliant man. Fun loving, but brilliant. He knew what he was doing."

"But he was drunk?" the judge asked.

"Well, Your Honor. I'm not sure I ever saw Wes McCulloch drunk, but you know as well as I do that he could outdrink just about anybody in this country, and he had been out hunting with some of the boys that day."

The judge nodded. "You may proceed, counselor."

"Did he ever revoke it, so far as you know and believe?" Ashley asked.

"Not that I know of, Ash," he replied.

The judge turned to Wilson, who had been standing with his hands clasped in front of his large girth with a smile on his face.

"Do you have anything, Mr. Wilson?" the judge asked, glancing at Lily Poe.

"Your Honor, Mrs. Poe joins in the application and says the will ought to be probated."

"Her joinder is not necessary, Mr. Wilson," the judge said. "The document is admitted to probate as the Last Will and Testament of John

Wesley McCulloch, deceased, and Laura McCulloch, his widow, is appointed independent administratrix. Bond is waived and the court will dispense with the appointment of appraisers. Does counsel anticipate any problem with having an inventory to me within ninety days?"

"No, Your Honor," Ashley replied.

"Then ninety days it is. Are there any other matters to be decided?"

He swiftly looked from Ashley to Wilson.

"No, Your Honor," Ashley said.

"No, Your Honor," Wilson quickly replied.

"I want to see counsel in chambers," the judge said. "This court is in recess."

Lily looked away from the judge for the first time and stared directly at Wilson for a long moment. Her lips were pursed. She turned quickly and walked through the railing gate and down the aisle out of the courtroom while Wilson stood looking after her.

The judge watched her leave, then went around the edge of the bench and descended to the floor. Ash asked Laura to wait for him and followed the judge through the jury room to the small office that served as his chambers. Wilson followed. The office was warm from the heat of the jury room stove that stood near the connecting door, and the judge took his worn coat off before taking a seat behind his desk. He reached into a bottom drawer, pulled out a whiskey bottle and a shot glass and placed them on the desk. He poured a full shot and downed it, wheezing and wiping his mouth against his shirt cuff. Ashley and Hadley Wilson remained standing.

"Hadley, you don't have a lick of sense," the judge said tartly. "Why did you bring that woman into my courtroom?"

"Why, Judge," Hadley began.

"Don't 'why Judge' me, Hadley. You had no call to do it and it served no purpose other than to make those two women uncomfortable. You should have known better."

"I was just representing my client's interests," Wilson said weakly.

"Bullshit!" the judge shouted. "Did she have any testimony to offer?"

"Well, she could have, Your Honor. In case Mr. Maitland here asked the court to deny probate."

"Deny probate!" the judge said. The doors leading through the jury room to the courtroom were still open and the judge's voice was loud enough to be heard outside the small office. "Did you consult with counsel about that before this morning?"

Wilson looked briefly at Ash.

"No, Your Honor. I didn't see the need."

"You didn't see the need," he said, his voice now lowered in volume and pitch. "A man of honor would see the need. And a man of honor would have avoided such a useless confrontation. All you had to do is ask Ash what he intended to do. You could have done that before the case was called. Besides, you didn't need to have your client here anyway. Was she a witness to the will?"

"No, Your Honor, but she knew the decedent's handwriting well."

"I am sure she did, but when there are witnesses' signatures on the document, it cannot be probated as a holographic will. Surely you knew that, counselor." His voice dripped with contempt.

Wilson said nothing more, but stood still before the desk with an air of stoicism, somewhat red-faced.

"Get out of here," the judge said. "Before you appear again in this case, you are to confer with counsel and me. And you are not to bring that woman into the courtroom again without my permission. Do you understand?"

"Yes, Your Honor," Wilson said.

"Very well. Good day, gentlemen."

Wilson left quickly through the door to the hallway. Ashley turned to walk back to the courtroom, but the judge said, "Ash," and he turned back.

"You know I am very fond of Lily, and I know you are also, but I could not let that son of a bitch get by without an ass chewing. He knew damn well what he was doing. I'm sure Lily didn't appreciate it either."

"I know, John," Ash replied. "I think you did the right thing."

The judge regained his bemused expression.

"I was not seeking your approval, counselor. Just letting you know."

"I understand, Your Honor," Ashley said.

"You tell Laura I chewed him out, will you?"

"I sure will, John. Thanks."

The judge waved backhanded, and Ash went back in the courtroom to see his client.

TWELVE

B ILLY WOKE WITH A START. HE HAD DOZED OFF LEANING AGAINST
the south wall of Hobart Key's cabin. The sun was high in the sky to
the south, warming the wood. Forgetting about his shoulder, he leaned
to his right to push up. The pain made him wince and immediately lean
back. He clasped his right wrist with his left hand until the pain subsided,
then struggled to his feet and stepped inside the dog run to the door on
the right, pushed it opened and peered into the dim room where he had
left Gruder. Two narrow shafts of light from the gun slits on the south
side of the cabin, delineated by the smoke from the fireplace, framed the
rough table in the middle of the room. He leaned in and looked around
the door and saw the Indian woman seated on the floor facing the bed
where Gruder still lay sleeping. She was motionless, her broad back covered by a dark blanket.

He stepped inside and waited until his eyes adjusted to the dim light.
Gruder lay on his back, covered by a red blanket up to his chin, his eyes
closed. Billy had the impression that he was dead. He looked like dead
people look when they lay in their coffins in the parlor, like his daddy
looked in the candlelight that rainy night at home, which now seemed so
long ago. He thought that Gruder had died while he had been asleep on
the porch and that somehow it was his fault for not being awake and by
his side. He walked slowly to the bed, forgetting about the woman who
sat cross-legged on the floor by the end of the bed. When he was standing
near Gruder's head he could see that his face was moving as he breathed,
and he could make out the movement of his breathing beneath the red

blanket that covered his chest.

He turned slightly, and the woman's dark eyes met his. She was holding an eagle feather in front of her, in two hands. Her face was solemn and calm. It was as if he was a mere part of the room, part of the world that existed outside of her, not affecting her, not requiring recognition. He felt a chill and backed away. She did not turn to look at him as he left the room and pulled the door closed behind him.

There was no sign of Key. Billy walked to the rear of the house and saw that the gray mule and Jimmy were grazing in a natural close. He found their saddles and bags lying against an outbuilding and decided he would saddle up and ride to find Hays and his uncles, but when he tried to lift the saddle with his left arm, he found that he was too weak to lift it over the mule's back. After a couple of tries, he dragged it back against the wall of the shed. Gray stood looking at him calmly, as if waiting for him.

"Not right now, old fellow," he said. "I'm going to rest a bit more."

When John and Wonsley returned to the store, they found Hays sitting around the fire outside the lean-to with several other men, including the two who had been there when they arrived earlier that morning. The bearded man that Hays had backed up was seated on a log in the circle with the others. A couple of the men looked up as they approached, and Hays stood to meet them, then gestured to them to step aside with him. When they were far enough from the others, he stopped and turned to them.

"They're saying there are two or three different bunches around here," he said. "The ones at Pegleg and one or two others up the valley between here and there. Our men might be with either bunch or they might have taken off. That fellow over there, name of Key, trades with them."

John and Wonsley looked at the men around the fire again. Key, in his dirty buckskins, was sitting among them, drawing in the dirt in front of his feet with a stick.

"We saw him," John said. "He said he was coming up here."

"He said he can find out about Morgan from the bunch down at Pegleg, but he wants to go alone."

Wonsley shifted his weight from one foot to another.

"Are we gonna go after them?"

Hays cleared his throat.

"I am going after them," he said, looking at the ground before him.

"You gentlemen are welcome to come along if you wish."

The three men stood in silence for a moment, Hays still looking down. Finally, Wonsley spoke.

"You want me to follow Key, Cap'n?"

A trace of a smile crossed Hays's lips.

"That's what I would like for you to do. Just make sure he doesn't see you. We'll follow him to his cabin. He says he has Gruder and Billy there and that Gruder's been shot."

"Yeah, he told us," John said.

They saddled up and followed Key to a point where they forded the river just downstream from Bradford's store, then down a trail on the north side of the river. It took them about an hour to reach the creek valley where his double cabin lay. As they crossed the creek, they could see that someone was leaning against the side of the house in the late morning sun. Billy saw them as they crossed the creek. He stood and raised his left arm. They came up and he took them in to see Gruder, who was awake, but not talkative. They sat around in the smoky room, quietly exchanging stories of what had happened since their paths had split. Billy told them about Gruder getting shot and the fight in the brush with the man with the rifle. Wonsley told Billy and Gruder about rescuing the girl. The Indian woman sat on her stool on the other side of the small room. Key stood aside, in the corner by the fireplace, barely visible in the dim light, listening. After a while, he came over near the cot. They turned to look at him.

"I best be gettin' on over to Pegleg. It would sure help if ya'll had something to trade. I gotta have something to give them."

John looked at Hays as he spoke.

"I have a horsehair lariat I can let you have," he said.

Key rubbed his bearded chin.

"That's a little of a problem there," he said. "That's more like what they would want to trade, not trade for."

John, still looking at Hays, showed the trace of a smile. "How about a tin pot?" he asked.

"Now you got it. That'll do good."

John turned and followed Key through the doorway. Wonsley raised himself from the crouch he was in.

"I'll go see him off," he said, exchanging a look with Hays.

"Don't forget to check my saddlebag," Hays said, his eyes darting over to the Indian woman. She sat on her stool looking down, apparently unaware of what they were saying. Then Hays said, in Spanish, "You will find that your vision will improve." The woman did not make any perceptible movement. Wonsley nodded as he left the room.

"I don't think she understands English," Billy whispered.

Hays raised one finger to his lips. He turned to the woman and said something Billy did not understand. The woman immediately looked up at Hays and replied to him.

"She knows who I am," Hays said, still staring at her. Then he said something else to her and she slowly stood and walked to the door. She paused as she opened it, then went out and closed it behind her without looking back.

After a moment, Hays turned back to Billy. "She understands English," he said, then turned to Gruder. "You able to ride?"

Gruder was still lying on his back with his head propped up.

"I can sure ride if I can get on," he said, grinning.

"Then let's get out of here," Hays said.

Key's bay was already saddled. He was down the creek bank toward the river by the time Wonsley joined John at their mounts. He approached the buckskin cautiously, patting his neck down to the saddle, then retrieved the spyglass in its leather case from the saddlebag. He moved to the paint, put the encased spyglass in the top of his rifle holster, and swung up. John came up to him.

"He's going to Pegleg. You can probably cut across that hill." He pointed across the neck of Wonsley's paint.

"You think he's to be believed, brother?" Wonsley asked.

John smiled.

"Not hardly," he said. "Leave us a clear trail."

"I will."

He turned downstream and was soon out of sight in the thick brush. When John returned to the dog run, the Indian woman was seated in the back in the wind, her blanket over her head. Inside, Hays and Billy were standing by the cot where Gruder was sitting up, barebacked, trying to pull a shirt on.

"What are you doing?" John asked.

"Gettin' up. Gettin' ready to go," Gruder said, his deep voice softer than usual.

"We're not leaving him here," Hays said.

John walked over to him and examined the cloth that was wrapped around his midsection. Billy had wrapped it around the wounds after taking the leaves off, which were stuck fast and required a good pull. He checked the wounds and they did not start bleeding again, so he tore another shirt from his bag and retrieved a fresh one from Gruder's bag for Gruder to wear.

John held the cotton shirt so that Gruder could slip his arms in and allowed it to fall over his head. Gruder then slowly pushed up from the cot, shaking. Billy reached to help him, but Gruder was up before he could touch him. He stood bent over at the waist, and for the first time Billy thought he looked like an old man. His balding head was down, profiling his prominent features in the dim light. He weaved slightly, and Billy grasped his left arm. Gruder quickly pulled away from him.

"I don't need no help, Billy," he said gruffly, with a touch of the old sarcasm in his voice. "Where's my hat?"

Billy retrieved it from the pile of saddlebags and handed it to him. He put it on with the front brim low over his face and peered out from under it at Hays.

"All right, Cap'n. I'm ready."

They moved out the door of the cabin with Hays in the lead and Gruder following behind John and Billy. Hays walked over to the Indian woman, who still sat against the back corner of the near cabin in the wind. He stood by her and said something to her that was soft but terse. She unwrapped the blanket from around her head enough to look up at Hays and spoke quietly to him, her dark eyes staring into his. She paused, and he replied to her, then turned away to the men who were waiting for him back up the dog run. He stepped quickly past them toward the horses in front of the house, and they followed him. He saw to his saddle cinch and the others did the same.

"She says he knows Morgan. Says he trades with him and he is going to warn him if we let him."

"She told you that?" John asked.

"She did. She doesn't appear to care much for Key. She called him a taker, or at least that's as close as I can come to the Comanche word she used."

"Wonsley will leave us a trail," John said.

John and Billy helped Gruder into his saddle against his protests, and they rode down the creek bank after Key and Wonsley.

Wonsley had no difficulty following Key's trail until it entered the river just downstream from the mouth of the creek. Although the river was up from the thunderstorm of the night before, the San Saba is shallow along most of its upper stretches, and Wonsley could see no tracks on the opposite side, meaning that Key had gone up or downstream. It also meant that Key thought or assumed that he was being followed and would therefore be on the lookout for his pursuer coming up or going down the middle of the river. It would be safer to cross over and look up or downstream in the trees along the riverbank. Wonsley urged the paint across and up the opposite bank, then upstream, leaning out and drawing a slash on an elm trunk with his Bowie knife before he turned, leaving a pointer in that direction. It was his guess that Key was going to the camp of the Honey Eaters, which he understood to be a few miles upstream, near where he had seen the woman the day before.

He kept a slow pace, keeping an eye ahead and paying particular attention to the edge of the river on his right and the edge of the tree line to his left. The woods at this point on the river were only about a hundred yards wide on either side. A profusion of light brown leaves blew in the north wind. To his left he could see the broad pasture they had crossed that morning. It seemed like it had been days ago. He moved slowly through the underbrush. After a few hundred yards, he saw a color, a small swatch that did not fit in with the rest of the foliage. He dismounted and dropped his reins and the paint froze in place. A few feet farther along on foot, creeping stooped below the tops of the underbrush, brought him to a point where he could make out the haunches of Key's bay, red-brown against the tan and green of the woods. He squatted and waited, watching the trees, until he noticed movement some ten feet up the trunk of a cypress growing at the water's edge. Key's buckskin-clad arm moved around the trunk from the other side until his hand clasped a branch. His shoulder came into view, then his bare head. He appeared to shift his weight, but otherwise became still again, perched in the tree at a point that gave him a clear view of the river downstream.

Wonsley sat down cross-legged under the branches of a small cottonwood and waited. Key remained motionless, the back of his head and his shoulder, arm and hand visible around the cypress trunk. After about fifteen minutes his shoulder moved up and his body came around from behind the tree trunk, his foot found a hold on a branch stub, and he crawled down the back of the tree and was on his bay quickly. Wonsley waited for him to gain a good lead again, then went back and grabbed the paint's reins. He proceeded on foot, leading the horse up to the point where the bay had been, then followed the tracks through the brush, while cautiously looking ahead in case Key pulled up again.

After about a half mile the woods along the river played out, and Wonsley hesitated at the edge of an open field that ran all the way from the low river bank to the hills to the southeast, a mile or so away. He could not safely traverse the field. He dismounted and climbed an old oak with the spyglass in hand. Perched on a branch, he surveyed the field. It was clear of trees across its entire width and he could see all the way to the foot of the hills and up and down them for a considerable distance. Upstream, the river came out of a copse of elms where the valley was narrower. There, at the south edge of the tree line, he saw lodge poles sticking up in three different clusters. More of them could have been hidden by the clump of trees. To the south and east of the tipis there was open ground, but the elms provided a small screen to anyone approaching from the opposite direction—across the river—and there appeared to be high ground there. He climbed down, mounted up, and retraced his trail a dozen yards downstream to a place where the bank was only a foot above a gravel bar. He nudged the paint into the water and across, up a slight incline and onto a piece of high ground that sloped gradually away to the north. He rode on the downslope out of sight of the lodges until he calculated that he had gone upstream far enough to be even with them, then dismounted and crawled to the top of the ridge with the spyglass.

There were two Comanche women and several small girls on the opposite side of the river down a two-hundred-foot slope from him. They squatted near each other on the shallow side of a gravel bar washing clothes. Cotton cloth and wooden bowls were strewn along the water's edge. The children were playing unwatched behind their mothers. Lying in the tall grass at the top of the ridge, he could see the light brown of the lodges through the trees. He looked at the angle of the sun. It was far to his right, and the lip of the spyglass would shield the lens and prevent any glare. He pulled it out and looked through the trees.

Moving it along the treetops then down, he brought the glass into focus on gold and brown leaves that still clung gracefully to the branches of
the elms, then moved down until the edge of one of the tipis sprang into
view. There were six of them, neatly lined up, three to a side. Key's bay
was hitched to a low branch near the second tipi on the left. There were
no people visible and no other horses. He put the glass down and looked
at the women at the water's edge. They were talking to each other as they
beat the clothes against stones in the shallow water. They were oblivious
to his presence, but there was no cover between him and their side of the
river and no way he could get any closer without being detected.

The sun was low enough to cast the shadow of the ridge on the water below. He could make out the shadow of his bare head and quickly
lowered it to blend in with the shadows of the grass. The women were
looking down and facing straight across the river, away from the shadows farther downstream. He moved back from the peak of the ridge and
quietly moved downstream. The paint stood still, grazing with the reins
falling into the high grass. He led him along the far side of the ridge.
When he was at the point he had intended, he crawled up to the peak of
the ridge again. Here, the grass was taller and grew right up to the edge of
a drop-off. The women were farther away, and he was out of their direct
line of sight. The three little girls were playing some sort of ball game.
He watched them from the tall grass. The sun was low enough for him
to be in shade below the crest of the higher part of the ridge to the west.
The spyglass would not make a reflection, and the little girls were looking
down at their game.

He pulled the glass up slowly and held it gently within cover of the
grass. He focused on an area in the trees and moved around until he saw
the brown of the nearest tipi. The rump of the bay was visible on the far
side of a tree. He passed over and went back to a movement: three men,
one wearing Key's dirty buckskins and the other two in long, dark coats,
were walking away from the tipis. One wore a bandana around his head.
The other was bareheaded, his long hair blowing in the wind. They took
long strides, Key following behind them, hurrying to keep up. In a few
seconds they were around the far tipi and out of sight.

They moved in a southwest direction, probably toward the horses. He
had caught a glimpse of a bag on the shoulder of the man wearing the
bandana. Wonsley scrambled down the backside of the ridge and back

to the paint. He grabbed the reins on the run and swung into the saddle. The paint stood still until Wonsley's butt hit the saddle, and he pulled the reins to the left. The paint instantly moved under him, turning back the way he came. Wonsley urged him on with his legs and body lean, and the horse moved into a smooth gallop down the slope to the point where he had crossed the river before. He kept on past that point and rode into the woods on the near side, slowing for the trees and underbrush, but still moving swiftly, outrunning the river, which was shallow here and swifter. A few hundred yards downstream large rocks jutted out from the hillside to his left, and he decided to cross while he could without having to double back.

He hung onto the paint across the shallow water, the hooves suddenly audible, a fast pulsation as the horse flew across, and he leaned into him and felt his quick adjustment to the stream, as he had so many times before. They came out on the other side as one, and he took him through the trees to the edge of the field and to his left in the clear, where the paint stretched out and covered ground. The trees to the left moved rapidly past. The paint ran well through the tall grass, even though the ground was still soft from the rain two nights before. The men were headed for their horses and could have been going in another direction entirely, but he had a feeling they were going southwest, away from him. He settled on this and focused his attention on getting back to tell the others, concentrating on his destination and the movement of the horse under him until they came to a place that caught his eye, and he straightened up in the saddle and pushed his feet down into the stirrups. The paint slowed smoothly, and he pulled into the trees along the path he had taken earlier when following Key. He missed the precise trail, but slanted back to it and was soon at the bank of the river where John and Hays were starting to cross from the opposite bank, with Billy and Gruder just behind them.

He waited for them on the near bank, and when John and Hays came up to him, he looked at Hays.

"Key warned them for sure and they're headed off. I think they're going upstream toward Bradford's."

Billy and Gruder had stopped behind Hays and John Baker, their horses standing in the shallow water. Gruder was noticeably leaning to his left. Hays turned back and looked at Gruder, but he spoke as if to both of them.

"I want you two to follow along at a walk. We'll meet up with you at Bradford's store. If we go past, we'll come back for you. Wait there and keep an eye on the trail where it crosses the river. If they went south, they may double back."

Gruder stared at him without speaking. Billy looked down at the stream.

"I mean a walk, Billy. You understand?"

"Yes, sir."

"And Gruder. When you get there you lie down and let that side heal. I don't want to have to nurse you all the way home."

He said it in a tone Gruder had heard many times before. A tone that said he had no time for discussion, that this was the way it was going to be.

"I hear you, Cap'n." Gruder replied, in the same way he had said it many times.

"Let's go, then," Hays said, and gestured for Wonsley to lead them. Wonsley turned the paint and as he turned dug his boot heels into the horse's withers. The paint came around running. Hays and John Baker were behind him on the buckskin and John's buttermilk mare. They cleared the trees in a hurry and were galloping over the open grassy field, the horses stretching their legs and feeling frisky in the cold wind. Wonsley headed straight for the south edge of the elm grove. They could not see the trees yet, but he had a good sense of where the lodges were. He had lost track of time and could not think of how long it had taken him to get back to the crossing where he met up with the others. The run back had seemed like it had taken a lifetime, but it surely could have only been fifteen minutes or so. The two they were after might have a half hour or more lead, and they would be in a hurry. They might get to the Bradford cabin almost an hour ahead of them. He leaned into the paint, and the horse stretched his stride a bit more.

After what seemed like a long distance, he could make out a tree line. As the tree tops grew larger, he could see a gap on the right where the elms came to the bank of the river. The sun was setting in the gap, a reddish gold in the clear air. By the time they reached the edge of the grove, he believed it had been an hour since he had seen the men. He looked back briefly at Hays, who waved him on. They galloped past the edge of the Honey Eaters' lodges. No humans or animals were visible. The flaps on the lodges on the south side out of the wind were closed.

He could see no smoke coming from the tops of the tipis. The village had been abandoned.

Linda Bradford had left the girl alone all day in the big bed. She kept the fire going in the large fireplace and put on a stew pot when she had finished with the second breakfast of the day, using some chunks of dried pork and some onions she had saved up to start off with. The girl slept soundly, although twice she sat bolt upright and stared around the room. Her eyes did not seem to focus on anything, and each time she lay back down suddenly, her eyes closing before her head hit the pillow.

She stayed in the cabin most of the day to keep an eye on the girl. Her husband came in for supper later than usual. The sound of his boots on the wood floor roused the girl, and Linda Bradford noticed that she was watching them, her head still on the pillow. Linda walked slowly over to the bed, afraid that if she moved too quickly she would frighten her. The girl's tired blue eyes looked up at her.

"You got some rest. I bet you'd like something to eat."

She helped her sit up. The girl grabbed the blanket to hold it to her chest, as Mrs. Bradford placed another shuck pillow behind her back. She looked at Adam, who was standing by the fire, then back up into Linda Bradford's eyes.

"Mr. B., I think we need some privacy," Linda said.

"Surely," he said, and picked up his hat and went out though the door.

"I know you have to go," Linda said to the girl. "I have a chamber pot here." She stepped to the wall to the right of the bed and came back with a white porcelain pot with a handled lid. The girl stayed propped up against the pillows, clutching the blanket to her breast.

"I'll go out if you can get it done by yourself. I don't think you can walk to the privy, and it's getting pretty cold out there." She paused, and the girl looked at the pot and then back at her. "Have you ever used one of these?" Linda asked.

"No," the girl said softly.

"Do you feel like you can make it outside? I can put some wool socks and a coat on you, and I can help you."

"Yes," the girl said. She started to sit up, and Linda pulled the blanket away. She had dressed her in one of her clean cotton nightgowns that she seldom wore. She had been saving it for something, although she had long forgotten why she had originally thought there would be some occasion worth saving it for.

"Your name's Martha, isn't it?" Mrs. Bradford asked.

"Yes, ma'am."

"How old are you, Martha?" The girl was light in her arms as she helped her stand by the bed, holding her by both elbows, her arm around her back.

"I'm fourteen, ma'am," she said.

She seated her at a chair by the table, took some wool socks from the chest in the corner and bent to put them on her feet. Her small, delicate feet were red and raw and two of her toes were blue from bruises. The scrapes and cuts on her legs were visible beneath the hem of the gown.

"You've had a time, I know," Linda said. "But the good Lord was watching after you. He sent those brave men to find you. Now we're going to take good care of you, and you'll be ready to go home in a few days." She finished with the second sock and looked up at her. "You're going to be all right," she said.

The girl's eyes filled with tears. She began to heave with deep sobs. Linda stood and put her arm around her shoulders.

"I know about your folks," she said. "And I'm real sorry."

The girl turned her face to her, and Linda took her in her arms and let her cry.

"I was scared," she said, into Linda's ear, the sound of her voice like the cry of a small animal. "I was scared."

She cried for a long time, until Linda's back was hurting from bending over and holding her. She spoke softly into the girl's ear.

"Can you get up now to go to the privy?"

Martha shuddered. Then with Linda's help, she rose and they made it out to the porch, a step at a time, and slowly to the back yard toward the well where Adam Bradford stood in the cold north wind, washing his hands. He turned and watched them go off at an angle toward the privy, where Linda held the door and the girl's elbow at the same time. She had not put a coat on, and the cold wind whipped through her dress and apron as she stood with her back to the privy, hugging herself. After a long wait, she turned, opened the door, and helped the girl back to the house, where the girl ate some stew and settled down by the fire in the rocker Adam had made, a heavy quilt over her lap.

Adam Bradford came in and had some stew while Linda sat on the stool opposite the rocker looking at the girl, who rocked and stared into the flames curling around the logs in the fireplace. Nothing was said. They watched the girl; the girl watched the fire. When Bradford had finished his stew and wiped the bowl with the rough cloth that served as his napkin, he stood and took his buffalo robe off its peg and wrapped it around his shoulders. Linda looked over at him as he approached the door. He was going out to have a smoke in spite of the cold, although he would normally have taken it inside.

The wind had died down, and he could see the half-moon under the eaves of the back porch. The still air always came as a surprise after a norther. It would be a cold, clear morning and a mild afternoon. He would be able to work on the fence in the south pasture, once he had seen to the visitors. Hays was not what he had expected. He had heard about his battles with the Mexicans and Indians and had assumed that he was a large, hardened man whose personal presence would inspire other men to follow him. Instead, he was small and quiet, and his features gave no clue to the ferocity for which he was famous. His reaction to bearded Hailey Morton that morning was not in keeping with his demeanor. It was sudden and instinctive, coming from something deep within, and his coolness was remarkable. As Adam Bradford filled his pipe in the moonlight, he wondered what this unusual man would do next.

He reached in his pocket for a match and had his thumb against the sulphur tip, then paused. He had heard something that did not sound right from down the trail to the southeast—a stick breaking. It was sharp enough to have been caused by a large animal, like a horse.

He held the match in his hand and waited silently. The edge of the porch roof cast a shadow over him in the pale moonlight, and he was sure he could not be seen as he leaned against the rear wall of the east cabin. It would have been uncharacteristic for Comanches to come up on his house now. They had been in the area for weeks, or at least two bands of them had, and he did not expect any intrusions from them. The young ones were always unpredictable, though. The Johnson family had been killed and burned out a little over a year ago, and that had been upriver, only a few miles from Fort McKavett.

He could see where the end of the path entered the clearing and squinted in the dim light. Patterns of shadow and moonlight covered the underbrush past the tree line. He scanned the entire area for movement. Then his coon dogs started barking, beginning with Jennie, the mama, who was always the first to alert on a hunt. There was no use in staying still anymore. He stood and quickly went to the door of the west cabin, opened it and reached inside for his rifle—a new Henry he had just brought from San Antonio that spring—and the leather bag with spare cartridges. He was back on the back side of the house in a few seconds, the bag hanging from his left shoulder and the rifle raised in the ready position, the butt just below his right shoulder.

The dogs moved from their place of rest by the far side of the west cabin into the moonlight in the backyard and kept up their baying. He held the rifle ready and scanned the tree line again. The dogs would not move on anything until he whistled. The five of them were alternately baying and pausing to sniff the ground around them, becoming more and more agitated—probably from the baying of the pack rather than any scent they had picked up.

Then there was a movement in the brush along the trail. It appeared to be about twenty feet inside the tree line, in a patch of moonlight, fleeting and sudden, too sudden to be natural. Then nothing for several minutes. He concentrated on the space where he had seen the movement. Two of the dogs stopped baying, as if bored by lack of encouragement or action. It occurred to him that his visitors could be making their way around to the front of the house. He slowly crept around the corner of the east cabin and down the dog run, keeping close to the wall. Linda had doused the lamp in the west cabin. No light came from under the doorway. The house cast a longer shadow on the front side, and the clearing reached a couple of hundred feet past the corral, giving a good view of the surroundings. He scanned the area, turning with his rifle at the ready. The dogs came around the outside of the east cabin, still baying, but not as urgently. They were gradually quieting down.

With his back to the moon he could see into the tree line better. He could make out a small post oak on the edge of the trail that lay well up under the larger oaks and elms, as well as the edge of a stone that he used as a landmark. He scanned the trees from right to left, slowly, making mental note of each space in the darkness before he moved on. The last barking dog spaced out his final wails, then stopped altogether. It was still and clear, the kind of night that was good for coon hunting, and the dogs were on edge anyway. The movement could have been a night bird. Telling the dogs to stay, he turned and stepped on tiptoes back down the dog run to the back porch.

He sat on the empty nail keg he used for a stool and leaned against the back wall of the east cabin, still in the dark and out of sight. He leaned the rifle against the wall within easy reach and reached inside his coat for a plug of tobacco and his pocketknife. He cut off a chunk, popped it into his mouth and replaced the plug and knife. He barely had the chew worked up when a voice called out from down the trail.

"Hallooo the house," it said, in the traditional greeting. He waited. Then again, "Hallooo the house. Mr. Bradford?" Then a pause. "It's John Baker."

"Hello," he yelled back as he stood. "Who's with you?"

"My brother Wonsley and Colonel Hays," the voice called back.

It was doubtful that anyone other than his companions knew the younger Baker's name, but Adam Bradford was still cautious.

"Come on out into the clearing so I can see you," he shouted back.

One by one, three men entered the clearing, leading their horses. Apparently familiar with the ritual of approaching a camp or cabin at night under hostile conditions, they halted once they were visible in the moonlight. Their shapes looked all right and only a couple of the dogs barked tentatively, then approached the men quietly. John Baker came up close to Bradford, and he recognized his features in the moonlight.

"The men we seek must have come by earlier," John said.

"I didn't see them," Bradford said. "But I heard 'em, and the dogs smelled 'em. You're not far behind."

Hays walked up beside John Baker. "Which way you figure they'll go, Mr. Bradford?"

Bradford hesitated. "I figure they'll go north. Head for open country."

"Will your dogs track 'em?" Hays asked.

"As far as they can go," Bradford said.

"Would you mind if we used them?"

"I'll have to go with you," he said.

"You got family to look after," Wonsley said.

"Wonsley, you can wait here for Billy and Gruder, then come on when you can," Hays said. It was more than a statement of possibilities.

"Yes, sir," Wonsley said.

Bradford grabbed his saddlebags, said good-bye to his wife, saddled up, and was ready in just a few minutes. Wonsley was sitting by the fire talking to Linda Bradford and stealing glances at the girl, who was bundled up in a rocker, staring into the fire.

They headed for the river, the dogs running ahead in wide arcs, crossing each other's paths over and over until the old bitch who had barked longest and most urgently at the cabin found their scent. She let out a wail that sounded like the crying of a spirit, and within seconds they were off, raising their voices in chorus after their prey.

When Billy and Gruder reached the Bradford place, Wonsley was at the edge of the tree line to meet them. Gruder was leaning over the saddle horn, his face impassive, but when he dismounted he grunted and stood still for a while before he turned and led the horse toward the hitching post by the back porch. Wonsley told them that they were to stay there with the women, silently heard Billy's protests, and was on his horse on the trail upriver before they entered the cabin. Linda Bradford met them at the door, and when Gruder hesitated before entering, grasped his hand and pulled him inside. She noticed immediately that he favored his left side and asked what had happened. John Baker had merely told her "Gruder and Billy would be along" and would stay with them. She lightly touched the stained shirt and he stood very still, looking at her but saying nothing. Then Billy said, "He got shot." She told Gruder to sit in the straight chair by the fire and take off his shirt.

Billy stood by the opposite side of the fireplace, next to the girl, who looked from him to Gruder as Gruder tried to lift his cotton shirt over his head and halted when his left arm did not respond, half straightened out in the sleeve. Mrs. Bradford pulled it up and off, revealing the thin black body wrapped with rags darkened by blood and wet under his arm. He winced from the pull on his arm as the sleeve came off and emitted a small, high-pitched sound. She leaned over and looked at the bandage in the firelight. It was soaked through. She turned to Billy and noticed his slung arm.

"Are you able to bring me a bucket of water?"

He straightened up. "Yes, ma'am."

"The well is right out back."

After he was out the door, she pulled the stool up to Gruder and sat down.

"I'm gonna take this bandage off and wash your wound and maybe doctor it," she said. "There's a cot with blankets in the other cabin and a place for the boy to sleep, and there's a wood stove with plenty of wood in the box."

"Yes, ma'am," he finally said. She cut his bandages away. When Billy returned with the bucket of water, she had him put it in the iron pot and swing it over the fire.

"It'll be ready in a minute," she said, then looking up at Billy, "Why is your arm in that sling?"

"I guess I sprung it," he replied, glancing at the girl, who was still bundled up in the rocker. She looked intensely at Gruder who sat looking into the fire.

"I'll take a look at that too," she said in a tone that sounded like his mother. "You may need a hot pack."

There was light in the east when the dogs began to backtrack on the near bank of the river, and they realized they had lost them. Going back downstream they looked at the opposite bank for a sign of where they had emerged, but they could have done so anywhere either upstream or downstream. It was impossible to track them farther. Hays rode up to Bradford.

"Can your dogs pick up their trail on the other side of the river?"

"Hard to say," Bradford responded. "They don't do so good over water. And it's hard to tell which way to go, except by guess. I'd guess they came out somewheres downstream from here and headed north. If you get much further upstream, you get close to the fort and they'd know that."

"We'll follow you," Hays said.

Bradford led the way downstream to a ford, and they followed the dogs on the other side down the left bank for several miles. Then the dogs veered off to the north, circled back to the edge of the river, then loped back north again until they began to separate, no longer following the old bitch leader. It was obvious that they had lost the scent and were following one thing and then another. The men kept downstream at a slow pace. Wonsley was again in the lead, looking for tracks, for the remainder of the morning, but saw nothing. There were areas where the grass grew on rocky ground, hiding any markings. Still Wonsley kept a steady pace and was not about to turn back. Finally, when they were almost to the spot they had crossed coming over from Hobart Key's place, Bradford pulled alongside Hays.

"We've gone past where they would have likely come to," he said. "There are three deep holes upstream from here. They would have got out before getting here."

Hays whistled to Wonsley, who stopped his horse and turned to look back.

"I think we oughta cross over here, Cap'n," Bradford said. "We can survey the other side all the way to the store. If they doubled back, we'll find their tracks. If they didn't, they're long gone."

Hays motioned to Wonsley and informed John Baker when he came up. They crossed where Bradford suggested and came back up the right bank with Wonsley again in the lead, but he saw nothing until they came to the ford near Bradford's store, where there were not only horse tracks, but those of numerous cattle. They rested at the store under the oak tree. A Mexican woman who worked for Bradford brought them some beans and tortillas, and they sat and ate. When they finished it was midafternoon.

"I guess we lost 'em for now," Wonsley finally said. Hays and John Baker gave him a look of agreement. "Maybe I better go check on Billy and Gruder." It was part question.

"That'll be all right," Hays said softly.

When Wonsley reached the Bradford cabin, Billy was sitting on the front porch, his arm still slinged. Wonsley dismounted.

"How's Gruder?" he asked.

"Asleep," Billy said.

Wonsley stood at the edge of the porch, shifting his weight from side to side.

"The girl's asleep, too," Billy said, looking past him down the clearing.

"Is she . . ." The question hung there.

"She's not talking much," Billy said.

After a long pause, Wonsley asked, "How about you? You all right?"

"I'm doin' okay," Billy answered, as if it wasn't a relevant question. He had the Remington on, the holster still around on the left side.

"Well, I better water this horse," Wonsley said, and he led the paint around the side of the cabin to the well and trough in back. Billy sat in the shade on the porch. The north wind had lessened, but it was still cool in the north-side shade. He had sat down there because that was the direction of potential danger, and the cool breeze helped to keep him awake. He had not slept much during the night. With the dogs gone, every sound stirred him, and it seemed like the east cabin in which he and Gruder lay had walls of paper. Gruder breathed heavy and mumbled in his sleep. When morning came, Linda Bradford came in, felt Gruder's forehead and said he had a fever, which awakened him. He tried to sit up, and she pushed against his chest to keep him from it.

"You need to stay there," she said. "You likely have an infection in that wound."

Gruder lay there and looked at her. She dipped a gourd of water for him from the bucket at his bedside and he drank eagerly.

"Only get up when you need to relieve yourself," she said. "And you let this young man know, so he can help you out back. I'll get some food for you in a minute and take another look at that wound."

Gruder let her nurse him. He stayed on the cot the rest of that morning and early afternoon but ate very little of the porridge she brought him, although she had put milk and sugar in it. She treated his wound in front and back with something that burned, then rubbed axle grease on it and applied a fresh bandage. He had trouble sitting up for her to wrap the bandage around him. Billy had to steady him.

On the dog run outside, she wiped her hands on her apron and told Billy to stay close and listen for him.

"He's likely to sleep, but if he cries out that means his fever's gone up," she said. "If you hear that, you come and get me."

Billy looked in on him a couple of times and found him lying on his back still in the same position, his eyes closed. Billy did not see the tired eyes open slightly when he closed the door each time.

After the paint had had enough water, Wonsley led him away from the trough to a grassy spot at the edge of the clearing, dropped his reins and left him to graze. He came back through the dog run, sat down beside Billy on the porch, and leaned against a wall. Neither of them spoke, and in a few minutes Wonsley drifted off to sleep.

THIRTEEN

"THIS ELECTION IS GOING TO PAVE THE WAY FOR PROGRESS," Thomas Coddington said, his full red face animated with seeming emotion. "Mark my words. There will be northern investment now. Mark my words."

He stood at the end of the bar at Dilley's in his usual place, drinking the bar's best whiskey with a beer chaser. John Joseph was behind the bar, his dingy apron draped over his paunch.

"I hope to hell there's somebody that shows up with money," he bellowed. "Ain't a goddamn cowboy around here who could buy a bottle." He glanced at the two men at the other end of the bar, who were nursing their beers. Both were young and lean, their hats cocked back on their heads confidently. "Shit. The judge don't even come here anymore. I may have to close down."

"That'll be the day," said the short, pudgy man sitting at the table by the door. He was wearing a bowler. The two other men at his table were quiet. "I bet you still got your first dollar, Dilley." Joseph glared at him. It was not the first time he had said it, and the man emphasized his nickname in the usual singsong manner.

"Running a saloon ain't all it's cracked up to be," Joseph said.

"Time's a coming," Coddington said, in his New England accent. "I'm telling you. Mark my words."

"You folks from up north gonna shut down the saloons I hear," the man in the bowler said.

The bartender's face stiffened under three day's growth of beard and his lower lip protruded even more. "That'll be the day," he growled.

"Only on election days," said Coddington. "Or that's what I hear."

"And you have your ear to the ground, don't you, Coddy," said the bartender.

"Coddington. The name's Coddington."

"He's got it to the ground, all right," said the man in the bowler.

One of the other men at the table by the door grunted his agreement.

"I'm not here to keep fighting the war," Coddington said curtly. "If some of you people would work for a change we'd all be better off."

The younger looking of the two cowboys, who had been leaning with his back against the far end of the bar, now turned to Coddington. He had an Army Colt snugged into his dirty blue pants on the left side, the handle showing its pearl face above the thin serape he used as a belt. The hat pitched back on his head was a remarkably clean, white Stetson, the brim raised in front. His brown, shoulder-length hair was sun-bleached around the edges.

The bartender noticed his move and turned again to Coddington.

"Well, Mr. Coddington. You don't talk much like a peacemaker," he said, glancing to his left at the young man in the Stetson. "Sounds like you hold with those Yankee nigger lovers who say all of the whites in the South ought to be run off."

Coddington had drunk just enough to be oblivious to the danger he faced.

"I'm no lover of the black race," he said. "But I believe this country would have been better off without slave labor."

"So you think we're better off now, huh?" said the bartender.

Coddington opened his mouth, prepared to expound, but noticed that the young man in the Stetson was coming his way. He stopped with his mouth open, his eyes straining to focus as the cowboy walked up to him and stopped a foot away, staring down into Coddington's frozen face, his expression calm and deadly.

Coddington glanced at the bartender, who said, "Mr. Coddington, I am pleased to introduce you to Mr. Hardin, a young man from Gonzales County, I believe."

"Pleased to meet you," Coddington said, extending his hand. The cowboy looked down coldly at the extended hand and made no move to shake it. He was only a boy, not more than sixteen, but he had a cold look about him.

"What were you saying?" he asked.

Coddington's hand was shaking. He looked down at it, as if it was not a part of him, then moved it a little too quickly. The boy grabbed Coddington's wrist with his left hand. The speed of the boy's hand was such that it seemed he had not moved it at all—as if his hand was there waiting for Coddington's before Coddington had even moved.

"I'm not armed," Coddington said, his voice an octave higher. The rest of the room was still and quiet. The boy held Coddington's wrist tightly, cutting off the blood flow to his hand. Coddington looked down at it, but the boy showed no sign of releasing it. His clear blue eyes steadily stared at Coddington.

"I'm sorry if I gave offense," Coddington said. His high voice and New England accent sounded out of place.

After a long pause, the cowboy released his wrist and said, in an overly polite manner, "I accept your apology, sir, but I hope it was also intended for these other gentlemen."

Coddington hesitated and looked cautiously to the table by the door. "Yes, indeed," he finally said. "I certainly meant no offense, and I apologize to all." His lower lip was trembling.

"That satisfactory to you gentlemen?"

There were murmurs of "That's all right" and "Sure" from around the room, although all voices were quiet and hesitant. The cowboy took a step back and, still looking at Coddington, asked, "We owe you anything, Mr. Joseph?"

"Not a thing. Those last ones are on me."

"We thank you kindly, sir," he said, and turned to the other cowboy. "You ready to ride, Jim?" The other young man nodded. "All right, then," he said, then walked to the door, tipping his hat to those at the table as he walked out, the other man following him. The quiet in the room stayed for a while after the door closed behind them.

"Who was that?" Coddington whispered.

"That was John Wesley Hardin. You're a lucky man, Mr. Coddington," the bartender replied.

FOURTEEN

GRUDER'S FEVER BROKE AFTER THE THIRD DAY AND NIGHT AT Bradford's house. Linda Bradford nursed him through it, with Billy's help. The girl, Martha, did not venture outside except to go to the outhouse, but kept in the Bradford's room, sitting in the rocking chair most of the time, rocking and staring at the floor. On the third day, a warm, sunny Indian summer day, Linda Bradford insisted that the girl bathe. She set up the washtub in a corner across the room from the fireplace and poured heated water from the fireplace into it. When the girl was reluctant to undress, she hung a line across the corner and put a quilt over it as a screen. After considerable argument, the girl finally agreed to let Linda help her off with her clothes.

The girl tried to cover up the dried blood on her thighs, but there were too many bad places to cover. Her hands shook as she hesitated, looking down at the scratches on her legs and the bruises on her chest, abdomen and pubis. She let herself be coaxed into the tub, then stood there, reluctant to sit down in the hot water, until Linda placed both hands on her shoulders and gently guided her down. Linda washed her hair with the homemade soap and gently scrubbed her back with the horsehair brush she had brought from Galveston three years before. The girl was as slow at washing as she was at moving around, and Linda had to guide her hands from time to time after they stopped, as if they had lost track of their purpose. Linda finally took the washcloth from her and washed her legs and between them, although the girl initially jerked away from her touch.

"Be still," Linda said impatiently, as if bathing one of her own children. The girl reacted immediately to this command, relaxed her arms and let them fall to her sides in the soapy water, as if it had been her mother's command to her as a young child. "If only their bodies could stay the same," Linda thought. The girl's breasts were full and the bruises on them stood out in the light from the window, somehow marking her definitely as a woman far more than the shape and fullness her body had taken on, and Linda thought of the years Martha had to face, the pain of childbirth and back-breaking work, if she was lucky. If she found a tolerably good man who would not beat her. It was not going to be easy for an orphan who had been taken by a half-breed to find a worthwhile mate.

Linda pulled her up and out of the tub by her elbow and dried her off, as if she were a four-year-old, and the girl continued to act the part, staring vacantly at the corner as Linda dried her. She helped her into the undergarments Linda had taken from the cedar chest. She put a gingham dress that had belonged to Linda's sister over her head and pulled it down around her. When Linda finished combing her hair, she stepped back to look at her.

"You're a fine-looking young woman," she said. "Look here," pulling the two-foot-high mahogany-framed mirror off the floor next to the wall and holding it up before her. The girl looked away. Linda hesitated, then put the mirror back against the wall. "I'm gonna need some help outside. I don't have any shoes to fit you yet, but it's a warm day. Come on." Linda picked up the ragged dress that the girl had been wearing. She had insisted on putting it back on in place of the boy's clothes she had worn while riding.

She left the tub and quilt in place and the girl followed her as she carried the soiled clothes out the door and to the back by the kitchen, where a good bed of coals was laid in under the iron washpot. Linda turned to her.

"These need to be burned," she said, in the same insistent tone of voice, and held the ragged dress out to her. The girl looked first at her, then at the plaid pattern of the dirty cloth, then back at Linda.

"It's your thing to do," Linda said. "There's the fire." She extended the dress toward her and Martha stared down at it for several seconds, then grabbed it quickly and threw it in the fire. It smoldered before giving off flame and they stood and watched it burn until it was nothing but gray ash and dark lines of smudge.

While they were standing there, Gruder came out onto the dog run. He had to duck to get through the door and when he stood up to his full height outside, he wavered a bit. Linda heard his step and turned to look his way. He was fully dressed with the spare shirt he had taken from his bedroll and held his hat in his hand. She went to him quickly.

"You're not to be up so soon," she said, with a hint of scolding and a degree of concern in her voice.

"As you can see, ma'am, I am up," he said quickly.

"Here," she said, pointing to a stump stool on the back porch corner. "Sit here and I'll get you some corn bread and fresh milk."

"Don't mind if I do," he said, trying to sound unconcerned, but after he sat and took his hat off and Linda brought him the corn bread in a bowl of milk, he ate it with obvious need, his hands shaking as he dipped the large wedge of corn bread into the milk and brought it to his mouth. He rested his elbows on his knees, his long legs elevating them above the low point where he sat. The girl had come up to him and stood just off the porch watching him eat. Linda watched him also, and when he had finished the corn bread, he drank the milk that remained in the wooden bowl in one long draught and then held the bowl in both hands, looking down at it.

"I'll get you some more. I can also fry up some bacon. We got some that's pretty fresh and smoked good."

"I don't want to put you out anymore, Miz Bradford," he said, without conviction.

"Don't you worry about that," she said, taking the bowl from him. "Don't you worry."

He turned from Linda and looked at the girl. She looked down when their eyes met.

"You doin' all right?" he asked.

"Yeah," she said softly.

"That's good," he said. "That's real good."

There was a silence. He was not inclined to say anything else to her and she did not speak, but stood looking down at her feet until Linda returned with another bowl of milk and corn bread.

"I'll get the bacon fixed," she said. "Come on, Martha, and help me." She headed for the smokehouse and the girl followed, leaving Gruder eating the second helping, this time at a slower pace. When he finished draining the second bowl, he decided to go to the well for a gourd of water and stood up too quickly, causing the dizziness again, and he swayed backward until his back hit the wall behind him.

"Damn," he said under his breath. He moved forward with a long step to the edge of the porch, then stepped down hard onto the ground, which caused his side to pain him. It felt like a wire had been laid in him, moving as he moved, but more rigid than the rest of his flesh. He had been guarding it unconsciously. Now he was fully aware that the movement he made off the porch involved straightening up and moving the wire where it did not want to go and that his plans to ride horseback that day were premature. He made it to the well by leaning to his left and taking short steps, but it infuriated him, and when he had pain in his left side as he raised his right arm up to grab the dipper, he said, "Dammit," to the dipper and himself and his left side and his stupidity in letting himself get potshot and disabled, when it was he who should be watching out for Billy and their flanks, not laid up and useless.

"Dammit," he said again as he dipped the gourd into the bucket. He was ashamed of being hurt, although he had been hurt many times, once far more badly than this, he thought, which was really nothing and he wasn't so damned old that a little nick should keep him as stove up as he was. Then he caught the first smell of bacon frying and the smell was so good that tears came to his eyes and he was suddenly embarrassed at himself for being so ungrateful. Mrs. Bradford was going to a lot of trouble for him and treating him like white folks, and he was out here feeling sorry for himself. He drank deep from the dipper and let the cold water run down his chin and the front of his shirt; then he replaced the dipper and turned back toward the house, moving a little more upright, but still stiff and taking small steps. When he reached the back porch again and sat on the stool, he was feeling better. He could live with the pain and he could walk, so he should not be impatient. He should let Miz Bradford wait on him just like Miz Laura had when he had been sick. Just like his Sadie did before she passed. And Cap'n Hays wouldn't need him anyway. At least not for a few days. And when he was healed up so he could ride, everything would be all right. No sense rushing it.

They had been at Bradford's for almost two weeks. Hays, John, and Wonsley had spent most of that time riding out with Adam Bradford in widening arcs from the immediate area, talking to settlers, looking for signs of their prey, but they found no trace of them. When they rode to Key's house, they found it empty of human beings and horses. The cabin floor was littered with debris, as if they had left in a hurry.

On the way back to Bradford's they rode into the small Comanche village where Wonsley had seen Key with the two men. It had been empty the day after Key was seen talking to them, but a few women and children were now standing near their tipis. Bradford waved his hat in the air as they approached. As they rode up, several of the women seemed to recognize Bradford's red beard. There were no men in sight, and the women held their children at their sides and stared at the men as they rode by. Wonsley recognized the woman he had seen gathering firewood, standing by herself at the edge of the clearing. Her round face was cold and still. Hays spoke to them in Comanche and later told his companions what the old woman said: that Morgan had blown off with the north wind, which was hard to read, but it probably meant he was headed in the opposite direction—south—if she actually knew. She was speaking as they rode off, but not to the other women. She was looking at the sky, talking.

Bradford's store was to have been a polling place for the election, but the Radical Republicans, who were backed by the army, had moved it to the front room of an abandoned house on the upriver road, miles from the settlement. General J. J. Reynolds, the commander of the Union Army in Texas, appointed only the supporters of Radical E. J. Davis as voting registrars. The lists were purged over and over until the real majority in the state became the minority. The election was held between November 30 and December 3. Military detachments stood at every polling place to enforce the Radical lists and exclude most Democrats and Conservative Republicans from voting. The Davis Radicals made sure to get all blacks they could to the polls, after assuring them that the Democrats and Conservative Republicans were their enemies and would have them back in the fields at hard labor if they had their way. "Forty acres and a mule," a slogan that was in currency throughout the South, was the Radical pledge to the Negro voters, although no public official ever promised it and no one could ever figure out where the rumor came from. The army had been ordered to close the polls in any place where trouble occurred. "Trouble" only seemed to occur in white counties. If a voter found his name stricken from the rolls and argued over it, the polls were immediately closed down. This cut the vote for Hamilton severely. In Navarro County, the registrar, realizing that a large majority would vote for Hamilton, took the registration lists and left town before the election. No votes from Navarro County were ever counted. In Milam County, the polls opened, but the votes were never counted and the results were never reported. In Hill County, the ballots were removed to another jurisdiction and counted by a single official, a Davis man, who reported a huge Davis majority, although the vote most certainly went the other way.

There was no canvass and the ballots were never made public. General Reynolds certified to President Grant that Davis had been elected, by a vote of 39,901 to 39,092. Only a small percentage of white people of voting age were allowed to register, and less than one-half of those that registered were able to cast a ballot. Despite the fact that affidavits charging fraud were sworn before magistrates all over the state, and even a number of US Army officers protested to Reynolds about the conduct of the election, Reynolds certified the entire Radical ticket, and Grant refused to investigate. Led by E. M. Pease, a dozen Republicans of known integrity petitioned Washington, but documented cases of serious fraud presented to Congress and the president were ignored.

Wonsley had tried to vote at the polling place, arguing that he was registered in Guadalupe County and was away from home on important business, but he had no documentation. The registrar, an unkempt little man wearing a dirty vest over a new white shirt, turned him away. John was waiting for him outside the yard of the house. When Wonsley came out he was visibly upset. He untied his horse, swung into the saddle and turned into the road before John had mounted. He said nothing until they were a mile down the road.

"Damned carpetbaggers," he said without looking at John. "How long you figure it'll take us to get home?"

"They won't let you vote there either, brother." John's voice had a sound of resignation to it that was unusual for him.

When they got back to the store, Wonsley walked up on the porch to Adam Bradford and asked, "Where's Colonel Hays?"

"He went down to the river about thirty minutes ago. Had a book and a map with him."

Bradford gestured toward the back of the store, where the river was obscured from view by the trees that lined it. Wonsley headed down a trail toward the near bank, but Hays was not to be seen. He looked for tracks and found a heel mark a few feet upstream. The overgrown path curved between young sycamores along the bank, and he soon came to a clearing where Hays sat on a cypress root facing the water, his back to him. His hat was lying on the ground beside him and his head was down. Wonsley crept up behind him, then realized that he should make some sound, so he cleared his throat and Hays immediately turned to face him, his right hand moving to his side.

He had realized too late that he was approaching too quietly and wished he had given warning of his approach earlier. Hays had been surprised. With his hat off in the late morning sun, he looked older than Wonsley usually thought of him. He was holding a worn cloth map in his left hand, but Wonsley only noticed this briefly. He immediately focused on Hays's face and the gold spectacles that hung low on his nose.

Both of them were frozen for several seconds, neither breathing, then Hays slowly reached up and removed the glasses. Wonsley wanted to speak, but could not bring himself to say anything. Hays's look changed from surprise to displeasure.

"Yes, Wonsley," he said, still looking into his eyes.

Wonsley mumbled, "Sorry Cap'n," then, "I was wonderin' when you thought we could get on home. I want to vote and they won't let me, here."

Hays's face softened. "I was thinking we should start tomorrow," he said. He pointed to the map with the hand that held the spectacles. "I was looking at a way that we might take, maybe that would run us into our man again."

Wonsley came closer, but did not look down at the map. In spite of his skills in the wild, he had no use for maps. He had often said to Billy that maps were for folks that didn't know where they were going and that they didn't have trails on them anyway, so why bother with them? Hays folded the spectacles slowly and placed them in a leather-covered case that he pulled from his jacket pocket. He examined it before placing it back, then looked up at Wonsley.

"I only really need these for close-up work," he said. "I still see all right otherwise."

FIFTEEN

L UIS HAD A DREAM ABOUT MARIA. SHE WAS DRESSED IN WHITE and her long black hair lay softly over her luminous white shoulders, as soft as he could remember, and her delicate lips were moving, talking to him, but no sound came out. There was sound, but it was like the rushing of a stream, so loud that it covered her small voice. She was smiling as she talked to him and doing something with her hands, but he did not want to look away from her beautiful face long enough to see what it was. She was young and he was somehow young listening to her, and although he could not hear her voice, he suddenly realized that it was not necessary, that he knew very well that whatever she was saying she was saying with love from her pure heart.

Then she looked beyond him and her hands stopped and her expression changed to one of fear, which he could not bear, so he tried to reach out to her to hold her against his chest, to feel her warmth against him and let her feel his strength, but he could not reach her, and she kept looking over his head at something that was behind him and then directly into his eyes and she was still talking, only he could not understand what she was saying because the sound of the stream was too loud.

Then there was another sound, one that did not fit in the dream and he opened one eye slightly. He was in his hiding place in the branches of a cottonwood tree high above Wallace Creek. It was not yet dawn, but there was a faint light on the ground and he could see the rocks and underbrush beneath him as well as the bottom of the trail on the hillside. He leaned slightly to his left to a place where he could see higher up the hill. He could detect no unusual movement. The wind from the north, though buffered by the trees, came down the creek valley with some remaining force and the leaves and branches and tall grass were in constant movement. The stream was over its banks, its swift brown water rushing impatiently down the middle and eddying on the edges over partially submerged weeds.

Then the sound came to him again and although he could not place it, it was made by a human, not by the wind or an animal. It was not that it was sharp or loud. Animal sounds could be sharp and loud. It was a tool being driven into dirt. A shovel or a hoe. Or a Bowie knife. He froze, blocking out everything but his hearing and his sense of smell. His breathing slowed. His heartbeat slowed.

After a long time, in which there was only silence, he heard a hoofbeat from the direction of the hillside and shortly after, increasing his concentration, he could make out the faint smell of a horse, slightly upwind and to the northwest, which would place it not far from the apex of the trail at the top of the hill. Another long period of silence followed, then the dull sound of something pounding in the damp soil of the hillside. The storm had washed the trail, and it was necessary to dig new footholds for horses. The digger would be crawling down the hillside with his back to him, leading his horse and reaching down from time to time to carve out footholds.

If Luis came down out of his tree, he could be seen and probably heard and his options would be limited. Better to stay in the tree and wait until he could see who and how many riders there were. His legs were drawn up in the fork of the limb and his rifle lay in his lap, its muzzle pointed in the direction of the hillside, so all he would have to do was raise it to his eye, cock and fire. The paint was across the creek on the other side of the pasture, tethered where he could graze. His roll was hidden under a log downstream. And he was downwind. There was no reason to move. He was confident he could stay in the tree all day if he had to, without movement or sound.

It took a long while for the man to work his way down the hillside and it was not until he was within twenty feet of the bottom of the trail that Luis was able to see him. Then, at first, he could only see his boots, which were homemade buckskin with tassels. Apache boots. The tassels swayed from side to side as he backed down the trail.

The boots came farther down the hill and he could see the man's brown pants, then the back of a drab wool coat; then he could see a long single braid of black hair against the lighter wool and the back of a neck and a hat, straight brimmed, and the man's left hand crossed in front of him, holding the reins. The man was not large, but his shoulders were broad and his legs were thick like Luis's. Luis knew he was the one he was seeking, although he could not have explained how he knew. It was as if he had seen the man before, in exactly the same position, coming down the hillside, his left hand grasping the reins, and this was what he had seen, not even remembering it until this moment. Then he saw the man's right hand, which held a wide-bladed tool and the vision had been fulfilled. It did not look like any tool he had ever seen, but he had heard it described. It was a bone-handled knife, with a wide, curving blade, only about six inches long. The edge was concave, like a miniature scythe. It had been used to slit throats.

A few feet from the bottom of the hillside the slope shallowed and the man, Juaro, put the knife away. He was quickly at the bottom and after leading the horse to level ground, he turned and looked around, standing fully erect, his black eyes quickly and thoroughly scanning from left to right. Luis had taken off his headscarf and his motionless head, speckled with gray flecks, blended in well with the cottonwood trunk. His pants and boots blended in. Nothing was loose to flap in the wind and cause an unusual movement. But the man's scan did not rise up to the height of Luis's position in the tree. He listened for a few seconds after his first look around, then led the horse away from the hillside, downstream, at an angle away from where Luis sat. The man's path took him beyond the low branches of a cypress tree and he was quickly out of sight, reappearing briefly before he crossed under the branches of another tree.

He realized that he might have lost his chance. His hesitation just as the man was turning around may have cost him his best shot. It had only been a two-second opening, but it had been there. He had been frozen looking at the face he had waited so long to see. Although he had never seen it before, he had memorized every description of it he had heard, and although it was not the face he had imagined, he knew it immediately. The low, heavy brow. The dark eyes and broad nose. The scar on his left cheek.

In only a few minutes he could hear the horse's hooves in the water of the creek, at a spot that was now two feet deep and in normal weather would have been six inches, a crossing known by the rider, who had mounted and was following the creek downstream. When Luis could tell that the man was out of sight, he climbed down the tree, dropping quietly in the leaves at the base of the trunk, and trotted in a crouch to the point where Juaro had entered the creek.

The churning water was dark brown, and the only way to tell where the man got out would be to search the bank on the other side, which would not be a safe thing to do. Better to retrieve his roll and get to his mount. He had staked him out of the way and did not expect him to be seen by anyone taking the trail downriver.

The paint was looking his way when he emerged from the high Johnson grass with his roll. The horse stayed still when he came up. He threw up the roll and tied it, tightened the cinch, and swung into the saddle. He headed at a walk down the valley, in the direction of Bandera, believing that he would find Juaro's trail where the Wallace entered the Medina.

SIXTEEN

LILY POE APPEARED AT ASHLEY MAITLAND'S PLACE IN THE LATE afternoon. Ashley greeted her in his shirtsleeves and asked her to step inside, but she suggested they sit on the front porch. It was not much of a porch, but the day was warm and sunny and Lily said that she couldn't stay long. She just needed to ask him a few things.

Two old straight chairs and a small table sat to the right of the door. He asked her to sit and offered her a drink.

"I'll take you up on that," she said, looking at him in a familiar way, with a fire in her eyes that he had not seen lately. He knew that she counted on him offering her a drink and that the occasional wanderer down the crude path that passed as Atlanta's main street would notice them sitting there. "And bring the bottle," she said, as he turned to the door.

He returned with a pitcher of cool water, two glasses and an earthen jug of corn whiskey.

"It's local, but I think you'll find it fair to middlin'."

She did not wait for him to pour. She grabbed the jug by the handle, pulled the cob out and poured two shots for them, then held her glass up toward him.

"To prosperity," she said.

Her smile was from her eyes, her lips firm as she raised her glass. They downed the shots and Lily set the glass down hard.

"I need to know about the will and what I need to do," she said quickly, as if to get it out of the way.

Ashley could see a horseman coming over the rise to the east, just over her shoulder. He looked down at his empty glass.

"The will's probated. I have an executor's deed for Laura to sign. She hasn't been by to sign it yet, but I think she just hasn't been over this way."

"What if she won't sign it?"

"She'll sign it. She has never objected to any part of the will. She knows it was what Wes wanted."

"She knows he was drunk," she said. "And that he was drunk a lot the last couple of years."

She picked up the jug and poured two more shots.

"I don't think you and I have had a drink to him, yet," she said, her lips slightly pursed. She held up her glass. He held his up and touched hers. They downed the shots and put the glasses down firmly. It was at least the tenth time they had toasted him since his death.

"Are you still going to be my lawyer?" she asked.

He looked steadily at her this time.

"She'll sign the deed," he said firmly. "Just give her a little time."

The rider was within a hundred yards now. He was riding a bay and leading a pack mule. Ashley shifted slightly in his chair as he spoke, to get a better view.

"How's the gin looking?" he asked.

"Good. You should come see it. But I need Gruder."

"They've been gone a long time," he said.

"You know why I didn't come to the funeral," she said, pouring two more shots.

"I do," he replied. He could sense the conversation falling into a familiar, more comfortable pattern.

"I've done nothing disrespectful."

He resisted the urge to comment about her going to the house to view the body, although she was the one who had told him about it, about sitting with Laura and Barbara Ann before the casket, the body surrounded by candles in the room with the sound of the rain against the windows, still persisting, as though it had not accomplished enough with his death; as if the rainy night had caused it and not his drunken state; and her shivering in his arms the night he died, telling him not to leave, not to go to the saloon. She had not mentioned it again, as if it had not happened. It was an unspoken understanding, a common thing between them, like the forgotten toasts.

The rider was now twenty-five yards away. He was bearded and wore a gray hat. The right sleeve of his coat was pinned, apparently covering an amputation above the elbow. He held the reins in his left hand, which was gloved. He was looking Ashley's way. Instead of following the worn center of the path, he was coming toward the porch. Lily turned to look.

The man was tall. His hair and beard were shaggy, but his clothing appeared to be new and of good quality. The horse was a Tennessee Walker, a good fifteen hands. He pulled the horse to a stop in front of the porch and took off his hat. His blue eyes had a familiar look about them. He held the reins and his hat brim in his gloved hand and was smiling at Lily. She looked at him uncertainly, then with a look of recognition.

"Is that you, Ev?" She stood up suddenly.

His smile broadened into a grin and he swung down from the horse and came to the edge of the porch. Ashley was frozen in his chair. Lily hesitated, looking at the pinned sleeve, her eyes no longer smiling.

"Oh, Ev," she moaned and leaned into him, her arms grasping around his neck. He looked straight at Ashley, his blue eyes weary and cold, although he was still smiling. It was a knowing smile. The once freckled, boyish face was tanned and dry above the beard and there were touches of gray in his sideburns. She clutched him by the shoulders with her strong, small fingers and stood back looking at him on the level, standing on the porch with him on the ground. She started crying. She held on to his shoulders and sobbed, staring into his smiling face.

"Aren't you glad to see me, Lily?" he asked.

She could not speak. It occurred to her that she had never broken down in front of anyone before and that this was uncalled for. She should regain her composure. This was silly. Absolutely silly. But she kept sobbing.

"I thought you were dead," she said. "We all thought you were dead."

Ashley stood and came over to the edge of the porch, his hands at his sides, hesitating. He reached for Lily, then thought better of it.

She was examining the young man's face, the sandy, shaggy hair and beard, then the place where his right arm had been. She dropped her hands from his shoulders.

"Oh, Ev." She sobbed again.

He took her with his left arm and cradled her against him, reaching around her slim waist.

"Here," he said. "You shouldn't go on like that. I'm not dead. I've come home."

Her shoulders shook with her sobbing. Ashley had never seen her like this. When he told her about Wes she had straightened her back and pursed her lips and asked, "Where is he?" with a determination that he had seen in her before. The night after she had viewed the body, she had been shaking, but the tears did not come. He had seen her angry, her pale features flashing a pink contrast to her dark hairline, but he had never seen her break down like this. It was as if all of her steel had melted in one instant. He placed his hand on her shoulder from behind.

"Lily, it's okay," he said softly, and patted her shoulder. She immediately drew aside, away from his hand and out of Ev Hardeman's grasp, turned suddenly and stared at Ash, her wet eyes glaring with the fire he was used to seeing, then, her back to Hardeman, she stepped quickly to the table and poured another shot of whiskey and downed it. She stood by the table with the glass held to her stomach, leaning forward as if she was in pain.

Both men waited for her to speak, or move, or give some sign of what she expected of them, waiting to follow her lead. After a long silence, she straightened up and reached into a pocket in her skirt, drew out a man's white handkerchief and dabbed her eyes, then turned to them with a look of uncertainty, trying to keep her lips from quivering. She forced a smile. "You shouldn't give me such a surprise. You surprised me, Ev. You just surprised me, that's all."

Hardeman looked down at his boots. He stood holding his hat in his hand in the street he had known so well in his youth. Ashley stepped forward.

"Welcome home, Ev," he said. "What Lily said is true. Your folks got word you died in a Yankee prison. That was obviously wrong. Come on up and have a drink with us. I'll get another chair."

He went inside and Lily sat tentatively by the side of the table. Hardeman stood his ground until Ash had returned with another rough straight chair and another glass, then he sat where Ash gestured, crossed his long legs and placed his hat on his knee. Ash poured a shot for him and reached for the water pitcher, but Ev waved him off. He threw down the shot.

"Have another," Ash said, reaching to pour again.

"Don't mind," Ev said. He downed the second shot.

He looked down as he spoke.

"I been up North. Boston." He looked up at Lily. "I didn't feel much like writing. Didn't have much of a hand." She looked again at the pinned sleeve. It had been neatly folded and pressed before the pin had been placed in it and the pin was brass, with a square head.

"You have anybody take care of you up there?" she asked.

He looked down as he spoke.

"I was in a Yankee prison. They cut off my arm to save my life. I was lucky, but I didn't think so for a long time. Then I got to know the doctor who cut my arm off. Turns out he was a good man. He came around to see me and look after me. Took a liking to me." He looked at Ash. "He had lost a son. About my age."

His eyes, to Ash, showed they had suffered pain and heartache, but there was something else, something he did not remember having seen in the boy who had left for the war. There was a serenity that was remarkable in someone of his age. Ash thought about it and remembered when Ev was born. He had been seventeen when he joined the cavalry. That would make him only twenty-four now, though the lines around the eyes and the slight graying at the temples made him look much older. But it was more than that. He looked you in the eye as only a man hardened by adverse experience would. As he told his story, Ash had the feeling that the boy he had known had not come back at all, that this man who was old beyond his years was an imposter, someone who had learned all there was to learn about Everett Hardeman, took that as a starting point, then built on it.

The way he told his story made Ash cringe more than once. How the doctor had befriended him and made him his intern in the camp, then talked the commandant into paroling him to him toward the end of the war when there was no South to go back and fight for anymore and many prisoners were let out to work in northern cities and towns so that their labor would be productive and they could help feed themselves. It was a tale of a foreign land, a land where the people were the enemy, where to live and work with them was to collaborate with them and therefore work against the South. But there was more to it. There was something about the way he told it that made Ash feel uneasy. He realized later that Ev's accent had changed, that he cut off certain words more crisply than Ash remembered. He had a hint of Coddington's New England accent, but mixed with the southern drawl it sounded different. And there was something else about the way he told his story. It was as if it had been rehearsed.

"Now I'm working for Colonel Pierce, from Boston. He and some others have bought out the railroad that stops at Alleyton and are set to bring it all the way to San Antonio. It'll come through here. I'm here to help facilitate. I'll be going on to Austin in a few days, but I'll be back."

He looked down at his lap and then at Lily again. She saw the look in his eyes.

"She's married," she said, putting her hand on his knee. "We all thought you were dead."

His eyes flashed with something that frightened her.

"Who'd she marry?"

She looked at Ash. He hesitated.

"Who is it?" His voice was harsher.

"Gil Adams," Ash said. "His wife died in '65. He needed a mother for his children."

"He's an old man."

"Oh, Ev. Everybody thought you were dead. Ada wore black for weeks," Lily said.

He stood, staring at her. His eyes narrowed as they did when he was a child, when she had first been attracted to him. He was always smiling in a certain way then, in the careless way that young people smile. She had not seen that smile this day and somehow felt that it was gone forever and she would never see it again.

He said goodbye to them politely, but his departure was abrupt. They stood on the edge of the porch and watched him ride west down the muddy street toward the creek. It was as if they had met him for the first time that afternoon, although they had both known him since he was an infant.

SEVENTEEN

THEY CAMPED IN A MEADOW ON THE UPPER GUADALUPE. THE sun was over the hill to the west, and the campfire was crackling and fresh. Billy had put the horse and mule up and was coming back from the edge of the meadow. He kept looking across the river to the southwest to a valley dotted with junipers and post oak. He placed the two saddles he was carrying on the ground a calculated distance from the fire, then laid the blankets out and turned to Gruder, who was hunched down at the fire's edge with his hands extended, palms down. It was cold and clear, the second week of January, and his gnarled hands welcomed the fire.

Billy's uncles had gone with Hays to follow up on a tip about Morgan up near the forks of the Colorado. They left Gruder and Billy at Bradford's after John had extracted a promise from Gruder that they would not leave until Mrs. Bradford said it was all right to do so. Three more weeks had passed before Billy joined Gruder's pleas for her to let them go.

"I know Cap'n Hays wouldn't want me stayin' here when I can ride. And I can ride," Gruder said to her. She was hanging up the wash in the late morning sun behind the smokehouse. She turned and looked at Billy, who had walked up with him, his hat in his hand. He had already buckled on his gun belt, and she noticed.

"Looks like you've already made up your mind you're going."

"They can use us at home," he said.

She turned to Gruder, who stood looking down at her.

"You're not fully healed. You'd have to take care not to bust that wound loose."

"I would, ma'am," he said quietly.

She knew he had been riding for a week, for short periods, and she had been watching him walk and help with light chores. He was still guarding his side and would occasionally wince when he did not know she was looking, but he had regained a lot of strength and she knew he was itching to go.

"If you feel you're up to it, you can go in the morning," she said, as if it was of little concern to her.

They could have gone due east from Junction City and saved at least a day, which would have probably put them home by the end of the week, but they both knew they were going back to the upper Guadalupe. Billy was responsible for the animals and the grub. Gruder had insisted on being the fire tender.

"Don't you want to sit by your saddle?" Billy asked, leaning toward him.

Gruder turned in his direction, as if he only barely heard him.

"Don't you want to sit down?"

He stared at Billy, then asked, "Did you get my saddle bag?"

Billy turned and reached for the worn bag, untied it, withdrew it from the saddle, and handed it to Gruder. Gruder fumbled the rawhide tie open, reached inside and pulled out the pewter flask, which he uncorked and drank from. He stayed in his crouch for a time, holding the flask in his hand, staring at the fire again. He slowly moved one foot and then the other until he was in a sitting position with his legs crossed, his eyes on the fire. He took another long swallow.

"I was in Galveston at the end of the war," he said. "I was workin' the docks. Made foreman."

Billy was still standing. He had not heard this story before.

"At the end, many white men acted like animals," Gruder said. "They broke into the warehouses and took everything. Some even broke into homes and took jewelry and money."

He turned and looked at Billy.

"They put us on a train to Houston to the Labor Bureau, so we could be sent where we were supposed to go. But there was hardly anybody left there. Everybody was afraid because of the looting that was going on. There were soldiers loose in the street. We stood outside the station and watched them and they paid us no mind. We weren't worth anything to them anymore."

He turned back and stared at the blaze.

"You know, some coffee would hit the spot."

He paused and smiled.

"You supposed to fix it, ain't you?"

When the coffee had boiled enough that they could smell it, Billy poured their tin cups full and they sat and drank by the fire.

The wind died down at dusk and the moon came up full in a clear, still sky. They sat without talking, Gruder occasionally throwing a branch on the fire from the pile he had gathered and stacked before dark. That day and the day before had been cold and clear and they had made good time at a leisurely pace.

After they had eaten a portion of the dried venison and biscuits Mrs. Bradford had packed for them, Gruder stretched out with his head against his saddle and his feet to the fire. Billy sat on a rock, looking across the meadow in the moonlight. A breeze came up from the northeast and he sat with his back to the fire, looking and listening. The river was a mile to the southwest, a narrow, shallow stream bordered by cypress and cottonwood trees that were a dark outline against the cedar-spotted hills. The smoke came over his shoulders as a luminescent stream in the moonlight, reaching out toward the river.

He was dozing when he heard it and at first he thought he was dreaming, then he stood and listened, completely awake. It was a slight, high sound, perhaps a coyote, but it was too long for a coyote's yip and too short for a howl and there was only the slight sound and then nothing for what seemed like a minute. Then he heard it again and it sounded closer. He began to walk toward the sound in the bright moonlight.

It came from downwind and it occurred to him that if it was her, she smelled the fire and was attracted to it and maybe his scent was mixed in with it. She had certainly smelled the mixture many times and would be familiar with it, but he did not hear anything else and after he had walked a hundred feet he stopped, thinking that the sound of his footsteps might be interfering with his ability to hear. His breathing was audible as he listened. He thought that he could even hear the sound of the wind in the huisache that spotted the meadow, but not the sound he had heard before. Then, from his right, came a clear series of three coyote yips and he wondered if that was what he had heard after all.

They had not discussed it, this understood thing, and he wondered what Gruder thought. At times he thought he knew that Gruder would be skeptical about the mare's chances of survival. All that he had said was that she had a chance and Billy knew if he asked, that is all Gruder would say and he did not ask—as much out of fear of being discouraged as anything else, though his mind-set was that she was out there and he would find her.

He looked for movement and saw none, then turned and looked back at the fire, where he could see Gruder's form lying before it, then he turned back and raised his hands and cupped them around his mouth and let out a shrill whistle, the same one he had always used to call her. After a short interval, a high cry came from the direction of the river, a sound that was familiar to him and it was not just from his imagination. He whistled again and this time it was a clear response that sounded even more like the mare's whinny.

He again started to walk toward the sound, this time moving faster, staring ahead, and he thought he could make out a dark shape ahead. He stopped and whistled again and the shape began to move perceptively and grow larger until he could make out her body, loping toward him in the moonlight.

"Julie!" he cried out, and she kept coming until he could see her, dark and smooth, moving toward him rapidly. She came to within a few paces of him and stopped, and his eyes were full of tears as he stepped forward and reached out his hand for her to feel, thinking for a moment that it was all a dream and she would disappear; then her soft, damp muzzle was touching his hand and he was reaching and petting her neck and she snorted as she often had when he touched her and he put his head against hers and stood there holding her, crying in the moonlight.

EIGHTEEN

T
HE GIN AND MILL HAD BEEN CLEANED OUT AND REPAIRED.
Lily Poe stood under the connecting shaft that ran from the main
building to the superstructure over the millrace, watching the rise of the
floodgate gradually increase the flow through the race and into the river
below. It was stopped at a point of best efficiency, according to Barger,
the man she had hired to engineer the repair and restoration of the mill.
The wheel, which lay horizontally, barely beneath the surface of the water
rushing by, began to turn, first slowly, then more rapidly as the force of
the river caught it fully. The vertical shaft coming up from the center of
the wheel turned the gears in the gearbox in the superstructure and the
entire series of gears, belts, and shafts came to life for the first time in
four years.

She turned and studied the entire length of the works, looking for
anything that seemed out of balance. Everything was smooth and quiet.
Barger came up behind her, said "Miss" in his deep voice, and momentarily startled her. She turned to him quickly and backed up a step.

"'Scuse, Miss," he said. "I didn't mean to scare you."

He was a tall, slim man with a soft face and a black moustache that
drooped almost to his chin. He had been too polite, too quick to apologize for the slightest error.

"Let's look inside," she said.

They walked through the portal past the open double steel doors into
the mill, into a large room with a concrete floor, where the main shaft inter-
acted with a series of gears and belts that drove the gin, the sawmill, and the

gristmill. The workers were standing around watching the movement, their tired eyes wide. After the weeks of cleaning and repairing, it seemed so ethereal—the structure and machinery at work in the great room. The quiet of the place, through which you would hear the occasional clank or thud of a dropped board or piece of steel, was now punctuated by a series of small sounds. The belts turning against pulleys and blocks. The gears grinding. A chorus.

She had expected Gruder weeks ago, but had found a young man who could work the negroes for her, a large, boisterous, light-skinned man who seemed to take over as leader without any authority but his ability to take over, who had begun directing the men in carrying out trash and sweeping without any word from her, while she was taking a delivery and only out of the area for a minute. When she asked his name, he was quick to give his first and last, "Lucius Jackson," instead of only the first name, the name that would have been used by limitation only a few years before, or at least the only name that was truly his then and not his master's. By the time Barger walked up to the scale house one afternoon claiming to be an engineer, Jackson had the entire grounds clean and was ready for direction about repairs that went beyond patching broken screens and mending things that were in obvious need. Unknown to her at the time, he had later devised a brace for a shaft that Barger took credit for and he had proved to be as innovative as he was energetic. He stood in the middle of the room in the forefront of the other men as she and Barger walked in. She stopped in front of him.

"Looks like we're ready to go," she said.

"Yes'm," Jackson replied, beaming.

"You go and tell Captain Parker's man Jim we're ready, Jackson. He can start unloading his warehouse on us."

Parker and a few others had stored up several crops of cotton, waiting for the day the gin would be repaired and reopened. There would be a winter crop for the first time. Farmers' and sharecroppers' families alike would profit from it. Lily Poe knew a buyer from Galveston that said he would take all the cotton she could gin. Although it would be a small crop compared to normal, it would get her started and stand her in good stead with the farmers for the coming year.

"I'll do it right away, Miz Lily."

"Wait," she said. He turned to her.

"Can you read and write?"

He looked down at his feet, not answering.

"If you can read and write and do arithmetic, it would be useful."

There was something about this young man that caused her to say this before she had thought it through. Normally she would have been more reticent.

"I can," he said proudly. "But that wasn't always a good thing."

He looked her in the eye, without wavering or looking away.

NINETEEN

THE SHERMANS HAD JUST SAT DOWN TO DINNER, THE NOONDAY meal. The door to the cabin was open and Ezra Sherman sat with his back to it, letting the cool breeze come across his shoulders. His stepson Pete sat opposite him and was looking out the door and said, "Papa" before Ezra could see the shadows from the doorway. The men were inside immediately, before Ezra could reach for his rifle over the doorway, six of them filling the cabin with their smell. Martha Sherman sat next to her husband. Their four children, including Pete, sat around the table.

Of the six, a young muscular man with long black shoulder-length hair was obviously the leader. A shorter man wearing a bright piece of cloth around his head seemed to be second in command. The other four split behind these two as they surrounded the table. The one wearing the head cloth took Ezra's rifle from over the doorway. The young leader held a Colt pistol in his hand.

"God's Heaven!" Ezra Sherman said, gripping the table edge hard with both hands.

"Don't show nothin'," Martha said. "Don't scare." She stared across the table at the young man with the Colt. He wore a blue jacket and a red bandana around his neck. Although he looked Indian, there was something about his face that looked out of place to her. He was smiling.

"That's right," he drawled. "You don't want the goddamn dumb Indians to think you're scared. They might kill somebody." His voice was like a white man's. The sound gave her a chill. Her youngest, a two-year-old boy, began to cry. She squeezed his arm until he stopped.

The young man with the pistol said something she did not under-stand to the man with the headscarf, who stood behind her. She then felt the man touching her red hair from behind, fingering the bun she had twisted it into before cooking dinner. She shied away from his hand, leaning toward her husband, who rose slightly from his seat. The one with the pistol extended it toward Ezra Sherman's forehead and fired. Ezra's skull was blown apart. His body was thrown backward and fell into the doorway. The move was so sudden and the force and noise of the shot so intense that the other men in the room jumped back from around the table. Martha was frozen, her arm around her two-year-old.

Ezra's brains were scattered in the blood that lay on the floor and across the threshold and his face was a swath of dark red that one would not have recognized as a face at all, but perhaps some kind of red cabbage-like plant. The leader still held the pistol where he had fired it and was staring at the barrel, which was red with Ezra's blood, as were the knuckles of his hand. He stared, childlike, as if taking in a new experience for all it was worth. The smile had not faded. He looked back at Martha.

"Let my children go," she said, then, in a voice from her depths, "Please." She had been on the frontier since she was a girl, having come from Mississippi with her brother and his family. Unlike her husband, an easterner who knew little of Texas, she knew the Comanche ways. "Or take them with you," she said, knowing that it was rare that a two-year-old child was taken along. She had heard of Comanches skewering white babies on their lances and tossing dead infants around in a spirited game of catch-ball, laughing happily all the while at the good medicine over their enemies they were making.

The smile disappeared.

"You will all go," he said.

She stood up slowly, holding her breath in. Pete stood up more quickly, which caused the brave nearest him to flinch.

"Come, children," she said, her voice quavering, and lifted the two-year-old into her arms. Pete was ten and his sister Nancy was eight. Harvey was six and feeble-minded. Nancy stood up and took Harvey by the elbow and they all rose.

They had to go past Ezra's body to get out the door.

"Take my hand, Harvey," Martha said. "Just look ahead, children." She turned to avoid the overturned chair that lay beside what remained of Ezra and was thinking that she had to find a way to get the children out of there. Hand in hand, the children followed her past their father's body. It was impossible to keep from stepping in his blood and Harvey, barefoot, looked curiously at his feet as he was pulled through the doorway. When she and the children were outside, with only the leader and the man with the headband outside the cabin, she yelled, "RUN" and began running down the hill toward the creek. Carrying Frankie, the two-year-old, slowed her, and the young leader caught her by the hair after she had taken only a few steps. She yelled "RUN" again and "DON'T STOP."

It was misting rain and his hold on her hair caused her to lose her balance and fall back into the wet dirt, holding the little boy to her chest with both arms. The other children kept running without looking back. The other four men were out of the cabin now and one of them had a lance. He thrust it at her as she went down. The blade went between her ribs.

The man with the headband grabbed her baby and jerked him out of her grasp as she hit the ground. He flung the child into the air and he landed with a thud in the wet dirt. The one with the lance pierced the child's back and ran him through with the steel blade, then lifted him on the blade into the air and let out a war whoop, before flinging him away into the brush at the edge of the yard.

The young leader let go of her hair as another man grabbed her wrists and pulled them up above her head. Two others were tearing at her skirt and spreading her legs and she was hoping that they all were here and that none of them were chasing the children. They tore her skirt and undergarments off. The young leader was the first to rape her. She tried to concentrate on the pain in her side instead of the pain of what was happening, but she was unable to and she heard herself scream, which seemed to excite him more and when he was finished, after a lifetime, the one with the headband was next.

After they had all taken a turn, they left her lying on her back, but tied her wrists to a tree trunk. They then ransacked the cabin and the smokehouse. They got into the molasses barrel and the flour, smearing themselves with whiteness. One had taken her feather pillow and cut it open and was spreading the feathers in the yard, which floated in the mist like snowflakes. She wondered why she was still conscious, why she couldn't faint.

They had found Ezra's whiskey jug and were passing it around, laughing at each other with their whiteness and feathers. Then the leader said something in a gruff manner and they took sacks they had filled and placed them on their horses and mounted up, except for the leader, who walked over and looked down at her. He bent down and grabbed her hair, pulling her up into a sitting position. He unsheathed his knife and started cutting around her hairline, the sharp knife cutting into the flesh covering her skull, turning her head by the handful of hair he held, until he had cut all around, then he jerked violently, but was unable to get her scalp off. The man with the headband, who was stockier and stronger, came over and put his foot on her shoulder and grabbed her hair away from the young leader. He grunted as he ripped her scalp from her skull.

Another one stabbed her again with a lance as he walked by, this one being a deeper thrust than the first, and she felt overcome by pain that became generalized and unbearable before she passed out. They then rode their ponies over her and she regained consciousness enough to hear them yelling and the sound of the horses' hooves, though none touched her. When Pete and the other children came out of hiding after the men were gone, they could see the imprint of the hooves all around her.

She lived for four days, tended by neighbor women, and was conscious enough to describe her ordeal in detail. Hays and the other men arrived three days after she died. It was clear from the descriptions of the men that it was Morgan and the man who had been with him, as well as four more they had picked up somewhere along the way. The boy, Pete, was particularly descriptive, even down to the fact that the man with the headband was wearing a bandage around his middle under his open coat.

The Sherman place was north of the San Saba, in Palo Pinto County, and it had taken them two days to get there after they got word of the massacre. The locals were for getting up a posse and joining them in their search, but Hays did not like the look of the men who were volunteering. They looked and acted like farmers, did not sit their horses well, and he doubted their ability to shoot from the saddle. Hays asked them to show him the Sherman cabin, then said he and his men would go their way and they could go theirs, thus increasing the possibility of running across those whom they were seeking, although he knew that the farmers would have to be extremely lucky to find them, as, for that matter, would he.

TWENTY

S HE WAS GATHERING FIREWOOD LATE IN THE DAY. THE SUN WAS already over the ridge beyond the river's high banks. The boy who had followed her was proud of his tracking and hunting skills. He was sure she had not seen him, but she turned and said his name quietly and respectfully, as if she had known he was there all along. He came out of the brush, his head down.

"You want to ask me something," she said, tying a bundle of wood with a rawhide thong.

"Abuela," he said, not noticing her wince at the use of the Spanish word. She did not like the tendency of the young to use Spanish. "I want to ask you about the white man, Capitan Yack."

She finished the knot in the rawhide and stopped and looked at him.

"You carry this bundle," she said.

He picked up the bundle of wood she indicated and she threw the one she had tied over her shoulder, holding it by the end of the rawhide. She then started downstream along the water's edge. He followed behind her until they reached a place where a rock cliff overhung a large boulder in the middle of the trail, and she sat down, dropping the bundle of wood beside it. He knew the place because his father had told him about it. It was an ancient council place. High up inside the concave rock overhang one could see crude, ancient drawings. He sat before her, crossing his legs. She waited for him to speak.

"I have heard tell that Capitan Yack is a devil," he said. "I want to know about him. They say he was one of the men that came to the camp."

"I will not talk to you in Spanish," she said in their native tongue. "But I will tell you more than about that man. It is about our people more than about him."

"Forgive me, grandmother," he said in Comanche. "I will be blessed by your words."

She stared into his eyes and they did not waver.

"Then I will tell you," she said. "Long ago, the Spaniards came and tried to make slaves out of other people, but our ancestors took some of their horses and left the great mountains, because they could ride better than anyone. The people were everywhere and the Spanish could not keep up with them. They were too brave and spirited and the Great Spirit was with them. Then some of the women mated with the Spaniards and there were some mixed people."

"The Mexicans?"

Her brow furrowed slightly.

"It is more complicated, but there were Mexicans among them. They were the brown people. Then the white men came to Texas. They took the land for their own, saying they owned it and the people had no right to hunt on it, so the people fought and defended their rights. The Mexicans changed their minds about the white men and decided they wanted them to leave Texas, but they lost one battle and gave up. So the white men became the Texans and they continued to fight and kill the people.

"The Mexicans made gifts to the chiefs so that they would kill the Texans and drive them away, but the Texans killed many warriors as well as women and children in a great battle on Plum Creek and the people decided to talk to the white men. Many chiefs were invited to San Antonio to talk and went under a flag of truce, according to the white man's rules, but once they were inside a large house, the white men said they could not leave and they had to fight to escape. Many of them died after the treachery of the white men. After that, it was kill or be killed."

She paused. He was leaning forward, intently listening.

"Diablo Yack was their best killer. He killed many warriors. Then he disappeared. Now he is back, because the curse is not over."

"The curse?"

"There is a curse on the people for mixing blood with the Spanish and later with the white men. That is why the white men killed the buffalo and why they will not stop until all of the People are dead."

"Why was Diablo Yack here in this place?" he asked.

"Because of the one they call Leo," she said. "He is part of the curse on the people because his blood is all mixed up and he does not know who he is."

"Then who is he, grandmother?"

"Some say he is a demon, sent by the evil one to fulfill the curse and cause an end to the last of the People. Others say he is a savior, who was sent to do away with the white man once and for all."

The boy was drawing in the dirt with a stick, looking down at it.

"What do you think?" he asked.

She stared at him without speaking until he looked up at her.

"I think they are both bad men and they will kill many more before they are through," she said. "And the people will die off because there will be nothing left to eat and no way to get any food. The white men will see to that."

She stared at him for a long time, her wrinkled face splotched in the late afternoon light coming through the tree branches. When she was a girl she believed that a savior of the people would come and that he would be a boy much like this one, who would grow strong in body and spirit, who would become a great leader and the white men would fall before him, but no real leaders came. There were many chiefs, but they had no answer for the white men. Other enemies had stayed away from the People because they were afraid of them. If they encountered the People and tried to interfere with their rights they were tortured and killed and their children made captives, which caused them to respect the People, but the white men came after them, just like Diablo Yack, without letting up.

Her name was Setting Moon, because she was born as the full moon was setting, but she now believed that her name meant that she was to see the end of her people. The People had always been safe wintering in this valley of the San Saba, near the place the white men called Pegleg. The whites had left them alone. Now Diablo Yack had been here and was after the one with mixed blood and the People were as diluted as the blood that ran through his veins. Each band was growing smaller and had to range farther to find food. She could foresee a time when the few survivors would be rounded up like the white men's cattle and penned up. Her extended family, the Penateka, or Honey Eaters, were down to a small number already. They had split up to survive and the different groups had not kept up with each other. In a sense, they had already ceased to exist as a people.

The boy looked up at her with the wonder of youth in his face. If she had still believed that a savior would come, she might have believed that he could be the one, but she was no longer a girl and it was hard to imagine such a thing in wintertime.

TWENTY-ONE

HAYS AND THE BAKER BROTHERS HAD BEEN OVER A GREAT DEAL of territory and on January 30, Hays told them it was time to break off the search for Morgan and get the girl to her relatives in San Antonio. After missing him by only a few days in Palo Pinto County, they had followed up several questionable leads to no avail. Hays decided that the trail was too cold and they would have to wait for more word. It was likely they would hear about Morgan again. There were fewer Comanche raids now, because there were fewer Comanches, and the odds were that the next raid they heard about would involve Morgan.

Linda Bradford hated to see the girl go when they came for her and offered to let her stay and she would raise her as one of her own, but Hays said she was better off with family. They were his wife's kin and although he knew little about them, he understood that there was a couple in San Antonio who had lost an infant girl many years ago and would welcome her at their home, so after a half a day and a night, they put the girl astride a paint pony they purchased from a local man and headed south. Adam Bradford told them about a trail that went due south from London Lewis's place that would save some time. The girl, Martha, rode like a boy, wearing pants Linda Bradford had provided, and did not slow them up, though she seldom spoke and sometimes had to be asked more than once before she would respond to questions.

They started early and rode until near dark each day and at dusk on the third day arrived at Leon Springs, where they camped for the night. Hays had only told the girl that he was taking her back to her family. He had furnished no details and she had not asked. Wonsley told her they would be in San Antonio the next morning, and she would be going to her new home. She was sitting cross-legged on a rock near the fire.

"Do you know your kinfolks in San Antone?" he asked.

"No," she replied.

"Cap'n Hays says it's your aunt and uncle Johnston."

The girl continued to stare into the fire. Wonsley stood near her, his hands extended out for warmth.

"It's your mama's sister. You never met her?"

"Wonsley," said John Baker, sitting opposite the girl, in a voice that meant for him to quiet himself.

"Your aunt Kathy," Wonsley continued. "You don't know her?"

"No," the girl replied, as matter-of-fact as the first time she said it.

John stood up, looking coldly at Wonsley.

"All right," Wonsley said, turning his back to the fire, away from John, but still looking in Martha's direction. It was awhile before she spoke.

"I ain't never met her," she said, her voice barely audible.

"Just wondered," Wonsley said, looking away from her.

It was a short ride to San Antonio, and they were on the outskirts by midmorning. When they reached the Johnston house on Soledad Street, Hays dismounted and went to the front door while the rest of them sat their horses. He had sent word the night before, and they were expected. The Mexican maid opened the front door and admitted him. He was met in the parlor by his sister-in-law, Katherine Johnston, and two other ladies, old friends of the Calvert family, Mrs. Elliot and Mrs. Lockman. Ellen Elliot had introduced him to Susan Calvert in 1843. After their marriage, he and Susan had stayed with Mrs. Elliot from time to time, and Susan stayed with her while Hays was with the Rangers in Mexico during the Mexican War.

The ladies were standing when he entered. They were silent at first, looking him over. His beard and hair had grown since he had left California and were peppered with gray. Katherine Johnston stepped up to him and extended her hand.

"Colonel Hays. It's been a long time."

"Yes, Kathy. It has."

"Is she with you?"

"She is. She's outside."

She followed him out the front door to the gate in the yard fence where the Bakers and Martha were still astride their horses. She looked from Martha to Wonsley and stopped and waited, until Hays walked up to the girl's horse and turned back to her.

"This is Martha Roberts," he said. "Your niece."

The girl's red hair was done up under the leather cap she was wearing. The dust that covered her made her face shine a light brown in the morning sun. The cotton pants and shirt she had been wearing for three days were too large for her. She looked like a boy. John and Wonsley dismounted, but she stayed in the saddle, looking first at the grey-haired woman in the blue dress who came up to her and then toward the house where the other two women were standing by the doorway. Katherine was looking her up and down. The girl's face and hands were dirty. She slumped in the saddle, looking at her aunt without expression, as if in a daze. The woman hesitated, then reached out to her. The girl shied away.

"Martha. I'm your aunt Katherine," she said.

Hays stepped in front of Katherine and reached for Martha's waist. She let him lift her out of the saddle and when she was standing on the ground, she took her cap off. Katherine took a step back, her nose crinkling. The girl's skin, under the layer of dust, was freckled, and Katherine could see her red hair, her mother's hair, under the dust. Her light blue eyes also reminded her of her dead sister, whom she had not seen in years, since Katherine and her husband moved from Seguin. Mr. Johnston had not approved of Mattie's husband, Seth Roberts. He had borrowed money that he had not paid back, which lowered him in Johnston's eyes. When news of their deaths reached the Johnstons, it was confirmation that no good could have come from Mattie's marriage to Seth, if they had actually been married. The family had not been invited to a ceremony; one day Roberts simply announced that they were married. Johnston claimed that they were common-law wed, if that, and then only because Mattie was pregnant with Martha at the time. A common-law marriage was not a marriage in the eyes of God, and Martha was probably a bastard child.

When the messenger from Hays came the night before, Johnston was in an uproar over the girl. She was ruined by the Comanches, as far as he was concerned, and had no business being in their home. Katherine had to promise to find another place for her to reside before Johnston would even agree to let her stay with them temporarily. Now, looking at the girl, it seemed that he was right. Some women had lost their minds as a result of assaults by Indians and the girl, standing mute before her, seemed to be addled. She did not know what to say to her.

"She's family," Hays said to the girl. "Your mother's sister."

Martha began to cry silently, tears making streaks down her dusty cheeks.

"Oh you poor dear," Katherine said, putting her arm around the girl's shoulders. "You come in the house with me. I'll do for you."

She turned to Hays.

"Will you and your men come in, too, Colonel?"

"No, Kathy. We'll be at the Menger."

"We'll have Epifania fix a warm bath for you, Martha," Katherine said.

The men stood their ground as Katherine led Martha slowly through the gate. Mrs. Elliot and Mrs. Lockman stood aside as they entered the doorway, then Mrs. Elliot came to the gate.

"Jack Hays, it's been a long time. How is Susan?"

"She was well when I left Oakland, Mrs. Elliot," he replied. "Here are John and Wonsley Baker, sons of Eli Baker."

"Oh, I certainly remember Elder Baker and Mrs. Baker. How is your mother?"

"She's well, Mrs. Elliot," John said.

"I can see you are Baker boys," she said, smiling broadly. She turned to Hays. "I don't know how long Katherine can keep the girl, Jack. Mr. Johnston is a problem, I'm afraid."

"How so, ma'am?"

Her face clouded over.

"You know what some men are like after women have been with Indians," she said.

Hays stared at her.

"She could stay with me, Jack. I could use some help around the house."

"I will call on you this afternoon, Mrs. Elliot. I appreciate your offer."

"After siesta, then?" Mrs. Elliot asked.

"Yes, ma'am. I'll see you then."

They mounted and rode down Soledad Street to the Main Plaza, then turned onto Commerce Street and headed east. Hays had been back to the city only briefly since he had left for California twenty years before, passing through on his way to Seguin after hearing of his sister-in-law's death and the abduction of her daughter, and he had come in at night and left at sunrise the next day. Now he saw new buildings and houses in place of others that had been there before, and some where only vacant land had been. There were still street vendors and pedestrians, but the street was much busier. They had to navigate around buggies and wagons. The burro carts that had been there before, as Mexican as Saltillo, were not to be seen.

At the bridge, they stopped to look down at a number of women and girls washing clothes in the river. Their brown skin, black hair, and colorful skirts were juxtaposed against the clear stream in the morning sunlight. There was a breeze from the south and it was warming up.

In front of the Menger, a black man and a Mexican came to hold their horses as they stepped down. John and Wonsley followed Hays through the doorway and into the lobby. Wonsley had not been in the hotel, and John had not been there since the war. Hays had stayed there for the first time on his way through to Seguin.

Wonsley stood and turned, looking at the black iron columns and the iron-bannistered balcony surrounding the lobby. His cap still on, he slowly turned around in place. He had never seen a room like this before. The dark mahogany furniture with red cloth, the deepest red he had seen. The marble vases with palms. The tall grandfather clock that showed the date as well as the time.

The desk clerk recognized Hays and said, "Welcome back, Colonel. How many rooms would you like?"

"Three, please."

The men came in with their saddlebags and the desk clerk did not require their signatures on the register.

TWENTY-TWO

BILLY AND GRUDER HAD BEEN HOME FOR ELEVEN DAYS WHEN word first came of the Baker brothers. Billy was cleaning leather for his grandfather when the boy from the telegraph office rode up. He heard the horse approach and came around the side of the saddle shed to look. The boy, Walter Gentry, rang the bell on the yard gate and before long his grandfather Baker came out onto the front porch and beckoned the boy to come to him. Walter handed him the telegram, and Eli Baker thanked him and tipped him a nickel. He put on his bifocals and stood reading it over, then looked Billy's way.

"They're in San Antone," he said. "They're safe."

"Did they catch up with Morgan?"

"Don't know, Billy. John says they'll be home tomorrow."

"Is the girl with them?"

"It doesn't say, Billy," he replied, looking over the top of his spectacles at him.

His grandfather went back into the house and Billy walked back to the shed. It had warmed up and it was a clear, sunny day, not a day to be inside cleaning saddles and bridles. He had already planned to check on Gruder when he finished and decided that he had done enough for one day. He put the jar of saddle soap and rags away, put on his hat and latched the door behind him.

He mounted Julie with his left hand on the horn of the saddle, keeping his right arm down. He still felt a twinge when he raised his arm and had come to be protective of it. The river was at its normal level and it was easy to ford. He turned on the trail that led upstream to Gruder's cabin. It would soon be time for plowing, and the field hands were working in the field that lay beside the trail. It would be one of the first to be plowed. His mother had told him that she would expect him to be working. She could no longer afford to hire full help, and the number of sharecroppers had dwindled. He would be starting on the McCulloch land he was passing, although he was not sure his shoulder was ready for it.

Gruder's cabin was in a spot surrounded by live oaks. Billy's father had given Gruder his choice of a place to build, and he had chosen this spot, which was on a rise near the river. It was a one-room log cabin with a porch across the front. Gruder was not there when he rode up, but he found him down at the riverbank, fishing with a long cane pole.

He came up behind him as quietly as he could, but he knew Gruder would hear him and know it was him approaching. He always did. This time was no different.

"Hello, Billy," he said, slightly turning his head. "You're just in time for some fish for lunch." He reached and pulled up a stringer with three good-size catfish on it. "I was thinking you might come to see me."

This was not the first time Billy had eaten with Gruder at his house. When he had told his cousin Sally about eating at Gruder's house, she wrinkled her nose and asked, "What did you eat?" as if it was hard to imagine anything decent being served at the house of a black family. Gruder's wife died in childbirth before Billy was born, and Gruder had implied that Billy was the replacement for his lost son, who was stillborn. Both mother and son were buried in a piece of high ground near the cabin. As he followed Gruder up the hill past the graves, Billy told him about the telegram and wondered aloud about the girl and whether Hays would leave her in San Antonio.

"She's got family there," Gruder said.

"Don't she have family in Seguin?" Billy asked.

"Hardly," Gruder replied. "The only Calvert left in Guadalupe County is James, and he's a widower. Cap'n's likely to leave her in San Antone."

Billy built the fire while Gruder cleaned the fish, which were soaked in buttermilk and rolled in cornmeal, then fried in lard, along with some corn pone. The fish was served with pickled onions and cucumbers, the way Gruder always served fried catfish. The smell and taste were unlike anything else Billy had ever experienced. There would be times when he would look back on these meals with Gruder as being from an unrecoverable world. The meals in his family were not always elaborate, and during the war there were scarcities, but he understood the advantages of relative wealth that the Bakers and McCullochs enjoyed, along with many other landowning—former slaveholding—families. He had tasted the everyday meals that poverty provided. He had learned the concept of not owning anything, except maybe the clothes on your back, if you were lucky enough to have a kind master. He had eaten dishes that many white people had never tasted, made from hoarded staples and often with meat the white man did not want. Possum stew. Jackrabbit stew. But there was no way that anything on a plantation-house table could exceed the perfection of Gruder's fried catfish filets. He added unknown ingredients to the cornmeal that he took from jars in pinches. Billy never discovered what they were. Gruder, when asked about them, would only say, "Oh, some African stuff," with a slight smile. One day Billy said, "I don't think that's African stuff. You been telling me that since I was a little boy, but I never heard anybody else talk about African stuff. It's just some spice, like from our kitchen." Gruder would just maintain his thin smile and continue to prepare the cornmeal.

The filets were always cooked to just the right texture, the cornmeal coating golden around the steaming white flesh. When there were fresh tomatoes, they would be on the table, although not sliced. There were no servants at Gruder's house and no one to slice the tomatoes for you. If you wanted them, you sliced them yourself. It was like camping on the trail. Each person did something to help out, but nobody waited on anybody else.

There were no tomatoes on this day, but Gruder always had some green peppers he kept in the cabin in a tow sack, and with the corn pone, cucumbers, and onions, they made a meal. When they finished, Billy helped clean up, then Gruder lit his pipe, and they sat at the rough table under the oak tree next to the cabin. After awhile, Gruder cleared his throat.

"Lily found her an engineer and a foreman while we were gone," he said. He called her "Miss Lily" to her face.

"She got the gin started up," Billy said.

"Yeah, and they've ginned all the cotton in the warehouses."

"I thought she'd asked you to be foreman."

"She did. She sent word it was still open, whenever I felt like it, but there's no ginnin' work right now, anyway."

Gruder's chickens were grazing nearby. Their sounds were peaceful and comforting.

"Do you think they got him?" Billy asked.

Gruder puffed on his pipe and squinted at him.

"I guess we'll find out," he said.

John and Wonsley rode up at dusk. Their long hair and unkempt beards were a surprise to their mother, who hugged them and showed them inside to the dinner table. Eli Baker did not ask questions, but sat and listened to their story of the pursuit of Morgan and the rescue of the girl, and of leaving her with Mrs. Elliot. When they were finishing slices of apple pie and the maid, Effie, was clearing the plates off the table, Leonie asked about Hays.

"He's all right," John said.

"He's doing good," Wonsley added. "He let me do most of the tracking."

Eli gave John a look.

"That's quite a compliment, son," he said. "He's the best there is."

"Or used to be," Wonsley said.

"I wouldn't be talking that way," Eli said. "He was letting you do it, but that doesn't mean you or anyone else could out-track him."

"He was wearing glasses, Pa," Wonsley said.

Eli glared at him. John looked up from his plate.

"I didn't see any glasses," he said.

"He was readin' a map. Down by the river one day. I saw him. He said he just used 'em for readin', but he was wearin' 'em."

They were silent for awhile, then Leonie spoke.

"Wonsley, you are not to tell anybody that," she said. "It would not do to tell anybody that."

"I won't, Ma," he said. "You're the only folks I've told."

"I need to get on home," John said, staring at Wonsley. "Walk out with me, Brother." He rose and hugged his mother again, shook hands with his father, and he and Wonsley went outside to John's horse, which was tied to the hitching post at the yard fence.

"You didn't tell me about the glasses," he said. "So I take it that you won't tell anybody else."

"I won't," Wonsley said. "I promise."

"You're gonna want to tell the story of the chase and getting the girl. Just make sure you don't forget. Hays has enemies."

"I won't," Wonsley said. "I sure won't forget."

TWENTY-THREE

H AYS HAD BEEN AT THE MENGER FOR ONLY A NIGHT AND A DAY and word was out that he was in town. He had settled Martha with Mrs. Elliot, but was not quite ready to leave. There were many sources of information in San Antonio and he had no leads on Morgan's whereabouts, so it made sense to stay for a while. He had wired his wife that he was all right and would be staying at the Menger for a few more days. He was eating breakfast in the dining room when a short man with graying sideburns came up to his table.

"Colonel Hays, I'm George Sweet, editor of the *Herald*. Welcome back to San Antonio."

"I've heard of you, Colonel Sweet. Won't you join me?"

"Thank you, Colonel. I have breakfasted already, but I'll have some coffee."

Sweet sat down at the table. Hays continued with his bacon and eggs.

"I've heard you're looking for someone, Colonel," Sweet said. "I may be of some assistance."

The waiter offered Sweet coffee from a pewter pitcher. Sweet turned the cup over and the waiter poured it full. "Just the coffee," Sweet said, then repeated, "I've heard you're looking for someone."

Hays looked up from his plate.

"Have you heard who I'm looking for?" he asked.

"I've heard you're looking for the renegade that killed your sister and brother."

Hays finished his plate and dabbed his lips with his napkin.

"What information do you have, Colonel Sweet?"

Sweet cleared his throat.

"The word is that there is an actress in this city that he is fond of. She is quite a looker. He has been here to see her and he's bound to be back."

"Where would I find her?" Hays asked.

"She works the Cosmopolitan. Goes by the name of Mary Olive. . . . Do you plan on staying in San Antonio for long, Colonel?"

"I don't plan on it," Hays replied.

"That's a shame, Colonel. You have many admirers in this city; many folks who are grateful for your service."

"You served under Ben McCulloch, didn't you?" Hays asked.

"I had that honor, yes sir. I was with him in Arkansas."

"He was a good man."

"He was, indeed. I saw Henry McCulloch the other day. He lives in Seguin."

"Thank you for the information, Colonel," Hays said. He signed the tab and stood, his hat in hand.

"Colonel," Sweet said. "I would really appreciate an account of your recent adventures. For the paper."

Hays stared at him.

"It is a private matter, Mr. Sweet. It should stay that way."

"Our readers would really like to know, Colonel. It's news, you know. The public has a right to know, after all."

"It's a private matter," Hays said.

He turned and left Sweet. Once out the front door, he turned left and walked to Commerce Street. The shops were just opening. Young men were sweeping the sidewalks. There were stone buildings where wooden huts had been. In 1842, when he and the other men pulled out for Mexico, the street had been muddy and the day cool. There were cockfights on Sundays with the padres in those days, and as the men rode by on the far side of Market Square, they turned in their saddles as they passed. The people gathered around the fight formed a dense circle, many of them wearing red bandanas around their necks that stood out among the white shirts and pants. Some of them were jumping up to get a better view. There was to be a fandango later that night, where the young people would dance and drink wine. Past the Square, interspersed with the shops, *jacalas* appeared—most of them open stalls where the vendors packed up their wares at the end of every day, loaded them onto carts, and took them home west of San Pedro creek. Bankers and store owners, white men who lived by the river, took nothing home with them that required a cart. And some did not go straight home.

They had moved out with Hays and the Rangers in the lead, past the padres and the young women standing apart from the cockfights, their young admirers standing by them, trying to look and sound sophisticated. It had been a gray October Sunday in 1842.

At Main Plaza, he turned onto Soledad and eventually came to Mrs. Elliot's front gate. She came out when called, and Martha came to the door, looking his way. Her face was drawn. There were hollows around her eyes that were not apparent before.

At Mrs. Elliot's suggestion, he approved of her going to school at Ursuline Academy, where the sisters would welcome and care for her. He said he had already made arrangements with his San Antonio bank for her support. Mrs. Elliot was to send him a wire if more money was needed, and he would wire it to her bank. He would be joining his brother, Harry, in New Orleans in a few days, but would be back soon.

After they had talked, Mrs. Elliot gestured for Martha and she slowly approached them. Mrs. Elliot talked to her about the sisters at the academy as if she were a grown woman, and Martha responded with a nod. Hays put his arm around her shoulder as he took his leave. She stood stiffly beside him.

He walked back to Main Plaza and turned west at the corner where the Cosmopolitan bar stood, passed the Military Plaza and the Governor's house, and eventually came to Market Plaza where the cockfights had been held. Vendors were unloading their carts and setting up their stands. He wandered past them, pausing occasionally for someone who looked familiar, then passing on after looking more closely and realizing his mistake. It had been over twenty-five years. None of the people, not even the young ones, were there anymore.

He and his men had led the army to Laredo and then across the river, doing scout duty for Somerville's main force. They had been the last to abandon the three hundred at Mier, but he obeyed his orders and came home with his men, except for Walker and Wallace, who had gone on with Fisher and the others to capture and imprisonment. It was strange that in spite of everything that had happened, he had not been killed or captured. Perhaps it was because he had never expected it, never admitted the possibility that it could happen. Or maybe it was just luck. Dumb luck.

He walked back to Main Plaza and noticed that the front door to the Cosmopolitan was open. The interior was dark and smelled of stale beer. A black man sweeping the floor in front of the bar turned and looked at him as he entered.

"Bar's not open yet, sir," he said.

Hays walked up to him.

"Whose place is this?" he asked.

"Mr. Jack Harris just bought it," the man said.

"You work here long?"

"Five years, Cap'n."

Hays looked at him more closely.

"Do you know me?" he asked.

The man stared into his eyes in the dim light.

"I don't think so, Cap'n," he said.

"What time does the bar open?"

"Bar opens at noon, boss, but the girls get here about nine in the evening."

"When does Mr. Harris show up?"

"Oh about nine, usually. The first show is about nine."

"Thanks," Hays said and turned and walked out.

That evening Hays, in a new suit of clothes, was standing at the bar at nine when Jack Harris entered. Harris wore a black suit with a vest, but no tie, his white shirt buttoned at the neck. He was a large man with black hair and long sideburns. He walked up to the end of the bar and greeted the bartender, who nodded toward Hays and said something. Harris stepped around the end of the bar and walked over.

"I'm Jack Harris," he said. "Sam said you were asking for me."

"You are the owner?" Hays asked.

"I run this place," Harris answered.

"I was looking for a girl who might work here," Hays said. "Name of Mary Olive."

"And who might be asking, sir?"

"My name is Hays," he said.

Harris hesitated.

"Not Jack Hays," he said.

"I'm afraid so," said Hays.

Harris's face lit up.

"I have heard a lot about you, Colonel. I guess everyone in San Antonio has heard of Jack Hays."

"Do you know this girl?" Hays asked.

"Why are you looking for her?"

"I understand she may be an acquaintance of a man I am looking for."

After studying Hays's face, Harris turned and looked around the bar area.

"I don't see her here now," he said. "But she should be along directly. Can I buy you a drink, Colonel?"

"Certainly," Hays said.

Harris motioned for the bartender.

He stayed and talked to Hays, but did not drink. He had been a policeman in San Antonio until recently and filled Hays in on what happened in town during the war. Cotton traders and slave chasers made bars and police business active pursuits. He had pulled off-duty jobs at various bars through the years, came to know several of the bar operators, and opened his first bar on Market Street. He and some silent partners had recently purchased the stone building at the corner of Commerce and Soledad, intending to convert the saloon into what was to be known as Jack Harris's Vaudeville Theatre and Saloon. At the present time, the group was awaiting funds to build a two-story addition in the back to house the theatre. In the meantime, Harris had brought a few actresses with him who worked the bar for a percentage of the drinks they could entice patrons to buy. They participated in musical entertainments at the back of the room, accompanied by a man playing the piano. Mary Olive had been around for a few years, but Harris had been on the verge of running her off several times.

"She's a hophead," he said, looking over the room. "Not very reliable when she has some of the poppy."

After some more history, Harris responded to a wave from the bartender and excused himself. Although it had been nearly empty when Hays entered, the place was beginning to fill up, mostly with young men in cowhand clothes and a few vaqueros with their riding quirts hanging from their belts. Here and there stood young men who looked like clerks or storekeepers. Several of the bar girls had entered, wearing white, gray, or black stockings, knee-length pleated skirts, and peasant blouses with lace-up bodices. A poker game was going on at a rear corner table, with three men and one small woman who wore a dark green dress.

He tried to remember how long it had been since he had tasted whiskey. It went down with a bite, but it was good whiskey, and he ordered another. The bartender refused payment. He said it was on the house.

She came in the side door off Soledad at nine forty-five, wearing black stockings and lace-up boots and a red bodice that accented her slim waist. She was dark, her hair in ringlets. She moved with a smooth, self-assured gait, smiling at several of the men who spoke to her as she entered, and crossed the room toward the bar. Hays stood near the front door, at the opposite end of the bar from where Sam, the bartender, stood talking to two customers. She walked up and said something to Sam, who retrieved a wine glass from the back bar and filled it with red liquid. The two men, who had parted when she approached and flanked her on both sides, reached into their pockets simultaneously to pay for her wine. Sam looked from one to the other and finally accepted a coin from the hand of the younger one, who appeared to be about Wonsley's age, his gray suit a little outgrown, his shaggy blond hair stringing out from under the back of his black derby and over his high collar.

Sam looked in Hays's direction, then back at the striking young woman, who stood smiling without speaking to the two men, who were both talking to her at the same time. A smile remained on her face, accenting her profile, but she did not appear to be saying anything to them or responding in any other way. She was facing the bar, but not looking at Sam either. She seemed to be looking at something in the back bar mirror, perhaps her own image.

After a long while, Sam moved into her line of vision and said something to her, his head slightly nodding in Hays's direction. She paused, then turned and looked down the bar toward him, staring for a few seconds. After speaking briefly to the older of her two admirers, she started walking toward Hays, looking directly at him as she approached. She came close and then stopped.

"You looking for me?" she asked, still smiling.

"Are you Mary Olive?" he asked.

"That's my name," she said.

"I would like to talk to you," he said.

She stared into his eyes, unblinking, as if looking for something, then said, "You can buy me a glass of wine."

"My pleasure."

Sam was already there with two bottles and another wine glass and refilled Hays's shot glass.

"Shall we take that table by the door?" she asked, and did not wait for his response. He carried the wine and whiskey and followed her to the table. She took a chair by a front window and allowed him to sit with his back to the wall.

"It's about Leo, isn't it?" She took a long sip.

"Yes," he said.

"I haven't seen him in months. Don't know when he'll be back. The only reason I know he's still alive is that you're looking for him."

She looked him over, from the new black hat down the string-tie front of his vested suit to the new black boots he wore.

"You just get into town?"

"Yes."

"Got some new clothes, huh?"

She looked away, across the length of the room, over the hats of the men seated at the other tables. The smile disappeared.

"You a friend of Jack's?"

"Just met him."

"Sam said you was a friend of Jack's. You're a lawman, aren't you?"

"No."

"Or been one."

He downed his shot.

"I guess you could say that."

She turned and looked at him again.

"Guess that's why you're a friend of Jack. All you laws stick together."

She took another long swallow from her glass before asking, "What's he done?"

"He's done murder. And kidnapping."

Her hand was grasping the stem of the wine glass.

"Don't tell me that," she said, her voice no longer smooth.

"It's the truth."

"I don't care. I don't want to hear it." She looked down at her lap. "I guess you want to kill him."

Sam was at the table with the bottles and refilled their glasses, then asked if Hays would like a snack.

"Snacks are free," Mary Olive said. "You might as well have some. That's the only thing free around here." She gave Sam a look.

"There's a spread at the end of the bar," Sam said.

After Sam had returned to the bar, she took another sip of wine and leaned forward.

"I don't want to know anything about it," she said. "The less I know the better. And I don't know where he is. I don't know nothin'."

"When did you see him last?"

"I don't know. Months ago. In the fall, I think. Why?"

"I think he'll be back to see you," he said. "It may be soon."

He was smiling for the first time, and she noticed.

"You're a dirty old man, aren't you? Look at you grinnin'."

The corners of his mouth turned down. He stood up.

"Miss Olive, it was a pleasure to have met you. I had better be going."

"Already?"

She looked up at him, then down to her lap again.

"You haven't even offered me any money to sell him out," she said softly.

"Would you take it?" he asked.

She looked up at him, smiling again.

"I might take it."

"I think you might. But that doesn't mean you'd do anything but warn him. And you'll do that anyway, if you're a mind to."

"Who'd he kill?" She was no longer smiling.

"Family," he said. Then he turned and walked out of the bar.

TWENTY-FOUR

---·—·◆·—·---

I T WAS A BRIGHT AND SUNNY MORNING, A GOOD MORNING FOR washing, and Ada Adams was hanging her wash out when Ev Hardeman rode over the wooden bridge of the small creek that fronted the Adams place. He could see her as he wound down the lane from the bridge. He had dismounted and walked around the corner of the house before she heard him. When she turned around and saw him, she stood staring at him, frozen, holding the sheet she was about to hang on the line with both hands in front of her.

She was as beautiful as he remembered, but paler, and there were lines around her eyes. Her dress was drab and lifeless, not at all like the summer dress she had worn to the picnic years before.

She looked from his face to his pinned sleeve.

"Hello, Ada," he said.

He was standing in front of her, alive, bearded, wearing an expensive suit. A purple cravat. Polished brown boots. His right sleeve was pinned up where his arm and hand should have been. He was holding his hat in his left, gloved hand, and she stared at the expensive-looking kid leather of the brown glove.

"I heard you were back," she said.

She looked at his face and studied it, then looked back at the pinned sleeve.

"I thought you were dead." Then, suddenly, with pain in her voice, "Where were you? Why didn't you write me?"

"That's hard to explain."

"Hard to explain? You could try."

Her face was hard, her eyes moist.

"After I lost my arm, I wanted to die. And I was a prisoner."

"I thought you were dead. We all did."

"I know."

"Why did you come back? You should have stayed away."

"I'm sorry, Ada."

"You're sorry."

She turned and moved as if she was going to hang the wet sheet on the line, but stopped and held it against her.

"I'm married now. You shouldn't be here."

"I had to see you. I've thought about you every day."

"You should have written, Ev. You should have written."

"I guess so," he said.

"You better go, before my husband comes back. He went to town and he'll be back soon."

"I'm not afraid of your husband."

She turned and faced him.

"You should be. He's a jealous man."

Tears had streaked her pale face. Her black hair was done up loosely in back. She looked like a figure in a painting he had seen as a child. She stood holding the sheet in front of her, her blue eyes fixed on his. The pain of the years stared at him from her eyes, seven lost and irretrievable years. The feeling of futility he thought had left him in New England came back in a rush.

"I'm not afraid of anybody or anything," he finally said.

He remembered the look on her face when the troops rode out of camp in 1863, bound for Tennessee. They had spent six months together. Six giddy, exciting months. She was standing by the rail fence bordering the road at Staples, holding the gold sash from his dress uniform that he had given her. Her eyes were wide and hopeful, although they both thought then that the war would not be over for a long time and that they might never see each other again.

By the fall of 1863, the hope that the North would sue for peace had largely evaporated, and most private opinion in Texas was that the struggle would go on for a long time. Some even doubted the South's chances of ultimate victory, but that was never expressed in public. They would fight on until the last Yankee had been expelled from their land. Word had it that the Texas cavalry and infantry were being sent to Tennessee because the Yankees were not capable of invading Texas, but there were those who suspected the truth—that the Confederate Army was short of men in the East.

He had asked Ada to marry him, but they were both underage and her mother refused to consent. She said it was her father's place, and he was off at war. When her father came home, he would consider the matter. Ev said he would take her away, but he could not run away from the Army. Ada said she would wait for him.

She put the wet sheet in the basket and wiped her hands on her apron, then turned to him again. He stood and looked at her and she brushed a lock of hair back from her forehead.

"I'm sorry you saw me like this," she said. "I look awful."

"No. You don't look awful," he said. "You're beautiful."

She looked down at his boots.

"I kept your picture until I was wounded," he said. "Then I lost everything. Except your memory."

"Oh, Ev. This is too hard," she said. "You'd better go."

"I'm not going to forget you," he said. "I'm not going to accept this."

"Stop. Just go."

She would not look up at him and after waiting for a long while, he finally turned and walked back to his horse. He mounted and rode up the lane and over the bridge without looking back. As he turned onto the main road, a large, swarthy man on a black horse, coming from the opposite direction, noticed him, but Everett Hardeman did not see him.

TWENTY-FIVE

THE PLACE WAS SO LOW AND RAMSHACKLE THAT IT DID NOT LOOK like a saloon. There was no sign so designating it, and its wooden walls blended into the surrounding ground along Griffin Avenue, giving it the appearance of a moderately sized dwelling, or maybe even a storehouse. The dirt floor inside was scattered with an assortment of tables, barrels, chairs, and stools, many made from cypress stumps, and the bar itself consisted of two rough-hewn cypress planks laid side-by-side over stacked flagstone pillars. There were cowboys and soldiers drinking, and a few who could not be easily identified or categorized. There were poker games at two of the tables.

It was one of a number of saloons in the Flat, just down the hill from Fort Griffin. Luis found a spot at the end of the bar where he had stood for several nights running. He was a bit late tonight and was concerned that his man might have already shown up. He had been following the man called Juaro over much of Texas, but had not confronted him. After trailing him into Fort Griffin several days ago, he had decided that the best place to camp was by the Tonkawa village on the other side of Collins Creek, so he had made his way there at dusk, greeted the elders, and obtained permission to camp nearby. He found that a group of Lipans were also camping there, with the permission of the Tonkawas, and he laid his bedroll near them. The next morning he learned from several of the younger men in the village that the man called Juaro had been to the Flat many times and was known to frequent Shaunessy's Saloon, where he enjoyed sitting at a poker table.

The bartender, he was told, was Shaunessy himself, a large, balding Irishman who wore a holstered Colt. The first night Luis had walked to the end of the bar, where half-breeds and Mexicans were usually expected to stand. Shaunessy came over and looked him up and down, as if trying to decide if he was going to allow him to stay there. He was dressed like the Apache he was and the bar owner did not normally allow Indians, not because of any innate prejudice, but because they were notorious for being violent drunks who could not hold their liquor. But the blue bandana around the old man's head and his cotton shirt with the shirt tail out and belted did not look like the garb he was used to seeing on a Tonkawa or Lipan, and Shaunessy hesitated, then asked him, in Spanish, if he was a "breed." The old man smiled and replied that he was some kind of breed, he thought, but he was not sure. For some reason, the reply and the old man's smile, coupled with his appearance, gave Shaunessy no reason to suspect trouble from him, so he served him the beer he ordered and on subsequent nights served him again, only one beer that he nursed for the couple of hours he stood there each night, each night leaving a portion of it flat in the mug.

Juaro had entered on the three previous nights, taking a seat at the only table in the place that could be considered a real table, the round one at the other end of the bar near the door, where the largest poker game was going. Although Juaro had never seen Luis, Luis had an unreasoned fear that the man would somehow recognize him and stood frozen at his end of the bar the first night, only taking a sip of beer when he felt sure that Juaro was concentrating on his poker hand. When Juaro headed for the back door that led to the walled trough that served as a urinal, Luis turned away from his path.

Sometimes it was hard to separate the dream world from the real world in his memory. His vision of the man with the scar on his cheek had been quite vivid, though it had proven inaccurate as to the details of his features, and he somehow felt that Juaro would also recognize him, as if the man he had been seeking all these years existed in the dream world and could therefore see Luis in it as well. But Juaro had not noticed him, and when he came in after twenty minutes or so on this night, he took his seat at the table and did not look in Luis's direction at all.

For the fourth night in a row, Luis watched him at the poker table. He was seated facing the door. The scar that ran from his left earlobe across his cheek to his chin was a pink slash across his brown face. He wore a holstered pistol on the left. He kept his straight-brimmed black hat on while playing. His single braid of black hair fell across his back to the top of the chair back behind him.

His movements were deliberate. When it was his time to deal, he held the cards close to his shirt and reached slowly with his left hand extended before dropping each card. He seldom spoke to the others in the game, who were the same ones each night, although the others carried on a constant conversation among themselves, the bartender, and those who entered by the front door. Watching him, Luis developed a feel for him that filled out the impression he had from his dreams. He was methodical, purposeful, without conscience. He did not change expression while he played and "call" was the only word he uttered during the game, except for an occasional word or two in response to questions or comments from the others, who appeared to be cautious in addressing him. He drank beer and motioned to the bartender when he wanted another glass.

On each of the previous evenings, Luis had intended to follow when Juaro left the bar, but each time he was frozen in the spot where he stood. It was not cowardice, but just that the time was not ripe. He had not been meant to follow him yet, but perhaps tonight would be the night. The moon would come later tonight and perhaps he would be able to follow him without being detected. And it was not a matter of fearing death, because he fully expected to die when Juaro died, and his soul would see Juaro's in hell. But he did not want to die without taking Juaro with him.

Luis could not tell if Juaro was winning or losing, although he occasionally won a pot and raked the coins and bills to his side of the table. Each night he had played for about two hours, then stood without speaking, picked up his money from the table, and walked out the door. Although Luis had never seen him looking in his direction, he had felt his eyes upon him and sensed that Juaro knew he was there and knew what he had come for. It was a matter of destiny, after all, and the cards would fall where they would fall, when the time was right.

On this night, after only an hour or so, Juaro raked his pile off the table and walked to the bar. He stood at the opposite end from Luis, near the table, and when Shaunessy came down to him, he shoved a stack of coins toward him and asked for paper money.

"You leavin' us?" the bartender asked.

"I think so," he said.

When he had his bills, he looked Luis's way before turning and walking out the door. Luis sensed that Juaro may have been setting him up, but he feared that if he did not follow him, he would lose him again, as he had done many times in the past few months. He took a last sip of beer, then went out the back door, past the urinal stall and the privy to the alley, then turned left and moved to the corner of the building facing the side street. The moon was low in the east and the building cast a shadow to its rear, where he stood and waited before looking around the corner slowly.

There were two horses hitched at the posts at the side of the saloon that blocked his view and shielded him from Griffin Avenue. He listened for the sound of a horse moving and heard nothing, then waited until his eyes adjusted to the light. Squatting so that he could see beneath the horses, he moved in a crouch out toward the street, then remained crouched as the horses moved away from him slightly. The street appeared to be empty. He waited, listening. He could hear the horses breathing and the sound of a cloth flapping in the breeze from the south, which blew in his face. The south wind had brought an early spring warming trend and he was grateful for it and hoped that he was downwind from his prey. He cautiously moved beyond the horses so that he could get beyond their smell, hoping that he could detect Juaro's smell if he was still out there. Breathing in, he scanned down Fourth Street and toward the south down Griffin Avenue, which he could see through the upright studs of the partially finished Meyer's saloon on the opposite corner. He could detect no movement or notable scent.

It was logical that Juaro would be walking south down Griffin Avenue or east on Fourth Street, but he may have gone north when he left Shaunessy's, or even doubled around back, or was perhaps waiting across the street from the entrance for Luis to come out. There was an elm tree behind the Meyer structure, and if Luis could make it there, he would have a safer view of the corner. He moved sideways slowly, still in a crouch, across the street to the shadow of the tree.

He reached under his shirt in back for his Smith and Wesson Number 1 and pulled it out. It was only a .22 caliber, but was accurate and easy to conceal, so he had brought it with him along with his hunting knife, which hung from his belt in a scabbard. He held the pistol as he scanned the corner again from this new perspective.

Across the street from the entrance to Shaunessy's, the Busy Bee and Bowers' Saloon were lit up, and there was a lantern hanging on a porch post at the Busy Bee that threw a faint circle of light out into the street beyond the three horses tied up in front. Other than the horses' manes and tails moving in the breeze, there was no movement. Still in a crouch, he crawfished to the edge of the partially finished building and squatted down by the edge in the shadow of structure, where he was able to move slowly toward the edge of Griffin Avenue for a better look up the street past the saloons. After looking down the front of Shaunessy's and not detecting any movement, he closed his eyes and listened.

He heard muffled sounds coming from the saloons and the sound of a windmill turning in the distance, then the sound of a board creaking from behind him on the porch floor of the unfinished building at the same time that he smelled him, a rank, unwashed odor coming from up- wind. He turned quickly and fired at the black shape that was coming at him and managed to get off two shots with the .22 before the shape was on him, its left arm raised, the curve of the blade flashing in the moon- light briefly before it reached his throat. Then he was back with Maria and she was holding him in her soft, white arms, which were bare to the shoulder as he had remembered them when she wore the white night- gown that was so filmy that her lithe body was a suggestion as she walked, and the sun was rising over her shoulder and she was smiling at him as in the old days, and he was young again and there was no pain, only the joy and relief of being where he had always known he would be someday.

The saloons emptied at the sound of the shots from his pistol, and they found him in the lamplight from several lanterns, lying with his life's blood still pumping from his jugular onto the sand of the street, his Smith and Wesson clutched in his hand. They did not find Juaro until the next morning. He had made it to the river and was lying face down in the shallow water of the ford at the end of Griffin Avenue.

They were buried side by side among the other dead in the Fort Grif- fin Cemetery, with wooden markers that bore inscriptions describing them as unknown Indians killed in a knife fight. No one bothered to investigate the matter. Deaths in the streets of the Flat had become com- mon in the spring of 1870.

TWENTY-SIX

———··———

M RS. ELLIOT'S SEWING CIRCLE MET EVERY WEDNESDAY AFTER-
noon. It was an offshoot of the Ladies' Sewing Society, which began meeting in the vacant building adjoining Lavanburg's in the summer
of '62. During the war the ladies knitted socks and made other articles
of clothing for the soldiers after an appeal from the army in Arkansas
that indicated that many of the men were barefoot and lacked a change
of shirts. Then the list of beneficiaries was expanded to include poor
families of soldiers in Bexar and surrounding counties. Many women and
children were left attending to farms and businesses after their men went
to war and had little means with which to buy clothes for themselves.

After the war was over, they continued to meet weekly at alternating
homes of the ladies, but Mrs. Elliot, one of the founders of the Ladies'
Sewing Society, was considered the unofficial leader and on a Wednesday
afternoon in March they had the usual light lunch at Ellen Elliot's table,
then retired to the parlor to discuss their current and future projects,
agree on which lady would be working on which articles of clothing for
the coming week and for whom they were intended, and as usual, to
begin sewing and knitting together while discussing the events of the day
and exchanging anecdotes about people and places.

Katherine Johnston was there, as well as Mrs. Lockman, Mrs. Roberts,
and Mary Maverick, who arrived late because she was caring for Mr.
Maverick, who was ill. She commented on a visitor Mr. Maverick had
the previous evening.

"Your brother-in-law came to see us last evening," she said to Mrs. Johnston. "The colonel has not changed much, although he has grayed a bit. He is the same quiet, generous soul I knew from the old days, and he was very solicitous of Mr. Maverick and his condition."

"I heard he also paid his respects to Señor Navarro," Mrs. Roberts said.

"He said he had been to see Señor Jose Antonio," Mrs. Maverick replied. "He is planning on traveling to New Orleans today and wanted to pay his respects before leaving."

Katherine Johnston looked up from the sock she was knitting. "I was not aware that the colonel was leaving San Antonio," she said.

"He's going on business," Mrs. Elliot said. "He'll be back in a month or so."

"Isn't he still looking for that outlaw?" Mrs. Lockman asked.

"From what I know of Colonel Hays, he will not rest until that murderer is brought to justice," Mrs. Maverick said. "He told Mr. Maverick that he was meeting his brother, Harry, in New Orleans. Harry was a general in the army during the war. He said his brother wanted his help and advice regarding a business matter, but he didn't say what it was about."

"I think it is more of a family matter," Mrs. Elliot said. "But the colonel is not one to talk about his business."

The ladies tended to their sewing and knitting quietly for a few minutes.

"How is the little girl?" Mrs. Johnston asked. She had been at Mrs. Elliot's for over an hour and had not inquired about her niece.

"She is doing quite well, considering," Mrs. Elliot replied. "The sisters are very strict, but kind. She is walking to and from school now."

"Was she not before?" Mrs. Roberts asked.

"No. She wouldn't budge, so I had Alonzo take her in the carriage. On Monday, she was home before he left for her. When I asked her about it, she said she got off early. I talked to her about it and she said she had just as soon walk when the weather was good."

"Is she talking more now?" Mrs. Johnston asked.

"Only when you ask her something and then only if a nod or a mumble won't do. The child doesn't seem to be shy. She's curious about things. She just doesn't want to talk."

"I knew of a case like hers," Mrs. Roberts said. "During the war. You remember the fair at the Menger? This woman, a Mrs. Brown, a widow, donated some clothing that belonged to her late husband, who died back East at one of the battles, and she brought her little girl with her, who just would not say anything at all. I tried to talk to her for the longest time, but couldn't get her to say a word. I asked her mother if she was a deaf mute and she seemed to be insulted by that kind of talk and left with the little girl quite abruptly. I didn't mean anything by it, of course, but the girl, who was about twelve or thirteen, seemed to be mute. I heard later that she was the apple of her father's eye, so I guess his passing was too much for her."

"Martha will talk if you ask her a direct question," Mrs. Elliot said. "But she never smiles. I think the massacre and what happened to her afterwards must have been terrible for her."

Mrs. Lockman noticed that there were tears in Mrs. Johnston's eyes. "Katherine. We shouldn't be talking about this," she said.

"It's all right," Mrs. Johnston said. "We never talk about it. Maybe it's good to talk more."

"I don't know how you stood it," Mrs. Roberts said. "What a terrible tragedy."

"She's had a visitor," Mrs. Elliot said. "I mean, other than the colonel."

"Who?" several asked at once.

"Wonsley Baker," Mrs. Elliot replied. "They visited last Sunday, here in the parlor."

"How old is Wonsley?" Mrs. Roberts asked.

"I think he's in his early twenties," Mrs. Elliot said.

"I don't think he's that old," Mrs. Johnston said. "More like eighteen or nineteen."

"He seems quite taken with her," Mrs. Elliot said. "He was very polite and dressed in his Sunday best."

"Well, it was Sunday," Mrs. Lockman said, which drew laughter.

TWENTY-SEVEN

ASHLEY MAITLAND WAITED UNTIL THE NOON HOUR TO WALK to the Plum Creek post office, which was about two miles up the creek from Atlanta. It was a brisk spring day and he was in the habit of walking instead of riding when there was no hurry and the weather was good. He picked up his mail, and then he started back down the dirt path that led to Atlanta and his home and office. After about a mile, he looked up to see Everett Hardeman approaching him on horseback. When he was near him, Hardeman stopped his mount.

"I heard you had come this way, Ash," he said. "I want to visit with you."

"Sure, Ev," he replied. "Come along and we can have some lunch at Garcia's."

"I don't really want to take time for that, Ash. I've got to leave for Galveston tomorrow and have a lot of things to do. But I wanted to talk about the new session of the legislature. I heard they're going to reconvene near the end of the month."

"That's what I hear," Ash said.

"I'm told you have some influence there and I wanted to offer you a position with the railroad interests I represent."

"I don't know if I have any influence," Ash replied. "I do know some of the men in the legislature."

"Well, I heard you had the ear of many of them."

"Possibly. But what would you want me to do?"

"Colonel Pierce and some other investors are wanting to form a new railroad company and need to obtain a charter. It'll be a good thing for

219

this area. This is where the line is going to go. We've made a deal with Mr. Josey for some of his land and there's an agreement to build a new town. It'll be good for the whole area."

"Come along, then, Ev. We'll talk as we go."

They proceeded down the path, Ash walking beside Hardeman's horse.

"I understand that a new charter must be obtained through the legislature and not every application gets a fair hearing," Hardeman said. "This is too important to this area for it to be left to chance."

"What do you mean by that, Ev? I can't guarantee a vote on anything."

"Maybe not, but I understand that the lieutenant governor is an acquaintance of yours and that he is the man who needs to be on our side. And there's plenty of money to go around, Ash."

"Maybe you didn't hear. The lieutenant governor just got elected United States senator. He'd never been sworn in as lieutenant governor anyway."

"I heard about that. But isn't Campbell in place of him?"

"He's the president pro tem of the senate," Ash replied. "He'll preside and have the same powers, that's true."

"And you know him, right?"

"I don't know that you're talking to the right man," Ash said. "You know why they're reconvening don't you?"

"Yeah, I know. The loyalty oath."

"Exactly. We've ratified the constitutional amendments and elected senators. Now we're going to have a loyalty oath."

"But it hasn't been decided yet," Hardeman said. "You might have some influence on that, too."

"I doubt it. Nobody who had anything to do with the Confederacy could be elected to public office or vote for delegates to the constitutional convention, under the Reconstruction Act. That means there are no rebels in the legislature. I doubt that the loyalty oath will be any different from the federal one we've had already."

"But you know a lot of those people," Hardeman said. "They're Texans."

Ash stopped and Hardeman stopped his mount.

Ash looked up at him. "David Campbell is one of the worst Radicals. Hertzberg wants to introduce a bill for frontier defense and give Davis the right to impose martial law. Campbell will probably support that.

They're mostly a bunch of bastards, Ev. I may know Campbell, but we are not on the same side on most things."

"Even the Radicals want progress," Hardeman replied. "A railroad that links New Orleans and San Francisco is something all Texans should want to get on. Your being there might do some good. You can tell them what you think about the defense bill. And I know hiring Negroes as state police is one of the issues."

"You're right, Ev," he said after a moment. "I shouldn't give up on it."

"And you can lobby for the railroad at the same time."

"I guess I could," Ash said, starting to walk again. "What does it pay?"

"I am authorized to tell you that anything within reason that you may expect is what it will be," he replied.

"I'd have trouble objecting to that," Ash said.

TWENTY-EIGHT

M ARY OLIVE LIVED IN A ROOM OVER A CHINESE LAUNDRY ON
the west side of town. She entered the street-level doorway that
opened onto the stairs to the second floor with a short, rotund man close
behind her. She found the candle on the shelf just inside the door and
turned to the man for a match. He had promised her laudanum, and
although he would not show her the bottle he said he had in his pocket,
she was in need. Her regular was nowhere to be found, and after several
glasses of wine at the Cosmopolitan she had decided that it was worthwhile to find out if he was telling the truth. She had reached the stage
where her skin was crawling and it was hard to keep her hands still so she
allowed the man to follow her the six blocks to her home, although she
had not seen him before that night and would ordinarily have rejected
his advances out of hand.

He followed her up the creaky wooden stairs in the candlelight, then
down the hallway to her door. She reached in her purse for her skeleton
key and fumbled for it, then, on a feeling she suddenly had, turned the
door handle and pushed. The door opened. The candlelight's arc moved
across the floor by the washstand and iron bed to the lone chair on the
far side of the room, where a pair of boots came into view. She recognized
the buckskin and the fringe immediately and drew in her breath.

The man from the bar pushed against her from behind and she took
a step inside the room, then turned around and shoved him back into the
hallway. He was unsteady on his feet and staggered back, then regained
his footing and shoved her aside. As he stepped inside she held the candle

up so that the light shone across the room, revealing the dark young man with long black hair sitting in the chair by the window. He stood up slowly and came toward the short man, who, after hesitating and starting to say something, stepped back through the doorway into the dark hallway. By the time Morgan had reached the doorway with long, leisurely steps, the man was scrambling back down the hall. In a few seconds, they could hear the sound of him stumbling down the stairs toward the street.

Mary turned toward the nightstand and put the candleholder down on it, next to the glass lantern, then turned around to face him.

"What do you think you're doing?" she asked.

He smiled. It was a thin smile without any joy in it.

"I came to see you," he said, his voice a low drawl.

She turned and took the chimney off the lantern, then held the candle to the wick, her hand shaking so much that she had to make several passes with the flame before the wick ignited. She replaced the chimney and adjusted the flame until the room lightened, then turned toward him.

"You shouldn't be here," she said in a shaky voice. "I don't want to see you."

He reached for her waist and she backed away, hitting the side of the washstand, but he moved swiftly and grabbed her around the waist and pulled her to him, holding her close and looking into her face.

"What's the matter?" he asked, his voice hard and brisk.

She shivered in his grasp and she knew he could feel it.

"You left months ago without a word. As far as I knew, you was dead."

He continued to stare into her eyes. She turned her head.

"You're lying," he said calmly. "You better tell me."

"Let me go," she said, pushing against his chest.

He turned her loose and she moved to the end of the bed and grasped a post of the iron bedstead. She could not control her shaking and had to hold onto something. Tears welled up in her eyes.

"You're too cruel," she said. "I don't want to see you. I don't know why you won't leave me alone."

"That's not it. You like being with me. And I brought you a present."

She watched his hand slide into his pocket and come out with a small brown bottle with a blue cork. She closed her eyes and a tear ran down her cheek. Her head sank forward, then she slowly reached a shaking hand toward him.

"Now, see. I ain't so bad."

He held the bottle out of her reach and she stepped toward him, but he backed away, smoothly retreating from her grasp, then he allowed her to come closer, but held the bottle up, out of her reach.

"Please," she said.

"What is it you want to tell me?" he asked, smiling his cold smile.

"There was a man here looking for you."

She was close to him and could smell his foul breath and for a moment she thought she would gag.

"A man? Who was he?"

"I don't know," she said.

He grabbed her wrist and held it hard, hurting her.

"You know," he said evenly. "Who was it?"

"Some old ex-Ranger," she said.

"What was his name?"

"Please," she said again, her voice weaker. She was looking up at the bottle.

"Not until you tell me."

"I can't remember now, Leo. Maybe if my nerves were calm," she said.

"You're lying," he said, raising his voice. "You should know better than to lie to me."

She was still looking up at the bottle, her face contorted with pain.

"Hays," she said. "He said his name was Hays."

"Hays? Jack Hays?"

"He didn't say his first name. I swear. He didn't say it." She paused, then again, this time whispering, "Please."

He slowly lowered the bottle and she took it from his hand as soon as she could reach it. She turned to the washstand and set the bottle down, then picked up a glass which she held shaking in her hand while she poured it half full of water from the pitcher. She uncorked the bottle and poured a shot into the glass. It clouded the water and she stirred it with a spoon, then gulped it down.

He waited as she stood by the washstand, her eyes closed and her eyebrows raised, her lips pursed. She steadied herself with one hand on the stand. After a few seconds, her features relaxed.

"When was he here?" he asked.

She waited, a faint smile upon her lips, then opened her eyes. She held her head higher and the lines had disappeared from her face.

"A few weeks ago."

"Why was he looking for me?"

"I don't know," she said. "He said it was a family matter."

"A family matter? What does that mean?"

"How the hell should I know?" she answered, her head still held high.

He reached for her and pulled her to him.

"You better never lie to me again," he said, holding her around her waist. She was small and his body felt huge against her, bringing back a feeling she had felt before. It had fear in it, but something else to boot. Something that she could not resist. She went limp in his arms. He kissed her roughly, holding her so tightly that her breath left her and the feeling, coming back from the past, intensified. She knew then that she could never get away from him as long as he lived. And the laudanum held her fast in its grip and she knew that she would not want to do anything that would take that from her, that relief, the smoothness that made everything else seem insignificant. She held her arms around his neck as he carried her to the bed.

TWENTY-NINE

———◆———

ASHLEY MAITLAND WAS ON THE FLOOR OF THE SENATE CHAMBER, standing next to George Paschal, who had shown him in. The senators, pages, lobbyists, and various unidentifiable men were milling about talking, and it was hard to hear Paschal over the din. Ash leaned closer to hear.

"They are debating the immigration bill," Paschal said. "Some bright Republican thought we should spend some taxpayers' money to get more Yankees and Europeans to come to Texas. You're just about to see a first for the Texas Senate. Gaines has offered an amendment. It would send an immigration agent to Africa as well. He is about to speak."

At the podium in front of the president's desk stood a tall black man wearing a black suit. The president pro tem began pounding his gavel for quiet, but the din continued. A few men looked toward the desk, then continued talking. The gavel pounding continued. Finally the voice of the president pro tem could be heard above the din.

"The senate will come to order," he shouted. Then again, "The senate will come to order or I'll have the sergeant at arms clear the chamber."

Paschal touched Ash's shoulder and Ash leaned in to listen to him.

"Campbell is going to see to it that he gets a chance to speak even if it's to an empty chamber," he said.

The gavel pounding continued. A few of the men in the room made gestures for quiet around them and some of the senators took their seats at their desks. The talking lessened gradually, and then ceased.

"The chair recognizes the senator from Washington County," Campbell said loudly. A murmur and rustling of feet as some of the men standing in the aisles walked to the edges of the chamber and the remaining senators sat down. The man at the podium stood straight, looking over the room, until the aisles had cleared and all of the senators were seated.

"Mr. President," he began. "This bill proposes to provide for a superintendent of immigration, at a cost of thirty-five hundred dollars per annum, of the public money of the poor people of this state."

His voice was deep and could be heard across the chamber. Ash noticed that he stood quite still, with both hands on the podium, as if used to speaking in public.

"This bill also provides that there shall be one agent for the United States and two for Europe; one of the latter for Great Britain and the other for Germany. Now, Mr. President, if this legislature can impose a tax on the poor colored people of this state, and take their money, and send to Europe for the British and the Germans, and to other portions of the broad globe, and not extend this hand of fellowship to the African, I think it is hard—that we, the colored people of the state of Texas, who have to work to till the soil of Texas, to make the cotton and corn—it is hard then to have the benefits of the taxation taken away from us, and have immigrants brought here to this country, to purchase the land that we have worked so hard to cultivate."

The men at the press desk to the side of the dais were writing rapidly, taking down every word.

"We have cut down the trees and pulled up the stumps; and, Mr. President, I offer this amendment in behalf of the colored people of the state of Texas, though I do not think that it will be adopted by the Republican Party. But I will show to the colored Republicans of this state that I have tried to do for them that which has not been done. The whites have overlooked the point, and I have tried to call their attention to the matter, and they have failed to support it; but I hope the day will come when the colored people will get justice. It seems to me, Mr. President, that it is no more than right that the bill should be so amended as to let the colored people have one agent to Africa."

Paschal grabbed Ash by the elbow and gestured for him to step outside the door. Ash followed him into the hallway. Paschal turned to him.

"He and George Ruby, the other colored senator, don't have a lot of influence, but they will probably support a railroad charter. I've arranged a meeting with them this afternoon after the session."

"He seems quite articulate," Ash said.

"He is literate. Learned from smuggled books. He ran away during the war and they caught him out West. He so impressed his captors that they kept him at Fredericksburg for the duration. Never told his owner they had him and kept him working for the Germans."

"I guess there are a lot of Republicans in his district."

"It's like everywhere. You know how the election went. But he drew a lot of white votes, too. As you can hear, he's a good public speaker. Let's go hear the rest of it."

They returned to the chamber and regained their places against the wall. Gaines's voice had gained momentum and he now spoke with added force.

"Mr. President, it has been said by the Democratic members of this senate that it would seem to them that the black men have no inherent rights in the United States; that they ought to be back again in the ports of Africa; but, in reply to this, I have to say that the blacks have as much right here as the whites. The United States belonged to the Indian. He is the only American. This is his native home, the place where he was born. But by unfair means, it seems that they were all driven away, and their homes taken from them. Now, if the Democrats of the state of Texas will agree with me that they will go back to Great Britain and the Germans to Germany and the French to France, then I am willing to go back to Africa—to my old home. The Democrats think that it is hard for them to sit in the state senate with the colored men and go to school with them and live with them, yet they will not stop sleeping with the colored women and getting children by them. I think that the little colored children and white children play together every day and sometimes at night and they get along well. Why, then, can't they go to school together? Let the Democrats remember that old times have played out and new ones have taken their place. Look to the future and see what it will bring!"

There was a silence, then a smattering of applause. One man rose from his chair on the right side of the chamber, applauding vigorously. He appeared to be a mulatto, with dark hair but a rather light complexion. He had thick sideburns that met his heavy mustache. Paschal pointed him out to Ash.

"That's Ruby," he said.

Later, Ash and George Paschal met with several senators in an anteroom to the chamber, including the senator from Guadalupe County, Thomas H. Baker, Eli Baker's nephew; and Senators Sam Evans, A. J. Fountain, and S. W. Ford. Matthew Gaines and George Ruby were not yet in attendance. Ford had been admitted after A. J. Evans's election had been declared by the senate to have been procured through intimidation and threatened violence against the colored voters of Falls County. Baker was chairman of the Elections Committee that had declared Evans ineligible and recommended giving credentials to Ford. Matthew Gaines was also a member of the committee. The men were standing around the large table in the center of the room engaged in conversation when the two black senators entered.

Fountain, a tall man with thinning brown hair, extended his hand to Gaines.

"Fine speech, Senator," he said. "I thought it put the immigration bill in the real light it should have been shown in all along."

"Thank you, Senator. But I was deadly serious."

"I know you were, Senator," Fountain continued. His smile framed his overly serious tone.

George Ruby walked around the table to Ash and George Paschal, who were standing at the end by the window. He extended his hand to Paschal.

"Mr. Paschal," he said. "Is this the man you wanted us to meet?" he asked, looking at Ash.

"It is, Senator. This is Ashley Maitland."

Ashley shook hands with Ruby, noticing his slight frame and small hand.

"Pleased to make your acquaintance, Mr. Maitland," Ruby said. His voice had an unfamiliar accent. "You wanted to talk to us about a railroad?"

Paschal chuckled. "Senator Ruby gets right to the point, as you can see, Ash."

"I see and I don't mind at all," Ash replied. "Yes, Senator. I know there are some problems with the railroad issue in the legislature and I'm not taking sides on that. I am here representing a new company. We just want a charter so we can connect San Antonio to Galveston."

"There is already a line from Galveston to Alleyton. What's to happen to it?"

"We have a contract to acquire it, Senator."

"And will you acquire the debts also?" Ruby asked.

Ash studied the face before him. Ruby's eyes were steady. His facial features were relaxed. This man had been head of the Union League in Texas, had worked for the Freedmen's Bureau, and had the reputation of being a skilled politician. Ashley had expected to meet someone who would be somewhat clever and a bit devious. His demeanor was to the contrary. He was more than clever and quite direct. Ash needed to choose his words carefully.

"Our company will assume all legitimate debts," he said.

"Including the debt to the school fund?" Ruby asked.

"If it is a legal and legitimate debt, yes indeed, sir."

Ruby was also studying Ash's face. He extended his hand again.

"Then I will support your charter request, Mr. Maitland, if everything else is in order. I appreciate your straightforward answer."

"Thank you, Senator."

Matthew Gaines had made it around the table. Paschal introduced him to Ash.

"It's a pleasure, Senator," Ash said.

"Thank you, Mr. Maitland. Mr. Paschal speaks highly of you," Gaines said.

"I greatly enjoyed your speech today, Senator," Ash said.

"Oh? What do you think of the immigration bill, Mr. Maitland?" Gaines asked, his eyebrows raised.

Ash hesitated. Gaines was as direct as Ruby.

"I have no politics this session other than railroads, Senator," he replied.

Gaines studied his face, looking into his eyes.

"Very wise, Mr. Maitland. If you want to lobby for an issue, you don't want to get on the bad side of anyone on any other issue."

"Mr. Maitland represents some interests that are trying to build a railroad from Alleyton to San Antonio," Ruby said. "What is the name of the company, Mr. Maitland?"

"We hope to call it the Galveston, Harrisburg and San Antonio," Ash replied.

"A good name for a railroad," Ruby said.

"Have you heard about the Militia Bill, Mr. Maitland?" Gaines asked.

Again Ashley hesitated. He certainly knew about the two bills that the governor was pushing. Democrats were generally opposed to them. One, the Militia Bill, would create a state guard consisting of volunteers under the ultimate command of the governor and give the governor the right to suspend the right of habeas corpus and declare martial law. It was not a secret that blacks were to be appointed to the force because, the Republicans argued, blacks were the main victims of the violence that was occurring, particularly during elections. The official Democrat position was that the bill would be unconstitutional. The bill also provided that every able-bodied male between the ages of eighteen and forty-five would automatically become members of the reserve Militia, but service could be avoided by the payment of fifteen dollars per year. The other bill would establish a state police force to be commanded by the state adjutant general, who was appointed by the governor. All sheriffs, deputies, constables, marshals, and chiefs of police would be considered part of the force and thus under the command and control of the governor's appointees.

"I have heard about it, Senator," Ash replied.

"I would be interested to learn what the Democrats really think about it," Gaines said.

"I don't have a position on that bill either, Senator, but I think there's a lot of opposition to it across the state."

Ruby spoke up.

"We know what's being said, Mr. Maitland. That it's going to be a nigger police force."

Gaines turned to him.

"Senator, we may think that, but how many Democrats have you discussed this with?"

Sam Evans, who had walked up, said, "You have discussed it with me, but I'm not a Democrat."

Ruby smiled at him.

"Senator Evans, you keep saying that and I will concede that a Conservative Republican is not a Democrat. At least not on the surface."

Gaines turned again to Ash.

"Mr. Maitland, I would like the opportunity to speak to the Democrats on this issue. I believe Governor Davis is a good man and is trying to do what is right by all the people, not just the colored people, but I also know there are a lot of white folks that won't admit that the war is over and they will do anything to keep the colored people down. Law and order is all we are asking for. And an equal opportunity."

"I believe you, Senator. I am sure you appreciate the fact that these kinds of things are going to take time."

Ruby spoke up.

"After years of bondage, Mr. Maitland, our people have waited long enough for justice."

The conversation had taken a turn that Ashley regretted. He had feared that something like this would happen.

"Senator, if I had the power, I would do something about it, but nobody has the power to change a way of thinking that is so old."

"That's true," Gaines said. "That's true. But we can begin by enforcing the law."

"I certainly agree with that, Senator," Ashley replied.

George Paschal stepped forward.

"Gentlemen, I asked you to meet Mr. Maitland so that he could explain his company's charter request. I don't think he can solve all our political problems."

The three senators who were standing at the end of the table with Ashley and Paschal and the others in the room were suddenly quiet. Paschal's words hung in the silence.

Ashley then gave the little speech he had intended to give all along, mentioning the people, including Colonel Pierce, who were involved in the project, their financial capability, and the plans for the line after it reached San Antonio. It was to be a six-year project. The senators expressed their pleasure in meeting with Ash and after pleasantries were exchanged, he and Paschal left the room. Walking down the hallway, Paschal cleared his throat, but did not speak.

"I think that went well," Ash said.

"I don't know," Paschal replied. "I think those fellows, particularly the Negro senators, will drive a hard bargain when it comes to the details."

"I would expect no less of them," Ash said. "Is Gaines a preacher?"

"He is, indeed."

"I thought so," Ash said.

THIRTY

E LI BAKER PULLED UP IN FRONT OF THE MCCULLOCH HOME AT
dawn in his wagon. It was pulled by his mules, Job and Jessie. Eli
whistled loudly, and in a few seconds Billy came running out the side
door. His grandfather had asked him to accompany him to Lockhart to
help him pick up some supplies. Billy crawled up to the wagon seat beside him, and they proceeded up the road. Billy was used to being silent
until his grandfather spoke to him, and other than a "good morning" the
old man said nothing until they were a few miles south of the town. After
they crossed Clear Fork Creek, Eli turned off onto another road that Billy
had not traveled and headed in a northeasterly direction.

"There's something I want you to see," Eli said. "I should have taken
you here long ago. It's about time you saw it."

Billy knew not to ask what it was that his grandfather wanted to show
him. He had heard "You'll see soon enough" a number of times. They
were crossing a plain and the sun was up in the east, the dew sparkling
on either side of the dirt road before them. He could see the tree line that
defined Plum Creek ahead of them, and when they were within a few
hundred yards of the trees, they turned right onto a faint trail. After a
while, his grandfather pulled up and tied off the reins. The field that lay
before them was covered with grass that brushed the bellies of the mules,
but there was no structure or other landmark visible, just the meadow
rolling slightly downhill to the creek to the east.

"I want to tell you about the battle," his grandfather said. "It started
here." He reached his open hand before them, sweeping it across the

vista. "This is called Comanche Flats, and this is where it began. The Comanches came up from the southeast on this side of the creek. They had been raiding on the coast and were on their way back to the Hill Country with their squaws and their children and their captives and a whole lot of stolen horses and mules and goods. About two hundred Texans met them here and chased them all the way to the Hill Country."

Billy had heard his grandfather and others talk about the battle for years, but he had never been here before. He remembered almost everything he had heard about it, but he never tired of hearing about it again.

"And you were here, Grandpa?"

"I was here," he said. "So were your cousins, Ben and Henry McCulloch. Jack Hays was here, too. And Bigfoot Wallace and Matthew Caldwell."

He turned slightly on the wagon seat to face Billy.

"The Comanche chiefs were dressed up in some of the goods they had stolen. A few of them wore top hats. They had tied colored ribbons on their horses, on their manes and tails, and they had a huge *caballado* of horses and mules they had loaded with their plunder. Some estimated they had three thousand stolen animals. I don't know if it was that many, but it was a huge number and you could see the dust they raised before you could see them.

"They had burned Linnville to the ground and killed a number of people there. Then they burglarized warehouses full of goods and loaded them on horses and mules and started back toward the Hill Country. We met them here on horseback and harassed them for several miles up that way."

He turned and pointed to the northwest.

"We cornered them near Clear Fork and dismounted and closed in on them. It was a great slaughter. The Comanches have never come back in force this far south since that day."

He was sitting next to Billy on the wagon seat, staring at the meadow before them, as if he could see the battle taking place all over again. His eyes were moist.

"We didn't lose a man," he said, his voice deeper than before. "Though some were injured. The Indians shot and killed a woman they had taken captive, while she was trying to run away, and they shot Mrs. Watts with an arrow, but she survived. They were savages. They had their women and children and old men with them and had them herding the horses and mules, trying to keep them away from us. They had never done anything like that before and they haven't since."

"Done what, Grandpa?"

"Come down that far south with their families. The Mexicans put them up to it. And they were spoiling for it after the Council House Fight."

"What was that?"

Eli smiled. He knew Billy had heard the story many times before, but never tired of hearing it again.

"Twelve Comanche chiefs were killed at the Council House in San Antonio earlier that year. They started the fight, but the Texans ended it."

He turned from staring at the meadow and looked Billy in the eye.

"You can never trust an Indian or a Mexican," he said. "Don't ever let them get in a position of power over you."

Billy had heard that before, too.

"I want you to understand what it took to hold on to what we have. What we worked so hard to get. Very few had any money to speak of when we came here. Your grandmother's folks were dirt poor. I had worked in Tennessee and saved up some money to get here, but I walked the whole way, and my brothers who came later did the same. Nobody ever gave us nothin'. God helps those who help themselves."

His grandfather paused as if waiting for him to speak, but he had nothing to say. He did not know how old his grandfather was, and when he had asked him, years ago, he merely replied, "Real old, Billy. Real old." He was dressed as he always dressed when going to town or receiving company—in his black suit and starched white shirt and black string tie. He wore his polished black boots that he reserved for this outfit. Billy noticed that the old man's tanned hand against the white cuff of his shirt was spotted with what he had heard were called liver spots. He found it hard to imagine being as old as his grandfather, and his stories of the past were like tales of ancient times, when things were clearer and easier to understand. And adults talked about those old times—the battles, the marriages and miscarriages, the deaths, as if they had happened yesterday, not in a past that preceded his existence; back into a time when there were fewer people, and they struggled to survive. Now he would overhear the adults talking in another room about the war and the freed slaves and the savagery of the Comanches, as if these were things that children should not know about. But he had been on the hunt for the kidnapped girl and was now a man. His grandfather was talking to him as if he was still a child, which seemed strange and out of place to him. It was as if his grandfather was stuck in a particular time and space and the world was moving on.

"What about the slaves, Grandpa?" he suddenly asked, surprising himself by the question, as if it had sprung out of him unconsciously.

His grandfather kept looking at the meadow ahead of him, as if still lost in thought, then, blinking, seemed to be thinking about what Billy had asked.

"The slaves? It was a curse upon us and it's good that it's over. But we should have been the ones to end it. We shouldn't have had it forced on us."

He turned to look at Billy.

"What made you think of that?"

"I don't know. It just came into my head."

"It wasn't what the Yankees said it was, for the most part. But it's good that it's over. I fear there will be a lot of blood spilled yet over it, though. I wonder why you are thinking about that."

"I was thinking about the people the Indians captured, I guess. Weren't they like slaves?"

Eli Baker looked back to the meadow. He did not speak for a while, then said, "It wasn't the same thing."

"Because the captives were white?"

He turned and gave Billy a look that he had not seen before, a look that gave Billy a chill.

"No," he said, forcing the words out slowly. "Because the Comanche tortured their captives and treated them badly. When they finally brought Matilda Lockhart back to San Antonio, just before the Council House Fight, she had bruises and sores all over her and her nose had been burned off." He paused for emphasis. "Her nose had been burned off. They would wake her up in the night by burning her. A fifteen-year-old girl."

There was a fire in Eli Baker's eyes that he had not seen before.

"Don't compare whites to Indians," he said. "There's no comparison."

Billy had heard about his great-grandmother's capture by the Comanches, but was not thinking about it when he spoke out earlier. He regretted what he had said.

His grandfather untied the reins and slapped them hard against the backs of the mules.

"It's time we got into town," he said, and turned the wagon toward Lockhart.

THIRTY-ONE

EVERETT HARDEMAN WAS LEAVING THE BANK. HE STEPPED OFF the wooden sidewalk to the hitching post and was about to mount up when Gilbert Adams approached him from the courthouse lawn across the street. Adams wore a full beard with gray streaks, and his hair was long under his flop hat. Although it was late spring, the faded red sleeves of his long underwear were visible below the rolled-up sleeves of his blue cotton shirt. Ev kept his hand on his saddle horn and did not turn toward Adams at first, but as Adams walked up to him, it became clear that he was coming to speak to him and he finally turned and faced him.

"Mr. Hardeman," Adams said. "Good day to you."

"Hello, Mr. Adams," Ev replied.

Adams shifted his weight from side to side and looked down at his worn boots for several seconds before he spoke again.

"I understand that you came to see me some time ago, but I wasn't home. My wife said she didn't know what you wanted, but I figured I'd hear from you before now."

Adams eyes narrowed. He waited for Hardeman's response.

"I'm usually home about supper time," he finally said. "That's the best time to catch me at home. Not in the morning."

Ev still did not speak.

"I was not aware that we had any business to discuss, but I'm here now and am at your service," Adams said coldly.

"I did come by your place, Mr. Adams," Ev said. "You know I represent the railroad."

"I heard that," Adams replied.

"Well, I thought you might be able to help us out."

"How's that, Mr. Hardeman?"

Adams was as still as a statue. Ev looked down at his polished boots and noticed a scuff mark he had not seen before. He hesitated.

"How's that, Mr. Hardeman?" Adams repeated, cutting off the words sharply this time.

"Wood," Ev said. "The railroad will need wood. You have a good bit of timber on your place."

Adams's eyes narrowed.

"I wasn't aware you was scouting for timber," he said.

Ev hesitated again. He met the man's stare for only a moment, then looked away and nodded at a man who passed on horseback behind Adams.

"I haven't been advertising it," he finally said. "I figure the railroad would be better off making only a few deals. Wouldn't want the price to be driven up by small loads. We'll need a steady supply and would want to depend on it."

Adams kept up his unwavering stare.

"You might have to hire a crew, but I hear there's plenty labor available now."

"How much you willin' to pay?"

"How about two dollars a cord?"

Adams looked down at his boots.

"Can't hire nobody and make money on that," he said.

"Three dollars?"

"I'd say five," Adams said.

"Five? I've never heard of anyone paying five."

"How much you gonna need?" Adams asked.

"As much as you can cut and haul."

"When's the railroad gonna be here?"

"We're probably a couple of years away," Ev said.

Adams stared at him again, this time with wider eyes.

"You're lining up wood a little early, ain't you?"

"I'm supposed to be looking out for the railroad's interests," Ev said. "Just trying to line everything up."

"Uh huh. Well, I'll think about it. In the meantime, if you want to see me, wait until after suppertime. Be seein' you."

Adams turned and walked away. Hardeman stood and watched him walk down the street, mount his horse, and ride away without looking back.

THIRTY-TWO

ISADORE FRIEDMAN HAD COME TO CALDWELL COUNTY BY FOOT from New Jersey in 1850, pushing a sales cart all the way. He had loaded up a stock of shoelaces, salve and liniment, thread and yarn, buttons and ribbons and a miscellaneous stock that found eager female customers ever so often, so he was able to keep going, sleeping in the open in summer and under whatever he could find in winter. He had devised a tarp that fit onto the back of his cart that served as a tent. He usually looked for bridges when he first hit town and would explore the ground under them before dark.

He avoided saloons and other gathering places such as churches. There were few Jewish temples in the towns he passed through, and he was reluctant to expose himself too much to the Christians. He felt free and fulfilled, knowing that his future was before him and he had the ability, learned and inherited, to succeed. He also had the ability to calculate what it took to make a profit and the experience to know that if sacrifice was called for and the situation was clear, it had to be done.

He would usually set up his cart near the post office or the bank. In some towns, the law would not allow him to set up at all, so he had to roam the main streets, pushing his cart. He would hold a sign up when he did not feel he was being watched by the law. It read, "Good Quality. Cheap." The goods he offered were of good quality, and he underpriced every merchant in every town he visited.

He was in good health most of the time, and there were established Jewish merchants in many of the towns who lent him a hand. He reprovisioned in St. Louis and took a hotel room for the night. It took him almost an hour to get his black suit brushed and cleaned, but he was dressed by seven and ready for the opera, which began at eight. He would leave civilization the next morning. That evening in the balcony, he felt like he was on the edge of a cliff, the balcony providing the image.

When he reached Plum Creek, he camped in the creek bottom a few miles from Lockhart. He went into town early the next morning, looking for breakfast, and found a small café just off the square where they served up eggs and coffee and friendly smiles. After breakfast he walked around the square. The buildings were wooden and crude, but functional. Within a block he found a general store owned and operated by a Jewish merchant who, after coffee, offered him a job and a place to stay. In six months he had been promoted to manager of the hardware department, and in another year he was made manager of the entire store, such as it was. By 1855 he had saved enough money to make a down payment on a commercial space for himself, on a corner lot that was vacant, and in another year he had saved enough to contract to build a small building. He opened Friedman's on January 1, 1858.

He had made many friends in town and his customers recognized his integrity and perseverance. He was able to cover his note the first month, and the business grew steadily. He had planned the building so that it could be expanded to cover the whole lot, which, like other lots on the square, was narrow and deep. At the time of secession, he had been in his newly expanded building for two months. It was the first real department store in town, and the saloon, with an entrance from the alley in back of the building, was an instant hit. He had free lunches, sandwiches, and sausages, and his drinks were cheap and not watered down.

A week after he returned from Austin, Ashley Maitland sat at the rear table at Friedman's in mid-afternoon. The saloon had the coldest beer in town, and it was a hot May day. Friedman had rigged a series of ceiling fans that were operated by a black kid riding a bicycle frame connected to a series of pulleys. It was twenty degrees cooler in the high-ceilinged saloon than outside. Friedman and two other men, regulars, sat at the table. It was Friedman's table and it was understood that there were no poker games at the owner's table. Ish Friedman, who never drank alcohol, sipped on a sarsaparilla. Ash and the other two nursed mugs of beer.

Pittman, the older of the two, had been asking questions.

"What's going to happen to Lockhart when the railroad comes?" he asked.

"It'll still be the county seat," Friedman replied.

"But there's going to be a new town, I heard," Pittman said.

The younger man, Stevens, who had hardly spoken since he sat down, said, "I heard that too."

"How about that, Ash? You gonna be the mayor?" Pittman asked.

"It won't be where I am," Ash said, just before taking a swig from his mug.

"I heard everybody was going to move to the new town," Stevens said.

"I might do that, Sam. It's going to be the end of the line for awhile. Lots of folks will be coming through."

"And everybody needs a good lawyer," Ish said, his eyes bright.

"There should be a lot of real estate changing hands. I don't guess you would know anything about that, Mr. Friedman?" Ash asked.

He knew that Friedman had acquired a fair amount of real estate in the area, some from farmers he sold to on credit who wound up deeding him land. Ashley was also aware that Friedman always paid a fair price and in the end usually gave the farmer the benefit of the doubt. He paid for the balance of the purchase price, after deducting what was owed him, partly in cash and partly by promissory notes that carried a fair rate of interest and on which he had never defaulted.

"You'd have to ask Mr. Josey about that," he replied.

It was well known that Josey had made a bargain with the railroad that granted a large swatch of land to what was now being called the Galveston, Harrisburg and San Antonio Railway, but kept the land around the townsite for himself. He stood to profit greatly by the transaction, and he was not a popular citizen among some of his neighbors, who secretly wished that they had made such a deal themselves. Ashley had heard talk of how the "Jew made a bargain with the Devil," and no good would come of it. There were preachers who warned of the evils that would come with civilization, as if only the good and just folks had had the courage to settle this part of Texas when it took hauling people and goods in wagons over dirt roads and trails to get to the area, and hard labor to build once they got there. Ashley had heard this sort of thing before in other places and in other times. It was the well-worn song of the old pioneer, who viewed the wilderness as part of his heritage and cherished relative ignorance when it came up against the hard realities of civilization. Even the war did not have the effect of dislodging this attitude from some, in spite of the clear evidence it brought of the unstoppable energy of the new pioneers, who would build railroads and telegraph lines over the entire continent and connect, eventually, the last vestige of the wilderness to the cities of the east and their civilizing and necessarily tarnishing influence.

And it had occurred to Ashley that it was an energy that was unstoppable because it was fueled by that aspect of human nature that had always existed and would always exist—the urge to move and build, to propagate, to spread out and find one's destiny. And the old were often slow to grasp the concepts of the young.

But Friedman was not one of those who resisted progress. He was one who valued opportunity.

"I wish I had had the foresight to invest as Josey did," Ash said. "There is still money to be made."

Friedman was quietly sipping his sarsaparilla, smiling.

"It ought to be good for business here, too," Pittman said.

Then Lily Poe walked into the bar. She was wearing a white summer dress with a lace bodice and carrying a parasol and a matching bag. She stood still by the doorway for a minute, until her eyes adjusted to the dimness of the shuttered room; then she saw them at the rear table and walked their way. All four men stood up as she approached and offered her a chair. She took a seat against the wall between Friedman and Maitland.

The bartender approached before anyone said a word. The men at the table were puzzled.

"Do you have lemonade?" she asked.

"Yes, ma'am, I can make you some."

"Then that's what I'll have," she said. "With a shot of bourbon on the side."

"It's good to see you, Lil," Ashley said. He waited for a response, but she just continued to smile at him. Then it gradually became apparent to him that she was tipsy.

"Glad you came to see me after all these years," Friedman said.

"You're welcome," she said.

Pittman and Stevens were transfixed. Her bonnet was a bit awry, but otherwise she was as beautiful as she had ever been. Her hair was pulled back into a bun under the bonnet. She leaned back in the chair.

"I was looking for you, Ash," she said.

"Oh?"

"I want my deed."

"Lily, let's move to another table so we can talk," he said.

"I don't want to talk. I just want the deed."

"All right. You know, I've told you that you have title irrespective of the deed."

She stared at him, still smiling.

"I want the deed," she said.

"I don't have it."

"Well, who has it?"

"You know who has it," he said.

She stopped smiling.

"Then I'll go see her," she said.

"No. Don't do that. I'll see her tomorrow. Let me see what I can do."

The bartender came with her shot and lemonade. She downed the shot and took a long swallow of the lemonade. Some of the liquid dribbled from the corners of her mouth.

"I know what is going on," she said. "You haven't even asked her, have you?"

"I've asked her. She always changes the subject."

She smiled again, her eyebrows raised.

"She can get away with that with you, can't she, Ash?" She looked around at the other men at the table. "Sorry, gentlemen. I didn't mean to interrupt a pleasant conversation."

"That's all right, Miz Lily," Pittman said. "We was just killin' time anyways."

"And this is a good place to do it," she said, her voice suddenly raised. She turned to look at Friedman. "Ish, I'll have another shot."

Ish gestured for the bartender, who brought the bottle of bourbon that was reserved for special guests and poured her another.

She raised the shot glass. "Here's to business," she said.

Later that evening, at dusk, Ash approached the McCulloch home. He was weary after a couple of hours of beer drinking and the ride in the late afternoon sun from Lockhart. He pulled up outside the gate and sat his horse for a while, considering whether this was a good time to see Laura. Then the front door opened and she appeared on the front porch, then walked to the gate to meet him.

"Good evening," he said.

"Hello, Ash," she said. "What brings you by here?"

"Lily came to see me this afternoon," he said.

"Oh. I see. Well, you'd better come on in."

Once they had stepped into her front parlor, he realized that it was the first time he had been in the room since he had come to see Wes McCulloch's body. She gestured toward a chair and took one herself.

"She wants her deed, doesn't she?" she asked.

"Yes. She came to see me at Friedman's."

"At Friedman's? What was she doing there?"

"Looking for me."

"I see."

"You know, you don't have to give her the deed, Laura, but it is customary and some lawyers think it a necessity."

She was staring down at her hands, clasped together in her lap.

"Why did she come to the probate hearing?"

"I think that was Hadley Wilson's fault," he said.

"You think so, Ash? I don't. I think it was her idea. You know Hadley Wilson. He would have no control over Lily."

He shifted in his chair.

"Can I offer you some tea or water?" she asked.

"No, I'm okay," he said.

"Or maybe a drink?"

He hesitated.

"Here," she said, standing up and walking to the cabinet by the front window. She pulled a bottle of bourbon out and poured a good quantity into a crystal glass, then brought it to him.

"Thanks, Laura," he said, reaching for it.

She returned to her seat. He took a swig from the glass.

"I'll sign the deed," she said.

He wanted to say that she did not have to, that the will was insulting enough, that Wes McCulloch should have been shot long before he hung himself in a tree, but it was another series of thoughts he wanted to express to her and never did. It was as if she was too good. Too good for him, at least. Somehow he had never been able to think of Wes McCulloch as not being good enough for her, which made no sense to him. Lily said Ash had always had a crush on Laura, and although he denied it, Ash was often hesitant to tell Laura what he was thinking, as if he did not have the right to give her his view of things. He had not asked her about the deed since he had given it to her.

"I'll get it," she said. "You can act as notary. It will be fitting. His best friend and his wife."

The next evening at Lily's he did not mention the deed. She had invited him the evening before as they left Friedman's, after he had helped her into her buggy. He came back to the kitchen as always, received his hug from Barbara Ann, and stood by Lily as she tended to things on the wood stove.

He was always impressed with her energy. She was almost never still.

"How about a couple of drinks?" she asked.

"Surely," he said and went to the liquor cabinet in the parlor. A pitcher of fresh cool water from the cistern stood on top of the cabinet, with two solid bar glasses. He mixed bourbon and waters for them and returned to the kitchen.

When she turned from the stove he handed her drink to her, and she raised her glass.

"To happier times," she said.

"I'll drink to that," he said, and raised his glass.

He told her he had the deed in his pocket and would record it the next day. He had to go to Lockhart anyway. He would have the original back to her in a week.

She smiled at him.

"You're a good man, Ashley. I hated to ask you."

"Oh?"

"Yes. But I had to have it. Wes would have wanted me to have it."

She was obviously relieved. They enjoyed a pleasant dinner.

THIRTY-THREE

T HE SCHOOL FOR GIRLS AT THE ACADEMY LET OUT AT THREE IN
the afternoon. Most of the girls left in groups of two or three, but
Martha Roberts always left alone. Other girls had tried to befriend her,
but found that she would not communicate, except with the nuns. One
nun in particular had taken her under her wing. Sister Rosella was immediately drawn to the girl. She had first noticed her on the playground,
sitting apart from the other girls. Sister made a point to have Martha
assigned to her afternoon class, usually walked with her to the edge of
the academy grounds, and saw her through the wooden gate as she left
for the day.

Sister Rosella said good-bye to her on a Thursday afternoon as she
walked out the gate and walked to the path along the river. A group of
three girls were ahead of her. It was a hot May afternoon and she took
her time along the river, then took the path leading toward Soledad Street
as usual, but stopped and turned after a few steps. She was not sure,
but thought she had heard something behind her. She had the feeling
that she was being followed. There were tall reeds interspersed among
the cypress and cottonwood trees along the river, and the wind from
downstream moved the foliage back and forth. She saw no one, but was
frightened and ran up the path until she reached the street. She crossed to
the west side into the shade of a log house and stood still against the wall,
looking across the street at the spot where the path ran between a storage
building and a low rock dwelling. Then she realized that she should not
be standing still and turned south, walking at a fast pace.

It was only a couple of blocks to Mrs. Elliot's house, and she ran the last hundred yards. When she reached the front door, she was out of breath. She landed on the porch with both feet, and when Ellen Elliot heard her from within and opened the screen door, Martha ran past her to her room. It was not unusual for Martha to say nothing to her when she came home from school. In fact, it was seldom that she had anything to say unless asked, and then her answers were brief. It was hard to get her to talk about her schoolwork or her classmates, although when asked, she said that she liked school. But she was almost always moving slowly, never running, and this time her face was flushed from running and there was something else there, in her eyes.

Mrs. Elliot turned, opened the door and looked up the street from where Martha had come. There was no street traffic. She stood there for a while, waiting, but nobody appeared. Then she walked quietly down the hallway to Martha's room.

Martha had been given the room in the rear of the stucco house. Its window faced the gulley where the riverbed had once been. It was overgrown with trees and grapevines, but there were paths that the locals knew, shortcuts that respectable people did not take. Martha was seated in the chair by her desk, looking out the window, still breathing heavily. Mrs. Elliot hesitated before speaking, but after Martha did not look her way, she cleared her throat.

"Martha. What is wrong?" she asked.

"Nothing," she said, still looking out the window.

"You look like you've seen a ghost."

Martha turned to look at her.

"I didn't see anything," she said, tears welling up in her eyes. "I didn't see anything."

"Martha . . . " Mrs. Elliot spoke carefully, keeping her voice low and calm. "I know something happened, Martha. I'm here to help you. But you have to let me help. You've got to talk to me if you want me to help."

"I don't want any help," she said, looking out the window again. "I don't need any."

Mrs. Elliot hesitated again. She had learned not to force Martha to talk. Occasionally Martha would come to her afterwards and tell her something Mrs. Elliot had inquired about earlier.

"All right, my dear. But you come tell me anything you want to. Okay?"

Martha continued to look out the window.

"I'm going to leave the door to your room open. I'll be in the front room if you need me."

The girl continued to stare out the window and did not speak. At suppertime, Mrs. Elliot was hoping that Martha would say something about what had frightened her, but she was overly quiet. In fact, Mrs. Elliot was reminded of the time when she first came to live with her. She would hardly look up from her plate and picked at her food only after questions about her not having an appetite. This night Martha went to bed without eating more than a few bites.

Mrs. Elliot had received a wire from Colonel Hays saying he would be back in town soon. She decided she would send her hired hand, Alonzo, to the Menger the next morning to see if he had returned from New Orleans.

Martha was usually up before Mrs. Elliot, sweeping the kitchen and hallway floor and performing her other assigned chores, but that morning Mrs. Elliot did not hear her steps in the kitchen, and when she quietly opened the door to her room, the girl was fast asleep on her single bed, the sheet pulled down and her legs bare under the hem of her nightgown. It looked as if she had tossed and turned half the night before finally falling asleep. Mrs. Elliot decided not to wake her and gently shut the door.

Alonzo was already in the garden in back and she quickly sent him on his way to the Menger. He reported back in about thirty minutes that the colonel was expected any day now, but had not yet arrived. Mrs. Elliot finished her coffee and roll and quickly dressed. She asked Rosa to keep an eye on Martha, telling her only that the girl was not feeling well, and headed for the academy. She took the route down Soledad to Augusta rather than by the river path and entered the main entrance just before eight o'clock. She inquired after Sister Rosella, knowing that she would be the one to talk to. She had already talked to the sister about Martha on several occasions. She found her on her way to her first class.

Sister Rosella said that Martha seemed normal when she left the day before, so something must have happened to her on the way home. She said Martha had taken the path along the river, as she usually did when the weather was good. Perhaps the sister should come and see her this evening. Mrs. Elliot said that she would be welcome in her home at any time, and this evening would be fine. She invited her to supper. They agreed that she would call around eight.

Sister Rosella rapped sharply on Ellen Elliot's screen door a few seconds after the hallway clock struck eight. She wore a summer habit, grey and a lighter weight than the ones that were worn in cold weather. Sister Rosella grew up in Madrid, in a poor family, one of seven children. She was used to the heat.

Martha hardly spoke at dinner, as usual, but the presence of Sister Rosella had an obvious effect on her. She quietly responded when spoken to, with only a word here and there, but her eyes were brighter and her voice had lost some of its sand.

After dinner, when they were seated in the parlor, the sister accepted a glass of sherry and some coffee, and they spoke of current social and charitable gatherings and the relief effort for widows and orphans of the war. Mrs. Elliot was glad that it was rare now that there were conversations about the war. Sister was happy that most of those who had been scarred were healing, through God's grace.

After a respectable time had passed, Sister asked Martha what had happened to her the day before, very simply and quietly. Martha looked down at her lap, then at Sister Rosella, the pain in her eyes again.

"I just thought I heard somebody. Or saw something," she said. Her lower lip was quivering.

Sister Rosella reached across the couch and took her hand.

"It might have been nothing, but I was scared."

Sister Rosella looked her in the eye.

"You should tell us when something like this happens," she said. "We cannot help you if you don't tell us."

Mrs. Elliot said, "I have some cakes that are very nice. Rosa made them special, so let's enjoy them," and gestured to Rosa, who had a silver tray held high and was smiling sheepishly.

When Hays arrived at the Menger that evening, he was given Ellen Elliot's message, which asked him to call as soon as he could. Shortly after nine, he knocked on the screen door.

Mrs. Elliot introduced him to Sister Rosella, who said she had heard wonderful things about him. Martha was sitting on the edge of her chair.

Hays was dusty from the stagecoach ride. He stared at Martha.

"What's happened, girl?" he asked, his voice calm and flat.

"Nothin'," she said. "Nothin' happened."

"Was it him?"

She turned away from him.

"Was it?"

She said, "I don't know if it was anybody."

"Where did this happen?" he asked the sister and Mrs. Elliot.

"Coming home from school yesterday," Mrs. Elliot said. "Somewhere on the river."

"I'll be here tomorrow to walk you to school, Martha. And I'll bring you back."

She smiled for the first time.

"Tomorrow's Saturday," she said. "There's no school on Saturday."

THIRTY-FOUR

B ILLY TIED JULIE TO A LOW BRANCH OF A MESQUITE TREE NEAR
the riverbank, took off his clothes, and hung them over the saddle
horn. He grabbed the end of the large grapevine from the fork of the
cypress tree where it was wedged and walked up the incline of the bank,
then launched himself out over the water, swinging up until he reached
the peak of the arc where he let go and was suspended in the air for a
moment before coming down into the water in a ball, head first, which
made the biggest splash. No one was there watching him, but it did not
matter. It was the way he liked to do it and although he had done it many
times, he still felt the same thrill in his chest that he had felt the first time,
at the very apex of his swing, as he hesitated for that moment high over
the water, before starting his downward motion. He came out of the ball
he had made as he hit the water, straightening out and stretching so that
his momentum propelled him deep, to the point that he could feel the
gravel bottom with his fingertips, and his momentum turned his body
over so that he looped in the water and came up a few yards downstream,
his head bobbing up just behind his feet. As far as he knew, it was his
trick and his alone. None of the other boys could do it.

The cool water had the shock effect that it always had on a hot day,
and he swam downstream on his back, looking up into the late afternoon
sun through the branches of the pecan, elm, and cypress trees. He had
been coming to this place since he was small, and although the river
changed with floods and drought and trees toppled into the water as the
river undercut earthen banks, it was still the same place. He could swim

the deep part until he came to another gravel bar, where eventually he would put his feet down to the bottom in shoulder-deep water and wade until it was knee deep.

The day had been unusually hot for May, and it had been hot for several days, portending a brutal summer. Gruder had said it might be another one like '57, when it did not rain for sixty days and all of the crops were burned to a crisp. The temperature topped one hundred degrees fifteen days in a row in August that year, Gruder said, and it was so hot in the afternoon that everyone lay around in the shade or got in the river to cool off. Billy wondered about the early Indians. They had to hunt and tend their crops to survive, but they must have spent a lot of time in the river in the summertime. He had found a number of arrowheads at an outcropping of flint near a place on their farm where, according to his father, the course of the river had once run. The place was on a high outcropping that would have overlooked the water. Now the former riverbed was a pecan orchard, but the swale which had been the riverbed was still visible. In wet seasons, the river in flood stage would cut through where it once ran regularly, and there were ponds of water in the low places in the orchard after it receded. He had once seen a mountain lion drinking from one of them. The lion raised his head and looked in his direction as he approached from the high ground and looked down, and he felt sure that the lion saw him, but he kept still. After what seemed like a long time, but was only a few seconds, the lion lowered his head and drank from the pond again before turning and slowly walking to the edge of the brush line, where he disappeared. Billy had wondered if he would see the mountain lion again. Gruder said that mountain lions took the same path over and over again and that their range covered many miles, so that it might be a year before the lion was back in the same place. He came back a year later to the day and climbed an oak tree that stood on the edge of the hilltop overlooking the place, but there was no pond there that year, and although he sat on the branch of the oak for most of the day, keeping still, the lion did not come.

He floated on his back with the current, looking up at the clear sky through the overhanging branches, and suddenly thought of Ada. He had not seen her since he returned. It was strange that she married Gilbert Adams, who had two sons not much younger than Billy and not that much younger than their new stepmother who, the last time he had seen her, looked pale and defeated. Her hair was bedraggled and she hardly spoke to him, looking down at the ground most of the time. Mr. Adams was there in front of Friedman's, loading the wagon with the help of his sons while Ada stood dutifully nearby, waiting for him. She had changed so radically from the beautiful, free-spirited girl he had known that he hardly believed it was really her. Floating, he again remembered swimming with her in Plum Creek, that summer before the war. Her wet, dark hair. Her blue eyes, laughing at him as he stared at her body. He daydreamed of going to see her, to talk to her, perhaps take her away somewhere, then he came out of his daydream. She had just turned twenty-three and he was sixteen. She was a married woman and he was but a boy. She was his cousin, but that should not matter. They were not close kin. His father and her mother were something like third cousins. He did not remember exactly, but Gruder had said, laughing, when he told him he was going to marry her one day, that she was his kissin' cousin and that would be all right, but he didn't think a pretty girl like her was going to wait for Billy to grow up.

He put his feet down and stood up in shoulder-deep water. Some of the family cattle were ahead, drinking in the shallow part of the gravel bar. When the river was low they waded across and had to be retrieved from the McKean place on the Guadalupe County side. A couple of the cows looked his way briefly, but soon returned to their drinking. He kicked back and began swimming back upstream. The current in the San Marcos was always strong, and it took considerable effort to make any headway when swimming upstream. He eventually turned and swam belly down, his long arms pulling the water at a faster and faster rate. His right shoulder had healed to the point that he was able to pull hard with his right arm, although he could still feel a twinge now and then when he moved it away from his body, so he reached overhead for his strokes and came down straight and followed through with his hands and arms straight down.

When he reached the place where he had jumped in and climbed up the cypress roots, he was looking down and did not see the man on horseback waiting for him, until he straightened up. Ashley Maitland sat his roan stallion beside Julie. He was wearing a straw hat and a white Mexican linen shirt rather than his usual suit and string tie. He smiled at Billy's obvious surprise.

"It's a good day to be in the river," Ashley said.

"Yes sir, it is," Billy said, still catching his breath from his swim.

"I'm on my way to see your uncle John," Ashley said. "I was meaning to come by and see you and your mother, too."

"Yes, sir."

"There's going to be a dinner and ball for Colonel Hays," he said. "In San Antone. You are all invited."

"Me too?"

"You too, Billy. Everybody who is anybody will be there. Some of the young men of San Antonio are putting it on, although I think Colonel Sweet of the *Herald* probably put them up to it. It'll be at the Menger ballroom. A pretty fancy affair, I expect."

"Will Martha be there?"

Ashley's smile returned.

"I expect she will," he said. "I hear she's a looker."

"She's all right. I just wondered, 'cause she's pretty young and all and I figured if I'm invited, maybe she would be too."

"I'm sure she will be," Ashley replied. "It's going to be week after next, on the third of June. I'll be by later to see your mother and extend her invitation, but you can tell her in the meantime if you want to. I guess you have some clothes you can wear, don't you?"

Billy looked down. He had forgotten he was naked. He reached toward the saddle and grabbed his pants. Ashley laughed as he turned the roan.

"I'll see you at your mother's house later," he said. "Tell her to expect me around seven."

THIRTY-FIVE

H AYS WAS AT MRS. ELLIOT'S PROMPTLY AT SEVEN-THIRTY ON Monday morning. He accompanied Martha up Soledad Street and then down to the river path and walked with her along the river until they came to the Augusta Street Bridge, then up the bank to the Ursuline Academy, where she was met by Sister Rosella at the gate in the stone wall. He had not seen or heard anything out of the ordinary along the path. He had asked Martha where she saw something and she was unsure, but she finally pointed out the place along the river where she thought it had happened. After leaving her at the academy, he searched the brush between the path and the river and found a narrow footpath near the bank. Anyone taking that path would be obscured from the main path by high reeds and brush. It was a well-worn path and there were many footprints in its dust. He took the path in a southerly direction. It followed the riverbank beyond the path that Martha and the other girls usually took to Soledad Street, then wound around with the bank until it reached Houston Street, beside a small lake formed by a low dam in the river. He retraced his steps and noticed a small path that veered west and took it. It wound up the incline beside the river until it approached the rear of Mrs. Elliot's house. From the path, he could stand and see the window to Martha's room. He made his way through the weeds and brush toward the Elliot house, keeping a close eye on the ground for signs of someone having walked there. He found where the grass had been disturbed by footfalls, but the impressions were indistinct. Then, only twenty yards or so from the window, he could make out a footprint in a bare spot and bent to look at it. He reached inside his shirt pocket and pulled out his gold-rimmed spectacles. He could make out most of a right footprint, and it was clearly made by footwear that did not have a heel. He recognized it as having been made by an Indian moccasin.

He searched extensively in the area near the house, but found no other signs, then returned to the path and followed it back to Houston Street, where he stood and looked up and down the street at the busy morning traffic. There were men on horseback, a few peddlers with carts, wagons pulled by mules and numerous pedestrians, many wearing palm sombreros and the white cotton shirts and pants of the Mexican peasantry. There were boots and huaraches, but no moccasins.

He accompanied Martha home from school that afternoon. They did not see or hear anything unusual. Later that evening, after supper, he paid another visit to the Cosmopolitan. There were only a few customers, who were outnumbered by the bar girls. He ordered a beer at the bar and waited. After about an hour, Jack Harris entered from the front door, immediately saw him and came over to him.

"Good evening, Colonel," he said, extending his hand. "It's good to see you again."

Hays shook hands with him.

"What brings you in tonight?" Harris asked.

"Mary Olive," Hays said. "I hope to talk with her again."

Harris stared at him for a long moment.

"I haven't seen her in weeks," he said. "I had to send her home one night and she has not returned. I suspect the poppy to be at fault, frankly. I think I told you. The girl's a hophead." He spoke without hesitation.

"Do you have an idea where she might be?" Hays asked.

"I'd look in the establishments along Market Street if I were you, Colonel. I still have a place there, Jack's Saloon. I don't think she'll be there. I pretty much told her what I thought of her behavior the night I sent her home. I'd be surprised if she showed up at my place. There are a number of other saloons, though. You might try Joe Foster's place, the Gem. She used to go in there some."

"Do you know where she lives?"

"Lives? Stays, as the negroes say, is more like it. I have no idea, Colonel. She got kicked out of the room she had when she worked here. Landlord came by looking for her."

He visited several of the saloons on Market Street that evening, including the Gem, and inquired after her, but the proprietors and bartenders he spoke to had not seen her. He also asked if any strangers had been in that looked like they might have Indian blood. No one said they had seen any. After he left the Gem, the head bartender, who had overheard his conversation with Joe Foster, told his second in command he needed to check on something and was taking a ten-minute break. He was gone for closer to thirty minutes.

On each subsequent morning and afternoon that week Hays accompanied Martha to and from school. On Wednesday, she repeated that she was not sure she had seen or heard anything out of the ordinary. He did not tell her about the moccasin print he had found.

On Thursday morning, he stopped at the gate with Martha as Sister Rosella greeted her. Sister Rosella extended her hand to him, palm down, as she had on each previous morning, and he held it and shook it lightly, still not quite sure if that was the proper thing to do. Then he spoke directly to Martha.

"I am afraid there is going to be a dinner and ball in my honor a week from Saturday," he said. "Martha, I would like for you to come as my guest, and I would like for you to bring Sister Rosella along."

Martha's face lit up. She turned to Sister Rosella.

"Can you come, Sister?" she asked.

"I don't know," the sister said.

"I had hoped you would honor us with your presence at dinner," Hays said. "I know Martha would like for you to come."

"Oh yes, I would," Martha said. "Please do."

"I suppose I could come to dinner," she said. "But I have to be in by ten."

"Good," Hays said. "You will be my guest. And you are welcome to stay for the ball if you can."

"Oh, I couldn't do that," the sister replied. "But I would love to come to dinner."

"I will arrange for a young man to call for you and escort you home after dinner," he said. "I would not want you to be walking along the streets after dark."

"I am not afraid to do so, Colonel. I would hope that my habit and my Lord would protect me, but I appreciate your offer and will accept. Thank you."

"Dinner is at eight and I will confirm with you next week who will be calling for you," he said. "Thank you for accepting."

"Thank you, Colonel, for the invitation. I will be looking forward to it."

"I will see you this afternoon, Martha," he said, then put on his hat and turned to go.

"Thank you, Uncle," Martha said.

He paused. It was the first time she had called him Uncle.

"You are welcome, young lady," he said.

After he left Sister Rosella and Martha, he walked down Augusta Street across the river bridge and eventually to St. Mary's Street, which he followed south until he again came to the river, where it formed a large horseshoe curve that led east near Alamo Plaza, then eventually back west. He had taken the path back as far as the Menger, but not beyond, and decided to see where it ended. It was a pleasant May morning. A norther had blown in the evening before, breaking the hot spell, and he could walk comfortably in his suit. The path led him past the old village called La Villita, then west, where the river ran to the rear of Market Street. On the left bank were orchards broken up by wooded spots. Just downstream from a wide, shallow part of the river, where there were gravel-based islands barely topped with silt and spotted with young cottonwood shoots, there was a low-water crossing made of stone, where the river narrowed and provided a natural place for a crossing over shallow water. It had originally been only a ford, used for centuries. It had been laid over with stones and concrete, forming a small, shallow dam. The water pouring over at its deepest point on the crossing was about six inches deep, and he easily waded across.

He turned back east on Market Street and walked past the bars, which were empty and not officially open, although if you tipped the porter he would serve you a beer from last night's last keg. He then walked past a laundry and a blacksmith shop. This was a street that servants and the poor frequented during the day. There were no dress shops or millenaries. He entered the Gem. The shutters had not been opened from the night before and he had trouble seeing in the dim light. He stood staring into the room for a moment, then heard a sweeping sound from the back of the room near the faro and monte tables. He could barely make out the white cotton shirt and pants of a man pushing a broom. He gradually came into the light from the doorway. He was short and dark.

"May I help you, sir?" he asked in Spanish.

"I am looking for a young woman," Hays replied.

"It is early, friend. You should come back after dark." The man's smile widened.

"I am looking for one particular girl," Hays said. "She might have worked here, or she might have been with a Comanche."

The porter stopped smiling.

"I can't help you, Colonel." This time in English.

"Do you know her?" Hays asked in Spanish.

"I know her. She was here ten days ago, with two of them. I don't know where they are now."

"Do you know where she was staying?"

"She used to be out west of the creek," he said. "But I heard she got kicked out. You looking for the half-breed?"

"Yes. Was he one of them?"

"He was. They were with her."

"What about the other one?"

"A little guy. Short and stocky. Looked Apache."

"Lipan?"

"No. Not Lipan. Some other kind I never seen before. He was a bad-looking man."

"How about the half-breed?"

"You never seen him? He's a tall, skinny man. Long hair, but no beard. Mean."

"Were they drinking?"

"No. They came to get some stuff for the girl."

Hays reached in his pocket and pulled out some coins and handed them to him. He accepted the money.

His next stop was Jack's, Jack Harris's old saloon. The porter was a graying, potbellied man. He was behind the bar, a cigar stuck in the side of his mouth.

"You remember a girl named Mary?" Hays asked. "I'm looking for her."

"You mean the doper?" the porter asked.

"You remember. The dark-haired girl."

"I remember," he said. "Beautiful girl." He took a drag on the cigar.

"Yes. You seen her?"

"Not since you was here the last time, boss. I'd tell you if I had."

"When was she here last?"

"I already told you."

Hays stared at him. The man was leaning against the back bar, one elbow up.

"I don't remember what you said," Hays said.

"It's been weeks," he said.

"I thought you said a week."

"Not a week, boss. I don't think so."

"That's what I remember," Hays said.

"Whatever you say, boss," he said, puffing on the cigar.

"Who's selling to her?"

"I don't know that," he said.

"You know where she gets it. I'm willing to bet on it," Hays said.

The man's eyes narrowed.

"Oh?"

Hays pulled a gold coin with an eagle on it from his vest pocket and gently laid it on the bar.

"There's a guy that works the joints around here," the porter said. "Goes by the name of Charlie Boy. He's an idiot. At least that's his game. Usually comes in around midnight, here, and later around the street."

He reached for the coin. Hays's movement to grab it was a blur. The man froze, then looked up.

"Where does she live?" Hays asked.

"I don't know that, boss. Honest, I don't."

"If you were looking for her, where would you look?"

"I'd ask around," he said. "The houses in the west end would be a start. She's gonna sell it. That's my guess. Her man's gonna put her to work. That's just my guess. But that's where I'd start lookin'."

Hays held the coin out between his thumb and forefinger.

"Where would you look first?" he asked.

"Sallie Brewer's. On Concho Street. That's where I'd start," he said, squinting at the coin.

Hays laid it back on the table. The porter reached for it slowly this time, watching Hays's hand as he reached. When he had it in his grasp, he withdrew his hand quickly into his pants pocket.

When Hays knocked at the two-story frame house at ten, a black woman opened the door. She looked him up and down.

"I'm looking for a woman goes by the name of Mary Olive," he said.

"You Colonel Hays ain't you?"

"Yes."

"I saw your picture in the paper. Come in, sir."

She opened the door wider and stepped aside. Hays took off his hat as he entered.

"If you wait here, Colonel, I'll tell Mrs. Brewer you're here."

He waited in the paneled hallway for a good while. The parlor to the left was elegantly furnished. Leather couches. A fire screen. The marble fireplace mantel displayed carved ivory elephants suspended in the reflection of a large mirror in an ornate frame. Finally, he heard someone coming down the hallway. A tall, thin woman in a dark dress approached him and extended her hand.

"Colonel Hays, it's an honor. What can I do for you?"

"I'm looking for Mary Olive," he said.

"Is she in trouble?"

"No. Not with me. I am interested in who she might be with."

"I can't help you, Colonel. I haven't seen her in several weeks. I hope she's alive. I don't know that she is."

"Do you know where I might find her?" he asked.

"I don't, Colonel. I never knew where she lived."

She showed him the front page of the *Herald* before he left. It had a contemporary drawing of his face and an announcement that there would be a dinner and ball honoring Colonel Jack Hays, formerly of the Texas Rangers, at the Menger, on June 3. Bar to open at 7 p.m.

Hays spent the rest of the day walking around San Antonio making inquiries, to no avail. But when he entered the lobby of the Menger that evening, the desk clerk waved at him and said, in a stage whisper, "Colonel Hays."

Hays approached the desk and the clerk told him that the sheriff was waiting for him in the bar.

"He said to ask if you would care to join him for a drink."

He thanked the clerk and tipped him. In the dimly lit, dark-paneled room the sheriff was leaning against the bar, talking with the bartender. Hays had known Jim Fisk since he had been the city tax collector in the forties. He had followed that up with a stint as an alderman, and was then elected sheriff in 1866. He had been married to a young woman from the Ruiz family. When his wife died, he married her older sister.

The Ruizes were originally Irish. Their ancestors came to Mexico under the Irish spelling of the name—Reese. Hays was a friend of the family. Fisk turned to him as Hays approached the bar.

"Hello, Jack," he said. "It's good to see you."

They spoke of the past and mutual friends. Fisk had always shown a great deal of respect toward Hays, and Hays appreciated it.

After a while, Fisk got to the point. "I hear you're looking for someone," he said. "I've had a couple of my men looking around on your behalf."

Hays visibly stiffened.

"Don't worry. They're good men. They're just asking their usual contacts. I might have something for you in a few days."

"Do you know who I'm looking for?" Hays asked.

"I know that and why you want him," Fisk said. "That's well known around here. Everybody knows the story about the girl and how you saved her," he added. "I just wanted you to know that I'm gonna help you all I can. I won't try to get to him first if you want the shot, Colonel. I'll help you as much or as little as you want."

"Let me know what your men find out, Jim. I appreciate the help."

"I'll let you know," Fisk said.

"You might be able to help with another thing," Hays said. "I have been told there is a man who sells opium in the bars around here, a man they call Charlie Boy."

"That's right," the sheriff said. "I think he's in jail right now, if he hasn't sat it out. I can check on that for you."

"I would appreciate it," Hays said.

"You think he might know where the girl is," Fisk said.

"That's right."

"He probably doesn't know. His customers usually come to him. Would you like to walk over to the jail with me and see if he's still in there?"

"I would," Hays replied.

Fisk finished his beer with a long swallow, and Hays followed him out the back door of the bar through the livery stable yard onto Alamo Plaza. From there, they walked to the Commerce Street Bridge. Fisk was tall and had a long stride. Hays found it hard to keep up with him.

"You might find the girl when she runs out of dope," Fisk said, as they walked across the bridge. "I'll run my traps in the bars for her. Charles Smith is not the only source she has."

"Why is he in jail?"

"Drunk on the street. That was last night. He may be out today."

They were quiet the rest of the way down Commerce Street. They turned the corner at Main Plaza and were soon at the entrance to the jail, a low stone building with narrow barred windows. Inside, the sheriff asked the sergeant at the main desk if Smith was still there.

"He is, Sheriff. He may still be asleep. Never seen a man sleep so much."

The sergeant accompanied them through the cellblock door and past several cells on each side of a narrow hall until they reached the drunk tank. At the end of the hall a deputy was asleep in a chair propped against the wall. The sergeant started to say something, but the sheriff touched him on the shoulder to quiet him, then walked up to the sleeping deputy. He was an older man with white hair and a beard and a large, bulbous, red nose. He was snoring quietly. The sheriff placed the toe of his boot under one of the upraised chair legs and pulled it forward. The chair slid down the wall, but the deputy jumped at once and landed on his feet, his eyes still closed. When he opened them, he was in a crouch, reaching for his empty holster. Hays recognized him.

"Dad," the sheriff said. "I'm going to get you one of these days if you keep sleepin' on the job."

The man stayed in the crouch, then slowly straightened up.

"Wasn't asleep, Jim. Just resting my eyes."

"This is Colonel Hays, Dad."

"Hays," the man said, squinting at him. "Shit. I'll be damned if it ain't. How you be, Jack?"

"I'm all right, Ephraim," Hays said.

Ephraim McLane had been part of a Ranger expedition led by Henry Karnes against the Comanches in 1839, having enlisted in Wilson's company of spies from Galveston County. Hays was leading a party of surveyors attached to Gonzales's company, a part of the expedition, and had been the leader of the spies that found the Comanche camp on the Pedernales. They attacked the camp just before dawn, while the Comanches were sleeping. Twelve Comanches were killed. None of Karnes's party were lost. Hays and his surveying party decided to return to Austin after the skirmish. The commander of McLane's company, Wilson, resigned his command and followed Hays and his party of surveyors a few days later. McLane, an enlisted man, was elected to succeed Wilson as captain.

McLane was for going after the Comanches who had fled, but it was decided that the entire regiment of two companies would return to Austin. McLane's company was disbanded upon its return to Galveston a short time later.

Men are elected captain in the Rangers, particularly in the spy companies, for different reasons. It was not clear why McLane was chosen over others superior in rank, but Hays had been told he was very vocal about pursuing the Comanches and was overruled by Karnes, who was in charge of all the companies in the expedition.

Hays also knew that McLane had been on the Davis expedition into Mexico in '42 and had heard inconsistent reports about him: that he was given to rash action, but he was a leader of men.

"Damn, Jack," he growled. "I thought you was dead."

"Still kicking, Ephraim."

"You looking good, too. I wouldn't have recognized you though," he said. "Hell, you're a greybeard."

Hays smiled and looked at Fisk.

"I see Captain McLane hasn't changed a bit," he said.

"Not a bit," Fisk said.

"Just as ornery as ever, you damned right," McLane said. "Still just as mean, too."

Fisk turned to the desk sergeant.

"Where is he, Joe?"

"Just here, Sheriff," he said. He turned to the drunk tank, which looked like every other cell in the jail, except it was bigger and was the only one that held more than one prisoner, at the moment. Three lumps of near-manhood were asleep on cots. By the window a young man sat on the edge of his cot looking out the dark window opening. He was lanky and bushy-haired with a full mustache. Two lanterns in the hallway provided the only light. Hays walked up to the barred cell door. The sheriff was beside him in a moment.

"Smith?" The sheriff's voice was deeper than before.

The young man turned to look over his shoulder at them, his half-lidded eyes accentuating his flat expression.

"Come here, please," the sheriff said, and the young man stood up slowly, turned, and walked over to them.

"This is Colonel Hays, Charlie. Maybe you've heard of him?"

"I don't think so," he said.

"He's looking for Mary Olive."

"I haven't seen her lately," Charlie said.

"Charlie. Don't lie to me," the sheriff said.

"I wouldn't lie to you, Jim," he said. "I saw her maybe ten days ago. I don't know where she lives." The sheriff looked at Hays.

"You know where she might be working?" Hays asked.

The man did not avert his eyes as Hays looked at him.

"Sheriff," he said. "You know all the dives I know. You can show the Colonel where he needs to go."

The sheriff stared at him. He turned to the desk sergeant.

"Let him out, Joe."

Joe unlocked the cell door and opened it, and Smith came out of the cell into the hallway with them. His rumpled clothes were fashionable, and his boots were shined. Though he wore a day's growth of beard, his tie was still knotted and his collar was straight, but as he drew near the smell of stale alcohol wafted from him.

"Charlie, you can help us more than that," the sheriff said. "Colonel Hays is looking for a man she may be with. She's not in any trouble."

Smith looked at Hays with the same unwavering stare.

"I'd try Ignacia Cortez," he said. "Near the stockyards. She gets the dirty vaquero trade. Mary may have sunk that low."

"I'll put a man on it," Fisk said.

"How about me, Jim?" McLane said, from behind him. "I've been in this jail too long."

"What do you think, Colonel?" Fisk asked. "Dad here's been serving a little penance for some alcoholic adventures of his own, but it's probably time to let him out in public again. Assuming you can behave, Dad."

"I'll take him with me, but I prefer that he not wear a badge," Hays said.

"That's easy," McLane said. He took his badge off and handed it to the sheriff. The sheriff did not even look at it.

"Put it in your pocket, Ephraim. I can't accept. That would mean you resigned. Jack, you sure you don't want me to handle this?"

"I'm sure, Jim, but thanks."

They walked back into the office, and the desk sergeant unlocked the large bottom drawer, pulled McLane's Colt out, and handed it to him. It was an old Walker Colt that bore significant signs of wear. Smith was standing by the desk. He backed up a step when the pistol came out. McLane checked the cylinder for loads, then holstered the Colt with a seamless move.

"Jim, it's been good working for you," McLane said. He put the badge on the desk. "You don't pay worth a damn, but you're an honest man. I have no complaint."

Fisk looked at Hays, then back at McLane.

"You take care of yourself, Ephraim," he said.

"You going there now?" Smith asked.

"It would be a good time to go, Jack," McLane said.

"I'm heading that way," Smith said. "Maybe I can help."

"You wouldn't be looking for a free meal would you, Charlie?" the sheriff asked.

"I might be," Smith said. "I might have some business there."

"You can come along," Hays said.

Fisk shook his head. "Up to you, Jack," he said. "But I don't know that he'll be a bit of help to you."

"It won't do any harm, Jim." Hays said. "He can go along with us."

"Very well, Colonel Hays," Fisk replied. "Let me know if I can be of further assistance."

They shook hands. Hays, McLane, and Smith left the sheriff and his deputy staring at them as they walked out the front door. They proceeded along the south side of Main Plaza and down Dolorosa, then south on Flores to the intersection with Nueva Street. Ignacia Cortez's place was a short distance east on Nueva, on the north side of the street. During the short walk, Hays and McLane questioned Smith about his knowledge of Mary Olive. Smith had been supplying her with laudanum. She could have purchased it at any pharmacy, but Smith sold it on the cheap. He explained that he had a special source of supply. She had been a customer for about a year. He always saw her in bars, at the Cosmopolitan or other saloons around Main Plaza or on Market Street. When told she had introduced herself as an actress, he laughed. He had seen her participate in a musical revue once, as a chorus girl. He actually liked her. She was pretty and she always laughed at his jokes.

The Cortez house was a two-story frame structure with a covered porch that ran from the front around the curved right corner of the house and down the side. There were soiled rattan couches and chairs on the porch. A single lantern hung over the front steps. There was no bell pull at the front door, and Smith stepped in front of the other two, opened the screen and inner door and stepped in. Hays and McLane followed. The hallway inside was dimly lit. The sound of a piano came from the parlor to the left, and Smith strode in and walked to the far corner where an empty fireplace was flanked by a black man with a derby hat playing an upright piano and a sideboard with several bottles of liquor, glasses, and a plate of sandwiches. A couple of worn couches and a number of straight-back chairs were occupied by some obviously drunken men and several whores who were sitting in a group together, slightly apart from the men. Smith headed straight for the sandwich plate. He had already taken a bite out of one by the time Hays and McLane crossed the room. One of the women stood up and came over to Smith at the sideboard.

"Charlie Boy," she said, in a high voice. "How's my sweet Charlie Boy?"

She put her arm around his neck. He leaned back away from her, smiling.

"Well, Miss Edna," he said, his voice livelier than it had been up to now. "What a fine figure of a woman!"

He beamed at her, holding her away from him by her arm with one hand, with the sandwich in the other. His previously flat features had taken on an exaggerated comic look, his eyebrows raised and his lips spread into a manic smile. Edna had seen better days, as had the sad dress she wore.

"Would you like to do a little tradin', honey?" she asked. She pulled his hand off her arm and stepped back slightly, raising her head. "You got somethin' for me?"

"No, Edna. I'm all out. Maybe tomorrow, but I'll have to have cash. You know I can't afford to trade."

"Aw, Charlie Boy," she said, draping her arm over his shoulders.

He pulled away from her and stepped over to Hays and McLane.

"I don't see her around here, Colonel," he said to Hays. "But she may be upstairs."

One of the men, a ruddy-faced man with two or three days' growth of beard, stood up and started weaving their way.

"Who you boys lookin' for?" he asked in a slurred voice. He stumbled, then straightened up and took a last long step. McLane moved forward a bit so that he was between the drunk and Hays. "Y'all got a special one here?" the drunk asked.

"We're doin' okay," said McLane. "Don't need any help."

The drunk took a step back, still unsteady on his feet.

"You ain't talkin' about my Mattie Belle," he slurred. "I got her for the whole night."

A frazzled blonde in a camisole stood up from the nearest couch. She also weaved a bit.

"I ain't your whore," she said. "You ain't got no money left anyway."

The drunk turned to her.

"I'll take care of you, you stupid bitch," he said, stumbling toward her.

McLane grabbed his arm. The drunk took a swing at him with his free hand. McLane caught the blow with his forearm and slapped the drunk across the face so hard that his feet slipped out from under him and he fell to his knees. In a swift movement, McLane kicked him in the groin, causing him to fall to the floor with a grunt. He curled into a ball and began to vomit on the worn rug.

Hays and Charles Smith stood motionless by the fireplace. The other men and women in the room were standing, looking down at the man on the floor. McLane turned to them.

"Anyone else?" he asked.

They stood in silence. After a while, Hays turned to the woman who had been talking to Smith.

"We're looking for Mary Olive," he said. "Do you know her?"

"Mary? I know her. But she ain't here," she said, her eyes rolling glassily. "Why you lookin' for her?"

"Do you know where she lives?" Smith asked.

"She's with that half-breed," she said. "He's a mean one."

"Do you know where they are?" Hays asked.

"I might," she said.

Smith turned to Hays.

"She might, Colonel," he said. "She'll want something for the information, though, won't you, Edna?"

"Something for my trouble is all," she said.

Hays pulled a gold coin from his pocket and held it between his thumb and forefinger. The woman stared at it.

"Colonel, huh?" she said. "You can get a little extra for that."

"Just where she lives," he said.

She reached for the coin and he held it away from her hand.

"She was at the Carnation two days ago," she said. "She was with both of them."

"Both of them?"

"The mean one and his friend," she said. "He's pretty mean hisself."

"Where is the Carnation?" he asked.

"It's a cheap hotel not far from here," McLane said. "We can be there in no time."

"Very well," Hays said. He handed the woman the coin. She took it and immediately turned and moved away from them, toward the corner of the room.

"Can I come along, Colonel?" Smith asked.

"Certainly, Mr. Smith," Hays replied. "You might be of some help."

The Carnation was a ramshackle structure that had been built as a hardware store. After the death of the owner it was sold, and the new owner put in partitions and turned it into a hotel. It catered to the lower class of travelers and women who had need of rooms at day rates. There were some more or less permanent residents, older men who had reached dead ends, but most of the rooms changed patrons on a much more regular basis, once a day or even once an hour.

The small lobby had a narrow desk built under the stairway on the right as you entered the front door. There was an outside door on the side, by the bottom of the stairs. A small kerosene lantern on the edge of the desk was lit, but no one was there. A set of double glass doors, the only visible concession to artistic considerations, split the wall to the left. They led to a narrow ground-floor hallway. The lantern cast its light on a single door in the back wall, which was ajar. McLane stepped over to it and gently pushed it open, his hand on the handle of the Colt. Inside the small room a man lay on a cot, asleep. He was thin and pale and lay sprawled on his back with his mouth open. A faint wheeze came from somewhere deep in his throat.

McLane stepped into the room and Hays and Smith followed. McLane kicked the heel of the man's boot off the edge of the cot, which caused a convulsive movement up his frame. McLane whipped out his pistol and held it in the man's face as he sat up.

"You the clerk?" he yelled.

The man sank away from the pistol.

"Hey!" McLane yelled. "Are you deef?"

"Yes," he gasped. "I'm him."

"We need to look at your register," McLane said.

The man sat up, his eyes fixed on the pistol.

"We'll follow you," McLane said, holstering his weapon.

The clerk staggered from the cot through the doorway to the lobby. He slipped behind the desk and pulled out a large register, bound with a worn green cover. His hands shook as he opened it. They moved forward to look. Hays came first and squinted at the book in the dim light from the lantern. He stepped aside for Smith, who had been peering over his shoulder. Smith pored over the pages. There were only twelve guests registered, five of them with repeat marks that indicated a residence of more than one day. Smith immediately recognized one of twelve days duration, a Mr. Ross.

He turned the book so the clerk could see.

"They paid for a month," the clerk said. "Two men and a woman."

The room number was shown on the register. Smith put his thumb under it.

"Looks like 'em, Colonel," he said.

"Have they been in today?" Hays asked.

"I haven't seen 'em in days," the man said. He was shrinking back from the desk, deeper into the cramped space under the stairwell.

"Is it upstairs or down?" McLane asked.

"Upstairs. In the back," the clerk replied.

"Are the rooms nearby occupied?" Hays asked.

"No. They're the only ones back there."

"Let's have your skeleton key," McLane said. "Unless you want to go up there with us."

The clerk reached under the desk and pulled out a large key ring with a number of keys. He turned them over one by one, looking closely at them, then grasped one, unhooked it and held it out to McLane, the key shaking in his hand. McLane grabbed it and stepped back from the desk, looking at Hays. Hays stepped in front of him to the stairwell. He started up the stairs, which creaked loudly, the sound startling in the silence. McLane and Smith followed closely behind. A railing bordered the top of the stairwell on the second floor, opposite several rooms, then the hallway opened wider toward the rear. All of the rooms were on the left, with windows to the right every ten feet or so. The rooms were consecutively numbered from 201 to the last door, 210, the one they were looking for. When they were within twenty feet of the door, they caught the smell. It was unmistakable to Hays and McLane, who stopped briefly, then continued moving forward slowly down the hallway, their pistols drawn. Smith stopped and stayed where he was when the smell first hit him. He pulled out a handkerchief and held it over his nose.

Hays stopped short of the doorway and stepped back for McLane. McLane stretched his arm out and placed the key in the lock, being careful to keep his body back from the door, against the wall. He slowly turned the key in the lock, then, after gesturing toward Hays with his pistol, turned the handle and threw the door open. Both Hays and McLane crouched around the edges of the doorway, their pistols pointed into the room. The door slammed loudly against the wall inside and came halfway back toward the doorway, its shadow from the hallway light moving across the figure on the bed. Hays stepped quickly into the room and rapidly turned from right to left, his gun hand extended. McLane was in the room on the other side of the doorway in an instant, scanning the room. When it was apparent that the body on the bed was the room's only occupant, Hays lit a candle on the bedside table so they could see. She lay on her back, naked, on the blood-soaked bed. Her throat had been slit from side to side, and her blood had dried on the side of her chest and shoulder and on the bed sheet where it had pooled. Her eyes were swollen shut from a severe beating and her lips were blue and swollen, indicating she had been beaten long enough before her throat had been slit to allow blood to flow to her wounds.

"Oh my God," Smith said from the doorway.

A disheveled cot stood against the wall by the door, opposite the bed. A table and two chairs, the only other furnishings, were scattered, one of the chairs resting on its side. There was an overturned chamber pot next to the bed, its contents spilled out on the bare wood floor. Scraps of her clothes lay about the room on the floor, torn and scattered, as if they had been torn off her. A small empty brown bottle without a label lay on the floor near the table, and cigarette butts had been stomped out all around.

Hays could not recognize the battered features as belonging to the young woman he had met at the Cosmopolitan. He turned toward Smith.

"Can you identify her?" he asked.

Smith took a step inside the doorway, then hesitated.

"If it's Mary, she'll have a tattoo," he said, his voice muffled by the handkerchief.

"Where?" McLane asked.

"On her right shoulder," Smith said.

Her shoulder was away from them, against the wall. McLane walked to the bed, leaned over the battered body and pulled the bloody shoulder of the girl toward him. A small yellow blossom peeked through the streaks of dried blood.

"It's some kind of flower," McLane said.

"It's a tulip," Hays said.

"That's it," Smith said. "It's her."

THIRTY-SIX

———•◦•———

L AURA MCCULLOCH WAS MEASURING BILLY FOR HIS NEW SUIT. His aunt Cassie was writing the measurements down in pencil as Laura called them out to her.

"I can't believe you've grown so much," Cassie said.

Laura called out his sleeve length.

"Thirty-six?" Cassie asked. "I can't believe it."

He had been measured by his mother before, but not in years. Store-bought clothes were expensive. He had worn some of Wonsley's hand-me-downs, and they had made do for a long while without Laura having to sew for him. The one suit he had that he had worn to his father's funeral was now too small. When she had forced him to try it on the week before, he could barely get into the coat and the sleeves ended at mid forearm. Now he needed a suit for the dinner and ball.

"You are going to be quite the man of the hour, you know," Cassie said. "The girls are going to be after you. You better watch out."

He started to speak, but his mother jabbed him in the ribs before moving the tape measure around his waist.

"Thirty-two," she said emphatically, then leaned back and looked at him. He turned to her. "I think he's grown up too soon," she said. "He's missed his childhood."

"He's quite the young man," Cassie said. "Who are you escorting to the ball, young man?"

"How about you, Aunt Cassie?" he replied.

Cassie blushed. She was his father's sister. An old maid schoolteacher who had never been found attractive to the opposite sex. She was tall and broad shouldered, with strong features. Her intelligence and sharp wit had not met their match in a man.

"You need to take a young lady," she said. "Not an old maid like me. You can get any girl you want, I'll bet."

"He doesn't need to escort anyone other than his mother," Laura said.

She gestured at him, indicating she had finished her measurements. He stepped back.

"I didn't know you wanted to go," Cassie said.

"I believe Colonel Hays is due the honor," Laura replied. "I think I would like to see him one last time and see him receive the honor due him. Billy has agreed to escort me."

"I thought perhaps Mr. Maitland would ask you," Cassie said.

"He alluded to it. I suggested he should accompany Mrs. Poe and her daughter. Billy will be glad to have the girl as a dancing partner."

"Mother," he said. "I don't . . ."

"An excellent idea," Cassie said. "But you surprise me, Laura."

"Oh? I don't see why."

Cassie made a guttural sound, then handed the piece of paper containing the measurements to her.

"I understand that the widow Moore will be accompanied by her daughter Ada, but not by her daughter's husband," she said.

"You know that Mrs. Moore and the Johnstons are kin," Laura said.

"That's true," Cassie replied. "But I should think Mr. Adams would accompany them."

"Cassie, hush. You shouldn't be saying that. You know Gilbert Adams."

"I know him, all right," Cassie said, her eyebrows raised.

After his aunt left, Billy asked his mother what she had meant about Gilbert Adams. She turned from the cloth she was marking on the dining room table.

"Don't pay any attention to Cassie," she said. "Mr. Adams is a good man. He's just set in his ways. He wouldn't be going to a dinner in San Antonio, or anywhere else."

"I don't see why she married him," Billy said. "He's an old man."

"It's a sad situation," she said. "Hard times."

"I don't understand it," he said.

Gruder was waiting for him out back. He was polishing the family carriage, which sat next to the carriage shed, where it had been since his father's funeral. It was a four-seater and had cost a pretty penny when new. Billy walked over to examine it. Gruder had removed the dried mud spatter left over from the drive to and from the Highsmith Church on that rainy day in November, had made the black finish and leather seats shine, and had even polished the brass fittings, which sparkled in the morning sun.

"Where will you stay in San Antone?" Billy asked.

"With a friend," Gruder said.

"Are they gonna let you attend the dinner?"

"I'll be there," Gruder said, rubbing a spot on one of the brass rein guides.

"I mean at the table."

Gruder turned and gave him a familiar look, one that he reserved for times when he knew Billy was stepping out of bounds, but could not say anything. Then he turned to polish a brass headlamp.

"I'll be there," he said again.

THIRTY-SEVEN

E PHRAIM MCLANE HAD TO BEND OVER TO GET IN THE DOOR, HIS hand holding the Indian blanket aside. It was barely lighter inside the room than the pitch-dark night he had just walked through, and he stood looking until he could make out the prone figures through the dim smoke. They lay on handmade wooden cots, a few feet apart. A few were listlessly puffing on pipes, but the rest were lying on their backs with closed eyes and beatific expressions on their faces. The room was littered with wads of paper and other debris. The cots were raggedly unarranged, with small tables for the pipes and the opium nearby. He waited.

After a few minutes, a small Mexican man wearing a rumpled black shirt slowly moved into his view from the dark in the back of the room.

"Is there something I can do for you, Captain?"

McLane gestured toward the room of smokers.

"You got any dopehead Apaches here?"

"Apaches?"

The little man started to chuckle, his dark eyebrows raised.

"I'm looking for an Apache."

"I don't see no Apache," the little man said.

"He's a killer. I want him bad."

"I'll see what I can do," the little man said.

"I'll just take a look around," McLane said, as he walked farther into the room, between the cots, stopping and looking over the edge of each cot at the face of each sleeping man. Several had oriental features and one of those wore a black silk skullcap that he recognized as Chinese. One of them was a mere boy, probably no more than sixteen, with a pockmarked face.

"What do you think you're doing, Ciro? This is just a child."

"He's nineteen, Captain. At least that's what he said."

McLane turned to look at him.

"You get him out of here when he wakes up," he said. His voice was coarse and heavy. "I don't want to see any more kids in here, Ciro. I'll shut you down if I see any more."

"Yes, Captain," the little man said. "I don't want no trouble with the law."

"I'm looking for an Apache," McLane repeated. "He has a habit. I know he's been here. You better tell me the truth."

Ciro smiled.

"What does he look like, Captain?"

McLane grabbed a handful of the man's shirt and pulled his face close. "Look, you little bastard," he said. "You know what a goddamn Apache looks like. Don't give me that shit."

Ciro's eyes widened.

"He was here the other day, Captain."

"What day?"

"I think Thursday, Captain. I'm not sure. A few days ago."

"Where did he go?"

"I don't know, Captain. I swear I don't."

"Was anyone with him?"

"A girl," Ciro said. He was trembling.

"What girl?"

"One of those whores from over at Blanca's. I don't know her name."

"Is she one of your regulars?"

"She comes here some," he replied. "I don't know her too good. I think she's called Susie."

"Is that what he called her?"

"No. I don't know. I didn't hear him call her nothin'."

"Had he been here before?"

"Not when I was here, Captain. That's the first I saw him."

McLane was still holding him up by his shirtfront. Ciro's heels were lifted off the dirt floor.

"Now, why didn't you tell me this to begin with?" McLane asked.

"I'm sorry Captain," he replied. "I guess I forgot a little."

"You see him again, you slip out while he's sleeping and let me know. I stay at Barnabee's. If I'm not there, go to the sheriff's office and tell the deputy you need to find me."

"Okay, Captain."

"You understand? *Comprende?*"

"Yes, Captain. I understand."

"You know what I'll do to you if I find out you're lyin', don't you?"

"I'm not lying, Captain. I told you all I know."

"What about his name? Do you know his name?"

The little man hesitated. His face had paled.

"I think the girl called him something like 'Pussycat'," he said. "Something like that, maybe 'Gatito', en Español."

"Was she speaking Meskin?" McLane asked.

"Sí, Captain. She is Mexicana."

McLane slowly lowered him and released his shirt, then pushed his extended index finger against Ciro's chest.

"I better not find out you're lyin' to me," he said. "I better not find that out."

"I ain't lying, Captain."

McLane looked around the room again. The pungent smell of opium was all too familiar to him. It permeated the room and he felt a little light-headed. He looked down at Ciro's face again, then turned and pushed his way through the blanket in the doorway.

He had not shared the information he had discovered about Morgan's man with Hays. He wanted to find him on his own, and now he felt he was near. Blanca Romero's house was a real dive, where the whores were cheap and a drunk would likely be rolled if he took his pants off. It was only a couple of blocks from Ciro's place. McLane instinctively felt the handle of his Colt with the heel of his hand as he walked.

He entered Blanca's through a side door he knew about and stepped inside the rear hallway that led to the kitchen. On a slow night, the girls usually sat around the kitchen table drinking coffee. Most of the nights at Blanca's were slow. He could hear some female voices as he approached the open doorway to the kitchen. Three of them sat around the table, playing cards in the light from the table lantern. Blanca, with her bleached blonde hair pinned up in a sloppy bun, stood at the stove stirring a large pot, a cigarette dangling from her mouth. She turned as he leaned in the doorway. As she looked at his face, her brown eyes narrowed.

"What you want?" she asked in a hoarse voice.

"I'm lookin' for someone," McLane said. He looked at the women at the table. "Any of you Susie?"

"What's she done?" Blanca asked.

"How about it?" he asked, still looking at the three at the table.

"She ain't here," Blanca said.

One of the women, a brunette with drooping eyelids, was staring at her coffee cup. "She went off with that goddamn Indian," she said without looking up.

"Shut up, Nancy," Blanca said. "It ain't none of your business."

"I don't give a shit," Nancy said. "She's a dope head like me. But I don't take up with no Indians."

"Where did they go?" he asked.

"Hell if I know," the brunette said, looking up at him. "She didn't consult with me none. None at all."

"Shut up, Nancy." Blanca gave her a stern look, her cigarette punctuating her hoarse words. She looked back at McLane.

"They might be at Ciro's getting a fix," she said.

"Just came from there," McLane said.

"Look, Dad. I don't want no trouble and I don't want you shootin' no Indian in my place. I bet if you go back to Ciro's, they'll be there before the night's out."

"Who told you you could call me Dad, whore?" he asked, his voice up a few notches.

She turned back to the pot and stirred rapidly. Her voice was barely audible when she said, "Sorry, Captain."

He turned back to the brunette.

"Where is she right now, Nancy?"

She looked in Blanca's direction. Blanca continued stirring without looking around.

"She said he was gettin' her a room at the Menger," she said. "But of course that's bullshit. I'd look at Henry's if I was you."

Henry's was a flophouse about a mile west, in the poorest part of the west end. It was known in law enforcement circles as a haven for petty thieves and pickpockets who were on their last legs.

"Why Henry's?" he asked.

Nancy looked up and gave him a heavy-lidded smile.

"Cause that's about the end of the line and that's about where they are," she said.

It was past midnight by the time he reached Henry's, and his legs were aching as he stepped onto the creaky wooden front porch. The building was a low one-story adobe with unfinished cedar posts raggedly holding the roof of the porch up. There was no screen on the wide-open front doorway, and McLane stepped inside with his hand on his holster. The narrow hallway was lit only by a dim lamp high on a wall toward the rear. He hesitated on the threshold. There were six doors, three on each side of the hall. The old man who usually sat on the porch in summer to collect rent and point down and outers to their rooms was nowhere to be seen. There were no keys to the rooms, only catch latches on the inside of each door, and McLane was prepared to kick in all of the doors, but the sound of the first one would likely wake everyone who was not past the point of being awakened by noise, so it was important to choose the first one wisely. The floor creaked as he walked on it, and he decided that, of the six doorways, he might as well pick one of the first two, which were opposite each other. There was no rear entrance, and if his man came out from one of the back rooms, he would have to run toward the front and pass by McLane. It was easier to try the handle of the one on the left and hold his pistol in his right hand as he tried to open it, but the rooms would likely all be darker than the hallway and he would be outlined in the doorway as he stepped in. If the Apache was awake and waiting for him, he would be an easy target, and he would not be able to see inside in the dark. Then he remembered that the front four rooms had four cots in each one, where a man could pay ten cents for the rental of a cot for the night. It was not likely that the Apache had taken his whore to one of those rooms.

He walked down the hallway toward the two rear doorways. The lantern was hung on the wall to the right. He moved to the door to his left, unholstered his Colt, turned the knob and pushed. He crouched as the door swung open, the hinge creaking loudly as the shadow of the door moved slowly across the room until he could see an iron bedstead. He stepped quickly in and to the left against the inside wall, out of the light coming from the hall. He could see the bed, where a portly man lay fully clothed. He was lying on his back with his mouth open, sound asleep.

There was a table and a chair in the room, nothing else. McLane turned out into the hallway again and approached the opposite door. The floor squeaked under his boot heel as he stepped toward it. He instinctively crouched on hearing the sound. The sound of a gunshot from behind the door instantly followed and McLane could feel the air around the bullet as it passed inches above his head.

He plunged toward the doorway and crashed through it, knocking the door open as he rolled through, coming up into a crouch again and firing at the gun flash he saw before him. He fired four shots in rapid succession in the direction of the flash, then waited, still in a crouch. In the dim light from the doorway, the smoke from the pistols rose in small clouds toward the ceiling. As it gradually cleared, he could make out the shapes of two bodies on the bed. They were still. He slowly stood to get a better look, his Colt extended toward the shapes.

The man had been hit in the neck and was bleeding profusely. His glassy eyes stared toward the ceiling. His body was jerking and with each jerk, the fountain of blood flowing from his throat gurgled. The woman had been hit in the chest and lay sprawled over the far edge of the bed, as if she had tried to pull away as the shots were fired. Her lips were moving, trying to form words, but a red foam ran out of the corner of her mouth as she tried to speak. Her arm swung over the edge of the bed in a movement that seemed out of place, as if she was moving it back and forth, still trying to push herself off the bed and away from the gunfire. The man's dark hair lay askew on the crumpled sheet. An Apache bandana lay where it had fallen off his head. It matched the description McLane had been given. He grabbed the bandana and turned and staggered out the doorway. He did not think he had been hit, but he was dizzy and weak and there was a throbbing pain running down his left arm. Doors opened as he wavered down the hallway, still holding the Colt in one hand and the bandana in the other. Startled faces stared out at him as he passed through the front door and out into the pitch-dark night.

THIRTY-EIGHT

⎯•◦•⎯

THEY PULLED ONTO ALAMO PLAZA AND GRUDER STOPPED THE team at the front entrance to the Menger. After Billy and his mother had descended from the carriage, Gruder helped the doorman unload their luggage, then drove around the corner to the livery stable, where the horses would be unhitched and fed and watered. No mention had been made of where and when Gruder would join them inside, and Billy was determined not to ask. The lobby was impressive with its iron columns and balconies on three sides and giant potted plants and paintings. Billy had been to San Antonio a couple of times, but had never been inside the Menger. He did not want to be seen staring up at the balconies and tried to look up from time to time without raising his head. After registering at the desk, his mother encountered two women she knew and stopped to talk to them, which gave him a chance to step to the side and look up at the balconies and around at the large paintings on the white walls. As he turned, looking, he finally saw a boy about his age in a uniform, a suit with a short jacket and matching pants with a small pillbox hat, standing at the end of the hotel desk, staring at him. The boy leaned against the edge of the desk, his grin displaying a missing front tooth. He seemed to be looking at Billy's pants and homemade suit jacket.

Laura finished her conversation and Billy followed her and the young bellman to their room on the second floor. After their luggage was situated, they came back down to the lobby and to the door of the ballroom, where they hesitated.

The room was a rectangle, with large windows on each side. A long table covered by a white tablecloth was set between two rows of white columns in the middle of the room. A shorter table formed a T at the far end for the head table. Large candelabra and place settings with folded cards had been spaced along the length of the main table. Black men wearing white jackets were standing nearby. A seven-piece orchestra playing a waltz was seated in the corner on the right. An oak table to the left against the windows overlooking the patio served as a bar, with bottles, glasses, large pitchers of water, and bowls of crushed ice. A group of men stood around the bar, only about half of whom were bareheaded. Billy was sure his mother noticed the ones who had failed to take their hats off.

On the opposite side of the room, a number of people were standing near two punch bowls situated on a table among crystal cups, next to a table with bottles of wine and wine glasses. Billy followed Laura as she approached the punch-bowl table. The bowls had small wooden signs in front of them labeled in calligraphy. One read *Punch*, the other *Not*.

Hays, wearing a dark gray suit with a vest, was standing at the light punch bowl beside Sister Rosella, who stood between him and Martha. Martha wore a green dress that set off her blue eyes and showed off her red hair. Hays was beaming, turning from Sister Rosella to Martha to Mrs. Elliot as he listened. He noticed Laura as she approached.

"Colonel Hays. It's a pleasure," she said, extending her hand.

"It's good to see you, Laura."

"I saw you briefly at Wes's funeral," she said. "Very briefly."

"I'm sorry. I couldn't stay long that day."

"I know."

"It's good to see you, too, Billy. Mrs. McCulloch, I don't believe you know my niece, Martha."

"I remember you from years ago," Laura said. "You wouldn't remember. You were a babe in arms."

Martha looked different. She was smiling. She actually smiled while looking at Billy, before looking down.

"And this is Sister Rosella," Hays said.

Billy and Martha were alternately looking at each other and down at their feet while Laura and the sister lightly shook hands and Hays introduced Laura to Mrs. Elliot. A few other groups of three and four people each stood around the room amid the white iron pillars. The ten or so men at the bar table, including an older man with a white beard and long straggly white hair, were downing shots.

When Billy turned back around he caught Martha staring at him. She even held the stare for a moment after he turned to look at her, then quickly looked away.

Wonsley came up behind Billy and tugged at the back of his suit jacket. He wore a blue homemade suit, a white shirt and a string tie, with a brown derby hat hanging back on his head. His blonde hair hung over his shoulders. He was clean-shaven for a change. He was with John and Susan Baker, who stood smiling beside him. Greetings were exchanged.

Susan looked quite different from the last time Hays saw her at the hog pen. She was a beautiful woman, smaller than he remembered. Her smile waned when she looked at him. John Baker hugged his sister Laura and clapped Billy on the shoulder.

Not taking part in the conversation, Wonsley and Billy drifted off to the side. They both looked around, each surveying the room, then glanced at each other and slowly made their way to the bar table. As they approached, Jim Fisk stepped out from the group.

"You must be a Baker and a McCulloch," he said.

"I'm a Baker and he's a McCulloch," Wonsley said.

"I've heard of you two," he said. "I'm Jim Fisk. How would you boys like a beer?"

"Glad to meet you, Sheriff," Billy said. "I'm Billy McCulloch."

"I knew your father," Fisk said. "And you must be Eli Baker's youngest," he said to Wonsley.

Wonsley nodded.

"How would you boys like a beer?" the sheriff asked again.

Billy and Wonsley looked at each other.

"Anybody who can chase a bunch of renegades all over the Hill Country can damn sure have a beer," Ephraim McLane said. The boys did not know him, but had noticed his white hair and beard from across the room. He turned and grabbed a couple of glasses, drew from the keg at the corner of the table, then handed the beers to them and picked up a newly filled shot glass. "Here's to Colonel Hays and his band," he said, lifting his glass.

McLane's voice was heard across the room. The other men at the bar table lifted their glasses and the men and ladies at the punch bowl turned and lifted theirs. Billy's eyes met his mother's and it was obvious she was looking at the beer glass in his hand. She hesitated before smiling her approval and he took a long swallow in toast with the others.

Ev Hardeman stood at one end of the table bar, off by himself. He had hung his hat on the rack by the door and stood facing the doorway, a long step away from the man nearest him. He had noticed everyone who had entered since he arrived. The ladies were wearing summer dresses. Many had their hair up in back, some tied with ribbons. About a third of the men wore store-bought suits. A few were obviously wearing their Sunday shirts and newly cleaned pants.

Ashley Maitland and Lily Poe entered, followed by Barbara Ann. Hardeman met them inside the doorway.

"I am so glad you accompanied these two lovely ladies tonight," he said to Ash.

"It is surely my pleasure," Ash replied.

Ash began to extend his hand to Hardeman, but realized it might be awkward. Ev saw his movement and reached his left hand out to shake. Ash extended his left hand, but his movement was halting and hesitant.

"It's okay, Ash. I'm used to this," Ev said. "I can easily shake your right with my left."

Lily extended her hand, covered with lace flowing from the cuff of her dress. Ev took it and held it lightly, bowing.

"I think your drawl has returned, Ev," she said, smiling.

"You are lovelier than ever, Lily," he said. "And who is this young lady?"

"This is Barbara Ann, Ev. She was quite a bit younger when you saw her last."

The smile left his face.

"A lot of time has passed," he said.

A couple entered the doorway behind them and they stepped to the side to let them pass. Ash nodded at the man and he nodded back, but it was only a polite greeting, not a sign of recognition.

"How about a drink?" Ash asked Lily.

"I'd love one," she said.

Ev hesitated.

"Would you prefer some punch?" he asked, gesturing toward the punch table, where other women were standing.

"Ev, you know I prefer whiskey and I don't mind hanging out with men at a bar. You know that."

She glared at him.

"Then let's have one," Ash said.

They walked to the bar table, where the sheriff stepped up to greet them and the other men stood aside for them. Ash poured himself and Lily bourbons with water. Ev volunteered to get Barbara Ann a lemonade from a nearby table. After he returned he stood on the edge of the group by the bar table, his eyes again on the doorway.

Ash noticed Laura across the room. He turned to Lily, who was talking to George Sweet, and asked her to excuse him for a moment. She looked across the room at Laura and the others standing by the punch table, then smiled and nodded. Ash walked over to Hays and the women by the punch table and stood patiently while Mrs. Elliott finished a story she was telling, then extended his hand to Hays and bowed to the ladies. Hays introduced him to Mrs. Elliott, Sister Rosella, and Martha.

The room gradually began to fill as more people came in the doorway and spread out among the side tables. Ev kept his eye on the door. Finally, Mrs. Moore, Ada, and Thomas Coddington entered, Coddington coming in behind Mrs. Moore with a wide grin on his face. Hardeman was surprised that Mrs. Moore knew the carpetbagger, and he hesitated before walking over to them.

"Good evening Mrs. Moore," he said, bowing slightly. "And good evening to you, Mrs. Adams," he said to Ada, ignoring Coddington, whose smile vanished.

"I haven't seen you since you returned, Everett," Mrs. Moore said, looking at his pinned right sleeve, then quickly up at his face. "It's good to see you again."

"I should have called on you, Mrs. Moore," Ev said. "I apologize."

"Ada told me she had seen you and you were well," she said. "Do you know Mr. Coddington?"

He nodded. "Mr. Coddington and I have met briefly," he said. "Good evening to you, sir."

"A pleasure to see you again, Mr. Hardeman," Coddington said. "It's such a fine evening for a dinner and ball and I am privileged to accompany these two lovely ladies. I'm sure I will be the envy of all men this evening."

Ada was looking at Ev with her eyebrows raised, as if she could see his discomfort with Coddington and was enjoying it. Ev smiled at her, finally, and stepped aside and gestured toward the punch table.

"Would you ladies care for some punch?"

"Oh, I don't know," said Mrs. Moore. "I rarely partake, but perhaps a bit."

Ada gave her a look. Mrs. Moore's eyes scanned the tables at the edges of the room.

"I actually prefer wine," she said.

"So do I," Ada said. She was still smiling, looking at Ev. He noticed a slight discoloration around her right eye that barely showed under a layer of powder on her face. He had not known her to powder her face. He frowned when he saw it, and she noticed.

"I'll be happy to fetch two glasses," he finally said. "I think they have Texas wine."

"That will be fine," Mrs. Moore said. "That's what we're used to."

The ladies and Coddington followed Ev to the wine table, where Coddington excused himself and walked over to the bar. The men were crowded around the table, blocking his way, and he shuffled to the right and left, looking for an opening. Billy and Wonsley were standing outside the circle of men. They watched Coddington's movements with smiles on their faces. Finally, Coddington shoved his way into the crowd around the table, two men moving aside without taking notice of him.

Mrs. Moore asked Ev about the railroad. He explained that it would be three or four years before the railroad came through Caldwell County, but that it would be a great thing for the area when it got there. The area around Ada's eye looked puffy.

Hays took his leave at the punch table and walked over to the bar. Ephraim McLane met him at the edge of the circle surrounding Lily Poe.

"It's been a long ride, Jack, and we're not through yet," McLane said.

Hays was looking at Lily, who was engaged in conversation with several men. He asked, without looking at McLane, "Who is the pretty woman?"

McLane turned to look at her.

"She is a beaut, ain't she? That's Lily Poe."

He said it loud enough for her to hear and she looked their way, catching Hays's stare before he looked away. She excused herself to the other men and came over to where Hays and McLane were standing, the circle parting for her as she moved through. She extended her hand.

"Colonel Hays," she said. "It's an honor to meet you. I'm Lily Poe."

"My pleasure," Hays replied. "This is Captain Ephraim McLane."

She did not take her hand away immediately, leaving it clasped gently in his for a few seconds before she extended it to McLane.

"Captain," she said.

"Ma'am," he replied, shaking her hand up and down.

"I hear you got one of the murderers, Captain. I want to hear all about it sometime."

"My luck was holdin' out, ma'am," McLane said. "But the baddest one is still around."

She turned to Hays.

"I hope you don't mind my attending tonight, even though we had not met before. Mr. Maitland asked me to accompany him."

"We are all glad he did," Hays replied.

"I want to hear all about your recent adventures, Colonel," she said. "At a more convenient time, of course."

"Jack don't talk much about that," McLane said, giving Hays a look out of the corner of his eye.

"I would be happy to give you a full report, Mrs. Poe," Hays said, smiling.

McLane beamed. "I guess there's always exceptions," he said.

George Sweet rang a brass dinner bell and announced that dinner was served. The crowd took to table, with Hays, the Baker brothers, and Billy seated at the head table, along with Sweet, as Master of Ceremonies, and the two young men who had organized the dinner and ball. The waiters served the first course and poured wine and water into the crystal glasses at each place setting, although a number of the men had brought their drinks from the bar.

It occurred to Billy that he had not seen Gruder. He looked around the room and spotted him standing by a column near the door that led to the kitchen. He was wearing a white waiter's coat and stood with his hands folded. He was looking Billy's way and his look was a familiar one that indicated Billy should keep quiet. Billy turned back to the guests at the main table. Martha was looking his way, frowning. She was seated near the head table and he could not avoid her stare. Hays was seated between George Sweet and John Baker and had not noticed Gruder. Billy stood up and walked to where Gruder stood.

"You need to be at the table," he said.

"No, Billy," Gruder said. "I'm okay here. It's okay."

Hays turned and saw them, then stood up and walked their way.

"He should be at the table," Billy said.

"He should indeed," said Hays. He turned to a waiter who stood nearby. "Bring a chair over to the head table. Come on, Gruder."

Hays led them back to the table, Gruder following reluctantly.

"Ladies and gentlemen," Hays said. "This is Gruder McCulloch, an important member of our party."

He directed the waiter with the chair to the opposite end of the head table from where Billy and Wonsley sat, then stood by until Gruder took his seat.

Several of the men visibly stiffened. Conversation had ceased. A woman next to Mrs. Elliott sat wide-eyed with her mouth open. A man sitting near the opposite end of the long table next to Ephraim McLane stood up.

"I'm sorry, Colonel," he said. "But I cannot do you the honor of remaining." He turned and walked out the doorway leading to the lobby. Everyone watched him leave.

"Anyone else?" Hays asked in the calm, low voice Billy had come to know. He stood at the center of the head table, looking around at the guests. They were all silent. Hays sat down. He stared straight ahead down the long main table, his eyes fixed on the vacant far end. After a long silence, George Sweet stood.

"Ladies and gentlemen, as you know, we are here to honor Colonel John Coffee Hays for his years of service to Texas. Colonel Hays has been back with us for a while on a mission that he has undertaken with the characteristic courage and valor that he is known for. His exploits are known to most of us. He was at the Battle of Plum Creek and the Battle of Monterrey, where he led our Rangers. He fought the Mexicans and Comanches, who came to fear him and his valiant men. He is one of the finest men of our age. I give you Colonel Hays."

They all stood and applauded. Hays stayed seated for a long time, looking down the table at the faces turned toward him. He recognized a few of them, but most of them were unknown to him. It usually made him uncomfortable for so many strangers to seem to know him, but tonight was different. He reddened and stood uncertainly. He began softly.

"It has been good to see so many old friends and comrades. And the city has changed a great deal since I was last here. I appreciate you attending tonight and hope you enjoy yourselves. I want to thank Colonel Sweet and the others for arranging this. Your show of respect means a lot to me. I came here long ago, so many things have changed. I was a surveyor by trade, and we had to do what we had to do to protect ourselves back then. Ourselves and our families. Anything I have done has been out of necessity."

He looked at Martha.

"As for recent events, it is good that my niece, Martha, is here with us tonight. My thanks go out to the friends and family who are taking care of her. Also to her teacher, Sister Rosella."

He looked right and left, at the Baker brothers and Billy.

"I also want to thank my recent companions, John and Wonsley Baker, Billy McCulloch, and my old compadre, Gruder McCulloch, for their able assistance. But our job is not done. There is a murderer still at large. He has been here in San Antonio recently and may still be here."

Several of the women looked at Martha.

"Sheriff Jim Fisk and his men have been on the lookout, and my old friend, Ephraim McLane, has been very helpful. We think we have thinned out the bunch down to one man, but he's a bad one and we think he might have come here to recruit new members for his band."

McLane's hoarse voice could be heard at the opposite end of the table.

"He'll need some new ones now."

This brought a smattering of laughter and the tension in the room relaxed a bit. Hays looked down at McLane, then slowly around the table.

"I have a lot of friends here, I know, and I know there are some who are no longer with us that should be here. I . . . I hope you enjoy the evening." He looked down, then abruptly took his seat.

After a few silent moments the table again buzzed with conversation. They dined on wild turkey, quail and ham, sweet potatoes, macaroni, and steamed cabbage, followed by apple pie and ice cream. After most had finished their desserts, George Sweet stood and announced that the table would be cleared shortly and the ball would begin.

Hays chose Martha for the obligatory first dance and had to talk her onto the dance floor. Although unsteady at first, she followed him well through the waltz. After a few turns around the floor, other couples joined them. On the third dance number, Ev Hardeman came and stood by Ada. Mrs. Moore, standing between Ada and Coddington, gave her a look. Ev stood quite still beside her through two more dances, showing no expression, then turned to her.

"I would like to ask you to dance, Ada," he said. "But I don't want to embarrass you. I don't have a right arm to hold you with."

She turned and looked him in the eye.

"I can hold you," she said.

She moved a step forward and reached for his hand. He took her hand in his and they stepped onto the dance floor between the columns. She put her left arm around his waist and they began to dance. Billy saw them from the opposite side of the room. Ada moved with Ev gracefully through every turn, although it was a struggle for her at first. It was strange to be the one holding him, her palm in his back, being in control of their movements, his left hand in her right giving him no leverage with which to move her. He tried to move closer to her, but she maintained a distance between them. He was looking steadily at her as they danced. She turned her head from left to right, looking at the other dancers. When the music stopped, they stood staring at each other.

"I'm sorry I didn't come back sooner," he said.

She turned without speaking and returned to stand by her mother. He walked to the bar table and poured a whiskey. Mrs. Moore noticed that Ada's eyes were moist and handed her a handkerchief.

Billy, feeling the two beers he had consumed, was standing by the orchestra. Martha had returned to her place next to Sister Rosella after her dance with Hays. She looked across the room at Billy, then looked away when she had caught his eye. He walked around the edge of the dancers until he was standing beside her. She turned and looked at him, her eyebrows raised.

"W-would you . . ." he stuttered.

"I would," she said immediately, holding out her hand.

They danced uncertainly until Billy realized that she could follow his staggering lead, then he gained confidence and found the beat of the music. Her red hair shone through the room as they moved around the floor. Her blue eyes were fixed on his while they danced, and her smile was broad and carefree.

Wonsley stood by the bar table next to Ephraim McLane, sipping on his third beer. McLane was talking about a raid against a Comanche camp that had happened in the distant past. Several young men were gathered around listening to him. He spoke between downing shots of whiskey, and his words were slurred.

"The Comanche don't hold with takin' prisoners, except for women and children," he said in his gruff voice. "They'll take them and raise them as slaves, helpers for the women folk, but they'll kill all the men and older boys. They ain't stupid. Don't want any grown men around to cause problems. So if you meet up with some of them, don't count on surrenderin'. Might as well fight to the death, 'cause that's what they'll do, except when they get spooked. Then they'll run like dogs. Hard to say what will spook 'em. Why, I've seen a lot of 'em spooked by silly things. Silly things, indeed."

"I heard they're scared of crazy people," one of the young men said.

"Oh hell yes. Bad medicine, they believe, to mess with a crazy person, because the Great Spirit has touched 'em. I know men who could act crazy and survive with 'em, but it's not like they'll take 'em along with 'em. More than likely they'll leave a crazy person to his own deserts."

Hays was standing in a circle of young men, including those who had arranged the festivities. One after the other, they asked him about the exploits they had heard about. The Battle of Monterrey. Enchanted Rock. Bandera Pass. He answered each question courteously and briefly, but did not elaborate. As for Bandera Pass, he took the blame for putting his men in a bad situation. At Enchanted Rock, he was lucky that the rest of the party found him in time, after his ammunition was exhausted. At Monterrey, his fellow Rangers made the difference. He was privileged to lead them. Finally, during a pause, he saw an opportunity to step away from the group. He excused himself and walked over to Lily Poe and Ashley Maitland.

"So what would you rather be doing than this, Colonel Hays?" Lily asked him.

He smiled and said, "I can't imagine any place better than right here, Mrs. Poe."

"Oh what tact, Colonel! Ash, you didn't tell me that the Colonel was such a diplomat."

"Oh, I think that depends on the company, Lily. Isn't that so, Jack?"

"Yes, Ash. It does," Hays said. "I have seldom been in such good company."

"Forgive me, Colonel, but I was wondering how long you would grace us with your presence here in Texas?" Lily asked.

"It all depends," Hays replied. "There is still work to be done here."

"Is that the murderer you referred to? Will he keep you here?"

"He will be caught," Hays replied. "It's just a matter of time."

"I know that Wes McCulloch thought highly of you," she said. "He mentioned you often."

"I had the privilege of having Wes as a friend," he replied. "He was a good man."

She turned to Ashley.

"I think I'm ready for another drink, Ash," she said. "Perhaps the Colonel would like to dance while you fetch it."

She handed her glass to him and Ash smiled his broadest smile and bowed, then turned toward the bar table. As Hays and Lily stepped onto the dance floor Laura McCulloch watched from across the room.

Mrs. Moore and Ada had excused themselves to go to the ladies' room and were returning down the hallway when they encountered Ev Hardeman coming from the lobby. Mrs. Moore's face was flushed with the several glasses of wine she had consumed. She greeted Ev by holding out her hand to him.

"Everett, I am so glad you are here with us," she said. "You were gone so long."

He took her hand and held it.

"I stayed away too long, Mrs. Moore," he said. "Would you ladies like to step out to the patio? There might be a breeze."

Ada looked at her mother.

"That might be nice, Mother," she said. "We could use some fresh air."

"Certainly," she said.

Torches were lit around the perimeter of the patio, and moonlight shone on the fountain in the center. Mrs. Moore stepped over to a stone bench near it and sat down.

"It is nice here," she said. "I think I'll sit for awhile. You two may want to walk around a bit, but I'm a little dizzy, so I think I'll sit."

She was smiling at them. Ada and Ev looked at each other. He held out his left arm for her and she placed her hand for him to guide her and they walked around the patio in the moonlight. When they were out of Mrs. Moore's hearing, he spoke.

"What's wrong with your eye?"

She stopped walking and turned slightly away.

"What do you mean?"

"Ada. You never wore face powder before. What happened? Did he hit you?"

"It was an accident," she said.

"What happened?"

"He didn't mean to," she said.

"So he hit you."

She did not respond. He grasped her arm.

"Ada. I want you to divorce him and marry me."

"What? I can't do that."

"Yes, you can. I love you. You know that. I'll always love you. And I can't stand thinking about him hurting you. If he does that again, I'll kill him."

He had raised his voice and Ada was afraid her mother could hear them.

"You and I are supposed to be together," he said. "We were meant to be together. I've got a good place with the railroad. I can support you and we can have a family."

"You don't know him. He'll kill you."

"No he won't. You can get Ash to represent you."

"Once he finds out, he'll come for you. I know he will."

He pulled her to him and held her.

"I will never let him hurt you again," he said into her ear. "I will never let anyone hurt you again."

She pulled back from his embrace, but he held her firmly until she stopped, then he kissed her lightly on the forehead and she started crying. He held her and kissed the tears on her cheeks, then on her mouth, and she responded and he could taste the salt of her tears as they kissed.

"We can't do this. It's a sin," she said.

He held her tight.

"It's a sin for you to be with him," he said. "We were meant to be together."

"I made vows," she said.

"We've all made vows we couldn't keep. I vowed to fight the Yankees to the death and wound up working for them. And then I didn't tell you I was alive, because I didn't think you'd want me anymore. You didn't know how he would be."

"Oh this just makes it hard," she said. "Don't do this."

This time she pushed with more force and slipped from his embrace.

"We had better go back," she said, out of breath, then turned and walked back to her mother.

"Are you ready to go back inside?" she asked.

Mrs. Moore looked toward Ev Hardeman, who was still standing at the edge of the patio, then back at Ada.

"If you are, my dear," she replied. "But what about Everett?"

"He's going to stay here for awhile and have a smoke," Ada said.

Ada helped her stand and held her hand as they walked back into the lobby. When they entered the dining room, a number of the guests had gone and others were saying their farewells to Hays and those gathered around the bar. The orchestra was still playing, but there were fewer couples on the dance floor.

Mrs. Elliott approached Hays and indicated that she, Sister Rosella, and Martha were ready to leave. He had told her he would provide an escort for them, and he turned to Wonsley and Billy, who stood nearby, and asked them to accompany them. Hays told Wonsley and Billy he expected them back at the hotel by eleven, in an hour. After Billy talked to his mother, they followed the ladies out of the ballroom, pausing with them for good-byes to several of Mrs. Elliott's acquaintances, then through the lobby and onto Alamo Plaza. It was a clear, moonlit night. Sister Rosella and Mrs. Elliott took the lead. Billy and Wonsley walked on either side of Martha, behind them. They crossed the bridge over the river and walked down Commerce Street. The stores were closed and the few residences were dark, but the saloons were open and the lights from their doorways and windows shone on the sidewalks. When they reached St. Mary's Street, Sister Rosella said she would turn and go from there to the academy.

"It's a fine night and we can walk that way with you," Mrs. Elliott said. "If that's all right with these two gentlemen."

Wonsley and Billy agreed and they turned down St. Mary's. As they reached the St. Mary's Street Bridge, Wonsley saw something moving in the shadows of the bridge superstructure that did not look right. He tapped Mrs. Elliott on the shoulder.

"Wait a minute," he said quietly. "There's someone up there."

Billy and Wonsley stepped in front of the ladies and peered through the moonlight at the other end of the bridge. There were cattails growing by the path that led up from the river, which could have been moving in the light breeze, but the movement Wonsley saw did not look like that. Billy thought he could make out a man's silhouette just beyond the steel beam that curved up from the base of the bridge on the right. He felt the handle of his pistol without thinking. Wonsley stepped forward and called out.

"Whoever is there, show yourself." His voice was higher than usual.

Wonsley did not carry a pistol and he had left his rifle at the hotel checkroom. He pulled his Bowie knife from its scabbard. A pecan orchard surrounded the street on the other side of the bridge, and the moonlight cast a patchwork of shadows across it, which made it difficult to tell whether the movement he saw was indeed at the end of the bridge or farther on. Then a tall man stepped out of a shadow and into the middle of the street at the other end of the bridge. He was about a hundred feet away, within easy pistol range. He stopped after stepping into the street, his hands at his sides. He wore a dark hat.

They stood there looking at him and he stood still, looking their way. The moonlight came from behind them and they could see that he was slim and long-legged. He wore a sash around his waist.

"What do you want?" Wonsley said. This time his voice was low and steady.

The man appeared to shift his weight to his left and his right arm moved, his hand moving up toward his waist. Billy pulled out his Remington. The man's hand went back down and his weight shifted back.

"*Yo no quiero nada,*" he said in a raspy voice that was barely audible. I want nothing.

"Then we're comin' on," Wonsley said. He turned to the women. "You ladies stay here."

"We better not leave them by themselves," Billy said, still looking at the man, his pistol pointed in his direction.

"We will follow you at a safe distance," Sister Rosella said. "Do you need help with the Spanish?"

"No, ma'am," Wonsley replied. "We can make do."

The bridge was a fairly new one, made of steel, with a superstructure that formed an arch on each side, peaking at the middle of its span. The moon was high in the southern sky and most of the north bank that lay before them was bathed in moonlight, but the river and the path beside it were in shadow from the high bank and buildings on the south side.

Billy and Wonsley stepped out and after they had moved a few feet, Sister Rosella, then Martha and Mrs. Elliott, followed. They walked slowly. They could hear the sound of their footsteps on the bridge and the faint sound of the river flowing beneath it in the quiet. There were no bird or insect sounds in the night, as if nature was waiting. The man stood unusually still in the moonlight, a part of the frozen moment they were in. Billy still held his Remington waist high, slightly in front of him. When they were within twenty feet of the man, they stopped, Billy stepping up a bit after Wonsley first came to a halt.

"*Queremos pasar*," Wonsley said. We want to pass.

"It's okay with me," the man said, without moving.

"You speak English," Wonsley said.

"*Sí, amigo. Tú hablas Español también, verdad?*" Yes, friend. You speak Spanish too, right?

The man's accent was pronounced, but had a strange intonation. His pistol was wedged at a casual angle into his sash in front. His black hair fell straight on his shoulders.

"Will you step aside and let us pass?" Wonsley asked.

The man was motionless, his hands hanging at his sides.

"*Este es un país libre*," he said. It's a free country.

Wonsley glanced at Billy out of the corner of his eye. Billy's hand was steady.

"But a gentleman would step aside to let the ladies pass," Billy said.

Silence from the man, then a murmur, then in his raspy voice, "That is true."

He still did not move, but even if he moved aside, they would be turning their backs to him after they passed and if they returned back down the street the way they came, their backs would be to him. And he might have confederates in the dark below the bridge. Then there was a sound behind them, coming from the other end of the bridge. Sister Rosella heard it first and turned to look. Two men were standing at the south end of the bridge with guns in hand. Billy and Wonsley briefly turned to look at them, then turned back to the man in their path. In the second they took to look back, he had pulled his pistol and now held it at his side, pointing in their direction. His smile was visible in the moonlight. He raised his pistol to fire, but Billy fired first. The bullet from the Remington struck him in the chest as he fired, causing his shot to pass over them.

"Get down," Wonsley yelled, as he put his arms around the shoulders of Mrs. Elliott and Martha, who were close to him, pulling them into a crouch. Sister Rosella, farther back, stood still in the moonlight, facing the two men at the other end of the bridge. Both of them fired at the same time, one of the bullets striking her in the forehead, the other passing over Mrs. Elliott's crouched body. The force and location of the shot pushed the sister's body backward and she fell against Mrs. Elliott, blood pouring out of the wound in her temple. Martha began to scream. Then they heard more shots, coming from behind the two men. The first one caught one of them in the back. The other man turned in a crouching position and fired down the street before another bullet caught him in the head. In seconds, two bodies lay near the south end of the bridge in the moonlight under a cloud of smoke from the pistols.

Billy slowly stood and looked in the direction of the man who had blocked their path. He was on his knees, his gun in hand, but held down at his side. His hat had been knocked off by Billy's shot. He was holding his left hand over his chest. Billy approached him slowly with the Remington held out in front of him. The man's eyes were closed, but when Billy was within ten feet of him, he raised his pistol again. Billy fired first, but this time the man's bullet tore into his left arm above the elbow, spinning him around. He stooped and fired again. His bullet hit the man in the face and he crumpled, falling forward. Wonsley was suddenly there with his Bowie knife, but it was obvious that the man was no longer a threat.

Wonsley turned to the women. Martha had stopped screaming and was standing, staring down at Sister Rosella's body, which had rolled off Mrs. Elliott, who still crouched down, her head damp with Sister Rosella's blood. Wonsley stooped to touch Mrs. Elliott on the shoulder.

"Are you hit?"

She looked up at him then. The shots still rang in their ears, although it was quiet. The pungent smell of gunpowder seemed to be all around them. She hesitated, not sure of her answer, then said, "I don't think so."

Billy moved slowly around them toward the two bodies near the south side of the bridge. One of them was moving, crawling slowly toward the side of the street. Then another shot rang out, and the crawling man's head exploded. Billy waited, then saw a man coming slowly toward him from the direction of the muzzle flash. He could gradually make out a tall-crowned hat on top of a head of long hair which shone white in the moonlight. Then it became clear that it was Ephraim McLane, who staggered a bit as he walked up to the two bodies.

"Everyone okay?" he asked in his low voice.

"They got the nun," Billy said. "There's another one at the other end over there, but I got him."

His voice was breaking. He had forgotten about the pain in his arm, but it suddenly came back with a vengeance, causing him to reach across his chest toward it with the Remington still in his hand. McLane wavered back and forth, then held his groin.

"They wing you?" he asked, his voice almost a grunt.

"In the arm. I'll be all right."

"Okay." He leaned forward then. "I'm going to have to sit down."

He staggered toward the side of the street. Billy holstered the Remington and followed close by him, and when he started to fall, he grabbed his arm and let him down easy, helping him into a sitting position on the gravel at the edge of the street, his legs crossed. Then the sound of rapid footsteps came from the direction of Commerce Street and several men were there, standing and staring, some with drawn pistols.

After a time, they carried McLane to a nearby saloon. He had been shot in the groin and was losing a great deal of blood. They put him in a chair near the bar, and the bartender brought a bottle of his best whiskey and put it on the table with a beer glass.

"On the house, Captain," he said.

McLane smiled.

"Hell, at least I get to die in a saloon. And a damned fine one at that."

The bartender poured the glass half full and McLane took a long swallow.

"Damn, Jake," he said. "You been holdin' out on me all these years. I never had nothin' this good here before."

A doctor was sent for, but by the time he arrived, McLane had passed out. The doctor had them lay him on a table. He opened the fly on his pants to get at the wound. It was low on his groin, just above the pubic hair. His pants were soaked with his blood.

Hays was there after a short time, standing by and looking at him as the doctor tried to stanch the bleeding. He noticed Hays and quickly turned back to his task. When he was finished, he turned to Hays and shook his head.

"It's a gut shot," he said quietly. "There's nothing to be done."

McLane lasted two more hours. He never regained consciousness. A memorial service for him was attended by hundreds, including a number of fellow Rangers.

The services for Sister Rosella at the Cathedral drew an overflow crowd. Martha could not be consoled. She withdrew and could not be persuaded to go back to school for more than a week. Finally, on a Thursday afternoon, she was visited by the parish priest, who sat and prayed with her. Mrs. Elliott left them alone in the parlor. The next day Martha returned to school, but she was unresponsive in class and stood apart from the other students on the playground.

Morgan's body was identified by the bartender from the Cosmopolitan. The two at the south end of the bridge had been seen earlier at Jack's Saloon. They were known thugs whom Morgan had recruited for a robbery. The sheriff concluded that they had been lying in wait for whoever might come across the bridge. Hays was not convinced, but he could not explain how Morgan would have known that the five of them would have taken the route to St. Mary's Bridge.

After a week of looking in on Martha and being assured that Mrs. Elliott wanted to raise her, Hays insisted on wiring money for her upkeep once a month. Mrs. Elliott finally agreed. She promised to write often and to get Martha to at least include a note. He then left for California.

THIRTY-NINE

B ILLY WAS FLOATING ON HIS BACK DOWN THE RIVER. THERE HAD
been no rain since June, and the water was clear and cool. It was
a hot afternoon in late August and he had sneaked off from working
cattle. He ignored the doctor's warning about keeping his bandage dry.
The wound had healed well enough, and the bandage was soaked with
sweat anyway. He had discarded the sling a week ago. Daydreaming, he
was back at the creek swimming with Ada. She approached the bank as
she always did in his dreams, her back to him, and as she stepped into
shallower water he could see the graceful curvature of her back and her
white skin, her wet black hair against it, and her face in profile as she
turned smiling toward him, catching him looking at her, and her but-
tocks and legs as she climbed up out of the water, and her feet, delicate
and fine. The genesis of his dream was now a clouded reality. It had been
so long since he had seen her in the creek, he was not sure if it had really
happened or was only a dream from the beginning.

Now she was married to an old man and was likely to stay married,
even though it was obvious that she was not happy. And Everett Hardeman
was in danger of getting into a fight with her husband that could lead to
the death of one or both of them. It did not seem real.

Everything after the death of his father, although lodged in his memory,
also seemed less than real to him. He remembered Lily Poe and Barbara
Ann coming to the house that night in the rainstorm. Hays entering the
church door at the funeral and talking to him in the cemetery. The long
trek after Morgan and the girl. Gruder's wounds and Billy's dislocated

shoulder. The waltz with Martha. The encounter with Morgan and the other men on the St. Mary's Street Bridge. It was all clear in his mind, but it seemed hard to believe it had all happened, and he felt the need to talk about it, if only to gain some perspective.

He had asked Wonsley about something that had happened while they were separated at the San Saba, about how they got the girl away from Morgan, but Wonsley just shrugged his shoulders and started talking about going on a coon hunt. His uncle John Baker was not someone he could talk to easily. So he had jumped in at the gravel bar above Gruder's house and was just now coming into the deep hole where he had fished with Gruder so many times, drifting past the old cypress log that had been there at the edge of the deep water for so long, its lone branch above water still warning of its location. He dog paddled over to the bank and crawled up the cypress roots he had ascended so many times before, emerging naked and dripping on the bank. Gruder was where Billy thought he would be, leaning back against the upper slant of the bank under the shade of the tree with his eyes closed. Billy knew he wouldn't be able to sneak up on him and was not surprised when the familiar voice called out his name, as if he had been seen in a dream.

"Billy," the voice said. And after a pause, "Staying cool?" Only then opening his eyes and looking straight at him as if his sense of hearing had been so good he knew exactly where Billy was standing without looking.

"I want to talk about something," Billy said.

Gruder leaned forward into a sitting position.

"You got that bandage wet, for sure," he said.

"It was wet with sweat anyway."

Billy whistled loudly and stood waiting and dripping until he heard a whinny from upstream. He whistled again, and before long he could hear hoof beats. Then he climbed to the top of the bank and Julie was there. His clothes were draped over the saddle. She had been careful not to spill them. She came up to him and he patted her neck, then put his shirt and pants on, leaving his boots hanging by their laces over the saddle horn, and returned to where Gruder was sitting. Billy sat down and waited. After a long pause, Gruder spoke.

"So you want to know about the girl?" he asked.

Billy was not surprised. Many of their conversations began with Gruder already knowing what Billy wanted to talk about.

"Yes. I would like to know what happened."

"They took her at night, during the storm. I thought you knew that."

"Yes, but how?"

"Cap'n Hays don't talk that much about those things, but it was at night during the storm and it was at the Pegleg. They tore through the back of the tipi and grabbed her."

"That was a hell of a storm," Billy said.

"It was," Gruder replied, smiling. "It was indeed. They couldn't see and they got one of them, but not the one we wanted. You got him. With the pistol your daddy gave you."

"Everybody keeps talking about it."

"That's the way it is. They'll keep it up until something else happens. And that won't be long."

ABOUT THE AUTHOR

W. W. McNEAL is a retired trial lawyer and a sixth-generation Texan. He lives on the family ranch in Central Texas with his partner, Cathy, along with two cats and a dog. The land has been in his family for generations, and the original 1850 deed to the property is in his possession. McNeal is also a songwriter who has been a student of Texas and local history for many years. *Plum Creek* is his first novel.